CHAINS OF LEGACY

THE CHAOS CYCLE #2

ML SPENCER

STONEGUARD PUBLICATIONS

CHAINS OF LEGACY
Copyright © 2020 by ML Spencer
STONEGUARD PUBLICATIONS

Cover by J Caleb Design
Edited by Morgan Smith
World Maps by Rela Similä
ISBN 978-1-951452-01-8

Arjul
Karog
Farath
Rajul Plains
Carash
Zagra Valley
Jur
Maghra
Orien's Finger
THE Malikari Empire
Tolath
Glen Farquist
Bel Arun
Qalm
Janul
Farrow
Auberdale
Karikesh
Nabad
Covendrey
Din Hollow
Cantridge
Smith's Forge
Isle of Titherry
Wertan
Meridan
Southwark
Bergin
Gandrish
THE
Kingdoms
Fells
Tivendale
Dandry
Foundry
THE Southern Continent
c. 1766 DCE

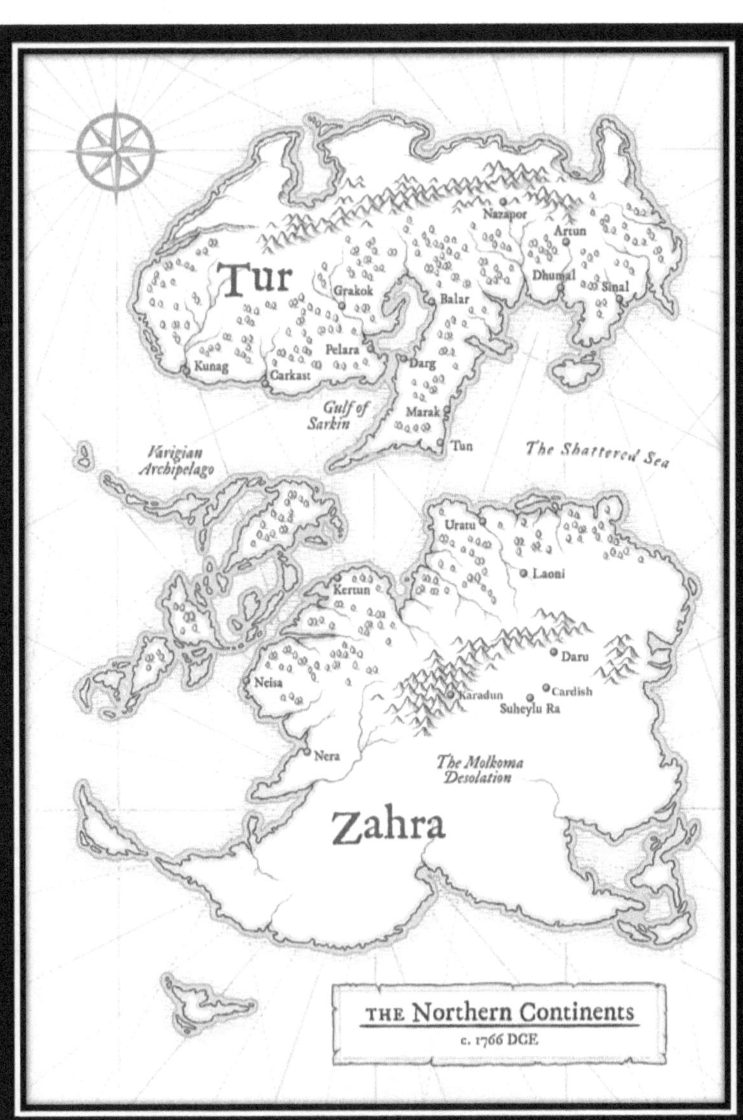

Tur
Nazapor
Artun
Dhumal
Sinal
Grakok
Balar
Pelara
Darg
Kunag
Carkast
Marak
Gulf of Sarkin
Tun
Varigian Archipelago
The Shattered Sea
Uratu
Laoni
Kertun
Daru
Neisa
Karadun
Cardish
Suheylu Ra
Nera
The Molkoma Desolation
Zahra
THE Northern Continents
c. 1766 DCE

WHAT CAME BEFORE

Rylan Marshall's young son was murdered, his daughter kidnapped, and a mage's power forced into him against his will. Gil Archer and his acolyte Ashra were charged with protecting Rylan. They brought him to the Lyceum in Karikesh, where Rylan learned he was the son of the infamous darkmage, Darien Lauchlin.

But before Rylan could settle into his new identity, the Turan Khar, a collective entity who uses mages linked by magical chains, laid siege to the city. Rylan was taken captive and whisked away to another continent, where a mage named Xiana was tasked with teaching him the use of magic. In order to do so, she led Rylan to Suheylu Ra, an ancient city populated only by dead, petrified people, so that he could merge identities with Keio Matu, the ancient Custodian of Shira who had brought his city to ruin in order to save the rest of the world from the Turan Khar.

While Gil was fighting a losing battle in Karikesh, the mages of the Lyceum were being captured and chained—made into willing weapons to be used against them. Because of Gil's poor choices, Ashra was captured. Plagued by guilt, Gil went alone into the Khar stronghold on a mission to get her back.

Across the world, Rylan joined with Keio Matu and inherited more than he bargained for: not just Keio's knowledge, but also his memories and emotions. But Xiana had been manipulating Rylan all along into becoming a weapon for the Turan Khar—the most powerful mage in their arsenal. Using his daughter as leverage, the Khar Warlord forced Rylan to don the chains that would connect him to their entire society.

Rylan and Xiana, linked, returned to the city to attack its defenders, including Gil and Ashra. Rylan was able to break free of the Warlord's control over him, killing Xiana in the process. He defeated the Khar Warlord and assumed his title, which ended the assault on the city. Linked indelibly to the Turan Khar, Rylan chose to depart with them.

1

IMPRISONED

The darkness went on forever, infinite and unyielding. There was no sound. No substance. No texture to the world, no odor to the air. His prison contained no walls, either physical or ethereal. Like the darkness, it was never-ending. He wasn't sure how long he had been there: days... weeks. Possibly months. Whichever—it didn't matter. The relentless darkness was accomplishing its purpose: he was going insane, and the faster, the better.

It was no more or less than he deserved, and certainly far better than the alternative. Sanity, as far as he was concerned, was a more grueling punishment than this prison of absence. He had suffered the memories too long already, far beyond his point of breaking. At first, he had yearned for death. But in time, it had become clear to him that death was likely no escape. What was death, but eternal emptiness? He had already looked upon the face of paradise, and then he'd betrayed it.

The only sensation left to him was pain, and he had learned to savor the experience. It had started with him digging his fingernails into his skin. He'd found the pain a welcome distraction, so he began clawing at his arms until they bled. At first, he did it just to deter his mind from the ache of the memories, to give himself something else to think about. But soon the pain became a staple, a necessity. An accomplishment. In the absence of other sources of stimulation, it had become the only thing grounding him in reality, the only way he could tell he was still alive.

Not that he wanted to be.

He had killed the woman he loved. No amount of physical suffering could distract him from that anguish. And yet, for some reason, he endured. The prison of nothingness hadn't defeated him yet, no matter how much he wanted it to. So he drifted forever in darkness. Sometimes sleeping, sometimes wakeful—it was hard to tell the difference. The nightmares were the same in both cases. They never went away; they scourged him always.

The face of his beloved haunted him still. As did her words: *The harder you try, the worse you'll fail, and the more people you'll hurt.*

No.

Those hadn't been her words.

They had belonged to another, someone else he had loved. Someone else who had died. Someone else he had failed.

Or perhaps the words had been spoken only in his nightmares, like the one he was presently inhabiting.

It was best not to think about it too hard.

He dug his fingernails deep into his flesh, finding the pain euphoric.

A light splintered his darkness.

It expanded slowly, yawning open like a doorway. He flinched at the intensity of the brightness and brought his hand up to shield his eyes. The light swelled until it enveloped him completely, pouring into his prison like scalding liquid. He edged away from it until he ran into a wall that hadn't been there before. A silhouette appeared in the light, tall and featureless, vaguely human-shaped. A hand clenched his wrist and urged him forward.

He staggered into the light, compelled by the rigid grip on his arm. Tears flooded his eyes and streamed down his cheeks. They had nothing to do with the light, and everything to do with the fact that something had changed. He had been delivered from the darkness. The touch of another's fingers on his skin after so long in isolation was overwhelming and exquisite.

He kept his hand raised in front of his face as he walked, but lowered it gradually as his eyes acclimated to the brightness. The man leading him down the corridor had skin the same color and texture as the walls. He was tall and thin, his features exceptionally angular, and he wore his silver hair in long braids threaded through metal rings reminiscent of chainmail. His dark robe was made from the hide of an animal that was utterly unfamiliar. It was smoothly scaled, like snakeskin, yet soft, like suede. He kept his eyes averted, his attention riveted on the corridor in front of them.

The sharp sounds of their footsteps echoed forcefully in the passage, ringing louder at every stride. The flood of sensations, though welcome, was also daunting. He felt lightheaded and unstable, like he could topple over at any time. Without the man's totalitarian grip on his arm, he probably would have collapsed already.

The long corridor ended at a door unlike any other he had seen. It was circular and spoked, like a wagon wheel, held together with iron fittings. Instead of knocking, his escort tugged on a long velvet rope that hung from the ceiling, and the faint sound of a bell echoed from the other side of the doorway.

They waited in silence.

His gray-skinned escort stood glowering at the door,

conspicuously avoiding eye contact. There was a bracelet on the man's wrist, thick, like a shackle. It was made of bronze and etched with a geometric pattern, and it had a ring affixed to the band that a chain could be attached to. That was significant, though he couldn't remember why. And that bothered him. He stared harder at the band on the man's wrist, struggling for recollection.

In a moment of insight, his eyes went to his own arm. He wore a similar band, though his was silver. The *A'isan,* it was called. An ancient artifact that connected him to the whole of the community. He couldn't feel them, though. Something must have happened during his long interlude in darkness. His eyes traveled to the skin of his arm, which was broken and scabbed over, and dark with dried blood where he must have raked it with his nails.

A cold feeling made him shiver. Made him sweat. He glanced at the man next to him. *A Darl*, a voice whispered in his mind. A man from the northern continent of Tur.

He winced.

The voice in his head hadn't belonged to him. It belonged to another man. He shivered harder, sweat dribbling down his forehead.

There was a grinding noise, and the door rolled open, revealing a large chamber lit by swarming colors that streamed in from stained-glass windows that ringed the walls. Dozens of lanterns hung suspended from a crystalline ceiling, emitting a muted, chaotic light. The walls shimmered as though carved from smokey gemstones.

The Darl man tugged on his arm, compelling him forward, and the door rolled closed behind them. He led him to the center of the room, where they paused under the equivalent of an indoor pagoda. He stood, wavering, his mind mired in a slimy haze. His gaze drifted from the crystalline walls to a floor carpeted by crimson rugs. Everything was a riot of glimmering light. It was too much. The colors and textures swirled together in a blur, overwhelming his ability to process it all.

"Leave us," a voice cut through the chaos.

A woman rose from a chair that appeared to be carved from an enormous, smoky crystal that looked grown from the wall behind it, just part of the shimmering tapestry. Not a chair, he realized, but a throne.

Not a woman, but an Empress.

Isaerae.

He dropped to his knees, bowing his head deeply. Her footsteps whispered toward him over the soft carpets. He squeezed his eyes closed, dreading her approach, and couldn't bring himself to look up. She paused, lingering over him, her proximity causing his body to tremble. Unable and unwilling to do anything else, he cowered before her. He clenched his hands into fists, squeezing them tight to stop his shivering. When it didn't work, he dug his nails into his flesh.

Isaerae reached down and lifted his chin.

Her mere touch scalded his face, and he winced. She wanted him to look at her, but he couldn't do it. It wasn't possible. She was too beautiful, and such an act would be profane.

"Open your eyes," she commanded.

"No..."

"Yes. Open your eyes and look at me."

Reluctantly, he peeled his eyelids open and forced himself to look up. Above him stood a young and beautiful woman with pale gray skin and eyes the deep purple of mountains at sunset. Her hair was long and silken, white and iridescent, glimmering, as though made of spun glass. Her presence radiated a frightful power almost painful to behold. Lowering his gaze, he trembled harder.

She smiled. "Rylan Lauchlin. Welcome home."

Was that his name? He frowned and thought about it for a

long moment before deciding that it was. One of his names. One of his many, many names.

"Rise, and be at ease."

He obeyed automatically, though he kept his head lowered, staring down at his Empress's feet. She wasn't wearing shoes. Her toenails were lacquered the same deep crimson as the rugs. The ermine-trimmed hem of her dark robe brushed the skin of her feet.

"Please. Sit."

She motioned to a half-circle of cushions spread out before her throne then turned and took her place before him, claiming her crystalline seat with regal grace. Rylan sank to the floor, purposefully avoiding her gaze. He sat cross-legged, hands resting on his thighs, his stare locked on the rug before him. It occurred to him that he wasn't wearing any garments. He sat naked before his Empress, clothed only in raw wounds and crusted scabs. A sudden heat seared his cheeks.

The shame was excruciating. Isaerae was beautiful, and he was wretched. The wounds on his body were an outward extension of the damage within. He couldn't heal what was inside; nothing could. But he could do something about his appearance.

Rylan reached out with his mind and clasped hold of the magic field. A tingling sensation filled him, making him tremble. He stared down at the injuries on his legs and arms and imagined them gone.

And, suddenly, they were.

The dried blood and scabs disappeared as though absorbed back into his body, leaving only new, pink skin behind. He wasn't aware of how he had accomplished the act, or of all the millions of little details his mind had attended to all at once in order to achieve that single instant of accelerated healing. If someone had asked him what he'd done, he wouldn't have been able to explain it. He just knew what to do.

Or, rather, Keio Matu knew.

Rylan scowled, staring down at his intact skin. He cringed at the thought of the other man who inhabited his body. That man had faded somewhat during his time in the darkness. Faded, but not gone away. All of Keio Matu's knowledge remained inside him, easily accessible, right there at his fingertips. But no matter how hard he tried, he couldn't remember a thing about Keio's life, other than what had been shown to him directly in the vision he had received in Suheylu Ra. It was better that way. It made living with the man a lot easier.

Rylan flexed his fingers, testing the elasticity of his new skin. His hands were smooth now, his skin almost like a child's, lacking the fine lines and blemishes two decades of work and age had etched there. Shifting his gaze to his legs, he saw that the rest of his flesh was likewise renewed. All of the injuries he had inflicted upon himself had been erased, at least outwardly. On the inside, though, he still bled.

He asked, "Why did you torture me?"

There was a long pause bloated by silence.

"We didn't torture you, Rylan."

He took a moment to ponder that answer. "Then who did?"

"You tortured yourself."

He glanced up at his Empress, regretting the action instantly. The strength of her presence quickly overwhelmed him, and he looked back down again. "I don't understand."

"You have been unconscious for weeks."

Rylan went cold. He fumbled through his memories of the darkness, but they were already waning. He glanced back down at the naked skin of his thighs.

"If I was unconscious, then where did these injuries come from?"

There was another pause.

"You wounded yourself, Rylan, but not with your hands. You turned your power on yourself. It was all we could do to heal you faster than you were flaying the flesh off your bones. The only reason you still live is because somehow, in your suffering, your mind managed to block the *A'isan.*"

He glanced down at the silver band on his wrist. He felt suddenly lightheaded, his pulse drumming against the inside of his skull. "Why would I do that to myself?"

"Because you betrayed the Unity, Rylan. You have sentenced us to death."

2

A CONFLICT OF INTEREST

ABOVE IN THE SKIES, A STORM WAS BREWING. DOWN BELOW THE city walls, spread out across the battle-scarred plain, another army was gathering, its appearance just as ominous as the darkening sky.

When Gil had first seen the long columns of soldiers cresting the horizon, his first thought was that it was the Turan Khar returning to finish them off. But this new army had no chained mages and had arrived before their walls in the usual way, which is to say, marching up the road before taking up position behind hastily erected earthworks, which they then spent the next several days reinforcing. Perhaps if Karikesh had even the semblance of their own army remaining, they could have done *something* before this new enemy became too entrenched. But after losing two-thirds of the city guard only a month before, the defenders of Karikesh hadn't had time to shore up their walls well enough to repulse an army of the size gathering below.

Not army, Gil reminded himself. *Armies.*

Looking down at the banners and insignias arrayed across the field, Gil felt his nerves growing cold. The soldiers encamped below were not part of a foreign expeditionary force. They were simply men whose fathers and grandfathers had tilled this self-same land—until they had been routed by the Malikari. The forces below were composed of the regular armies of Chamsbrey and Southwark, augmented by ranks of militia, soldiers who simply aspired to take back the lands of their ancestors. There was no better reason to bring war against another, Gil thought. He couldn't find it within himself to blame them.

But he could despise them.

It was a brilliant but underhanded strategy they were employing. The rulers of the Rhen's kingdoms had bided their time, letting the Turan Khar pummel the city of Karikesh. Then, when the city walls were reduced to open and bleeding wounds, their generals had advanced their forces and laid siege. Gil knew that if he had been in command of the Kingdoms' armies, he would have done the same damn thing. But after spending two weeks fighting to defend the city and the people who dwelled within it, it was heartbreaking to realize they had won the first battle just to lose the second. The Malikari had made Karikesh their home for over twenty years, and now, when they were at their weakest, they would be driven from it.

Gil rested his hand on the haft of the silver weapon he wore at his side, the magical artifact named *Thar'gon*. The air was crisp, threatening either rain or snowfall, and he could feel the chill of the metal through the leather straps that laced the morning star's hilt. But the talisman gave his mind no comfort, for he knew it wouldn't do him any good. The army below was not an enemy he could face. They were his own kinsman—by rights, he should be celebrating their arrival, not dreading it. But his experience fighting the Turan Khar had opened his eyes to the plight of the Malikari, and he couldn't wish this on them.

They had fought well and taken devastating losses. They deserved a respite.

He glanced at Ashra, who stood across from him, leaning against one of the shattered battlements of the defeated tower. Under her black mage's cloak, she wore a finely embroidered kaftan with flowing sleeves. He had never seen her in anything so elegant during all the time he had known her at the Lyceum. But ever since the disappearance of the Turan Khar, she had taken to wearing such finery, and her wardrobe seemed to be growing more expensive by the day. The gown she wore looked like it was meant for a formal occasion, perhaps a meeting with dignitaries or an audience before a king or queen. It wasn't an outfit suited for the city's crumbling battlements. To Gil, Ashra looked pretentious, and though he knew her reasons, he didn't like those either.

She had lost her father to the Turan Khar, along with both of her brothers. As Princess, Ashra was the only member of her family left to continue her father's legacy. The people of Karikesh had taken to calling her Sultana, and Ashra hadn't corrected them, despite the fact that she had yet to be properly crowned. That, more than the armies below, made Gil's blood run hot. Relinquishing his position on the battlement, he crossed the tower to stand at her side.

"What are you going to do?" he asked, just loud enough to be heard over the sound of the rising wind.

"I don't know," she responded.

"You need to walk away." He moved closer to her, making sure his voice couldn't be overheard by the officers who were standing behind them. "Right now, before this explodes in your face."

Ashra looked at him with understanding in her eyes, but there was a hard stubbornness there too. She glanced back out over the embrasure, seemingly to observe the ever-changing face of the armies below. "I can't. It's not what my father would have wanted."

Gil doubted that. He had known the Sultan long enough to guess that he wouldn't have wanted his daughter up on a tower overlooking a battle waiting to happen. Gil figured that was one of the reasons the Sultan had agreed to Ashra joining the Lyceum's ranks of mages: to keep her out of harm's way. But Ashra was just as headstrong as her father, and Gil was quickly growing frustrated.

"Your father wanted his *son* on the throne," he growled under his breath. "Not you."

Ashra cast a disparaging glance his way. "Regrettably, none of my father's sons survived." Her voice was caustic, as was the look in her eyes. She stood with her chin raised at an infuriating angle, staring down her nose at him, the way she used to do before becoming his acolyte.

"Ashra. A mage cannot rule."

She lifted a perfectly arched eyebrow. "Why not? If there is some law that says so, I've never heard it."

Gil felt like grinding his teeth. "It's an unwritten law."

She shrugged dismissively. "Well, if it's that important, then someone should have written it down."

She turned and walked away from him, moving to the far side of the tower. For no other reason than to avoid him, he was sure. He wasn't going to let her get away that easily, and he sure as hell wasn't going to be snubbed by his own acolyte and just let it pass. Moving after her, he planted his hands on the stone of the embrasure at her side.

"We are *mages*, Ashra," he reminded her. "We can't take sides. Magic shouldn't be used for battle, but if you assume the throne, that's exactly what they'll expect of you."

Ashra leaned back against the wall of the battlement, her leather-gloved fingers clasped in front of her. "This city would be ruled by the Turan Khar right now if it wasn't for magic being used in battle."

"That's different," he grumbled.

"How is it different?"

Inside, Gil felt like screaming. That or batting her over the head and dragging her down off the tower.

"Because the Khar were invaders."

"And *they're* not?" Raising her eyebrows, she nodded toward the army below with a look that dared him to contradict her.

"No, they're not," Gil snapped, taking the bait. "*You* were the invaders. This was their land before your father took it from them!"

Ashra recoiled as if struck, her dark eyes smoldering with anger and hurt. Stabbing him with a hateful glare, she asked coldly, "So, we're back to that, now?"

"Yes, we're back to that." Gil wanted to spit. "Gods, you're infuriating!"

He turned away from the ramparts, wanting to swipe out at the air in anger. But he halted himself, bringing a hand up to rub his eyes in a last, desperate attempt to find patience. He stood there for a minute until his breathing slowed, chewing on his anger. He decided to start over. Knowing Ashra as he did, he figured he was approaching this from the wrong angle. He decided to try reasoning with her.

Turning back to her, he said with the gentlest voice he could conjure, "Naia will never stand for this, you know."

"I don't need Naia's approval. The Malikari Empire was built by my father. It's *my* empire now. I'll rule it as I see fit. And if the Prime Warden doesn't like that, then she can move her academy to a different city."

Gil groaned audibly. Of course reasoning hadn't worked—it only worked with *reasonable* people. "It's not that simple. You're a mage, Ashra! You don't have the luxury to do what you want. You gave up that right the day you swore to protect the land and its people. That means *all* its people, not just the Malikari. A mage can't rule an empire—it's a conflict of interest."

She stared at him silently for a long moment, her gaze wandering over him. At last, she licked her lips and breathed a deep sigh. "I understand what you're saying, Gil, and you're right. It *is* a conflict of interest. Very well. I hereby resign my position as a mage of the Lyceum."

Gil's mouth flopped open. "You just can't *resign* from being a mage!"

Ashra raised her eyebrows, differing with him imperiously. "I can't help the fact that I have the gift in me, but I can no longer remain at the disposal of the Lyceum. I am a monarch now. Naia will just have to understand that. I can't be subject to her and rule the Malikari Empire at the same time."

Defeated, Gil blew out the last of the air in his chest, his frustration cooling into something different, something that felt an awful lot like fear. And the more Ashra talked, the colder that fear became. Somewhere, he felt sure, there was an invisible line in the sand, and she was coming very close to stepping over it. He didn't know what would happen if she did.

Softly, he said, "I'm telling you, Naia's not going to allow it."

"She won't have a choice."

"Pardon me, Your Grace," a man's voice interrupted from behind them.

Gil turned to find himself staring at Murat, the general in charge of the city's defenses. He wore a tall, red hat adorned with a feathered plume that looked much more suited to a noble court than it did to the battlefield.

The general waited for Ashra's invitation to continue, and then reported. "Madam, I spoke with General Hornsberg and General Knibbs, the commanders of the armies of Chamsbrey and Southwark, respectively. The generals asked me to inform you that they are ready to discuss the terms of our immediate surrender."

Ashra shot Gil an accusatory glare. "Do you still believe that now is a good time for me to abdicate?"

Gil took a step toward her, intentionally caging her in against the corner of the tower. "Yes. Especially now. You can't do this. We're talking about *war*. As a mage of the Lyceum, you can't lead an army into—"

"I am no longer a mage of the Lyceum!" She stepped sideways, dodging around him. "I am the sovereign ruler of—"

"You haven't even been crowned yet! For gods' sake, Ashra! I'm saying this as your friend: don't do this. Don't start down this road—it's not going to lead anywhere good. For one thing, it's taken us over twenty years to regain the public's trust. If it becomes known that a mage is in command of an army, we lose that trust. Next time, it may take us a hundred years to get it back."

Ashra's shoulders raised and then fell again as she exhaled a deep sigh. Her eyes lowered, and for a moment she stood staring vacantly out across the plain below, the wind rippling her hair about her face. At last, she looked back at him.

Quietly, she said, "I'm sorry for that. I truly am. But it's not my problem anymore."

She turned to her commander. "Murat Pasha, please go inform the generals of the Kingdoms that we are disinclined to surrender at this time. Inform them that, out of kindness and mercy, they shall be allowed one day to remove their armies to the far side of the river. If for any reason they fail to comply, tell them that act will be interpreted as aggression, and we will retaliate by slaughtering their forces to the man. Remind them that Malikar has never taken prisoners, and never shall."

The general brought his hand to his chest in salute. "At once, Sultana."

Gil winced at the title. There had to be dozens of people who would make better rulers and who weren't compromised by a mage's power. But one look at Ashra told him that the argument was over. She'd made up her mind.

"Do what you want," he sighed, "but just understand something. Mages have been executed in the past for defying the will of a Prime Warden."

Her mouth fell open. "Are you actually *threatening* me with execution?"

"It's not a threat, Ashra. It's a fact. And you really need to think about it."

With that, he turned away and stalked toward the tower stairs. When he reached the bottom of the steps, the two Battlemages who had accompanied him fell in next to him, their cloaks rippling like banners in the wind. As they gained the street, he paused and cast and infuriated glance back up at the tower, swiping a hand through his hair.

Turning to the taller of the two mages who accompanied him, he said, "Stay here, Ranick. Send a runner if anything bad happens. Leven, come with me."

Ranick screwed his face into a grimace. "What do you consider bad?"

Gil scowled. "Just about any decision she makes."

3

THE UNITY

Rylan touched the silver band on his arm, trailing his thumb across its cold, silken texture. The *A'isan* was an artifact, just like the chains that linked the rest of the mages of the Turan Khar. Only, the *A'isan* was the master of all bonds. The silver band defined the Khar Warlord—and he, it. It was what gave the Warlord the power to move armies, conquer cities, and chart the course of an entire society and every person within it. But somehow, he had managed to find a way to block the *A'isan*, to turn off his connection with the whole of the community. He could no longer feel their sweet emotions in his head, and his heart ached at their absence.

The Empress Isaerae gazed down at him from her crystalline throne with a look of sympathy. Rylan didn't understand how she could find compassion for him.

Tears clouding his vision, he whispered, "How did I betray us?"

With a forgiving smile, Isaerae informed him, "You withdrew our forces from the Southern Continent before we had a chance to collect enough of their mages. Now, we must sacrifice our own brothers and sisters to feed the hunger of the Sky

Portal, and we simply do not have enough. When we run out of mages, the Sky Portal will collapse, and our civilization will crumble into chaos."

Isaerae's smile was a painful condemnation. Rylan couldn't look at her after such a weighty accusation, so he lowered his gaze to the floor. He clenched his hands into fists, his stomach tightening, feeling the desire to rake his nails across his flesh, knowing that physical pain would be far easier to bear. An image of the Sky Portal filled his mind, even though he'd never seen it. He knew exactly what it looked like, for he had witnessed it through another man's eyes. The portal was a swirling maelstrom that dominated the sky, casting its menacing shadow over the world.

"Why must we feed our mages to the Sky Portal?" He shivered as cold fingers of dread traced down his back. He couldn't imagine such a fate.

"To uphold the covenant that we made with Xerys." Leaning forward, she gazed at him, maintaining that strange, enigmatic smile on her face. It was beautiful, just as she was beautiful—and terrifying.

Rylan spread his hands in an imploring gesture. "I don't understand. Why would we have made such a covenant in the first place?"

"To protect ourselves from you." Isaerae's smile deepened, a cold thing that seemed frozen on her face.

"From me?"

"From Keio Matu."

He winced, a cold dagger of shock slipping through his heart. "How?"

Isaerae narrowed her eyes, staring deeply into his face as if boring into his soul. "Keio Matu was the Custodian of the Wise Council. The core magic was sequestered by his command."

Rylan had no idea what she was talking about. Even the name was utterly unfamiliar. He had no recollection of it, and the man inside him wasn't helping. "I don't remember. What is core magic?"

"Residual magic left over from the creation of the universe."

He frowned. "Why have I never heard of it?"

"No one alive has. Since the destruction of Shira, knowledge of the core magic has been lost to the world. But, then again, you are as ancient as I. Everything you need to know is locked somewhere deep inside your head, should you dare to go looking for it."

He wished it were that simple. He didn't have access to Keio Matu's memories; just the man's knowledge of magic, along with some of his emotions. He couldn't speak to him or ask him questions, couldn't crack him open and take a look inside. Keio Matu was dead in every way that mattered, although something of his ghost lingered on, haunting the recesses of Rylan's mind.

Frowning, he asked, "What does core magic have to do with the Sky Portal?"

Isaerae reached upward with both hands, stretching languidly like a cat. Then she rose from her seat, her fingers trailing across the sharp planes of the throne's armrests. She stood before him as radiant as a goddess, her spun-glass hair glimmering in the crystalline light. She lingered over him, gazing down at him imperiously as he quailed before her, over-awed by her beauty.

"We were harvesting the core magic before Shira had any knowledge of it. It is the purest form of magic, the perfect power source, lacking the inconsistencies of the magic field or the brutality of the Onslaught. With it, we accomplished the Unification of our society and were able to overcome all of humanity's innate flaws and limitations. No longer did men have to struggle against each other for survival. No longer were we slaves to the base, self-serving thoughts that motivated our every action. Using core magic, we transcended the limitations of the human condition.

"But then Keio Matu discovered our power source and desired it for Shira. He created a reservoir and siphoned every last drop of core magic into it, locking it away for his own selfish use. While our society starved, Shiran society blossomed. Keio Matu left us no choice: we had to either act to take back our power source or descend into madness. We decided to act. But we didn't have the means of fighting a war against a nation as advanced as Shira."

"So you made a covenant with Chaos," Rylan concluded grimly.

"We needed some way to maintain our Unity in the absence of core magic."

Her explanation made him ill. Keio Matu had contributed to the demise of his own society. Had he done so intentionally, or out of ignorance? And did it even matter? Perspiration broke out across Rylan's brow. How many people had died because of Keio Matu's actions? How many more lives were yet to be sacrificed? The more he understood about the man living inside him, the more he wanted to take a dagger and carve him out.

He opened his mouth to speak, but the only sound that came out was a raspy gurgle. Clearing his throat, Rylan asked, "So the Khar Unity is dependent on Hellpower?"

Isaerae nodded. "Yes. In order to maintain the Sky Portal and keep it from collapsing, we must continuously feed it vitrus."

Rylan could only shake his head in disbelief. The Turan Khar had mortgaged their lives to the God of Chaos, and now their entire society was bound by chains of evil. Without the Hellpower, their civilization was destined for collapse... but the price of survival was the sacrifice of the same mages who made such a Unity possible.

It simply wasn't sustainable.

Gathering his courage, he asked, "So that's what we've been

reduced to? Roving the world in search of mages to feed to Xerys?"

"We don't have a choice."

He believed her, even though he didn't want to. She was his Empress, and her voice commanded every fiber of his being. And yet, he couldn't help but feel appalled. She was talking about sacrificing people he knew, people like Gil and Ashra.

"What we are doing... it can't be justified," he argued.

The Empress's expression hardened. Lingering over him, shrouded in a cloak of innate power, Isaerae seemed like a vengeful goddess descending from the sky. "It is justified. Our society is the pinnacle of human achievement and must be preserved at all cost. The lives of the mages we sacrifice are a small price."

Rylan didn't agree. "And when the last mage is sacrificed? What then?"

Her iron gaze held his own. "Then we descend into madness."

She called it madness, but he knew it was worse than that. What she described was the extinction of their entire civilization. Having known nothing but a sheltered existence within the Unity, the people of the Khar Empire could never exist apart as individuals. They were not mentally capable of surviving in isolation.

"Do you understand now?" Isaerae asked softly.

"Yes." Unfortunately, he understood every nuance of their situation too well. And he also understood how impossible that situation was. There was only so much mage-blood in the world. He gazed up into his Empress's beautiful, perfect face, finally recognizing the source of the sadness behind her smile. Isaerae understood, too. She knew they were already defeated, and yet she refused to surrender.

He admired her for that. Or blamed her. Or both at the same time.

She considered him with a cool and expectant gaze. "You are Rylan Lauchlin, son of Darien Lauchlin, but you are also Keio Matu. If there is any hope left for our Unity, it will come from you. You must open yourself wholly to the *A'isan*. You must assume your place at my side. You must become Warlord."

Rylan frowned down at the band on his wrist, groping to understand why she thought him suitable to the task. He was the son of a demon, and had made a dark compact of his own with the realm of Chaos. Who was he to bring hope to a dying civilization? Surely, Isaerae could find another man far more suited to be Warlord.

"Why me?"

Her enigmatic smile returned. "Because you defied Shiro."

"Why does that matter?"

"When Shiro became Warlord, he wrest control of the Unity from me. He became my *isan,* and reduced me to his subordinate—his *sayan.* No matter how hard I struggled, I couldn't reverse the link. Shiro was far too strong, and his control was absolute. The way I saw it, you were our only hope of defeating Shiro. And now I believe you are our only hope again."

Rylan held up his arm, displaying the silver band that encircled his wrist. "If I open myself to this, will you control me as Xiana did?"

The Empress nodded. "You will be my *sayan,* and I will be your *isan,*" she answered. "I will be in command of the link, but we shall share all with each other. We will be as husband and wife, and I will treasure you with all my heart and value your judgment. Together, we will be *kaiden-sumato,* and together we will rule the Khar Empire."

Rylan sagged, for he understood. He would once again be at the mercy of another mage in control of his mind and magic. But this woman was not Xiana. She had not lied to him or tried to manipulate him. Instead, Isaerae had been completely transparent and forthright, even when he didn't like the answers. He ran his thumb over the cold, silken surface of the band, shivering.

"And what will you ask of me?"

Reaching down, she helped him to his feet. "All I ask is that you be my partner in this life and commit yourself wholly to our cause. Find a way to free us of Xerys' covenant. Failing that, take us back to the Rhen to harvest its mages."

"And if I refuse?"

Isaerae smiled as though he had just plied her with a compliment. The expression was self-assured, almost gloating. "You won't."

Rylan considered the band she wanted to collar him with, contemplating it grimly. The smooth metal felt cold against his skin, chilling him in more ways than one. Looking at it brought painful and unwanted memories of Xiana to the forefront of his mind. She had chained him with a similar band and had used that bond to control him. He did not want to be controlled again.

And yet, somehow, he had defied her will. He had used the corrupt power placed within him by Xerys to kill her and sever that bond. He had accomplished what should have been impossible: he had slain his own *isan.*

At last, he understood why Isaerae had chosen him. The demon who assaulted him in the cornfield had given him a terrible and yet mighty gift. With it, he had overthrown Shiro Nagato and spared the people of Karikesh. Shiro had desired him for his capacity to destroy, just as Isaerae desired him for the same purpose.

But he still didn't know why the awful man in the cornfield had created him in the first place. *Someday I will call, Gerald. And you will come.* Those had been his words, his threat. Rylan doubted that man was done with him yet.

He squeezed his eyes shut, battering away the thought. No. He wouldn't be that demon's pawn.

He opened his eyes. Looking up at Isaerae, he told her firmly, "I won't sacrifice the Rhen's mages. I'll find another way."

She shook her head. "There is no other way. I understand, Rylan. It's a terrible choice. But it is our only choice."

He didn't believe that. He *couldn't* believe that. "Why not use the magic field to keep the Unity together?"

She scrunched her lips. "The magic field is too inconsistent. It ebbs and flows, compounds and nullifies. We must have a consistent and reliable power source."

She turned away from him and moved back toward her throne. Her long hair cascaded to her waist in silken waves. The gown she wore was open in the back, exposing the smoky skin between her shoulders. He had never seen such an exquisite woman before. Even without a chain between them, the Empress of the Turan Khar infected his mind, igniting a deep and hungering desire.

He looked away. "Will you force me to act against my will?"

"No."

It wasn't much, but it was enough.

For the second time in his life, Rylan closed his eyes and opened up his soul to another. And, in doing so, opened his soul to the Unity.

He wasn't prepared for the sensation, even though he had experienced it once before. The room around him drained away, twisting into darkness. He was overcome by a sudden dizziness, and he staggered. Suddenly, he could feel the presence of others there with him. Many others. Thousands—tens of thousands. Some alive. Most dead. He felt them all, an intimate and immersive connection. Warmth and solace poured into him along with a growing feeling of strength. Never before had he felt so accepted, so appreciated, so well-loved. Their faith in him was both staggering and humbling, and it was far more than he had ever earned or deserved.

They trusted him more than he trusted himself. A profound sense of belonging filled his heart, and he was overcome with gratitude and an urgent need to protect and shelter these people who had forgiven him and accepted him for all that he was, with all of his weaknesses and flaws. Defending them was the only important thing in the world, his reason for existence. He understood that now.

The Unity had to be preserved at all cost, at any price.

And it was now his duty to ensure that it was.

Rylan opened his eyes to find his Empress standing next to him, holding his hand. There was no chain linking them, but there didn't have to be for him to feel her moving into his heart, assuming the place that Xiana had once occupied—that his wife had once occupied. He was linked to her by a connection no physical bond could ever replicate. He could feel her moving through him, seeking, exploring, folding back his layers and discovering new depths beneath them. When she pressed her soul against his, he felt a thrill of contentment.

He basked in the gratification brought to him by her presence. The aching grief he felt for Xiana was washed clean from his mind, replaced by the joy at finding refuge in another beautiful soul.

No longer did Rylan question his choice. Isaerae was beautiful and strong, magnificent in every way, the only woman in the world deserving of adulation. Feelings of devotion bubbled to his surface while, deep inside, the warmth of desire stirred awake in his loins.

No.

He drew in a long, stabilizing breath. His gaze went to her, delving deep into her eyes. It took him long moments to realize that the desire he felt was merely an echo of her feelings for him, not his own. He did not want another lover. He would much rather worship Isaerae from afar. After all that he had been through, he was far too drained to give her anything more, at least not yet. Perhaps not ever.

It was time to test her honesty. Isaerae had promised not to force him to act against his will. He wondered if she would keep that promise.

She must have read his emotions through the link. Smiling reassuringly, she said, "Of course, I will never ask you for anything more than you are willing to give."

Instantly, the emotions he felt coming from her faded. Not gone, but muffled, as though the link between them had narrowed substantially. Rylan gasped, feeling suddenly destabilized. It took him a long second to realize that Isaerae had erected a buffer between them that had returned to him a large portion of his anonymity. He felt relieved. But at the same time, a feeling of loss crept over him, for he was aware of the kind of all-encompassing intimacy and comfort he was electing to forgo.

Moving forward, she took his hand in hers and pressed a kiss against his cheek. "Come, Beloved. I will show you to your chambers."

4

BESIEGED

IT HAD BEEN A FULL MONTH SINCE THE SIEGE OF KARIKESH HAD ended, and yet the streets of the city were still barely navigable. One improvised wooden bridge had been built over the Grand Canal, and it was barely stable enough to drive a cart across. That wooden bridge was the only connection between the devastated North City and the southern districts.

The neighborhoods surrounding the Lyceum had been decimated, most of the buildings razed to the ground. The streets were endless fields of debris that continued to be cleared to make room for the passage of soldiers and equipment going to and from the forward command center, which had been reestablished in Murkaq Square.

The mages of the Lyceum had built their own temporary campsite in the neighborhood just west of the square. It consisted of only a few dozen tents, which was all they needed, for the moment. Every available body had been sent to repair the city walls.

Behind the tents, the charred bones of the Lyceum lay scattered like picked-over carrion. Every time Gil stumbled across a chipped piece of enameled tile in the street, he felt a sharp pang of sadness, reminded of the splendor of the Lyceum's magnificent halls.

He made his way across the campsite, nodding greetings at the scattered people going about their chores. Woodsmoke was heavy in the air from the cook fires, and the persistent, sharp ringing of metal striking metal echoed from the surrounding ruins, the sound of work parties excavating the remains of crumbled buildings.

He crossed the camp to the command tent, which was really just an improvised wooden frame covered with oiled canvas the size of three or four of the surrounding tents put together. In the absence of the Lyceum, it had become the mages' administration center. Gil had a desk in there himself, which he'd scavenged from one of the nearby buildings. He rarely occupied it, using it more often to gain a scant few minutes of sleep than he did reviewing lists of requisitions and supplies, which were becoming fewer as the days went by. There was a scarcity of parchment in the city, a scarcity of everything, really, including people.

He found Prime Warden Naia behind her desk, surrounded by five black-cloaked mages including her acolyte, a small woman with dull brown hair. Upon sight of him, Naia motioned Gil over, then proceeded to ignore him while she finished her conversation with the bulky Malikari captain who was in charge of the soldiers guarding their camp. After she had sent that man on, she turned to the next petitioner, launching into what looked like was going to be a lengthy conversation. Frustrated, Gil conspicuously cleared his throat to get her attention. When that attempt failed too, he interrupted her midsentence.

"Can I speak with you?"

The Prime Warden trained an irritated look at him. "Can it wait?"

"No." Unfortunately, Ashra was being Ashra, which made the situation on the walls unpredictable.

Naia sent the rest of the men and women out of the tent with a wave of her hand. She turned to look at her young acolyte, who sat on a stool behind her with a leather-bound book in her hand that looked to be nearing the end of its life.

"Priya, why don't you go get some rest," Naia said.

The woman rose silently from her stool, bobbing a quick curtsy. She flashed Gil a disgruntled look as she passed him, walking out of the tent with her book clutched tight against her side.

The Prime Warden motioned for him to have a seat at one of the two chairs that sat in front of her desk. Grateful to be off his feet, Gil took her up on the offer, setting his morning star down and spilling into the chair with a heavy sigh.

"It's Ashra," he grumbled. "She's not stepping down."

At the news, Naia rubbed her temples wearily. "And you tried reasoning with her?"

Gil nodded. "I did. She's not having it." He leaned back in his chair, stretching his legs. He'd been up most the night, and spent most of that time on his feet. He'd gotten precious little sleep over the past week, with the reports that had been drifting in of another approaching army. The citizens of Karikesh, already war-weary, had taken the news with predictable panic. The looting had increased, with more petty squabbles escalating into bloodshed and murder.

Leaning her head heavily on a hand, Naia looked up at him through an aura of hair that had escaped her braid. Very seriously, she said, "I can't have a mage leading an empire into war."

"I know." Gil blew out an exaggerated sigh, feeling his stomach tighten. He already knew what Naia would say. He knew it because he would make the same decision himself, if he were in her place.

"Then there's nothing more to talk about," she said. "You have my authorization to take Ashra into custody."

He'd expected that kind of order, but he would've preferred a little more direction. Shuttered in her command tent, Naia was shielded somewhat from the atmosphere of the city. Perhaps she didn't appreciate the logistics of what she had just asked.

Leaning forward, Gil said, "I can't just go arrest her in front of the entire Malikari army. They're all running around calling her 'Sultana,' for gods' sake. So how do you recommend I go about it?"

Unmoved, Naia lifted her eyebrows. "It's not my job to figure that out. It's yours."

Of course it was. Over the past few weeks he'd been given a lot of impossible tasks, but this one seemed heavier than all the rest of them put together. Gil scowled at Naia, for the first time noticing how haggard her face looked. Her eyes were bloodshot and ringed by dark circles, her skin paler than he remembered it. Like him, the Prime Warden hadn't been getting enough sleep. There simply wasn't enough time in the day to get it all done.

"All right, then. I'll find a way to bring her back." He scooted the chair out and stood, scooping his morning star up off the floor, then he turned and started toward the entrance.

"Gil." Naia's voice stopped him.

Turning, he looked back at her over his shoulder.

"I'm sorry," she said with a look of sympathy in her eyes.

Gil left the tent, the apology not doing much to quench his guilt. Outside, he stood looking around at the encampment. There were a few people sitting around the fires, though not many. The scent of cooking food hung on the air, not strong enough to disguise the other, less palatable odors seeping from the surrounding buildings. They had done all that they could to clear the bodies from the rubble, but there were still victims they couldn't get to, buried under the fallen structures.

He walked up to one of the fires, where a few spits of meat were braced over the flames. They looked cooked enough for him, so he removed a spit from off the fire with a nod of thanks at the man tending them. Taking a bite, he recognized the taste of half-rotten horsemeat. He'd never particularly cared for horse before the war, and liked it less after eating so much of it recently. But the orchards surrounding the city were barren, and the Turan Khar had devastated the surrounding farms, reaping them of their food stores as well as their citizens.

Tearing off another mouthful of gristly meat, Gil made his way back toward the North City. It took him some time to wind his way back through the streets, as navigating the city had become far more difficult, with obstacles ranging from broken pavers to the remains of entire buildings spilled across major thoroughfares. As he walked, the devastation around him became more acute; the North City had been devastated by the attack, far more so than the districts south of the canal.

A group of about a dozen soldiers ran toward him down the center of the street, forcing him to dodge quickly out of their path. He took it as a sign that something had changed, and probably not for the better. The sounds of shouts echoed from somewhere far away, ringing through the streets. The crippled city no longer slept, but was stirring awake.

Gil quickened his pace as more soldiers jogged past him in the direction of the walls. Ahead, the sounds of shouts grew louder and more emphatic as the quarter around him broke down into chaos. He already knew what to expect by the time he reached the square in front of the Dog Gate. There, Malikari soldiers had formed a defensive line behind the freshly repaired gate, which was barred and reinforced by beams set against it at an angle. Men scurried along the tops of the walls and collected in the spaces where the wall had been breached, working frantically to plug the holes.

Gil noticed one of his Battlemages standing off to the side, watching the goings on intently but doing nothing to help. He changed his course, sprinting across the square toward the man.

"What's going on?" Gil demanded as soon as he reached him.

The Battlemage, Caston, nodded in the direction of the gate. "They're bringing up a battering ram, just moving it into position."

Gil grimaced. Naia's order to arrest Ashra couldn't have come at a worse time. Not only would she be surrounded by militant defenders, but her removal was likely to destabilize the entire Malikari command structure. He thought about delaying or even flat-out ignoring the command. But in the end, he decided leaving Ashra in place was the more dangerous course. They couldn't afford the risk that magic might be wielded as a weapon against soldiers of the Kingdoms. Gritting his teeth, Gil clapped Caston on the shoulder and moved around him, making for the tower stairs.

Taking the steps two at a time, he arrived at the top of the tower and stepped into the middle of a commotion. Fires had been lit along the walls, and archers stood ready in defense of the gate, with sheaths of arrows laid out ready for their use. A line of men had formed a human chain, hefting stones from crumbled areas of the wall and depositing them in a growing pile at the corner of the tower, most likely to rain down on the men tending the battering ram when it arrived.

Despite the turmoil, it wasn't hard to find Ashra standing amidst a cluster of men, looking even more out of place in her elegant dress than she had before. She was staring out over the walls, an intense look of concern on her face. Gil made his way over to her, weaving through the press of bodies that crowded the tower.

Grabbing Ashra by the shoulder, he turned her toward him. "You've got to get down from here. They're going to be at the gate any moment, and from there, it's going to get ugly."

Ashra shrugged out from under his grip, stepping back out of reach. "Then I'll stop them," she replied tartly, walking away.

Deciding to try one, last time to appeal to her sense of reason, he dodged in front of her, saying quickly, "If you use magic in battle, you'll betray everything the Lyceum stands for."

Ashra spun away from him. "I'm not having this argument again. Is that the only reason you're here? If so, then get down off my tower!"

Gil suppressed the impulse to slam his fist into the stone of the rampart. She was going to leave him with no choice, and that infuriated him. In the end, there was nothing else he could do. He unhooked the talisman from his belt and, holding the morning star at his side, strode forward to intercept her. Ashra stood in the corner of the tower, doing her best to ignore him, which actually worked to his advantage. She didn't see him coming.

Reaching out, Gil caught her by the arm. Before she could react, he reached within her and twisted something deep inside.

The expression on her face changed instantly, going from vengeful to slack.

He caught her as she fell against him and whispered, *"Vergis."*

The ground shifted under his feet, the tower disappearing.

5

____

FATHER OF ALL

RYLAN AWOKE TO A COLD MORNING SUN PEEKING TIMIDLY INTO the room through narrow windows he hadn't noticed the night before. The bedchamber was dominated by an enormous canopied bed with carved posts. Tiny crystals in the walls reflected the wan light coming in through the windows, creating a dizzying ambience. He looked around the room, seeing a few other items of note: a squat wardrobe and two chairs seated at a table that held a glass vase with fresh flowers. Everything seemed to be carved in a way that eschewed right angles. Even the wardrobe had a multifaceted girth.

He rose from the bed and stretched, feeling warm and languid, as though he had been sleeping for days. Opening the double doors of the wardrobe, he saw it was full of drawers. Curious, he pulled them open one at a time and was surprised by what he found. Within were many different tunics cut to fit a man, each perfectly folded. The garments were made of *oki*, the priceless silk of the whisper butterfly. The bottom drawers contained trousers woven of the same fabric. Lifting one of the folded garments, he was impressed by the weight of it. Xiana had told him once that *oki* silk was tough as armor. He believed it.

Selecting a black tunic and matching trousers, he pulled them on and stood holding his arms away from his body, considering the garments, grateful to find they were cut long enough to fit his tall frame. The thought occurred to him that this outfit might have once belonged to Shiro. It was possible, perhaps likely. He wasn't sure if that bothered him or not. In the end, it didn't matter. He couldn't go naked about the palace. He buttoned the tunic's high collar, then started the hunt for his boots. It took him a moment to remember that he had emerged without them from his prison. He had no idea where any of his belongings were, or if they had even been saved.

He needed to try to find them, and he also wanted to find his daughter. She was somewhere within the palace; he could feel her through his link with the Unity. She was asleep at the moment, peaceful and content. Wherever she was, she had been well-cared for.

He opened the bedchamber door and stepped out into a well-lit corridor. To his surprise, he found two men and a woman who appeared to be stationed in the hallway. Each wore and iron band on their wrist with a ring that could be attached to a length of chain. He could feel the power in them, and it was substantial.

They were mages. All three of them.

Two were Darl. The woman had dark gray skin, her hair gray with a lavender sheen, worn close-cropped in a style he had never seen before on a female. At her side, she carried a slender black staff that was longer than she was tall. The Darl man next to her head hair white as frost, worn pulled back from his face. The third man was older, balding, his skin a warm brown mottled by freckles. A wooly beard formed a soft fuzz over his cheeks.

At Rylan's appearance, all three mages lowered their eyes

and bowed their heads. The devotion they held for him came to his awareness through the connection they all shared, the bonds of the Unity. He wasn't surprised. It was simply the way it was meant to be, the natural compliance to hierarchy and structure that was fundamental to Khar society.

The muscular Darl man brought a hand to his brow, touching two fingers to his forehead. "Warlord."

Rylan took it for a gesture of greeting. He mimicked it quickly, asking, "Do you know where my possessions are?" He knew it was a small chance. He wanted his boots returned to him, along with his father's belt and the sword given to him by the Sultan.

The Darl woman immediately turned and strode off down the hallway. Rylan wondered if he should follow, but decided against it. Instead, he remained behind with the other two mages. He considered them critically, wondering who they were and what their relationship to him was, if any. After a moment, the woman returned carrying an oiled sack, which she handed to him.

Rylan thanked her and knelt to open the bag. Rifling through it, he was grateful to find that all of his possessions were accounted for. He donned the boots and strapped his belt on over the thick black tunic. The clothes he had worn during the battle were badly damaged, stiff with blood, the fabric torn and, in some places, charred. Not knowing what else to do with them, he tossed them into the bedchamber. Feeling whole again, he turned and nodded his gratitude at the woman.

He started down the corridor. To his surprise, the three mages followed. Rylan stopped and looked back at them. He had assumed they were guards posted to ward his chambers. All he wanted to do was find his daughter. He didn't need an escort.

"Why are you following me?" he asked, abandoning subtlety and most likely courtesy.

"Father, we are your cadre," the burly Darl man responded, bowing his head.

Rylan winced. The unchained mages Shiro had surrounded himself with had all addressed him as 'Father.' Perhaps it was a customary honorific, but even so, Rylan didn't like it. It made him sound like a priest. In all truth, he wasn't sure if he was comfortable with any title, after spending a lifetime resenting those who wore them.

"Don't call me that," he said.

The faces of all three mages became very serious, as though he had just set before them a weighty problem. For a moment, they appeared deep in thought. At last, the Darl man asked him, "You are the Warlord, the Father of All. What else would we call you?"

Rylan thought about it. He understood that his rank would have to be acknowledged, at least in public. Grudgingly, he told them, "You can call me Lord. Or Warlord. Whatever you like— just not 'Father.'"

All three mages glanced at each other. The woman shrugged, and the old man nodded slowly, fiddling with something he wore around his neck tied to a length of twine.

The Darl man said stiffly, "Very well. We will call you Lord. Or Warlord."

Hesitantly, he extended his hand. "Rylan," he said, then hesitated, not sure which of his two surnames he should supply. All his life he had been Rylan Marshall, using the name of his adopted parents. But that was their legacy, not his. "Rylan Lauchlin," he decided with a sigh of defeat. Xiana had once told him he could not run from his heritage, and it turned out she'd been right. "It's an honor to meet you."

The white-haired mage grasped his hand in a strong grip. "Thank you, Warlord. My name is Varik. I am your base."

The lavender-haired woman came forward, bowing slightly,

and saluted him with her staff. "Thank you, Lord. I'm Farash. I am your crown."

The older man dipped his chin. "I'm Jendo Mahr. I am your core."

Rylan wasn't sure how their respective relationships to him mattered—or what they meant—but he could feel the esteem they held for him through the bond. They did not question his status as their Warlord, even though he had wrested the title from their former leader. He wondered if these three mages had served Shiro in the same capacity. He didn't remember seeing them in Shiro's retinue, but then again, he had been overwhelmed at the time and incapable of noticing much of anything.

Rylan asked, "What is a cadre?"

Varik responded, "Warlord, we are here for you to draw on, should the need arise."

It took Rylan a moment to realize what he meant. The man was referring to the power within them—within all three of them. If they were linked to him with one of the Khar artifacts that resembled chains, their power could be combined. He supposed that if the four them all linked together at once, the sum of their power would be substantial.

"How can I draw on you?" he asked. "Don't we need chains?"

Jendo answered, "Through the *A'isan*, the Warlord is linked to every member of the community. Theoretically, you could draw on every mage of the Khar Unity. Of course, channeling so much magic would no doubt kill you."

Rylan didn't doubt him. That would be like trying to light a candle with a bonfire. He would probably melt just like the wax of the candle, should he try to draw so much magic all at once. The thought made him shiver.

He looked from one mage to the next. "Then, how could I

handle the power of all three of you? Wouldn't that be too much?"

Jendo shrugged. "I'm sure you can do it for a short while without suffering any lasting damage. We are each forth tier."

Rylan thought about it. "So, if I drew on all three of you at the same time, it would be like being..." He did the math. "Twentieth tier?"

Jendo nodded. "That's right."

"That's not too much?"

"It shouldn't be. Legend has it, your own father handled much more than that when he helped seal the Well of Tears."

Rylan winced. He'd heard the same legend. "Aye, but it killed him."

"Only because he couldn't rid himself of it afterward."

Rylan bowed his head, suddenly saddened by the mention of a father he had never known. He wished he could have met him. He had heard so many conflicting things about Darien Lauchlin. In the Kingdoms, his name was used to scare children into obedience, while the Malikari regarded him as a hero. It was hard to know who to believe.

He turned his mind to the three mages in front of him and sifted through possibilities. Combined, their power would be overwhelming. The accomplishments that might be possible...

He thought about what it would be like to use such dreadful amounts of power on a battlefield. The results would be truly horrifying, he supposed. But the advantage... No wonder the Khar had been able to advance from nation to nation, leaving complete devastation in their wake. The might of the Warlord alone would be enough to lay waste to entire villages.

"If I link with you, how does that work?" Rylan asked. "Does that mean the entire community will know everything I'm thinking and feeling?" Since making his compact with Isaerae, he had become protective of his emotional autonomy. He didn't want to sacrifice it, at least, not until he was ready—which he wasn't yet.

"No," Jendo shook his head. "Because you are Warlord, your link with the community works in only one direction unless you desire otherwise. That way, you can maintain your independence—which you'll need if you're going to be making hard decisions. If you link directly with any one of us—take me, for example —your private thoughts and emotions would be shared just between the two of us. It wouldn't go any further."

"That's good," Rylan mumbled, chewing on that information. Looking down at his worn boots, he wondered if these mages would know the location of other things that belonged to him. He asked, "Can you take me to my daughter?"

"Of course," Varik said with a slight bow. "Come with me, Lord."

Varik turned and immediately started down the corridor. Rylan fell in at his side, Jendo and Farash walking behind them. They wound their way through a series of hallways that made up the guts of the palace, arriving finally at a narrow white door. There, Varik stepped aside, motioning for him to pass.

"Your daughter is within," he said.

Suddenly apprehensive, Rylan opened the white door and stepped into his daughter's room. There, he halted and stood gazing around in mild surprise. It was the perfect room for a little girl: small but tidy, full of plush woven rugs, a petite bed just her size, and a corner stuffed with dolls and toys. His arrival had awoken a young woman who sat in a chair on the other side of the room. His daughter's nursemaid, he guessed. Rylan smiled and nodded to her in greeting.

Moving forward, he approached the small bed and crouched beside it. He searched inside a nest of blankets until he found a little girl with soft black curls beneath all that bedding. At the sight of her, Rylan smiled, warmth flooding his heart. Amina's sweet face was relaxed in sleep, her lips parted slightly. The sound of her rhythmic breaths was the most beautiful noise in the world.

"Baby," he whispered, and reached to wake her.

But then he stopped himself. Amina was sleeping soundly, and he didn't want to disturb that tranquility. He decided to return when she was awake, perhaps spend the day with her. He ran a loving hand through her hair. With a nod of thanks at the nurse, he rose and left the room.

6

THE ENEMY

GIL KNELT, SETTING ASHRA'S UNCONSCIOUS BODY DOWN ON THE ground, and then stood, glancing wildly around at the camp to get his bearings. The makeshift tents that surrounded him were arranged in long rows and occupied the entire street in front of the Lyceum's charred rubble. They had arrived in the exact spot his mental image had conjured: the cleared space in front of the Prime Warden's pavilion.

Reassured, he quickly fastened *Thar'gon* to his belt and hefted Ashra into his arms, resting her head against his shoulder. Then he just stood there, realizing he had absolutely no idea what to do with her. His planning simply hadn't gotten that far. Come to think of it, he really hadn't had a plan.

She would have to be confined, though the thought of physically restraining her made him want to cringe. There were few intact buildings left in the quarter, and none of them were prisons—at least none that he knew of. Certainly none that could hold a mage against her will. There didn't seem to be any good solutions.

Taking notice of them, two mages stopped what they were

doing and started toward them with looks of alarm on their faces. Gil shook his head, fending them off. They slowed to a stop and, shooting him and each other confused glances, eventually turned away and went back to what they were doing. Gil heaved a sigh, wishing there was something they really could do to help. But in this entire despicable situation, the only person who really could make a difference lay unconscious in his arms.

Adjusting Ashra's weight, he set out down the street, his boots crunching on broken cobbles as he wound his way around fragments of debris. His gaze was drawn to a three-story structure a couple blocks down that had somehow survived the assault that had leveled the surrounding district. The building stood alone and forlorn, its walls blackened by soot. Within it, they had stashed many of the relics that had been rescued from the Lyceum. The building was under heavy guard to protect it from the looters who had made a career of going from ruin to ruin, sifting through debris like vultures picking over carrion. The building was the most secure place Gil could think of, the only place where he thought he could keep Ashra safe from others—and from herself.

At the building's entrance, he greeted the two well-armed sentries guarding the door. Recognizing him, the men stepped aside to let him pass, although their confusion over the unconscious woman he carried was evident on their faces. Shifting Ashra's weight, Gil carried her into the dim interior, past rooms stuffed full of scattered objects that together held more power and mystery than any other such collection in the world.

Ignoring the storage rooms, he took a rickety staircase up to the second floor and carried Ashra down a narrow hallway, its ancient boards creaking under their combined weight. By the time he reached the room at the far end of the hallway, his muscles burned from the strain of carrying her.

Pushing the door open with his foot, he stopped and glanced around. It was as he'd hoped: the room was furnished, containing a bed and a decrepit dining table, along with various odds and ends. The storage rooms on the first floor had been shops, and the owners had made their homes above their stores. The residence Gil had chosen still contained the possessions of the people who had abandoned it. The soldiers downstairs belonged to the Prime Warden's personal guard, and their presence alone was enough to make sure nothing got carried out. That, and the wards that had been laid down to protect the collections of artifacts, made this building the most secure place in the city. What had become of the residents who had once lived there, Gil didn't know. They may have been simply turned out of their homes... or their bodies might be encased in the rubble of the surrounding district. It was impossible to know.

He laid Ashra on the bed's straw mattress and covered her with a thick wool blanket. Straightening, he stared down at her, frozen, unsure of what to do. He didn't have the ability to keep a person from touching the magic field—no mage did. There were scant few artifacts in the world that could accomplish that, and he didn't have any of them on him.

He wondered if Naia had managed to save one of the field dampeners that had belonged to the Lyceum. There had been only three of them, that he was aware of. One had been Quin's sword *Zanikar,* which the Grand Master had been wearing at the time of his death. But there were two others: one in the form of a knitting needle; the other, something that looked like a thimble, but with a small spike at the end. They all required at least a drop of blood to activate.

Wiping sweat from his brow, Gil resolved to go find Naia and see if she had managed to save one, perhaps stored in the collection of artifacts downstairs. Failing that, he would have to find a way to keep Ashra unconscious and out of trouble until he could figure out what to do with her. As he turned away from her and strode out of the room, he swallowed back a feeling of nausea that clamped down on his gut. What he was doing wasn't right, he felt certain. But then, leaving her to command an army wasn't right either. He had no good options, and that was the frustrating thing.

Leaving the building, he went directly to Naia's pavilion, finding it empty. So he ducked back out and stood glancing around the campsite, hands on his hips, at last spying her at the far end by the barricades, surrounded by a small group of mages. She was easy enough to spot, marked by the bright white cloak she wore, the symbol of her office. Despite the destruction and death constantly surrounding her, Naia somehow managed to keep that cloak pristine.

Gil crossed the camp toward her, breathing in the cloying odor of smoke mixed with decomposition and human excrement that tainted the air. At the sight of him, Naia dismissed the ring of mages that surrounded her, releasing them to their respective duties. Dusting her hands off, she walked forward to meet him with an expectant look.

"I got her," Gil said, answering her unspoken question.

Naia nodded in acknowledgement, her shoulders sinking as though bearing a great weight. Her eyes slipped past him into the distance with a troubled expression.

"They're going to be breaking through," Gil warned her. "There's no walls to stop them. When I was at the Dog Gate, I saw them bringing up a battering ram."

Naia drew in a deep and heavy sigh. "It's unfortunate. They've already suffered so much."

Gil couldn't agree more. He wished he could do *something* to help. After spending two weeks defending the city's residents from one enemy, it didn't feel right to just abandon them to another. "They have suffered more than their due. There's got to be something we could do. At least speak with their commanders. This is an underhanded move on their part."

Naia's eyes became stern. "It *is* underhanded. Which makes it strategically brilliant. You can't fault them for it. We can't take sides in this, Gil. It's not our place to interfere."

Gil clenched his fists, the frustration within him coming close to boiling over. "I know. It's just hard. What about Ashra?"

"Did you get to her before she did anything to compromise us?"

"I did," Gil assured her, scratching the whiskers on his cheek. "By chance, do you have a field dampener?"

Naia nodded absently. "I do." With a sympathetic smile, she reached out and pat his arm. "Go get something to eat. I'll have the dampener brought to you. Keep Ashra out of sight and under guard, at least until this battle's over. Once the Malikari have surrendered, we'll figure out what to do about her."

"Malikari don't surrender," Gil reminded her darkly.

Scowling, Naia said, "Then this is going to get very ugly."

As she walked away, Gil decided to do as she suggested. He found a campfire manned by one of the retainers who, he knew from prior experience, could prepare a meal of spitted rat without it tasting too much like rat. If the shortages went on, cats would be next on the spit. Those, they had in abundance. Dogs were in less danger of ending up on a dinner plate. They were used widely to protect property from looters and were the best way to search out bodies buried in the rubble.

He accepted a charred rat poked through a metal spit then sat down to eat on a large block of broken marble, part of what must have been a scalloped column. Rat was a meager meal and a bit tedious to eat; the bones were small and easy to miss. At least it stopped the belly from grumbling. When he was done, Gil tossed the spit in a pile of other spits and rose, wiping his hands clean on his pant legs. Now all he needed was a water barrel.

He turned to look for one, but was startled to find that Naia's young acolyte had come up behind him unnoticed, bearing a small leather purse in her hands. The acolyte's jaw was clenched, her eyes narrowed, as though she were terrified she might drop the purse.

"The Prime Warden wants you to have this," she said, offering the small bag to him with both hands.

Gil accepted the purse with a mumbled word of thanks. Opening the drawstring, he saw that it contained the silver thimble artifact he remembered. With a sigh of relief, he immediately turned and jogged back to the building where he'd left Ashra. People stared at him as he passed. Many of the faces looked nervous, and it took him a moment to realize why.

In the distance rose the unmistakable clamor of fighting in the streets, a sound he'd become all too familiar with.

Gil hurried his pace, sprinting into the building where he'd left Ashra, and jogged up the steps to the second floor. She was still sleeping peacefully, for which he was more than grateful. Kneeling beside the bed, he slid the silver thimble from its purse. All he had to do was prick her with the small spike at the end, and that would activate the dampening ward imbued in the artifact. Taking Ashra's limp hand, he slid back her sleeve and placed the thimble on his thumb, setting the spike against the soft skin of her arm.

Gritting his teeth, Gil pressed the spike into her skin.

A drop of blood appeared immediately. Hastily, he pulled the thimble off his thumb and replaced it back in the bag.

Ashra groaned in her sleep, fussing a bit. He set her arm down at her side then sat back, anxiously watching her sleep. Outside the windows, the sounds of shouts and fighting was growing louder. The Kingdoms' soldiers were advancing through the city much quicker than he'd thought they would. They were his own people, his own kinfolk, but Gil couldn't help feeling angry and bitter. The Malikari had conquered this land, but they'd had reason. He couldn't blame them for that.

Two months ago, he wouldn't have felt conflicted. But in the last few weeks, his feelings had changed. Gazing down at Ashra, Gil thought he knew why. Her face was beautiful. Fragile. It was no longer the face of an enemy.

Reaching down, he caressed her cheek.

7

NAZAPOR

RYLAN CLOSED HIS DAUGHTER'S DOOR, THEN TURNED TO THE three mages who stood awaiting him in the hallway. Varik and Farash leaned against the far wall, while the old man, Jendo, stood cleaning the grime from under his fingernails with a small knife.

"I want to look around," Rylan said. "Where exactly are we in the world?"

"Nazapor," answered Farash, arching her back to push herself off the wall. "The Darl ancestral homeland."

"Where is that?"

"On the northern continent of Tur," Varik clarified, hooking a thumb into one of the two straps that crossed his chest. One was a pack, the other some kind of a wide, flat sword that he wore slung across his back. He had a casual stance that was almost a careless slouch, and his arms were heavily muscled. Rylan suspected that he was the only Battlemage among the three.

The old man wore a milder expression, his eyes wise and patient. To Rylan, he had the look of a scholar or perhaps a diplomat. The tunic he wore was long, almost a robe. It had an odd swirling pattern to the fabric.

Looking from one mage to the other, Rylan said, "I'd like to go out and have a look around the city, but I'd rather not take all three of you with me. I don't want to stand out."

Farash grinned. "You'll stand out no matter what you do or who you're with."

Scowling, Rylan realized she was right. "I suppose I'll have to get used to attention."

All three mages of his cadre smiled as if they knew something he didn't. They probably did. Rylan fell in beside Jendo as Varik led them downstairs and out of the palace, into the bright glow of moonlight. On the other side of the doorway, Rylan stopped, pausing to stare open-mouthed at the city below him.

The palace stood on a cliff, overlooking a starlit valley that reminded him of a bowl of frosted crystal. Snow had recently fallen, and the entire world around them was covered in unrelieved white. A frozen lake dominated the center of the valley, spreading from a glacier to the north. The surface was crusted with shimmering buildings that appeared carved from ice. Moonlight reflected off the walls in a glittering display that made Rylan feel like he was looking down upon a sea of stars. He stared in unabashed wonder, deeply moved by the sight.

"What's down there?" he asked, nodding at the sparkling buildings that jutted from the ice like a forest of crystals.

Farash shrugged. "Homes, businesses. The usual things you'd expect to find in a city."

Rylan couldn't understand her nonchalance. Perhaps she had grown accustomed to the view and didn't appreciate what a beauty lay spread before her.

"I want to go down there," he said.

Farash and Varik exchanged amused glances.

"The lake's quite a distance, Lord," Varik said. "It's farther than it looks."

"That's fine," Rylan said. "The walk will do me good."

Farash shrugged, then waved him forward. "Follow me, Lord."

He was beginning to wish he'd chosen another honorific. Nevertheless, he held back his complaint and started after her, accompanied by Varik and Jendo, who seemed determined to walk at his side. The road that led down from the mountain was wide and descended gently toward the lake. Rylan paused and glanced back at the palace, curious to see what it looked like, and was rewarded with the sight of what appeared to be a crystalline castle that seemed to have grown from the side of the mountain. The sharp plains of its towers thrust upward into the sky like jagged spikes, dazzling in the moonlight.

"It's quite a sight," Rylan breathed.

He followed Farash as she started forward again. This time, Varik fell in behind them. Rylan walked at Jendo's side, finding himself very much at ease around the old man. There was something about his personality that reminded him of the Sultan, though he couldn't put a finger on it.

"Jendo's a Shiran name, isn't it?" Rylan asked, then winced.

That question hadn't been his own; he didn't have that kind of knowledge. Instead, it had come from somewhere deep inside his head, from the buried part of him that was Keio Matu. It was not the first time the man had stirred awake, although the times were becoming less frequent. Still, whenever it did happen, Rylan was always left feeling shaken.

"My mother was from Nagala," Jendo said guardedly. "But I was born and raised in Shira."

Rylan frowned, pondering the man's words. Shira had ceased to exist eight thousand years ago, when the Turan Khar had decimated the nation, cleaving it apart city by city. But then, the Turan Khar had also disappeared eight thousand years ago.

A sudden realization slammed into Rylan, making him halt.

He stared hard at Jendo, then turned his gaze to both Farash and Varik. Then he looked past them, down at the dazzling city below.

All of the Turan Khar had been swallowed by the Sky Portal, consumed into hell, where they had remained for the same eight thousand years, waiting for the Sky Portal to open again and regurgitate them back into the world. Looking at his three companions, he wondered if they were all as old as Shira itself.

Rylan asked Jendo. "Did the Turan Khar capture you?"

The old man corrected him with a strange, enigmatic smile, "They brought me home."

Rylan understood what he meant, for Jendo's voice echoed his own feelings. He had ceased thinking of himself as a man of the Kingdoms the moment he had willingly placed the iron shackle of the Unity on his wrist. As far as he was concerned, it was the best decision of his life. Thinking of the comforting presence of the community within his heart, he turned his gaze back to the valley.

Home.

The sparkling walls seem to beckon him. Following Farash, Rylan made his way down off the mountain. As their party approached the valley floor, they were met by people who were about in the streets. At the sight of him, the citizens of Nazapor paused what they were doing and turned toward him, bowing their heads in deference. Rylan was hit with the sudden urge to retreat, to run back up the hill and hide from the attention. He didn't deserve such reverence, and was quickly becoming overwhelmed by it. The farther they went, the more people collected around them, and he could feel all of them, each citizen individually. The flow of information was too much; he was drowning in it, smothered by heavy layers of emotions. He clenched his hands into fists and ducked his head, unable to make eye contact.

Jendo must have sensed his distress. The mage put a hand on his back, sending feelings of understanding and reassurance through the bond. The man's quick response brought Rylan some relief. He drew up and closed his eyes, struggling to collect himself.

"Do you want to go back?" Jendo whispered in his ear.

Rylan shook his head. "Not yet."

He willed himself to press forward. Their passage parted the crowd that was gathering ahead of them, anticipating their arrival. The further they walked, the wider the roads became. Rylan stared over the heads of the crowd, admiring the architecture of the buildings they passed. They were unlike anything he had ever seen. Most were made of smooth gray stone, while others looked carved from slabs of ice. Blue moonlight glowed from deep within the crystalline walls, illuminating the street in strange patterns and ghostly hues. As they approached the center of the city, the structures around them grew in size, jutting from the ground to either side of the street, their translucent walls scattering the starlight.

Eventually, they came to a large square paved only with lake-ice. From the center of the square rose a tall ice sculpture of a winged man holding a horn. Hundreds of people were gathered about the statue, and Rylan could feel their excitement even from a distance. By the time the crowd parted to admit them into their midst, the weight of their combined presence in his mind was nearly unbearable. He drew to a stop in the center of the square, too overwhelmed to continue. The people around him seem to blend together in a swirling haze, dark shadows against a glimmering, surreal world.

A loud screeching noise came from above, drawing his attention. Glancing up, Rylan saw several winged shapes that resembled serpents circling like hawks overhead. He instantly recognized the sound of their cries. A similar creature had hunted him in his flight from Farlow with Gill and Ashra a month before. He hadn't known then that he was being chased by a spy of the Turan Khar. Seeing them there, circling above him, was chilling.

Until they invaded his mind.

The creatures greeted him with feelings of excitement, recognizing their new master. One by one, they slid down from the sky, dipping toward him as if in salute. There were four of them in all: each slender and reptilian with bat-like wings, about the size of a cat. One in particular hovered over him, its wings beating furiously.

On impulse, he reached out his mind toward it.

Feeling his touch, the creature shrieked and dove toward him. Rylan cringed back, raising his hand to fend it off. Sharp claws bit into the flesh of his arm. He recoiled, jerking back, leathery wings beating his face. A forked tongue snaked out and licked his cheek. Opening his eyes, he saw that the creature had alighted on his arm like a raptor returning to the falconer. He stared at it in shock, and it stared right back at him with acute intelligence in its eyes.

It wasn't a bird, but it wasn't a reptile either; rather, something in between. It had a blue serpentine body with an exceptionally long, snakelike neck. It hopped from his arm onto his shoulder, curling its tail around his neck and digging its claws beneath his collarbone. He was hit with a strong feeling of contentment. Somehow, he knew that the creature was pleased with its new master and excited to serve him.

"What is it?" He reached a hand up to stroke its chest.

"A dracipiter," Varik responded, regarding it warily. "A winged demon of moderate intelligence."

Reaching up, Rylan tentatively stroked the leathery blue skin of the dracipiter's neck and was surprised by how soft its hide was. In response, the creature flicked out its black tongue and caressed his cheek, the feel of it sending shivers down his neck.

He asked, "What purpose do they serve?"

Varik shrugged. "Dracipiters mostly serve their own purpose. Sometimes they provide us with surveillance."

"Where are they kept?" He wondered if it would be possible to take this one with them. It seemed to like him well enough, and he was fascinated by it.

"Dracipiters are not 'kept,'" Varik said with a frown. "They belong to the sky."

The strange creature was rubbing its head against Rylan's whiskered cheek with a purring noise that reminded him of a cat. The creature on his shoulder spread its wings. The sharp talons gripped harder, piercing his skin. With a squawk, it leaped off his shoulder and took to the air, flooding Rylan with feelings of regret and apology for causing him pain. He watched it bank overhead before slipping away into the night with a graceful stroking of wings.

As he watched the dracipiter disappear into the dark sky, his eyes were drawn to something behind it: a dark mass of clouds that had swirled together into the form of a vortex with a dark eye at its center. Just the sight of it made his stomach clench with dread.

"What's that?" he asked, pointing.

Varik peered upward, his face suddenly grim. "Warlord, that is the Sky Portal."

8

A CITY OVERRUN

THE SOUND OF HIS NAME JERKED GIL AWAKE. HE SQUINTED HIS eyes against the light coming in through a window across from him. Had he fallen asleep? He batted his eyelids, trying to clear the heavy fog that clouded his head. Sitting up, he rubbed his eyes, the action bringing Ashra's face into focus.

She was sitting up in bed, glaring sharp daggers of hatred at him, confined by woven bonds of air.

"What did you do to me?" she growled in a voice cold as vengeance.

He'd seen that look in an animal's eyes before, but never in a woman's. It was the same look given him by a stray tomcat that some boys of the academy had trapped under a wooden crate. By the time he'd cleared the scoundrels away, the cat was hissing and spitting, and it raked his arm open when he'd lifted the crate to free it. He hadn't blamed the cat at the time, just as he didn't blame Ashra for hating him now.

"I dampened you," he said apologetically.

Her eyes widened with dread, and her jaw slackened. "What about the battle?"

"I don't think it's going well," Gil told her truthfully. He glanced at the window, listening. The sounds of fighting still echoed through the shattered streets of the quarter, closer than before he'd fallen asleep. The Kingdoms' soldiers must have found a way to cross the river.

"Gil, please," she begged. "My people need me."

He wished he could help her, but he couldn't. Frustration clenched his gut like a fist. "I'm sorry," he said. "I've got to leave you here for a little while. I'll be back."

He rose and started toward the door.

"What are my people supposed to do?" Desperation cracked her voice. "Go back to starve in the Black Lands?"

Gil paused in the doorway, turning back to her. "You've still got the rest of the North."

"For how long?"

Gil bowed his head, realizing he didn't have an answer for her. Helpless to do anything else, he left Ashra there and fled down the stairs to the ground floor. Outside, the sounds of fighting were even closer than he'd thought. The ringing of weapons and the cries of men seemed only a few blocks away. Alarmed, Gil hurried toward the end of the street.

Before he could get there, dozens of civilians spilled into the camp, streaming southward. Seconds later, soldiers wearing the black uniforms of Chamsbrey began collecting on the other side of the barricades at the end of the street. Gil ran toward them, trusting that his black cloak would identify him to the soldiers. There were already mages stationed near the barricades, two Querers and a Battlemage. All three looked alarmed, as if they had no idea what to do.

Taking notice of him, a small group of soldiers broke off from the rest and, ignoring the barricades, moved to intercept him. They met him halfway, and a man with a sergeant's insignia raised his hand at him.

"This is our camp," Gil snapped. "Tell your men to stay clear of it."

The sergeant, looking skeptical, peered past Gil to the rows of tents set up behind him. "Are you harboring any hostiles?"

The question took Gil off guard. He wondered what the man's definition of 'harboring' was. "Some of our servants and retainers are Malikari. They're noncombatants, and you can leave them the hell alone."

The man looked exceptionally unmoved. "You'll have to turn them over."

Gil set his jaw, stubbornly shaking his head. "They're our colleagues, our servants, and our friends. They're not going anywhere."

The sergeant stared at him deadpan. "The city is to be cleared of all foreign hostiles. Nowhere in my orders does it say, 'except for colleagues, servants, and friends.' I'm sorry, Master Whoever-the-Fuck-You-Are, but you'll have to find new help."

Gil could have put his fist through the man's throat. He also didn't care a whit what the sergeant's orders were—he outranked him. "No. Our people stay with us. Tell your men to skirt this area but don't come into the camp."

The man's eyes looked thoughtful. Perhaps he was considering his options. Once again, his gaze swept past Gil, and he stood for a long moment surveying the encampment behind them. He sucked in a cheek, his lips squirming into a frustrated scowl. At last, he gave a curt nod.

"You'll have your way for now, then," he conceded. "I'll tell my men to stay clear. But you'd better keep your people close. I can't vouch for their safety."

Gil didn't like hearing that, but he supposed it was the best compromise he was going to get. He turned away, walking over to where the other two mages stood at the end of the barricade. "I want you to stay here," he ordered them. "If any of this rabble tries entering the camp, send for me right away."

"You got it, boss," said a man named Harvor, who stood fingering a long knife as he stared past Gil at the soldiers.

Harvor was a good man. Gil felt better with him there; he could trust the intersection would be secure. Leaving the mages to their task, he crossed back through the camp to make sure the other approaches were being guarded. He didn't think the Chamsbrey soldiers would purposely target mages or their campsite, but it was hard to say what men heated with battle rage would do. The last thing he needed was misunderstandings, or worse.

There wasn't a lot of activity throughout the camp. It seemed most of the mages that remained behind were Malikari. He was glad to see them there and not out in the streets. He thought about telling them to shelter in their tents, but decided against it. As long as their perimeter was secure, they should be safe, especially with the black cloaks on their backs.

He stopped by the command tent and found Naia standing outside with three of her acolytes, surveying the situation with a grim face. Handing the purse with the thimble back to her, he gave her a quick summary of the situation.

"I don't trust them," Naia said, her face stern. "Reinforce every intersection. I don't want their soldiers coming anywhere near this camp."

From another street over, a woman started shrieking. The sound made Gil's body tense, every nerve tightening like harp strings. His first impulse was to run toward her—for that was the right thing to do. But war is seldom right, and the present situation was no exception. No matter how much he wanted to, he couldn't get involved. He squeezed his eyes shut and clamped his hands into fists as the shrieks grew frantic and then suddenly stopped.

He looked at Naia and saw her studying his face. She shook her head.

"I know," he said, so angry he wanted to spit. It had always been his job to keep people alive. Letting them die went against every instinct he had.

"I'll see to the perimeter," Gil snapped. "Just keep the servants well away from it."

He left the Prime Warden and hastened to the western end of the camp. There, he didn't have to worry about soldiers flooding in from the streets. The buildings on either side had been reduced to hunks of rubble that had spilled over, blocking entry from that direction. The only other entrances into the camp were at the north and eastern intersections, bordering the Kasri Souk. The souk had been devastated by the Turan Khar, but it was still a popular place for looters. He'd have to keep his mages out of it.

When he reached the barricade on the western end of camp, he found a group of a dozen mages gathered behind it, along with an equal number of Malikari regulars, some of the few who had managed to survive the battle with the Turan Khar. The sight of them there, mixed in with his mages, made Gil immediately nervous. The Kingdoms' soldiers might take it as a sign they'd picked sides. He didn't want to turn the soldiers out—an action that would surely get them killed—but he also knew he couldn't shelter them in the camp.

He drew up well short of the barricades, frozen by indecision, and looked beyond the small crowd to the intersection beyond. The fighting hadn't reached it yet. But by the sounds echoing off the walls of the souk, it wouldn't be long.

He made his decision.

Striding forward, he called to the Malikari soldiers, "You men! What are you doing?"

"We are preparing to hold the square," replied one of the men, older and taller than the rest. He bared an inch of blade from his scabbard.

"We don't need you here," Gil told him sternly. "There's

nothing you can do, anyway. Head on down the street until you see a large building on the left. Take cover there."

The soldiers glanced back and forth between each other.

"No," the man growled. Shaking his head, he drew his sword fully from its scabbard. "There is no honor in hiding."

Gil despised the rigidity of the Malikari honor code. Furious, he spat, "But there's honor in dying?"

"There is," the man answered solemnly. Turning back to his men, he raised his sword. "For *sharaq!*"

Before Gil could protest, the group of soldiers scrambled over the barricade into the intersection beyond and rushed north toward the sounds of the fighting. Within moments, the sounds of clanging weapons echoed through the streets. Then the noises stopped, and a heavy silence followed. Gil clenched his fists in rage. He had made a decision that had gotten men killed. It wasn't the first time, but this was different. This was a waste.

Minutes later, the intersection was overrun with black uniformed soldiers. Raising his hands, Gil strode forward to meet them before they could make designs on the barricade.

"That's far enough!" he shouted.

Heated from battle, a soldier surged toward him with a raised spear. One of his compatriots reached out and caught him by the pauldrons, dragging him back.

Gil shouted, "In the name of the Prime Warden, I order you to go no further! This is our camp!"

At first, they didn't listen to him. But then someone who might've been an officer raised his sword in the air, bellowing orders. The men with him turned and started southward, avoiding the barricade.

With growing frustration, Gil turned back but then stopped at the sound of screams. Whirling around, he glanced back across the barricade to find a group of soldiers chasing civilians out of one of the nearby buildings. The soldiers gathered the residents up on the side of the street and pinned them against the wall with crossbows trained on them. There were two women in the group, one holding a baby.

Gil immediately started toward them. He didn't know what they would do to the civilians, but he didn't trust them.

One of the men shouted, and the soldiers holding crossbows release their quarrels. Every male prisoner fell dead to the street, the women standing helpless, sobbing. The one holding the baby threw her head back and let out a raw, throat-shredding wail. Gil lurched forward, scrambling over the barricade and running headlong into the center of the street. Seeing him, soldiers whirled and turn their weapons on him, but then froze at the sight of his cloak. Gil made it halfway across the street before he realized why the mother was shrieking.

A crossbow bolt had struck her babe.

Without thinking, Gil moved forward and snatched the child from her grasp. Turning his back on the soldiers, he summoned the magic field and sent his mind burrowing deep into the tiny body in his arms, gasping in relief to find that the child was still alive. The quarrel had gone all the way through, which was good. Using magic, he snapped the iron head off and withdrew the shaft, then worked as rapidly as he could to staunch the bleeding. Within seconds, he held an unblemished child that was sleeping peacefully. He turned to the mother, but she wasn't there. Startled, he looked around.

And found her lying on the ground.

They had killed her and the other woman while he was distracted with her baby. Consumed by rage, he backed away from the men who had so coldly murdered an entire family.

"They were civilians!" he shouted at them. *"What the hell are you doing?"*

"Orders," said a soldier whose face was hidden by his helm. "No prisoners."

Horror-stricken, Gil stood paralyzed. He gasped, "Then drive them out! Don't murder them in the street!"

The helmed soldier scowled and spat on the ground. "No one leaves the city. That's the order."

Gil stared at him a long moment, processing the man's words, his brain grappling to understand the magnitude of atrocity that existed in that statement.

"We're taking back the North," the man informed him. "The *entire* North."

Gil glanced down at the bloody bundle in his arms, his anger overboiling. "You're murdering children!"

The soldier shrugged. "Children grow into adults."

Trembling, Gil hugged the child tighter against his chest, fighting back the urge to split the soldier in half. "What exactly are your orders?"

"My orders are to kill every man of fighting age and round up the women and children. If they resist, then we kill them." He shrugged. "They showed us no mercy. Fair's fair."

Gil shook his head, backing slowly away toward the barricade. "You're wrong," he growled. "They let us run. They took our land, but they left us our lives."

The soldier smiled blandly. "Well, we're doing things a bit differently."

9

THE CORE MAGIC

RYLAN TURNED OVER IN BED, WAKING FROM A DREAM IN WHICH HE held his wife in his arms. She wasn't there, of course, but for some reason, he could still smell her, as though she had been lying there beside him and had just risen from bed, her scent lingering behind on the sheets. Sitting up, he pushed back his covers and looked around.

The room was empty.

Dismissing his misgivings, he rose and crossed the room to the wardrobe and dressed in the dim light filtering in through the windows. The urgency of the situation gnawed on his consciousness. It was almost time again to feed the Sky Portal, to pay the God of the Netherworld his due. Someone would have to be sacrificed in payment, and his Empress didn't want it to be one of their own. Rylan didn't want that, either, but he also didn't want it to be one of the mages taken from the Rhen.

Somehow, he had to find a way to preserve them all. There could be no compromise.

Opening the door, he was surprised to find the three mages of his cadre waiting for him. Looking from face to face in confusion, he asked, "Don't you have anything better to do than stand in the hallway?"

"No, Lord," Jendo responded with a wry smile. "Our duty is to wait for you here every morning."

At his side, Farash offered an apologetic grin.

"Right," Rylan muttered, running a hand through his hair. "Then maybe you can help me. I need some way to get information on an ancient magic." To Jendo, he asked, "Do you remember much of Shira?"

The man looked at him with a guarded expression. "I do."

"Do you know anything about when I..." Rylan winced. "...when Keio Matu seized the core magic?"

Jendo compressed his lips, slowly shaking his head. "No. I had no part in it. Nor would I have agreed to it."

Rylan scratched irritably at his face in frustration. Looking at Jendo, he wondered if there were others like him, other mages in the Khar Empire that had worked more closely with Keio Matu. There had to be. The Turan Khar had conquered Shira, and they would have absorbed as many of Shira's mages as they could.

He asked Jendo, "Is there anyone alive who would have knowledge of the core magic?"

The old man glanced down and for a moment seemed to be studying the floor tiles with great intensity. "There is one man," he said at last. "A mage."

"What's his name?" Rylan pressed.

"His name is Maro, Lord."

Rylan felt a tingling stir of hope. "Do you know where this Maro lives?"

"You can find him yourself, through the link."

Rylan blinked. Of course. Through the *A'isan,* he had access to every member of the Unity, both collectively and individually. He didn't know who this Maro was, but one silent query sent the information reverberating back to him through myriad channels.

Absently, he muttered, "He's somewhere down in the city. Let's go. I want to speak with him."

They lingered only long enough for Varik to grab him a bite to eat from the kitchens before heading out. Outside the palace, the morning was pale and gray, and the sun glowed dimly from just above the southern horizon. Hundreds of lights glimmered up at them from the frozen valley bowl, the azure glow of street lanterns frothing with magelight.

Soft snowflakes drifted down from the sky, alighting on Rylan's shoulders, and his breath formed a cloud in front of his face. Surprisingly, the *oki* weave of his tunic kept out the chill of the air. He didn't shiver once, even when a biting wind kicked up, chasing them down off the hillside and into the winding streets of Nazapor.

They found the house they were looking for in one of the outer districts, pressed up against one massive arm of the glacier. The walls of the little house were made by blocks of a peculiar stone that reminded Rylan of smoked quartz, which seemed a common building material in the city.

He knocked on the door then stood waiting, shifting uncomfortably. When the door opened, he found himself staring at a woman with the same, dark complexion as Jendo. The tunic she wore was dyed with an intricate geometric pattern, her hair woven into many rows of thin braids. At the sight of him, she bowed her head deeply.

"Warlord," she said in a low voice, and went gracefully to her knees.

"Don't," Rylan commanded.

The woman rose with a confused look.

"I'm looking for a man called Maro," he said.

"Maro is within, Father." Motioning him forward, she moved aside to let him pass.

Rylan took a step toward the door but then stopped abruptly. It suddenly occurred to him that he understood what this woman had said, even though there was no way she could be familiar with Rhenic. These people were from another time, another place. They had to be speaking a different language. But somehow, he needed no translation. Looking from the woman to his three companions, it occurred to him that they were all from very different places in the world, and yet they communicated with him easily. The answer lay within the Unity, he realized. All members of the society shared a common mind, a common purpose, that transcended the need for spoken language.

Within, the interior of the house was dim, lit only by a single clay lantern that sat upon a small table. The floor was covered with rugs and soft mats, the room dominated by a large bed. A man rose from the floor and stood before them, bowing deeply. He was garbed in a long robe, his head wrapped in a thick turban. By his complexion, Rylan thought that he might have been originally from Nagala, Jendo's homeland.

"Warlord, I am honored," the man uttered in a deep and throaty voice.

The woman retreated to a corner of the room and knelt beside a kettle that hung over an iron stove sunken into the floor.

Approaching the man, Rylan offered his hand. "Maro, it's good to meet you. I heard you were from Shira. I'm looking for something that you may have knowledge of. Something called core magic."

Maro frowned, releasing Rylan's hand. "Father, surely you know far more about the core magic than do I."

"I don't know anything about it," Rylan admitted as Jendo came up to stand at his side.

Maro's eyebrows scrunched together, confusion deepening

his frown. "Father, you are the Custodian of Suheylu Ra. How do you not remember the power you usurped?"

Maro's tone of accusation wasn't lost on Rylan. He spread his hands in apology. "I'm not Keio Matu. He lives within me, but I don't have his memories. Nothing specific, at least. I can work magic because of him, but it's more like a reflex, like something I just do without thinking. I don't remember anything from his life. At least, nothing that matters."

"Then I'm truly sorry," Maro said gravely, as though Rylan had admitted some great failing. He could feel waves of sympathy radiating from the man, though he didn't understand why.

Maro extended his hand, indicating the rugs on the floor. "Please, Warlord. Come sit with me. Could we get you anything to drink?"

Rylan lowered himself to the rugs, while Jendo remained standing behind him. Maro sat cross-legged on the floor across from him and leaned back against the wall. He raised an earthenware pitcher, scooping up a cup.

"Please, Father. Drink."

Rylan wondered if the offer of drink was more than just simple courtesy. In Malikar, the offering of food and beverages to household guests was obligatory and greatly symbolic. This man had been gracious to allow them into his house, and Rylan didn't want to offend him simply because he wasn't thirsty. Maro poured him a cup of dark tea, placing it in Rylan's hand.

"I lived in Suheylu Ra, just as you did," he said. "But I wasn't anywhere near the Guardian Tower. I was an architect." He poured himself a drink and took a long sip. "The only thing I know about the core magic was that the Council was using it as an experimental power source. A large part of Shira existed under a vortex, where magic couldn't be used. The cities there were hundreds of years behind the rest of the nation. When the core magic was discovered, the Council saw it as a way of getting magic to those places that didn't have access to it. Among other applications."

Rylan took a sip from his cup, enjoying the flavor of the tea. It felt good on his throat, cold, and tasted of berries flavored with spice. "What other applications?"

"The mages of the Sanctuary were experimenting with a powerful defense grid."

Rylan raised his eyebrows in insight. "The Watchers."

Maro nodded and took a great gulp from his cup. "Yes. The Watchers used core magic to bend the lines of the magic field into focus."

Rylan rifled through his memories of the last moments of Suheylu Ra. Keio Matu had overcharged the Watchers and aimed their combined might at the Sky Portal, destroying it instantaneously. Rylan had no idea how they worked or how he had accomplished the act.

"Why core magic?" he asked.

"Because the magic field can't be used to change its own nature."

Rylan took another a sip of the berry-flavored tea. "I don't understand."

Maro explained, "The magic field travels over the ground in particular patterns that can't be altered... normally. The lines of the magic field are contoured by the earth itself. Core magic has the ability of influencing those lines. But unlike the magic field, it's finite."

Rylan leaned forward. "Where was it stored?"

"Not in Suheylu Ra." Maro shrugged. "That's all I know."

Rylan heaved a sigh, sitting back and setting his cup down on the floor. "Is there anything else you can tell me? Anything at all?"

Maro shook his head. "Nothing, Father. I'm sorry."

Deflated, Rylan nodded. He rose to his feet, offering Maro his hand. "Thank you for your hospitality."

This time, Maro returned his handshake without hesitation. "May you serve well, Father."

"Thank you." As Rylan moved toward the door, he nodded his thanks to the woman kneeling by the stove.

When the door of the little house closed behind him, he turned to his three companions, swallowing his frustration. "Well, that wasn't a complete waste of time, but it really didn't get me anywhere." Turning to Jendo, he asked, "Do you know anyone else who might have knowledge of the core magic?"

"Not that I ..." His eyes widened.

Suddenly, the old man lurched forward and slammed into Rylan, nearly knocking him off his feet. Rylan reacted immediately, sucking in magic and honing it into a killing blow as his eyes searched for an enemy.

Before he could find one, a flash of brilliant light overpowered his eyesight. At the same time, a torrent of pain slammed into him from Jendo's body, jabbing his spine. Rylan turned to see a fiery spear streaking toward him from across the street. He brought his hand up just in time, and the spear exploded in a fireball.

Panting, he lay Jendo down while Varik and Farash leapt in front of him, swords drawn. Rylan bared his own sword, turning slowly around, searching the shadows for sign of their attacker.

There was a deafening *whoosh.*

Suddenly, he was on fire.

Rylan dropped to the ground and rolled, sucking all the energy in the air into him as fast as he could. The air around him chilled and condensed into mist, and the fire hissed into nonexistence. Shaking, Rylan looked down at himself, relieved to find that the only thing burnt on him were his clothes.

"Where is he?" Rylan gasped.

"I don't know!" Farash shouted, raising her staff. "It's more than one! They must be chained!"

"Warlord, link with us!" Varik shouted.

Rylan did. Reflexively, he reached out through the *A'isan* and connected with the minds and gifts of the two members of his cadre that were still conscious. The power that filled him was instantaneous and overwhelming, so much so that he gasped, stiffening. For, at that moment, he became *isan,* the mage in control of the totality of their combined power. Harnessing his guardians' strength, he rushed forward, angling toward a row of houses, from where the spear of fire had originated.

At the sight of him, the shadowy form of a man slipped back through a doorway. Rylan pulled up, weaving a shield around himself as he lashed out with his mind.

The house exploded. Shards of burning crystal were flung into the air that rained back down to stab into the street like hailing daggers. He didn't know for sure whether his action had killed their attacker, but he didn't want to take the chance. He extended his shield to encompass both Varik and Farash as the two mages dashed across the street toward him.

"Who's doing this?" Rylan gasped.

"Who knows?" Varik panted. "No one in the community!"

Rylan wasn't sure about that. The commotion they were making should attract attention, but he saw no people anywhere in the surrounding neighborhood.

Behind them, Jendo cried out. Rylan growled an oath, turning to go back to him.

But Varik's hand caught his shoulder, yanking him back.

Another fiery spear streaked past him, just missing his cheek.

He heard a sharp cry, and then the part of him that was Varik went suddenly silent.

Rylan stood in shock in the center of the street. One of his companions lay dead before him, and he could feel Jendo's pain through the link. He turned slowly in a circle, searching for his attackers.

He heard them before he saw them.

The sound of feet crunching on ice came from all around, closing in from all sides.

Turning, Rylan saw that he and Farash were surrounded by pairs of mages linked by chains. There were at least a dozen of them, both men and women.

Rylan's blood chilled to ice water. He was left with only one member of his cadre, and even with Farash's strength, he was powerless against so many.

The encroaching mages stopped still a good distance away. A lone man stepped forward, bearing a war hammer in one hand and looking as though he had every intention of using it.

He stopped in front of Rylan, his dark eyes hard and vengeful. "Why did you betray us?"

Rylan frowned. "How did I betray you?"

The man lifted his weapon as though testing the weight of it in his hand. "You are supposed to be our Warlord. And yet you choose to feed us to the void!"

A man and woman stepped forward, the chain that linked them scraping across the ground. "You murdered our Warlord! You robbed us of the Rhen's mages! Now it will be *our* souls fed to the Sky Portal! It will be *our* blood spilled in sacrifice! *Betrayer!*"

"*Betrayer! Betrayer!*" The cry rose from all around them.

Rylan shook his head. "No. That's not what I'm doing—"

"Tonight it shall be *your* soul we feed to the Sky Portal!" growled a white-haired man linked to a pasty-white woman at his side. "Bring him!"

Two mages move forward, grabbing him by the arms. He didn't bother to fight; there were too many. Behind him, Farash was being likewise restrained, while Jendo lay bleeding to death somewhere behind them on the ground.

The men at his sides pushed him forward, and Rylan had no choice but to stumble after them. There was nothing else to do. Where were the rest of the people of Nazapor? Surely, they had felt his plight through the link. Yet no one emerged from the surrounding houses to champion him. The city streets were entirely, inexplicably empty.

"How are you doing this?" Rylan asked.

The white-haired man barked a laugh. "We serve the Unity. Not one man."

"What if I can stop this? What if I can close the Sky Portal?"

"It's not possible," hissed a black-haired woman who stalked at his side.

"I believe it is," Rylan insisted. "If I can free the core magic—"

"Silence!"

One of the men cuffed the side of his head. They were leading him through the empty streets toward the center of the frozen lake. Overhead in the sky, the clouds had turned violent and circulated eerily. While he'd been distracted, the day had grown cold and dark, and an awful silence clenched the city in its grasp. An icy fear shivered across his skin.

The clouds above rumbled, rotating around a dark vortex.

It was the Sky Portal, he realized, the thought bringing him close to panic.

And he could *feel* it. It hungered with a terrible need that ached.

Frantic, Rylan glanced around at the men and women surrounding him. He knew now what they intended to do with him. Thunder rolled across the sky, and a terrible wind picked up. Overhead, lightning arced across the clouds toward the gaping throat of the vortex.

The man next to him screamed.

Suddenly, the air was alive with the beating of wings. Something slammed into him hard, knocking Rylan to the ground.

Rolling, he scrambled on his hands and knees to the side of the street, where he squatted, glancing back. Behind him in the intersection, men and women flailed against writhing, snake-like bodies that darted between them, breathing gouts of flame. Screams of death rose, and bodies littered the street.

In a matter of seconds, only winged demons moved in the intersection, hopping from corpse to corpse, hungrily devouring a meal of charred meat. Razor-sharp teeth gashed through muscle and sawed through bones. Each dracipiter claimed a corpse, flapping and squawking with territorial displays whenever another came too close. When they had eaten their fill, they took to the air, bodies glistening and slick with blood.

Silence claimed the street.

Nothing moved. The freshly fallen snow was splattered with dark streaks of gore.

Picking himself up off the ground, Rylan jogged across the street to where Varik lay sprawled on the ice. Crouching next to him, he probed the man with his mind and sensed only empti-ness within. He bowed his head, closing his eyes, feeling suddenly, profoundly sorrowful. Farash came up next to him and knelt at his side. Without saying anything, she removed the iron band from Varik's wrist. Then she placed her hand on his forehead, muttering something that sounded like a prayer. She leaned forward and tenderly kissed Varik's lips.

Rylan stood and ran to Jendo. He found the old man lying on the ice, bloody and injured—but alive. Closing his eyes, he sent a flood of healing energy into him to make certain he stayed that way. All around, people were emerging from the nearby buildings, gathering to take in the scene with wide eyes and horrified faces.

Rylan looked up at the sound of a squawk.

He felt a rush of air as a dracipiter alighted on his shoulder, while another circled above him. A long tail curled around his neck, and a cold tongue licked the side of his face. A jumble of confused emotions tumbled into him.

He let his gaze travel from the serpentine creature on his shoulder to the glut of charred bones strewn about the inter-section. He stood there reeling, feeling suddenly weak and terribly cold.

10

SLAUGHTER

GIL HURRIED TOWARD THE COMMAND PAVILION, CRADLING THE unconscious child in his arms. As he walked, he stared into the slumbering face that had only moments before been close to death. The babe's bundling was saturated with blood, giving him chills. He stopped and closed his eyes. Reaching within, he imagined what the blankets would look like clean.

When he opened his eyes, they were.

Almost, he could imagine that nothing had happened. It could have been any babe in his arms, sleeping peacefully. Not a child that had been shot through with a crossbow bolt, whose mother lay dead in the street. Trembling, he clutched the child closer against his chest and hurried his pace.

Ahead, gray smoke rolled from a leaning building that looked on the verge of collapse. The sight made him shiver. He'd seen too much war in the last few weeks. Even the sight of something simple, like a building on fire, gave him a physical, visceral reaction. He felt every nerve tense, the hair on the back of his neck standing up. His heart thudded wildly, beating at his ribs.

Reaching the command pavilion, he stood in the tent's

entrance for a moment, letting his eyes adjust to the dim light of the interior. It took him a moment to realize that Naia was staring at him through the swarm of advisors gathered around her desk. Seeing his expression, she rose immediately, hurrying toward him.

"Why do you have a baby?" she gasped.

Seeing red, Gil all but flung the child at her. "Because soldiers killed her mother and shot her through!"

Naia's expression melted. Glancing back, she called, "Priya!"

Her prim acolyte skittered forward, moving as though a fire had been lit under her. Without hesitating, she removed the sleeping bundle from Gil's arms and stood awkwardly rocking, making soft cooing noises. Naia moved toward her and placed a hand on the infant's chest, closing her eyes. She stood like that for the span of heartbeats, at last turning back to Gil.

"What was your involvement in this?"

"I was just there," Gil snapped. "Look, we've got to do something. They're slaughtering everyone!"

Naia's face compressed in empathy. "I'm sorry, Gil. It's the nature of war."

Gil shook his head emphatically. "No. This is different. These people are beaten, but the soldiers aren't stopping." He drew in a sharp breath, all the frustration in him clenching his lungs. "They're murdering children, Naia!"

"Intentionally?"

"Yes, *intentionally!* They've been ordered to kill everyone in the city!"

Naia breathed a curse, the first one Gil had ever heard pass her lips. Her eyes went to Priya and the sleeping infant in her arms. Shoulders sagging, she brought a hand up to her face and rubbed her eyes. When she spoke, it was with all the weight of the world pressing down on her voice. "The minute we are perceived as supporting one side over the other, we lose all trust."

Gil could hear his pulse throbbing in his ears, and his head felt like a lit keg of black powder. "Prime Warden—"

Naia raised her hand. "What would you have me do? Send Battlemages to kill our own soldiers?"

She was right, of course, but knowing that didn't help. With a snarl, he brought his hand up to knuckle his brow. *This is so wrong!*

"Yes! It's wrong!" Naia agreed. "But if we intervene, it will only go *more* wrong."

She was probably right about that, just as she was right about everything else. But Gil couldn't accept that answer. Without saying another word, he whirled back toward the tent flap.

Naia's voice stopped him. "What are you doing?"

He turned to glare at her. "Something."

She nodded, resigned. "Then come here."

Grudgingly, he obeyed, although he really didn't want to hear anything she had to say. His mind was made up, and the last thing he wanted was someone in authority telling him what he couldn't do. But Naia's expression had softened, her eyes growing thoughtful.

Moving toward him, she leaned forward, whispering in his ear so that only he could hear, "Please understand: I can't condone anything you do. If you decide to act, you're on your own. Do you understand what I'm telling you?"

A faint tingling of hope stirred in Gil's chest. "I do. Just please—let me take Ashra."

She pulled back from him. Staring at him flatly, Naia asked in a voice loud enough for all to hear, "What did I just tell you, Warden Archer?"

At first, Gil was confused. Then the import of her words sank in. The hope in his chest flared like a candleflame invigorated by a gust of air. He couldn't help the smile that sprang to his lips. In all his years as a mage serving under Naia, he had never been more proud of her.

"Thank you, Prime Warden," he muttered, bowing low in gratitude.

"Godspeed, Gil."

Leaving the tent, he made his way back to the building where he'd left Ashra, trying to ignore the sounds of fighting ringing through the quarter. As he walked, he stared, fixated, at the sleeves of his white shirt, which were stained brown with the blood of the infant. He knew he could erase that grim reminder with magic, but decided against it. He left the stains there to remind himself of why it was necessary to do what he was about to do.

Jogging up the stairs to the second floor, he made his way quickly to the room where he'd left Ashra. When he entered, she looked up at him from the bed with red, watery eyes that burned with hatred. Without pausing, Gil lunged forward, dropping to her side to release her bonds.

"What are you doing?" she gasped.

"Getting you out of here."

He severed the magical bonds of air he had woven around her then dispelled the dampening ward. The gratitude on her face made him feel as though a mountain's worth of guilt had been lifted from his shoulders.

"Why?" she asked.

He swallowed. "Because I have to. Come on."

He took her hand and led her toward the doorway.

"What about Naia?"

"Don't worry about Naia."

In the hallway, he stopped, pausing a moment in thought. He brought his hands up and released the brooch that held his cloak. When the fabric fell off his shoulders, he gathered it in his hands and just stood there for a moment, staring down at it with a deep feeling of regret. Then, closing his eyes, he willed the color to change.

And it did.

The embroidered silver star disappeared as though seared from the fabric. Within seconds, he held a plain cloak the color of dark forest green, the kind any common peasant might wear. With a forced smile, he held up the cloak.

"Here. Put this on."

Ashra stared at him in confusion. "Why?"

Draping the cloak over her shoulders, he moved closer to pin it with his brooch. "Because I can walk freely about the city, but you can't—especially not in that dress. So you're going to pretend to be my wife."

Her mouth opened, her eyes filling with tears. Before they could fall, he chided her, "Why did you have to wear that dress today?"

"Because I wanted to make a statement."

"Well, you're making one. Unfortunately, it's not the kind we need right now." He tugged the fabric of the cloak together, making sure the dress beneath it was well-hidden. "Better," he said at last. He offered her his hand. "Walk with me?"

Smiling in gratitude, Ashra accepted it. "Where are we going?"

"To the gate."

"No. I can't abandon my people."

When she tried to tug her hand away, he tightened his grip. "We're not abandoning anyone. Just listen to me." He led her down the stairs as the boards cracked and groaned beneath their weight. "We've lost the city, so the only thing we can do is try to rescue as many citizens as we can. Right now, they've barred all the gates to prevent people from leaving. We need to open them, and make sure they stay open. Well, at least one gate. That's probably all you and I can manage."

She didn't respond immediately, not until they'd left the

shadows of the building and emerged into the street. There, Ashra paused, shielding her eyes against the sun and glancing around fearfully. The sounds of war shuddered the neighborhood around them, and black smoke poured from the nearby streets, darkening the air.

"All right," she gasped, choking on ash.

Nodding his thanks, Gil led her toward the barricade. As they walked, he held her hand tightly, knowing he couldn't let it go. She was Malikari, and therefore a target. He had to do anything he could to make her less of one.

"Pull your cowl forward. Keep your face down," he instructed. "Hopefully, they'll be looking at me more than you."

Moving around the barricade, he stepped into a street filled with debris. The walls of the surrounding district were chaotic, their bricks darkened by flames, their guts strewn into the street. Three bodies lay within eyeshot. There were no soldiers immediately visible; the fighting had passed through and continued on.

"We'll make for the Mouse Gate," Gil said to Ashra, heading for the street that led north toward the Waterfront. The boulevard was empty, but up ahead was a crowd of people who had gathered at an intersection. He hurried toward them, curious to see what had drawn them. But when they arrived at the back of the crowd, he couldn't see anything—there were too many people collected in front of them. So he led Ashra around the perimeter, until he found a hole in the crowd big enough to see through.

A line of men had been gathered in the center of the intersection. They were kneeling on the ground, their hands tied behind their backs. Chamsbrey soldiers stood over them. At the order of an officer, the first sword fell, severing a head as the crowd reacted with screams and sobs. Clenching Ashra's hand, Gil backed away, maneuvering her toward the nearest side street. She turned back at the sound of a scream.

"Just keep walking," he commanded.

He hurried her down the street away from the clamor of the crowd. She pulled against his grip on her hand, glancing back.

"Keep walking!"

A cluster of uniformed soldiers jogged past them at a dogtrot. The officer leading them eyed Gil up and down, his eyes going to Ashra suspiciously. Gil's chest tightened, apprehension squeezing his lungs. It wasn't until the sound of the men's footfalls faded behind him that he let out a long, relieved breath. He could feel Ashra's hand trembling in his.

The sound of a woman's terrified shriek sliced toward them from an alleyway.

"Keep walking,"

"I can't," Ashra moaned. He could hear the anguish in her voice.

"You have to. There's nothing you can do right now."

She let out a strangled noise that sounded halfway between a groan and a sob. More soldiers spilled out of a side street, spreading out and moving toward them. Gil made eye contact with the man nearest him, nodding politely. With any luck, they would mistake them for a married couple from one of the old Rothscard districts.

The soldier nodded back, walking past. Gil's nerves tingled in relief. Their guise was working, so far. The soldiers didn't look back as they continued up the street, picking their way around debris. Once the men were out of earshot, Gil turned to Ashra.

"I don't know how long this is going to work. Be prepared for anything."

She nodded but didn't answer. He walked at her side, past the tortured form of a building leaning precariously over the street. The sound of screams echoed from the neighborhood behind it. As they passed, the screams were drowned out by shouts, and then the shouts were drowned out by silence. Gil glanced nervously at Ashra, wondering how long she would be able to hold herself back. He couldn't see her face beneath the cowl, but he could feel the tension in her grasp.

When they reached the Waterfront, they came across a mob of soldiers chasing two Malikari men who fled wildly before them. The soldiers caught up with them halfway into the intersection, knocking them onto the ground and then kicking them brutally.

Ashra let go of his hand.

"*No—!*" Gil gasped, reaching for her.

But she was already gone.

Sprinting after her, he tried catching hold of her cloak, but missed. With a cry, Ashra flung her hands out in front of her, as though shoving open a door. Ahead, soldiers cried out as they were lifted off their feet and hurled through the air, their bodies impacting with the walls on the other side of the street. Their bloody victims staggered to their feet, reeling drunkenly before stumbling away.

The soldiers were already recovering. With growls of anger, those that could sprang to their feet and surged toward them, drawing their weapons. Gil staggered to a stop, feeling torn completely in half. The soldiers hurling at them were his own kinfolk. He watched as one swept out with his sword at a bleeding Malikari man standing in the street. The man's head went tumbling off his shoulders, his body falling in the opposite direction.

Ashra screamed and threw up her arms. Ahead, the fleeing soldiers collided with a wall of invisible knives. They were cut down between strides. Gil caught up with Ashra and clutched her shoulders, gripping her hard as he stood gaping at the carnage. He could feel the air physically leaving his lungs, leaving him weak and dizzy.

Ashra had used magic to kill.

All the years they had struggled to regain the public's trust in mages were now wasted. Everyone would know that magic had been wielded as a weapon against people of the Kingdoms. For a moment, Gil just stood there staring, his jaw slack.

Ashra whirled toward him, stark terror on her face. "I didn't mean to!"

"Doesn't matter!" Gil gasped. *"Run!"*

He ran first, tugging her after him, sprinting past the bodies that littered the street. Soon they were joined by other fleeing civilians, who came scattering into the road from alleys and side streets. Gil glanced behind, wondering where they were all coming from. He couldn't tell. All he knew was that he was grateful for the cover.

They ran with the panicked crowd until they reached the bridge that spanned the canal. Soldiers holding spears and kite shields lined the streets. Strangely, they were not attacking, instead waving the crowd past as if herding them onto the bridge. Gil slowed, his stomach tightening. He didn't know why the soldiers wanted them on the bridge, but there was nowhere else to go. Every side street was warded by ranks of soldiers who stood shoulder to shoulder, funneling them forward. Gil forced himself to keep running, even though his lungs burned and his sides screamed.

He was surprised when they made it over the bridge unharmed.

But then, suddenly, the crowd ahead of them stopped.

For a moment, every person in the street around him stood silent, eyes wide and glancing around. From ahead came the sound of screams. And then the entire crowd started stumbling backward, the people in front of him crushing him into the people behind.

A frantic man charged into him, moaning and babbling, and began battering his way past him with hands and elbows. Ashra cried out as she was shoved aside, his hand ripped from hers. He was forced away from her as an entire wall of people collided into him, forcing him back. He couldn't move. His arms were pinned against his sides.

"Ashra!" he screamed, frantically glancing about.

But she was nowhere in sight.

The crowd surged against him, crushing him up against a wall and squeezing the air out of his lungs.

"Ashra!" he wheezed.

But she wasn't there.

He'd lost her.

11

THE HUNGERING

RYLAN FOUND ISAERAE IN HER THRONE ROOM, A CRYSTALLINE queen seated upon a crystalline throne. She was surrounded by people: ministers and courtiers, many of them mages. Although the throne room was filled with people, it was also filled with silence. No one spoke, for there was no need for words. Through her command of the Unity, Isaerae would already know the concerns of every supplicant in the room, so there was no need to give them voice. Each person in the Khar Empire was spun from the same thread, each woven into the tapestry of their civilization.

Noticing Rylan, Isaerae looked up and met his gaze, acknowledging him before he could interrupt the ebb and flow of her silent discourse. He clenched his jaw in frustration, forcing himself to stand still and wait as his Queen returned her attention to matters of the Empire. He glanced at Farash and Jendo, who came forward to stand at his side, their gray tunics rent and darkened with blood. Both mages wore expressions of calm patience that were at odds with the anxiety that gripped his own spine.

He stood there a few minutes until, at last, Isaerae's eyes

opened, and she sat upright. As one, every person in the chamber turned and drifted toward the door, lowering their gazes in deference as they passed by. Glancing at Jendo and Farash, Rylan nodded his gratitude and dismissed them with a thought. Bowing, the two remaining members of his cadre departed on the heels of the others, the door closing behind them.

He gazed at his Lady, who sat contemplating him silently from her throne, one arm draped over a crystalline armrest.

"Why didn't you warn me?" he asked.

He made no attempt to hide his anger. Isaerae already knew his feelings, just as he knew hers. She was troubled by the situation—mostly by his own actions. She thought he had acted naively, though she understood why.

"If you had been listening to your children, they could not have taken you unaware," she scolded him.

Rylan understood what she meant. It was too easy to hide behind the distancing effect of the *A'isan*. If he had been paying better attention, he would have never been caught off-guard by the people who had risen up against him. He would have felt their unrest from the beginning, and could have dealt with them proactively. Varik hadn't needed to die.

Still, the whole event was confusing. It defied everything he understood about Khar society. "But how is it even possible that they could rebel against their Warlord?"

Isaerae brought a long, slender hand up, brushing aside a spun-glass lock of hair. Her eyes, the color of amethyst, regarded him sympathetically. "It is possible because the Unity is decaying, and the threads that connect us are beginning to fray."

Rylan had sensed the decay she spoke of but hadn't realized the extent of it. It occurred to him that the process must be accelerating, and it wasn't hard to guess why. *He* was the reason for the deterioration. The Sky Portal had gone too long unfed.

It was shrinking, depriving the Unity of its consistent power source. If it wasn't fed soon, their entire existence would collapse.

Isaerae looked at him flatly. "You need to start making the hard choices."

Rylan squeezed his eyes closed against the pain of unbearable guilt. The choices she wanted him to make were not hard—they were impossible. They were choices that went against every grain of his nature, choices no man should ever be asked to make.

She rose from her chair and took him by the hand. Leaning into him, she kissed him softly on the Isaerae and whispered, "The first time will be the hardest."

His throat clenched as he realized what she was asking of him. He glanced at her for confirmation.

She pulled back, still holding his hand. "Two mages survived the attack on you today. They are no longer assets to the community."

Rylan understood. If the bonds connecting these mages to the Unity had become so corrupt, then they were like a cancer. And, like a cancer, they would have to be cut out before their corruption could spread to infect the rest of their society. Their deaths were justified.

Closing his eyes, he reached out through the *A'isan*, groping through the warp and the weft of the Unity, searching for the two mages who had turned against him. They weren't hard to find; the fibers that connected the two of them ran counter to the rest, and he could feel their fear and anger trembling the web around them.

Isaerae was right. They were no longer assets.

"Come."

Rylan hesitated, guessing her intent. Nevertheless, he allowed her to lead him out of the throne room and into the hallway beyond, where they were joined by Jendo and Farash, along with the other mages of Isaerae's retinue who step to the side to let them pass. Rylan walked beside his Empress up the palace stairs to the highest floor. There, she led him out onto a storm-darkened balcony ravaged by winds. In the center of the balcony, Rylan halted, letting go of her hand and craning his neck to look up.

Above, a turbulent mass of clouds swirled violently around the dark vortex that was now centered above the palace. Lightning flickered, forking across the surface of the clouds, before being sucked into the mouth of the funnel. Wind rushed to feed the hungering portal, battering Rylan's clothing and lashing his hair against his face.

His blood went cold as he stared upward into the dark maw above. He could feel its need. It pulled at him greedily, as though yearning for his flesh. He glanced at Isaerae.

She held her hand out, indicating something behind him.

He turned to see the two surviving mages who had assaulted him. They stood in the center of the balcony, bound together by a single iron chain. One was a tall man with gray skin and a thick, dark beard; the other, a woman with smoke-gray hair that rippled in the wind. Both were staring upward into the hole in the sky with faces frozen by fear.

Talat.

That was the man's name, and Pedra was the woman. The knowledge of them slammed into Rylan, along with the sum of their raw emotions, a heady combination powerful enough to make him reel. Talat felt justified for what he'd done. He stared up defiantly into the mouth of the vortex above them. He wasn't afraid to die, but he didn't want to die *like that.* He clutched Pedra against him, saddled by both his own fear and hers. Whatever Pedra's feelings were about her own part in the attack was smothered by her terror. She stood gazing open-mouthed at the maelstrom, tears draining down her face, utterly unaware of Talat's attempts at comforting her.

Overhead, the swirling mass of clouds thundered their anger.

"Choose one to go today," Isaerae said. "The other will be held for later."

Rylan bowed his head and rubbed his eyes, his insides going cold. He was the Warlord, and it was his life that Talat and Pedra had attempted to take. It was his decision to make. But he had no idea which one to pick.

Pedra let out a sob. Talet clutched her harder against him, his own cheeks glistening.

"I'm sorry, Father," she whimpered. "I'm so sorry! So sorry…"

Rylan knew she was. He could feel her regret, and he knew her remorse was true, not something merely compelled by the fear of death. Pedra sincerely believed she had been led astray, and the shame brought on by that knowledge overcame her terror.

"Take her, Father!" Talat begged. "Don't make her watch me die, then sit in a cell waiting for her own end. That's cruelty."

"And what about you?" Rylan asked.

He could feel Talat's courage slipping. Every second drove another nail of fear into his body, cracking his resolve. Nevertheless, he was holding up, and Rylan couldn't help but respect him for that.

"I can wait," Talat said, raising his chin. "Do Pedra a kindness and take her quickly."

Rylan glanced at Isaerae, feeling sick.

"Choose quickly," she murmured.

Rylan bit his lip, shuddering in indecision. "How often does it need to be fed?"

Isaerae glanced up at the hungering maw, her crystalline hair billowed by the gale. "It depends on the amount of vitrus." She raised her voice to be heard over the wind. "A single sacrifice can keep the portal stable for a week. Sometimes longer, if the mage is of a higher tier."

Which meant there was no reason why they couldn't go together. Resolved, Rylan turned back to the two condemned mages struggling against terror in each other's arms.

"I choose them both," he said.

Talat released Pedra and, leaving her there, moved toward Rylan as far as the chain connecting him to Pedra would allow. Seeing his intention, Rylan covered the remainder of the distance, drawing up in front of Talat and gripping his shoulders. He paused, looking deeply into the man's eyes, letting the nobility he saw there settle into his soul. Not knowing what else to do, he kissed Talat's cheek.

"I'm sorry I raised my hand against you," the man said, wiping his eyes with his shirtsleeve. "I misjudged you. I understand that now. Forgive me, Father."

"I forgive you," Rylan said then stepped back. Turning away, he walked back to stand at Isaerae's side while Talat returned to Pedra and took her hand, lifting her fingers to his lips. He kissed her skin softly, holding her gaze with his own.

"Move back," Isaerae commanded.

Rylan stepped back with the rest of their retinue, pressing his body up against the crystalline wall of the palace, leaving both Talat and Pedra alone in the center of the balcony under the gaping throat of the portal.

"What's going to happen?" Rylan asked.

"Just watch."

He glanced up at the seething turmoil in the sky, his insides stiffening. A keening came from within the portal's depths, growing louder by the second, rising until it reached an earsplitting pitch. The fury of the wind increased, buffeting the palace. The clouds above swirled faster, the vortex sucking the breath right out of the air. In the center of the balcony, Talat and Pedra clung together in each other's arms.

The portal's wail became a shriek. Both Talat and Pedra threw their heads back, covering their ears and screaming piercingly. A terrible light lashed down from the heavens, consuming the balcony. Rylan threw up his hands to shield his face as the world glowed red through his eyelids. Talat and Pedra's screams became raw shrieks that overpowered even the rage of the wind.

And suddenly silenced.

Rylan opened his eyes, blinking furiously to clear the dark motes that circled his vision. Glancing up, he saw that the sky overhead was calm, free of any sign of clouds. The stars glimmered at him, echoing the glimmering lights of the valley.

Looking back at the balcony, he let his eyes wander to the empty space where Talat and Pedra had just been standing.

The man and the woman were gone. The only sign they had ever been there was a wet halo of blood.

12

——————

SURRENDER

THE TIGHT CLUSTER OF PEOPLE GRADUALLY YIELDED, GIVING GIL some room to breathe. He shoved his way out from the wall, glancing about frantically for Ashra. He finally got a glimpse of her, standing in the street, turning and glancing about wildly, calling his name.

"Ashra!" he shouted, squeezing toward her through the crowd.

When he reached her, he caught her arm an drew her close, afraid she might be separated from him again. All around them, panicked faces glanced nervously about, many of them bruised and bloodstained. Gil tried to peer over the people in front of him to see the cause of the bottleneck ahead, but the crowd was too dense.

"Let's try to see what's going on," he said.

Taking Ashra's hand, he wound forward through the press of bodies. Fortunately, the dazed crowd yielded fluidly before them. Most people seemed to hardly notice them, moving aside automatically as their attention was focused ahead, searching for the nature of the threat. The street was filled with the cries of babes and the sounds of moans and weeping.

It took a while to reach the side of the street. There, Gil climbed on top of a crate, where he was able to see over the heads of the crowd. Before them was a circular intersection where five different streets came together. Each street was blocked by thick ranks of armed soldiers. There was nowhere for the citizens to go. The Mouse Gate lay somewhere ahead, the closest exit from the city. But with the soldiers blocking the roadways, the fleeing civilians couldn't reach it. Looking back, Gil tried to estimate the number of people gathered behind them, waiting to pass. There had to be at least a thousand.

Glancing up at the sky, he saw that the clouds hung even lower than they had an hour ago. The wind was picking up, bitterly cold, stabbing sharp needles into the skin of his cheeks and tossing his hair around. It was a chaotic sky, uncannily echoing the turmoil below it on the ground.

"Stay here," he said to Ashra, releasing her hand.

She glanced at him in concern. "What are you going to do?"

"I don't know," Gil admitted.

"What are you *willing* to do?"

He bit his lip. "I don't know. Just stay here."

"But I'm the Sultana—"

"*Shut up!*" he growled, hoping to all the gods that none of the nearby soldiers had heard her. Leaning close, he whispered, "If you tell them who you are, they'll kill you. Now, for just once in your life, *do what I tell you.*"

Resentment flared in her eyes, but it faded quickly, at last burning out. Licking her lips, she nodded.

"Thank you," Gil whispered, more flustered than grateful.

Raising his hands, he moved away from Ashra and the protection of the crowd, crossing the square toward an age-worn soldier with a skeletal face who stood slightly apart from the rest, looking like he might be someone in charge. The soldier watched his approach warily. Frowning, he raised his hand and gave his men the signal to hold.

Gil nodded at him in greeting. "I'm Gil Archer, Battlemage of the Lyceum."

The old soldier looked him up and down as though he didn't believe him. It didn't help that he wasn't wearing a black cloak. But Gil still had the emblem of the chain on his wrist, the mark of the Acolytes' Oath, a symbol that was universally known. He rolled back his sleeve and bared his arm, holding it up for the man to inspect.

"I want to speak to your commanding officer." Gil tugged his sleeve back down.

The man glanced to the side, shifting uncomfortably. "Well, he's not here."

"Then get him here," Gil snapped. "Rapidly, Lieutenant!"

The man stiffened, looking torn. His eyes darted from Gil to the crowd behind him then back to the soldiers blocking the intersection. He turned back to Gil, staring at him fixedly.

"Corporal Hollis!" he shouted.

A young man scurried forward, one hand resting on the pommel of his sword. "Yes, Lieutenant?"

The officer kept his eyes fixed on Gil. "Run and inform the Colonel that there's a Battlemage desiring to speak with him."

"Aye, Lieutenant!" The man turned and sprinted away, disappearing into the deep ranks of the men behind them.

Gil stared hard at the officer until the man looked away, scowling heavily and shifting his weight from one foot to the other. Beads of sweat had broken out on his brow despite the chill of the wind.

They waited for minutes. The whole while, Gil stared intensely into the lieutenant's face while the officer looked conspicuously anywhere but at him. At last, a shout parted the ranks of men behind him, allowing a small group of soldiers forward. Gil turned to acknowledge the gray-bearded man who drew up in front of him.

The man spat gruffly, "Colonel Holisgrave of the Northern Division of His Royal Majesty's Armed Forces."

Gil offered his own name, choosing the most important-sounding version of his title. Cocking his head to the side, he asked, "Would you mind telling me exactly what your men are doing here, Colonel?"

"My mission is to secure the city," the Colonel answered in a harsh, authoritative tone.

Gil didn't like the man's callous answer. He also didn't like the unyielding hardness in the officer's eyes. This was not a man who liked negotiating. "Well, then. Your job is done here. These people are defeated. Call off your soldiers."

The Colonel raised a finger. "Are you trying to tell me how to run my army?"

Gil felt his ire rising. "Your men are indiscriminately killing civilians."

The officer shrugged. "Many of my men have lost fathers and brothers to this war. They're thirsty for vengeance."

That answer made Gil's fists tighten in anger. He snapped, "Exercise some control over your men, Colonel."

The officer stared at him deadpan. "I am. They're following my orders to the letter."

Gil glanced away from the vile man while he struggled to maintain his composure. He looked back through the crowd of helpless people behind him, his eyes coming to rest on Ashra. One look at her solidified his resolve.

He turned back to the Colonel. "Let them go."

"No. If I let them go, I'll just have to fight them all over again somewhere else."

Gil looked past the officer to the soldiers behind him. They had bloodlust in their eyes, to a man. They all had the look of wolves ravaging a dead animal. Gil figured it would take as much effort to pull these men away from slaughter as it would to drive wolves off a fresh kill.

He ground his teeth in indecision, glaring into the Colonel's eyes. The man had to have a conscience. It was buried deep, but if there was even a chance he could appeal to it, it was worth a try.

He said, "Two months ago, this city was home to almost half a million people. We lost over a third of that population to the Turan Khar, but that still leaves over three hundred thousand residents. Think about that, Colonel. Do you really intend to slaughter *three hundred thousand* civilians?"

The man leaned forward and let a dribble of spittle fall to the ground. Wiping his chin, he said to Gil, "There's no such thing as a Malikari civilian. Every one of them springs from the womb with a sword in hand."

Gil took a deep breath, summoning the last dregs of his composure. "Please. Let the civilians flee with their lives."

The officer spread his hands. "And where will they go? North to fortify other cities we'll be attacking in a few weeks?"

"They have to go *somewhere!*"

"No. They don't."

The response stunned Gil. For seconds he just stood there, unable to comprehend the magnitude of indifference it would take to say such words.

"You're serious," he whispered.

The Colonel had the audacity to smirk. "This was our land before they took it from us. It is our intent to take it back. *All* of it."

That was enough. There was no reasoning with this man. Gil could see it in the Colonel's eyes: the officer was incapable of compassion or shame.

But maybe, for the sake of expedience, he would be willing to compromise.

"Let the women and children go, along with the elderly," Gil offered. "In exchange, every man of fighting age will lay down his weapons and surrender." He had a hard time getting that last part out, for he knew he had just condemned every man in the city. But if the deaths of the fathers could spare the lives of their children and wives, he knew it would be worth it to them. It would be worth it to him.

Colonel Holisgrave paused long seconds without speaking, eyes staring into the distance. At last, he nodded. "I'll agree to it if they will."

"Let me ask," Gil swallowed the sour taste of bile rising in his throat. "Give me just a moment."

Feeling defeated, he turned and started back toward the lingering crowd. Ashra stood waiting for him along the side of the street, the cowl of her cloak pulled forward. The hood partially hid her face in the shadows, but it couldn't hide the trepidation in her eyes. He couldn't blame her; he felt the same.

Reaching her, he lowered his head and whispered softly in her ear, making sure the bystanders couldn't hear his words. "The Colonel and I have come to an agreement, and I highly suggest you accept it. He has agreed to let the women and children leave the city if all men of fighting age lay down their weapons and surrender."

Ashra flinched back, her features stiffening. "Malikari don't surrender."

"They'll kill everyone," Gil whispered. "*Everyone.* Think about it."

Ashra raised her head to look at him, the shadows of the cowl parting to reveal her face. Her jaw was set in stubborn lines, her eyes narrowed and cold as stone. "My father would never surrender."

She might be right, but Gil didn't think she was. Ashra's father had been a ruthless warrior, but a compassionate man who had never shied from showing tenderness for his daughter. Sayeed had fought to the death, and had expected the same from every soldier under his command. But Gil doubted he would have expected every civilian in Karikesh to lay down their lives for the sake of honor.

"Your father was not merciless," Gil argued. "He would have never consented to the slaughter of babes."

The hardness in Ashra is eyes softened at his words. She lowered her head, the cowl slipping forward again to hide her face.

"This is a black day," she muttered.

Gil agreed. "Yes. A very black day."

She stood for long moments in silence, staring downward at the ground, letting the frigid wind ruffle her cloak. In a small and defeated voice, she said at last, "Tell the Colonel I agree to his terms."

Gil let out a deeply held breath, feeling almost dizzy with relief. "You're doing the right thing."

She glanced at him sharply. "Then why does it feel so wrong?"

Because it was. The whole situation was wrong, but there was nothing he nor Ashra could do about it. He wished there was something he could say to her to take the burden of that decision off her shoulders. Ashra would have to live with it for the rest of her life, and there wasn't a damn thing he could do about it. Head bowed, he turned and crossed the intersection back to where Colonel Holisgrave stood waiting.

"They've agreed to your terms," he informed the officer.

The Colonel looked distrustfully past him, nodding at Ashra. "Who's she?"

Instantly, Gil's nerves sprang taut. "She's my acolyte."

The man snorted. "Does she speak for the Malikari?"

"The Malikari lost their Sultan. No one has replaced him yet."

"But she speaks for them?"

"For right now, she does."

The Colonel grunted. "Fine. Spread the word. Have all men

between the ages of fifteen and sixty lay down their arms and surrender themselves to the nearest uniformed soldiers."

"I'll spread the word," Gil said dismally, turning away.

"One moment." The Colonel nodded in the direction of the Mouse Gate. "We'll open the gates only after I've determined their men are complying with their end of the agreement. But if anything goes wrong—*anything*—those gates will close, and they won't open again."

Gil glared at him, wishing his stare could carve right through the man's flesh and pierce his heart. "Understood."

He stalked away as, behind him, Holisgrave started barking orders to his men. When he reached Ashra, Gil told her, "It's done. They'll be opening the gates. Have the word spread that every man must lay down his arms and surrender to the nearest soldiers. If anything goes wrong, they'll close the gates and slaughter everyone."

Ashra nodded. Then she turned and pulled her cowl back, revealing her face to the crowd behind her. At the top of her voice, she relayed the terms of the agreement in Malikari for all to hear. "The lives of your families depend on your courage and *sharaq!* In the name of honor and duty, see it done!"

There was no hesitation. The men within earshot raised their hands to their chests then turned and began moving back through the crowd, shouting at the top of their voices, cupping their mouths with their hands. Immediately, the gathered mass of people began shifting as the men turned and made their way toward the outside of the crowd, hands on their heads, leaving their women and children behind. Cries of dismay and keening sobs rose from the throats of those left behind.

"Gods forgive me," Ashra whispered.

A gust of wind came up, bitingly cold, raking at Gil's face with icy claws and making him shiver. He glanced up at the sky and was dismayed by what he saw. The storm clouds had gathered densely overhead, darkening the sky. The entire city looked bathed in foggy gray twilight.

Cries of "Open the gates!" were taken up in the distance. Far up the street, the Mouse Gate creaked open, the portcullis raised with a clatter of chains. The crowd behind them rushed forward, frantic to clear the gate before it closed. Gil clutched Ashra against his side, backing away from the panicked stampede. He turned his eyes toward the rows of prisoners lining the street, kneeling on the ground with their hands atop their heads, their relinquished weapons collecting in piles.

He knew what would happen to them. Just the thought made his gut wrench. As the crowd streamed past, he realized he had a decision to make. Every part of him wanted to go with Ashra, to keep her safe. But his duty lay here.

Gruffly, he whispered, "Go with them. I'll stay here and make sure they keep their part of the bargain."

"What about the mages who are Malikari?" she asked.

He hadn't thought about them. It was very possible their lives were in danger despite the protected status afforded to mages. "I'll talk to Naia about letting them decide whether to stay or leave."

It was starting to seep into him what it meant that he was staying behind and letting her go. For so many weeks, he had considered himself responsible for her. She was his acolyte, but it went deeper than that. During the war with the Turan Khar, his own actions had endangered her, and he still felt a terrible guilt. The thought of abandoning her now sickened his stomach.

"The Malikari mages will want to leave," Ashra said.

"Then they'll leave." He couldn't keep the sadness out of his voice. He did his best to smile, but his attempt failed miserably. "Go on, now. Keep yourself safe."

The sad smile Ashra gave him only succeeded in making him feel worse. "Thank you, Gil. Thank you for everything."

The flood of civilians still surged past them, though the crowd was growing thinner. If she didn't go with them now, she might be left behind.

"*Go on,*" he insisted.

Leaning into him, she kissed his cheek. The feel of her lips against his skin was both shocking and thrilling. He closed his eyes for just one second.

When he opened them, she was gone.

Gil stood with his hand pressed against his face, watching Ashra until she disappeared in the crowd, just another woman among hundreds of others. With luck, she should be safe. There was nothing about her to single her out, unless she did something to attract attention to herself.

He waited until the crowd thinned enough to let him retreat in the opposite direction. When he turned around, he was met with an appalling sight. Hundreds of men had gathered along the edges of the road, kneeling under the watchful eyes and sharp weapons of the soldiers. A light snow had started falling. He stood gazing at the prisoners through drifting snowflakes, overcome by a sadness so profound that he couldn't move. It was as though he were paralyzed, helpless to do anything but stand in the middle of the street, staring into the face of impending tragedy.

A tragedy of his own inception.

Distant shouts broke his attention, followed by the clatter of chains.

He whirled around, suddenly disoriented. The last of the fleeing stragglers stopped in their tracks and stood still, staring into the distance toward the end of the street. The air was filled with screams.

All around, the kneeling prisoners leapt to their feet and turned on their captors. Weapons went to work, swiftly carving their way into unprotected flesh. All up and down the street, prisoners fell to the ground, where they lay in expanding pools of blood.

"What's happening?" Gil shouted at a woman running past him.

She staggered and slowed, glancing back at him with terrified eyes. "They closed the gate! They're killing everyone!"

She only took a few steps before a soldier stepped in front of her and cut her down with his sword.

"Ashra," Gil gasped, turning back toward the gate.

13

THE NATURE OF THREAT

RYLAN DIDN'T REMEMBER FALLING ASLEEP. SITTING UP, HE looked around his bedchamber in confusion, not remembering how he had gotten there. He stood and gazed around the room, groggily rubbing his eyes.

Feeling lightheaded, he went to the water closet and ran some water into a bowl. Cupping his hands, he splashed it over his face and wet his hair. The feel of the wetness helped clear his head a bit. He scrubbed the sleep out of his eyes and swirled some water around in his mouth. Spitting it out, he found a towel and dried off as he wandered across the room to the wardrobe, selecting a fresh outfit.

He pulled his arms through the sleeves, but paused in the middle of the action, his vision suddenly filled with an image of the bloody balcony. For seconds, he couldn't move, just stood with his gaze pinned on something intangible in the air. Then the image disappeared, making him flinch. He started moving again, going through the motions of dressing not quite as quickly as before. His stomach felt weak.

He knew he had to do something. He wasn't sure what, but something. No other mage should ever have to be fed to that vicious, hungering thing. If core magic was the answer, then he would have to deliver it.

He opened the door to find Jendo and Farash waiting for him in the hallway. They had the uncanny way of always being there, whenever he was awake. It was almost as though they never slept. Both mages nodded at him in greeting, their faces grim. The loss of Varik must weigh on them heavily, just as it did him.

He asked Jendo, "How are you feeling?"

The old man smiled reassuringly. "I believe I'm quite fine. Thank you, Lord. You saved my life."

Rylan dismissed the idea with a wave of his hand. "No. You saved mine."

Reaching out, he took Jendo's hand, clasping it firmly. He did the same with Farash. "I am so sorry about Varik," he said, a knot forming in his chest. "It's my fault."

"No," Jendo shook his head. "It's no one's fault. It's a situation with no good answers, and all the bad answers are equally repulsive."

Though there was wisdom in that statement, Rylan still felt troubled. He was ultimately responsible for Varik's death. The guilt had a galvanizing effect on him. He knew he could no longer wait. He had to act, even if he had no idea where to look... or really no clear idea what he was looking for.

"We are leaving," he announced. He turned to Farash. "I want you to round up supplies. Pack enough food and water to sustain us for a week."

"Where are we going?" Farash asked.

"Suheylu Ra," Rylan answered, starting down the corridor. He could hear their feet rushing after him.

"My Lord, you've been there once before," Jendo protested, catching up with him. "Your body can no longer tolerate the corruption. You can't go back."

Rylan reassured him, "I went there before, but I didn't walk back out again. I transferred out."

Jendo examined him with a skeptical look. He cocked an eyebrow. "How will we be getting there?"

Raising the *A'isan*, Rylan answered, "I can transfer us to Daru. But then we'll have to walk from there. For some reason, you can only transfer out from Suheylu Ra. Something blocks anyone trying to transfer in."

Jendo nodded with a grunt. "The core magic. It has a repulsive effect."

Rylan nodded thoughtfully.

"Why Suheylu Ra?" Jendo asked. "Maro said the core magic wasn't stored there."

"I figure the Guardian Tower is a good place to start looking for information." Turning to Farash, he said, "Please. Get us some supplies. Enough for a week. We're going to have to cross the Desolation, and it's a long walk."

Farash inclined her head. "At once, Lord." Immediately, she started down the corridor.

Turning to Jendo, Rylan said, "I'm going to say goodbye to my daughter. And my..." His voice stumbled. He had almost said 'wife.' Feeling confused, Rylan dropped his gaze to his feet. Unbidden, his eyes wandered to the band that encircled his wrist.

The *A'isan*.

It wasn't a wedding band. And yet... somehow, it was. It sealed him to a woman in an unbreakable bond that united both their souls. Feeling even weaker than before, he left Jendo in the hallway and made his way to his daughter's room, thoughts swirling dizzily through his head. When he arrived at the door, he entered without knocking, then stopped and looked around.

The room was dim, although a muted light crept in through the window, casting its glow in a discrete square of light upon the rugs. All across the floor, Amina's toys lay scattered: colored blocks and stitched dolls with painted faces, cloth dogs stuffed with goose down; a wide assortment of various things. His daughter's bed, tucked away in a corner of the room, was cloaked in shadow.

Drawn by bittersweet feelings, Rylan move slowly into the room, stepping carefully around objects. The woman who watched over Amina sat sleeping in her chair, her head leaned back, quietly snoring. She had a blanket thrown across her lap, one arm dangling limply at her side. He wondered if she had meant to nod off like that, or if she slept there every night.

He felt bad that he didn't know. He stopped in the center of the room, turning toward his daughter's bed. In the faint light coming in through the window, he saw that the sheets were empty.

His breath caught, his body stiffening. A terrible fear lanced his heart.

Movement on his right caught his attention, and he whirled toward it.

Another woman stood with him in the room, holding his baby girl.

Rylan's first impulse was to rush her, but he caught himself. He had no idea what kind of threat this woman posed to Amina. She was staring at him flatly, cradling his daughter's head, as though patiently waiting for him to react.

Rylan did the only thing any father could do. Imprisoned by fear, he raised his hands. "Don't hurt her."

The woman stood rocking his daughter back and forth gently, cradling her head against her shoulder. Amina looked to be unaware, her eyes closed, her little face serene. Her chest moved slowly in the quiet rhythm of deep sleep.

A slow smile crept to the woman's lips. Her face was young —she looked barely out of her teens. Her light brown hair was tied in a bun in the back of her head. The dress she wore looked prim and dated, with a high collar, cut from black fabric in a style that had once been in fashion two decades before. It was something his foster mother might have worn to a funeral. Here in the palace in Nazapor, in his daughter's bedchamber, the dress looked frighteningly out of place. On this particular woman, it looked terrifying.

"What do you want?" he asked, his voice trembling. He glanced at his daughter's caretaker, who still slumbered in the chair. He didn't understand how she remained sleeping. If she *was* sleeping.

"Take that off," the woman said, nodding at the *A'isan* on his wrist.

Rylan complied immediately, removing the silver band and holding it up.

"I have a message for you, Gerald," she said, gazing down at his daughter's sleeping face. "Our master has been watching you from afar. He is pleased." Her smile brightened. "But then again, we expected no less. She's such a dear child, isn't she?"

With a loving expression, she trailed a finger down Amina's face. Rylan gritted his teeth against the impulse to lunge for her. His heart thundering, he stood frozen. He didn't dare move.

"Our master has a keen interest in the core magic," the woman went on, her voice low and gentle, as though afraid of waking the child in her arms. "He wants you to find it. And after you release it, you will come to him. Do you understand?"

Rylan's gaze was fixed on Amina. "Come to him, where?"

"You will know."

The woman kissed Amina on the forehead. The action enraged Rylan, pushing aside all clarity from his mind. Grasping the magic field, he lunged for her.

She was already gone.

Panicked, he fell to his knees to catch his falling daughter.

She dropped right through his hands, right through the floor.

Crying out, Rylan sprang to his feet, backing up against the wall. He stood there, his chest heaving for breath, his body shuddering in terror. His gaze darted frantically around the room.

Then his eyes fell on Amina, still slumbering in her bed.

A flood of breath gush from his lungs, and he slumped against the wall in dizzy relief. Staggering forward, he collapsed to his knees at his daughter's bedside, pressing his ear against her chest. Her heart was beating strongly, slowly. She was asleep. Just asleep. She was safe.

But she wouldn't be for long. His enemies knew where he was. Where *she* was.

Rylan covered his face in his hands, fighting back the white-cold grip of panic, until his heart eventually slowed its frantic pace. Thoughts swarmed through his head faster than he could catch them, and nothing he could think of would help the situation anyway. The man from the cornfield had found him. The man who had killed his boy.

He would not let him take Amina. No. Not her too.

He went to the chair where his daughter's caretaker slept. For failing Amina, he wanted to slap her awake. But he knew deep inside that it wasn't the young woman's fault. His enemies were powerful—far more powerful than a governess. Far more powerful than himself.

He had no choice. He would have to give them what they wanted.

He turned to leave and, as he did, a voice from behind startled him.

"Must've fallen asleep."

It was the voice of the nursemaid, groggy and muddled.

Rylan paused at the door. "It's fine," he said, softening his words. "I was just checking on my daughter."

"She's such a love," the woman said with a sleepy smile. "And so bright. You must be very proud."

Rylan felt tears gathering in his eyes. "I am."

He reached for the door handle but paused. "Take good care of her."

"Of course, Father."

He left the room without kissing Amina goodbye, for there were no goodbyes to be said. He wasn't going away for very long, and she would be there when he got back. She would be there, because he would make sure of it. He would give them no reason to harm her.

Staring down at the *A'isan* in his hand, he realized he couldn't put it back on. The moment he did, the community would know him for the traitor he was. Unless...

In the prison, he had found a way to turn it off. He could do so again. Closing his eyes, he slid the band back on his wrist, but kept his mind distant from it.

Relieved, he left his daughter's room and went directly to the throne room. He entered without knocking and stood gazing around the empty chamber that seemed alive with its smoky crystals. Isaerae wasn't there. He wondered where she could be. He could find her simply by opening himself to the *A'isan*, but he knew better. It wouldn't take her a second to recognize his change in loyalty. He couldn't risk that, couldn't risk being the next mage fed to the Sky Portal.

He decided to look for her in her chambers. Fortunately, his guess proved correct. She was there, standing on the balcony in the winter-crisp air, gazing down at her glittering realm. She didn't turn around as he approached her from behind, walking softly across the marble tiles. He drew up next to her at the railing of the balcony and, planting both hands upon it, shared the view with her.

"I'm leaving," he said, the wind ruffling his hair. "I'm going to go find the core magic. And when I find it, I'm going to release it."

His Empress turned to look at him unblinking, her long,

ice-white hair fluttering in the breeze. She was the most beautiful woman in the world, fair enough to make every other woman seem mundane. She gazed at him with eyes as deep and mysterious as the ocean, and just as treacherous.

Reaching up, she cupped his face with her hands. "You are closed to me. Why?"

"Because I'm leaving," Rylan answered, pulling back from her touch. "And I'm taking my emotions with me."

She peered harder at him, gazing deeply into his eyes as if trying to read his depths. When she couldn't, she conjured a faint smile. "Then go with my blessing, Beloved."

In that moment, Rylan had a powerful urge to kiss her, but confusion and guilt kept him from it. So, instead, he bowed formally and turned away, excusing himself from her presence. As he left the balcony, it was as though the last light of day set behind him forever. Tears welled in his eyes, and he swallowed to fight them off.

He realized he shouldn't love her, but he did. He loved her fiercely. She was his *isan,* his partner, his Queen...perhaps even his wife.

But whatever he felt for her, he loved Amina more.

He found Jendo and Farash standing in the hallway, like always. He donned the thick coat Jendo offered him, and thanked Farash for the pack and the waterskin she hung from his shoulder.

He told Farash, "I want you to stay here. I need someone to look after my daughter and keep her safe."

When the woman started to protest, Rylan cut her off. "My daughter needs you more than I do right now. She was already taken from me once. That's not going to happen again. Stay here. Don't let her out of your sight."

Concern tightening his face, Jendo stepped between them. "Do you have some reason to suspect your daughter is in danger?"

The question was too probing. Instead of tackling it head-on, Rylan decided to dodge it. "I can't leave without knowing she's safe."

Jendo didn't look too pleased with that answer, but the mage knew better than to question him. He nodded slowly.

"No harm will come to your daughter while you are away," Farash promised, then stepped forward to hug him.

Motioning for Jendo to follow, Rylan turned and started down the hallway. It took every scrap of courage he could muster to walk past his daughter's doorway without stopping to kiss her one last time. He brought a hand up to his face, hiding the guilt and shame that moistened his eyes.

14

BLOODBATH

Gil fought his way upstream against a panicked stampede of screaming people rushing past him, until the crowd stopped, as if they'd hit a wall.

At first, he didn't understand why. Then he realized: the soldiers lining the street behind them had cut them off from any hope of retreat in that direction. By the looks of the panicked mob swarming the street ahead, the Mouse Gate had been closed, barring their escape from the city.

The soldiers behind them opened ranks, admitting a contingent of archers holding longbows, who, together as one, raise their bows to the sky and nocked arrows. He didn't hear the command to release but, suddenly, the sky was darkened by a thick arrow cloud that whistled above their heads in a high arc then, reaching its apex, fell toward the unprotected citizens.

Gil threw up a light shield just in time as arrows splattered down on the crowd. Arrowheads *thunked* metallically off his shield, while others found purchase in the bodies of the civilians he couldn't extend the shield over in time. Multiple people screamed and fell to the street, clothyard shafts protruding at odd angles from their bodies. Some still moved, clawing and groping at the wooden shafts sticking out of them, while others lay motionless where they had fallen.

The archers had already loosed their second volley.

He couldn't protect them all.

Unhooking *Thar'gon* from his belt, he raised the magical weapon above his head, brandishing it with both hands. Its spiked, mace-like head glowed with argent light, rays of power slicing the air around it. People cried out and surged back from him, not understanding what he was trying to do. Using the talisman's great strength, he was able to maintain his shield as the arrows reigned down, stretching it thin to extend it over as much of the crowd as he could. This time, no one fell.

He stood firm as people fled around him, straining to maintain the integrity of the shield as he spun it out wider and thinner around them. Many of the people finally recognized what he was and what he was doing, realizing the enormous difficulty of what he was trying to accomplish. They pulled in close, clustering together under the growing shield that enveloped them all with dazzling light. Relieved, Gil let the shield contract. He reached out a hand and caught himself on a wall, gasping for breath.

Ahead down the street, he could see that the Mouse Gate stood open—they had only lowered the portcullis, its iron lattice sealing off escape. Bowmen stationed along the wall above the gate were already lobbing arrows into the crowd.

"Ashra," Gil gasped. She was there, somewhere beneath the raining shafts.

Scrambling forward, he twisted and dodged past the people clotting the road ahead of him. He scrambled to see around heads, vying for a glimpse of her, but it was impossible. The chaos was too turbulent.

"Ashra!" he cried, standing on his toes, desperately scanning over the crowd as bodies collided into him. *"Ashra!"*

"Gil!"

The sound of his name was like a siren's call, spurring him forward into the sea of teaming bodies. He couldn't see her, so he fought his way against the current of the crowd, struggling in the direction he had last heard her voice, praying to the gods she would call his name again. Tripping over bodies of the fallen, he staggered forward toward the portcullis.

At last, Gil caught a glimpse of her. It was enough. He redoubled his efforts, shoving and elbowing his way through the wall of people ahead of him, shouting her name. Turning sideways, he squirmed his way through the crowd and, reaching her, caught her up with both arms.

"Come on!" he gasped, summoning the shield of light. He took her by the hand and, raising *Thar'gon* over his head, waded with her back into the center of the crowd. Seeing his raised weapon blazing brighter than the sun, people cringed back, bringing their hands up to shield their eyes.

Gil stood for a moment in indecision, weapon raised and glowing, the crowd still roiling around him.

And then he acted.

"MOVE!" he cried at the citizens between him and the portcullis.

As people scattered, he brought the weapon back and swept it forward in a powerful arc aimed at the gate. The talisman's magic responded, producing a concussive blast of air that battered at the portcullis like the great arm of a giant, wrenching it off its track and twisting it with a terrible groan of tortured metal. The portcullis was left contorted in such a way that there was a small space between it and the jam of the gateway—enough to admit a thin stream of people. Gil brought his weapon back again, preparing for another swing, but people had already seen the opening and were scrambling into it, putting themselves between him and his target.

The opening wasn't wide enough. It was just a bottleneck

that would slow them down. Gil threw up his hand, creating a wall of solid light that halted the stream of people scrambling for the gateway, shoving them backward away from it.

Struggling to maintain both light shields at once, he shouted at Ashra, "Keep the arrows off us!"

Immediately, she wove a shadow web and cast it out over their heads like a net.

Gil raised his weapon again, sweeping it forward with all his strength behind it. The concussive blast shook the entire gateway, wrenching the portcullis backward, twisting the metal grille until it was entirely disfigured. Another swing ripped it clear of the wall, hurling it to the ground well back from the gate.

Dropping the shield, he let the crowd spill forward.

But the archers on the wall were swift to respond, rushing to the other side to lob volley after volley of arrows into the crowd as soon as they passed out from under the protection of Ashra's shadow web. Bodies collected in the road like felled trees, creating obstacles for others to stumble over, slowing the stampede of people trying to flee beyond the reach of the arrows.

Gil raced forward but stopped in the gateway, torn by indecision. He couldn't shield people on both sides of the wall at the same time, but he didn't want to leave Ashra. He swore out loud. In the end, he decided to trust her. She was a capable mage, far more capable than the people dying in the road.

"Go!" He shouted, motioning her toward the gate.

"We can't leave them!" she cried, staggering as people jostled into her in their rush to get by.

"You go! I'll stay!"

Her eyes smiled in gratitude, while her lips pursed in sorrow. Then she fled, casting her web before her to ward those civilians on the other side of the gate. Raising his weapon, Gil turned back to face the oncoming mob that split like a river into two streams that flooded around him. He glanced up at the archers stationed along the wall, knowing they were the greatest threat—a threat that would have to be eliminated. But there was no way to clear the wall of bowmen unless he used magic as a weapon against soldiers of his own nation.

Gil stood frozen by indecision, torn between two conflicting loyalties. He clenched his jaw, feeling physically ripped in half. He looked desperately at the crowd swarming by. His shield wasn't going to be enough to protect them all. As he watched, people on the margins of the crowd fell under the rain of shafts. Grimacing, he looked back up at the archers, feeling his resistance crumbling.

His attention was drawn to a woman struggling toward the gate, carrying a toddler in one arm, her other hand clutching an older boy that she was practically dragging through the crowd. Instantly, his mind was taken back to the babe hit by the crossbow bolt. Sobbing, the woman struggled forward through the mob of people shoving their way toward the gate, jostled by people rushing to get around her. She scooped the boy up off the ground and staggered, weighted down by both.

She wasn't going to make it.

Gil moved toward her, fighting his way across the current as panicked civilians shoved into him forcefully. A group of men barreled into him, knocking him backward off his feet. Before he could recover, a boot kicked him in the head, almost hard enough to knock him out. Groaning, he clutched his head and struggled to wrench himself off the ground. He staggered upright, reeling in dizziness, blood streaming from his head. He knew better than to heal the wound. At best, he would probably pass out. At worst, as confused and dizzy as he was, he might do more harm than good.

He left the wound to bleed and pressed forward through

the crowd. Reaching the woman, he took the boy from her arms, relieving her of one burden. The look of gratitude in her eyes was something he didn't think he'd ever forget. He urged her forward, using his own body to shield her from the frenzy of the crowd. His vision reeled, a spear of agony stabbing through his head every time someone jarred into him. The child in his arms screamed and struggled, and it was all he could do to keep from dropping him.

Then he saw the soldiers.

He didn't know where they came from, but suddenly they were there, forming a shield wall to physically block the gate, forcing the crowd back. Gil staggered to a halt, glancing around desperately for another solution.

More soldiers poured in from the sides of the square in front of the gate. They advanced into the crowd, boring a path toward him. Gil perceived them blearily, as if through a haze. It took him long seconds to realize the soldiers had no interest in the civilians.

They were coming for him.

Before he could react, he was surrounded by soldiers holding shields with spears level that him, ringing him in a circle that was slowly constricting. Gil turned around, taking a quick survey of the situation. It only took him a moment to realize that they had him, and there was nothing he could do about it short of murder.

"Please! Do something!" the woman next to him shrieked.

But he couldn't.

The soldiers closed in, spears trained on him.

He looked at the woman, hoping she knew he was sorry. The child in her arms was staring at him wide-eyed and wet-faced. He glanced helplessly at the soldiers then back to the child, his heart breaking in his chest. The boy was going to die with him—because of him—along with his mother and brother. And how many more people were going to die without his light web to protect them?

That was the thought that broke him.

Gil brandished his weapon, raising it over his head. "Get back!"

In response, the soldiers rushed him.

Gil brought *Thar'gon* down, it's concussive blast slamming into the wall of men and hurling them backward into the air. He swept the weapon around again, ripping apart the men who were still left standing. Blood and body parts splattered the street. The woman beside him wailed.

"Run!"

Clutching her arm, Gil scrambled toward the open gate, stepping and stumbling over fallen corpses. Arrows continued pelting his shield, reaping a harvest of civilians along its margins.

Gil swung *Thar'gon* in an upward arc, and the battlements overhead exploded in a shower of collapsing stone and tumbling bodies. The barrage of arrows ceased.

"Go!"

He handed the child back to its mother. As she fled, Gil pressed his body back up against the wall beside the gate, waving the mob of civilians forward while his eyes scoured the roofs of the buildings surrounding the square for signs of further resistance.

Another group of archers took up position on a balcony across the square, raising their bows. Gil hurled them to the street before they could release their shafts. The flood of people continued, pouring through the gate, trampling bodies in their urgency to escape. He stood by and waved them past, lashing out with magic at every threat that presented itself.

"Warden Archer!"

He flinched at the sound of his name. Turning, he found himself confronted by two of the Malikari mages who had worked alongside him at the Lyceum. Both were looking at him with eyes shadowed by grief and exhaustion. He couldn't imagine what they'd been through.

"Warden!" a man named Mahzar repeated. "What can we do?"

Gil blinked, realizing he'd been staring dazed into the man's face as though locked in a trance.

"Just help me defend the gate!" he shouted.

Mahzar nodded, shouting in Malikari to the mage who accompanied him, who turned to make his way across the flow of people to the other side of the opening.

"Warden, do you know what you've done?" Mahzar asked, his face slack with disbelief as his eyes took in the carnage that surrounded them.

"What I had to," Gil responded.

The man nodded, his expression rigid. "You acted honorably."

Gil stood dazed as the crowd finally thinned, the last few stragglers trickling through the gate. He stood with Mahzar until, eventually, the crowd ebbed, and the square lay completely still, empty but for the dead. He slouched back against the wall, resting his head against the rough granite, struggling to catch his breath.

"What now, Warden?"

He grimaced. He had no idea. There were still thousands of people in the city, but he couldn't just stand at the gate hoping for more to come. The people who had already fled would need protection, and the mages of the Lyceum would be facing repercussions for what he had already done. The enormity of the consequences they would suffer because of his actions sank into him slowly, making his skin prickle and his body go cold. It was possible he had condemned every last mage left in Karikesh.

He felt suddenly ill. He found himself at a crossroads, and

he didn't know what to do. He had made himself an enemy of the state and an enemy of the Lyceum. He realized that the best thing he could do was turn himself in. Maybe, if he surrendered, he could take all the blame, and the soldiers would leave Naia's mages alone.

"We should go," Mahzar prompted.

Gil shook his head. "You go. I'm staying."

"You can't. They'll kill you."

Gil grimaced. "Someone's going to need to pay in blood for this."

"It can't be you." The Malikari mage set his hand on Gil's shoulder. "Go. I will pay the blood price."

Gil shook his head. "That won't work. They've seen my face. They know who did this."

Mahzar raised an eyebrow, gesturing around at the surroundings square that was bathed in blood and echoing with silence. "Look around, Warden. There are no witnesses."

Perhaps Mahzar was right. But if he wasn't, then he would be wasting his life. It was too much of a risk.

"They're your people," Gil insisted. "Go with them."

"No." There was a stubborn set to Mahzar's jaw. "I will not go. If you choose to stay, then I will stay at your side, and we will fight and die together."

Gil glanced around, feeling confused and overwhelmed. Mahzar was trying to force him to leave by limiting his options. The other mage, Demir, came trotting toward them from the other side of the gate. When he drew up at their side, Mahzar clapped him on the back.

"Go with our Warden. I charge you with keeping him safe."

The man brought his hand to his chest. "I will, Brother."

Gil wanted to argue, but he saw there was no use in doing so. Malikari stubbornness infected Mahzar's eyes. He blew out a deep sigh.

"May the peace of the gods be with you," he said in formal Malikari, one of the few phrases he knew.

"And with you," Mahzar answered in Rhenic. "Now, go. Protect my people."

"I will," Gil said, hoping he had it in him to fulfill that promise. He felt a hand on his back and looked at Demir, who nodded toward the gate. Reluctantly, Gil turned away from Mahzar, hating himself and fighting back tears.

15

THE SALT FLATS

"All right," Rylan said. "There's going to be a moment of disorientation."

Jendo grinned at him mirthlessly. "This won't be my first trip, you know."

Rylan felt foolish. Jendo had been among the Turan Khar in the Rhen. When Rylan had killed Shiro, he had used the *A'isan* to transfer the entire invading force back to Nazapor.

He didn't have to think very hard to activate the *A'isan*. The knowledge of how it worked was intrinsic, part of the communal knowledge base of the Khar Unity. Closing his eyes, he visualized the small cabin he has shared briefly with Xiana. He could have taken them anywhere in Daru, but that was the place he remembered best. When he had a detailed vision of it fixed in his head, he concentrated on that image and commanded the artifact.

Rylan opened his eyes in time to see the palace fading around them, as though it were a curtain that became thinner before disappearing altogether. As Nazapor evaporated around them, the town of Daru coalesced, growing progressively more solid, like a half-remembered dream coming to life. One moment he was standing in the dim hallway outside his bedchamber, the next he was in the middle of a manicured garden, the warmth of sunlight heating his skin.

He glanced at Jendo, who stood with his thumbs hooked under the straps of his pack, looking around blandly, as if thoroughly unimpressed. Rylan glanced around, taking in their surroundings. They appeared to be alone in the yard of the little hut he had lived in, tucked away in a grove of trees away from town. He suspected that had been intentional, Xiana's way of keeping him separated from the town's occupants.

Looking at the hut, a deep and lingering sadness came over him. The last time he had stood in this garden, it had been with Xiana. They had spent the afternoon making love, and then had come outside to take a walk along the edge of the grove, hand in hand, taking joy in the experience of simply being together.

That had been one day before he had killed her.

She had been the woman he loved, the woman the man inside him had died loving. Eight thousand years ago, Ilia Osan had become Keio Matu's wife, and they had died together on the day the Turan Khar defeated Suheylu Ra. Xiana had merged with Ilia, the same way that Rylan had with Keio. And, just as she had eight thousand years ago, the woman he loved had died in his arms. Both times, he had been to blame.

"Wait here," Rylan said, trying to keep the sadness he felt from infecting his voice.

Setting down his pack and waterskin, Rylan followed the dirt path toward the hut. It was just as old and dilapidated as he remembered, its walls riddled with gaps and cracks. The door squealed when he opened it, shuddering the cottage and raining dust from the ceiling. He moved into the dim interior, the floorboards creaking under his feet. He stopped in the middle of the room, letting the smell of the place wake memories almost too painful to bear.

The sadness became a weight, as though his heart was filled with lead. He stood gazing around the little hut, taking in every detail. A tray with two clay pots still sat on the floor in the corner. On the far side of the hut was the thin rush mat Xiana had given him for a bed. Upon it lay the blanket they had made love beneath, the day she had convinced him to confront Shiro. She had lied to him then. But he'd also lied to her. He hadn't told her about the darkness within him, about the oath he had sworn to the God of Chaos.

The cracking of a board told him that Jendo had entered the hut behind him. Rylan turned toward him, using a thin fragment of a smile to wipe the sadness from his face. The look of understanding in Jendo's eyes told him he needn't have bothered. The old man reached out with an age-spotted hand and pat him on the shoulder.

"Let's get going," Rylan said, dusting his hands off on his trousers as if trying to scrub away his feelings. With a sigh, he followed Jendo out of the hut, closing the door on the memories it provoked.

"Which way are we headed?" Jendo asked.

"We need to go down the mountain. Which means we'll have to find some mules."

"Mules," the old man echoed, sounding less than pleased. "I never liked them when I was young."

"It's a long way down the mountain," Rylan explained.

"Oh, I know," Jendo said with a grimace. "That's why I'm not looking forward to it."

They left the garden and took the path that cut through the forest toward the village. As they passed people on the trail, they got looks. Most of the citizens of Daru had seen Rylan before, so his face was familiar to them. It was Jendo who seem to draw their attention. With his dark brown skin and strange clothing, it was obvious he was foreign.

No one spoke a word of greeting as they made their way

past fields left fallow for the winter. The people of Daru knew Rylan as *deizu-kan,* a Battlemage, and lowered their eyes and bowed their heads in deference as he passed.

They found the mule paddock next to the edge of the cliff, above the trail that led down from the mountain. There was no one around to help them, but no one tried to stop them as Rylan hunted down tack and saddled the mules, two dark brown beasts with white muzzles and black legs. The one Rylan had selected for himself tossed its head in complaint when he put his foot in the stirrup and swung his leg over its back. Resenting his weight, the mule spread its legs, extended its neck straight out, and brayed loudly. Jendo grinned, apparently finding humor in the situation. Rylan wondered if he would still think it humorous when they were halfway down the mountain.

It took some coaxing to get the animals going. The trail down the mountain was steeper than Rylan remembered, and the valley seemed even further beneath them. He wasn't normally afraid of heights, but the view was harrowing, and he sucked in a sharp breath every time his mount lost its footing. Jendo bounced and bobbed along in the saddle ahead of him, holding onto the high pommel with what looked like a death grip.

It was late afternoon by the time they reached the valley floor. The Desolation sprawled before them, a brutal and barren landscape dominated by parched, cracked earth. The waystation at the bottom of the trail was the same as Rylan remembered it, with its creaking windmill and sagging fence line. The sight of it inspired more memories of Xiana that he didn't want and didn't need.

They unloaded the mules and sent them on their way back up the cliff. Rylan had no doubt they would reach the top and arrive at their paddock safely. It was instinct, and also what they had been trained to do. There was no food or water for the mules at the bottom of the cliff; the trip was a one-way journey for any traveler who attempted it.

He decided it would be prudent to stay the night at the waystation. There was no sense striking out into the desert this late in the afternoon, not when he knew the landscape would only become more inhospitable. Beyond the cooled lava flows in the distance lay a poisoned salt flat called the Scalding Sea.

Not a place he would want to spend the night, if he had a choice.

They built a campfire out of posts that had eroded from the fence. Night fell while they sat around it, and a dense quiet stole over them, broken only by the sound of insects and the crackling of the flames.

After they finished a meager dinner, Rylan found himself staring vacantly into the glow of the fire, the memories of the day returning to haunt him. He pulled one knee up against his chest, wrapping an arm around it. Unbidden, images of Xiana filled his mind. And also of Ilia, which his subconscious managed to dredge up from Keio Matu's memories, yet another woman to torment him.

"Is everything all right, Lord?" Jendo asked from across the fire, snapping Rylan out of his trance.

"Stop calling me 'Lord,'" Rylan chided him. "There's just the two of us now."

"Are you all right, Rylan?"

His own name sounded foreign on Jendo's lips, something he would have to get used to.

"Yes," Rylan answered after a moment's hesitation, his eyes still fixed on the dancing of the flames. There was a loud crack as one of the logs split, showering the night with sparks.

Jendo sat looking at him, as if waiting for him to elaborate. He could wait all night, as far as Rylan was concerned. He wasn't one to trouble others with his problems.

"If you share the bond with me, I can share your burdens," Jendo prodded him gently.

"No." Rylan shook his head. "Believe me, you don't want them."

"I'm sure I don't," the old man said, raising his eyebrows. "But that is what I'm here for."

It was a kind offer, and Rylan didn't think Jendo meant anything adverse by it. But he couldn't risk it. His loyalty had been compromised, and through the bond, Jendo would sense that.

"I'll link with you when I have to," Rylan grumbled. "Not before."

With that, he stood and turned out his bed roll. He was tired; the day had been emotionally draining, and he'd had enough. He laid down and turned his back on Jendo and the fire, staring out into the darkness beyond the waystation until sleep finally took him.

It wasn't a restful sleep.

In his dreams, he was Keio Matu, and he was holding Ilia in his arms. She was leaning back against him, resting her head against his cheek, the silken softness of her hair smelling of summer and lilac. He wrapped his arms around her, clutching her tight against him, and ran a hand through her hair.

It was the same dream as always, the same that tortured him every night.

Every night, he held her tighter, desperate to keep her there, silently begging her not to go.

But every morning when he woke, his arms were always empty.

"That's Puna Ajaru," Rylan said, pointing toward the flat plain that expanded before them, smothered by a sour miasma.

"When I came through here before, I didn't know how to cross it. Now I do."

Jendo stood with back hunched under the weight of his heavy packs, staring out across the hostile landscape with a disbelieving look on his face.

"I've been here before," he said slowly, his jaw wilting as though it had lost all motivation to speak. "But it wasn't like this. Oh, no. It was a forest. Beautiful. Filled with every type of animal you can imagine, and some you probably can't." He shook his head, blowing a soft little whistle. "Eight thousand years. That's hard to conceptualize until you see it, actually see the changes." He raised his hand, pointing at the poisonous mist that blanketed the salt flats. "There's something beneath the earth here... a volcano, perhaps. Only, there was no volcano here before. I can't imagine one just appearing from out of nowhere."

Rylan said, "It's dangerous, but I can get us across. After that, though, I'm going to be relying on you. Do you think you remember the way?"

Jendo nodded. "I know where it is. Or, rather, where it was. Hopefully it's still in the same place," he added, as if the city could physically move around.

Rylan picked his way carefully over a wide lava flow. It was a miles-long hump of tormented dark rocks, one of several that crawled across the otherwise flat landscape. The black rocks were sharp and unstable, and had a habit of turning underfoot. He had to proceed slowly and choose his path very carefully to avoid falling or twisting an ankle.

He hopped off the last boulder into a bank of thick white fog that smelled sour like vinegar. Spread out in front of him was the Scalding Sea, a series of deep green pools of bubbling water bordered by chaotic bands of ochre salt. The miasma in the air rose from the pools, and from small, conical vents made of salt that steamed hot, putrid breath into the air.

As soon as his feet touch the ground, Rylan began coughing. He lifted his shirt up, covering his mouth and nose, using the fabric to filter the air. It didn't help a lot. Whatever the mist was poisoned with, his shirt did a poor job of keeping it out. Beside him, Jendo bent over and burst into a fit of coughing, as though his lungs were riddled with consumption.

Rylan knew they had to move fast. The fumes from the poison pools would scald their throats if they stood there.

There was a trick to the place Xiana had taught him. The air was clear where the lines of the magic field rippled across the ground. It was possible to cross the entire salt flat by following the field lines carefully.

Opening his mind, Rylan felt their way around the blue-green pools until he found the first field line. As soon as they reached it, the air cleared immediately. Jendo sank to his knees, holding his stomach, and coughed until his lungs cleared. His eyes were red and watering, his face tinged with gray. Rylan's own eyes were moist and stinging, and his throat felt like he'd been swallowing nails.

It took them minutes to fully recover. Then Rylan started out again, keeping his mind open and aware of the direction of the field. The gases stayed out of their path, almost as though they walk through a tunnel bored through the fog. Jendo glanced around as he walked, wide-eyed, as if struggling to believe what he was seeing. For the most part, the paths of salt followed the field lines, winding around the frothing pools.

"Keep an eye out for others. We don't want to run into any Lonesome Ghosts," Rylan warned, scanning the mist for signs of movement.

Jendo gave a loud harrumph to clear his throat, then asked in a gravelly voice, "What are those?"

"Nomads that wander the salt flats," Rylan explained, thinking of his last encounter with their kind. "They all have some kind of disease like leprosy, so they wrap themselves up like ghouls. They're not very friendly."

Jendo's eyebrows flickered, but his expression remained unruffled. "I'll watch for them," he muttered.

They walked on for hours, winding their way through the caustic mist. The salt crunched underfoot, and sometimes Rylan's boots sank deep into it. Navigating the flats was thirsty work. By midafternoon, he was starting to get worried about their water situation. His lips were cracked and stinging from all the salt in the air. And even though their path was mostly clear of the poison mist, they still chanced across the occasional pool of toxic vapor that they couldn't go around.

As the afternoon wore on, Jendo started to flag. He walked in silence with his shoulders slumped, his head bowed. He made no effort to keep up, so Rylan had to slow down and walk at his side. Hating to see the old man struggling so, he offered to take his pack. At first Jendo protested, but at last he relented.

Rylan decided to try to draw him out in conversation, hoping that would distract him. "Tell me about yourself, Jendo. What was your life like before?"

The old man didn't speak immediately. He seemed hesitant to answer, as though uncertain or distrustful of why the question had been asked at all. "Lonely," he admitted at last, smiling slightly. "My wife died soon after we were married, and no woman was ever good enough to replace her. So I worked. That's how I dealt with her loss. I worked at a hospital in Panao for many years. I guess I was a good healer, because I was invited to the Sanctuary of Suheylu Ra."

"Did we... know each other?" Rylan asked, uncertain how he should even phrase such a question. It was so awkward. He wasn't sure whether he should refer to Keio Matu as part of himself or think of the man as another person entirely.

"No," Jendo said with a dismissive gesture. "I never met Keio

Matu. Oh, I saw him about, every so often, but we never spoke, not once."

"What was he like?"

Jendo pursed his lips, taking a moment to think about it. "He was a competent leader, or so everyone kept telling me. Now, I'm... of a different opinion."

Rylan frowned, wondering what Jendo knew of Keio Matu that he didn't. "Why?"

"Well, it's his fault we're here right now, isn't it?" Jendo pointed out. "He made some bad choices that made life very hard for all the rest of us. Look around. Where are we going? Why are we here? I'll tell you why: because Keio Matu wanted to play with a power he didn't understand, and then had too much arrogance to surrender it when he needed to."

By the time Jendo's voice trailed off, Rylan found himself staring down at his feet with a troubled expression. He had never thought about it before, but it did seem Keio Matu's actions had broader repercussions than he had ever imagined. Letting his gaze travel across the tortured earth and its poison mist, he mumbled quietly, "I'm sorry."

"It's not your fault, Rylan. It's *his* fault. I don't know how much of him's in you, because whatever's in there seems buried pretty deep. But who knows? Maybe this journey's his chance to make up for what he did. At least, we can hope."

Rylan thought back to the vision he had experienced of Keio in the Guardian Tower, of the man's desperate choice to overload the Watchers and bring an end to Suheylu Ra. "He thought he was saving the world."

Jendo snorted. "He always wanted to be a savior. He just wasn't qualified."

Rylan nodded absently, falling into a deep, troubled silence, listening to his feet crunching on salt. He kept his gaze on the mist ahead, thinking they should be out of it soon. It had already seemed to go on too long, much further than it had the first time he had passed this way.

They walked for another hour, and all the while Rylan was growing much more uncomfortable. There was a pressure in his head that had been growing all morning, and now it was getting exponentially worse with every stride.

He said, "My head hurts, but it feels like it's coming from outside, not in."

Jendo looked at him with a confused expression. "We're entering a vortex. Don't tell me you don't know about them."

"I don't know what that is," Rylan said. "Is there something wrong with the magic field? Because that's what it feels like."

The old man glanced up at the sky as though begging for divine intervention. "How is it possible that a mage doesn't know what a vortex is?"

Rylan could only spread his hands helplessly. "Everything I do with magic comes to me like it's instinctual. It's not like Keio Matu's in my head explaining the world to me."

Jendo screwed his lips into a long-suffering grimace. "Well, then. I guess that leaves me to explain the world to you. A vortex is a place where the lines of the magic field swirl like a cyclone and become very violent. As a mage, you have to close your mind off from it, or it can kill you like that." He snapped his fingers.

"How big is it?" Rylan asked, looking around.

"Oh, they can get pretty big. Some are *very* big. Now, this one," he twisted his eyebrows and shrugged. "I suppose this one's about average."

"How do I close off my mind from it?" Rylan asked, rubbing at his temple.

Jendo didn't look like he knew how to answer the question. "You just do." He walked in silence, his jaw working as if chewing the inside of his cheek.

Rylan stopped walking. The pain was getting too much, and

Jendo didn't seem to be forthcoming with an answer. Closing his eyes, he concentrated, pleading silently with the man inside to help him out for once. He envisioned building a wall around his head, a nice thick wall with bricks. It didn't work.

"Here," Jendo said.

Rylan turned toward him. The solid punch the old man threw nearly took him to the ground. Rylan cried out and stood dazed, rubbing the side of his face.

Blinking in confusion, he asked, "Why the hell did you do that?"

The old man smiled at him. "How's your head?"

"It bloody hurts!"

"Not your jaw. Your *head.*"

It took Rylan a moment to realize what he meant. When he did, his eyes widened in surprise. He couldn't feel the magic field anymore. It was almost as though Jendo had knocked it right out of him.

"What did you do? How did that work?"

The old man shrugged. "You said everything you do with magic is instinctual. So I thought I'd give you a reason to act on instinct." With a smile, he turned and started walking.

16

FLIGHT

Gil trudged through a thick white fog that clung closely to the ground and felt cold and damp against his skin. The wind had died, and the twilight had taken on a foreboding stillness, lurking, expectant. Behind them, dark clouds of smoke billowed from Karikesh. Ahead of them stretched flat acre upon flat acre of fields clothed in winter white, denuded and stripped of all bounty. The Turan Khar had decimated the outlying fields weeks ago.

Gil spotted a farmyard off the side of the road. The farmhouse had been burned to the ground, along with the barn and all the other surrounding outbuildings. Small clusters of people had gathered across the yard, extending out into the snow-covered fields beyond: campfires of the Malikari refugees who had fled with them from the city. Gil stopped in the center of the road, taking in the scene. He had been bringing up the rear of the column for hours, and yet he didn't realize until now how many people they had actually managed to deliver from Karikesh. By the looks of it, there were thousands.

He wondered how many they had left behind.

A heavy weight settled over him. These people were now his to protect, but there were so many of them. Gil had no idea how he was going to do it. He looked at Demir, the Malikari mage who had accompanied him from the city. The man stood holding a sword in one hand and a dead chicken in the other. They had come across the chicken pecking at the frozen ground just off the side of the road a few hours back. Demir had stopped its heart and scooped it up by the legs, displaying it like a prize, proclaiming every chicken was going to count. Gil was starting to realize why.

Looking ahead at the encampment of refugees, Gil asked, "How are we ever going to feed them all?"

Demir shrugged. "I have no idea."

They continued up the road toward the farmhouse, Demir clutching his dead chicken. Snow was falling around them, collecting on the ground. The cold was starting to seep into Gil's skin, all the way to his bones. He hadn't stop shivering since they'd left the city, and the chill was starting to get to him. He rubbed his fingers together, the friction doing little to warm the ache out of them.

He nodded at the chicken. "How are you going to cook it?"

Demir shrugged. "I'm not sure I will cook it. I haven't decided yet."

"If you're not going to cook it, then what are you going to do with it?"

Demir's eyes were focused on the distance, looking out across the field, where smoke from the campfires formed a dark haze against the sunset. "Might give it away," he muttered softly.

Gil figured one chicken wasn't going to make much of a difference, but didn't want to say it. The scorched earth campaign waged by the Turan Khar had decimated the surrounding landscape. There would be no livestock or grain stores left to feed the refugees, not for many leagues. And they couldn't afford to stop for long. There were too many of them, and too little food. They would have to keep pressing forward.

He asked Demir, "If you do end up cooking it, what do you think you'll make?"

Demir's face grew very serious, as though he had been saddled with a very weighty decision. "Najaj," he said finally.

"What's that?" Gil had never heard of the dish.

"A recipe from the old lands. It was once prepared with eggplant, but now most use chicken instead."

Before Demir's people had fled the Black Lands, their culture forbade them to eat meat. Animals were simply too rare in a land without sunlight. It took far more acres to grow enough grain to feed a cow than putting the same acres to use growing vegetables for human consumption. But after arriving in the Rhen, the Malikari had quickly developed a taste for meat. The markets of Karikesh had been filled with the stalls of meat vendors, and the city had become known for its delicious odors of lamb or beef roasting over a wood fire.

"I'd like to try that," Gil said, staring down balefully at the chicken.

Demir nodded, ruffling the feathers of his prize as if comforting a favorite pet.

They were approaching the outskirts of the encampment. Ahead, clumps of people were scattered across the prairie, gathered in tight circles, struggling to keep warm. Few had blankets, and many had escaped the city without even the comfort of jackets or cloaks. The sounds of moans and weeping were carried in their direction by the wind.

They moved deeper into the encampment, crossing ground that had once been part of the farmyard. They waded into the sea of bodies, winding their way around clusters of folk, mostly women and children, though Gil was glad to see more men had managed to escape than he had previously feared. He scanned the crowd as he walked, searching for Ashra's green cloak. He was beginning to feel apprehensive. She could be anywhere in the broad camp, and he might have a hard time finding her.

His eyes were drawn to a commotion on his left. A group of people were standing in a circle, shouting and jeering, clapping their hands and whistling. Gil shot a concerned glance at Demir, who returned the look with a shrug. Curious, Gil decided to see for himself what was going on.

He made his way through the clusters of people to the outside of the crowd. In the center of the ring of men stood two naked Chamsbrey soldiers. Both wore horse bridles around their heads, and steel bits had been passed through their teeth, their cocks wagging back and forth like the tails of eager dogs. Two children held the reins of their bridles, snapping the leather straps between fits of laughter. Another boy held a horse whip, which he was using to flog the men forward, even though the soldiers were tethered to the ground. The backs of both men were heavily scored with welts, and blood drooled from their mouths.

Gil strode forward, stopping beside a man wearing the uniform of a city guard. "What's this?"

The man reported, "We captured two of their scouts. The children are making sport of them."

Another snap of the whip was accompanied by a shriek of agony. One of the two men doubled over, arms crossed in front of him, hands clutching his back.

It was a shocking spectacle, but Gil was more surprised by his own reaction to it. Two months ago, he would have been horrified by such a scene. But now, after all he had experienced, he couldn't summon even the barest scrap of pity.

He grimaced, more at himself than anything else. "Tell them to stop."

The guard's smile slipped, but he didn't argue. He shouted something at the children in Malikari, and instantly the laughing and jeering was replaced by hisses and boos coming from the gathered spectators.

Ignoring the crowd's disappointment, Gil stepped into the ring and approached the two bridled men. He stopped in front of them, letting his gaze wander over their welted bodies. Seeing him, both men's eyes lit with desperate hope and, even though they couldn't talk, they started issuing pleading moans through the bits in their mouth.

Reaching up, he unbuckled the leather straps from the face of the man nearest him, carefully removing the bit from his mouth. Immediately, the soldier bent over, spitting out long strings of blood and fragments of teeth. When he was done, he pulled himself upright, trembling violently, tears of relief spilling from his eyes.

Remembering the baby shot through with the crossbow bolt, Gil glared at him. "I'm not here to save you."

The relief drained from the man's pale face. He threw his head back and let out a moan then started sobbing wretchedly.

That was enough for Gil. He ended it quickly. The man's eyes rolled back in his head and he fell to the ground, his pain and humiliation ended.

Gil turned his attention to the soldier's naked companion. The man backed away from him, staring at him with a mixture of terror and disgust in his eyes, the bridle bit still shoved between his teeth. He let out a thin whimper then fell over dead.

Behind him, someone gave a grunt. Gil turned and found Demir looking on over his shoulder, nodding in approval. Gil turned and addressed the crowd of onlookers, commanding, "Next time, finished them clean."

There was a murmur of acknowledgment when Demir translated his words, but the spectators' disappointment was obvious. Slowly, the crowd broke up as people drifted back toward the fires, leaving Gil alone with Demir and two naked corpses.

When the sun managed to crest the horizon in the morning, many of the people who had fled from the city did not wake with it. The snow and wind had reaped a deadly harvest in the night. Gil had taken shelter with Demir in a hollow carved out of the ground, their bodies pressed together for warmth, and Demir's cloak wrapping both of them. If there had been enough wood, he could have used magic to light bonfires around the camp. Without fuel to burn, any fire he could make would lack warmth.

Gil hoped that the people who survived the night might have a chance of faring better, because of the clothing, food, and blankets they could scavenge from the dead. Their only chance was to keep moving. Demir at his side, he made his way to the north side of camp and set out walking down the road, hoping the thousands of people behind him would follow.

They did.

They traveled the rest of the day on foot, trudging through the snow. Every step he took, Gil felt a tug of apprehension. He kept glancing back down the long column of civilians who followed them, looking for Ashra, desperately hoping she was back there somewhere.

It took him hours to find her.

He recognized the soldiers surrounding her first, identifying them by their uniforms as Zakai, members of the Sultan's elite officer corps. He almost didn't recognize Ashra when he saw her. She was dirty and haggard, her hair and clothes in disarray. She looked nothing like the princess he remembered. There was a look of defeat in her eyes, an expression Gil would have never thought he'd see on her.

When Ashra saw him, she ran forward and collapsed into his arms. Gil held her, squeezing her tight as she cried against his shoulder. He struggled to hold back his own tears, consumed by a euphoric relief at finding her still alive.

"What are you doing here?" she gasped, wiping the tears from her eyes. "You're not supposed to be here!"

"None of us are supposed to be here," Gil said. "Are you all right? Are you injured?"

"Just cold and hungry, like everyone else."

He hated seeing her this way. He would have to do something—something fast. If they didn't find food and shelter soon, the number of people found dead every morning was going to start increasing exponentially. But he had no idea how to solve that problem.

"We'll figure this out," he assured her, giving her another squeeze. "I don't know how. But we will."

He turned to find Demir already engaged in conversation with a group of Ashra's Zakai. He figured he shouldn't be surprised to find they already knew each other. The Malikari mages in the Lyceum had usually kept to themselves. He didn't know a lot about Demir, other than the man's capabilities—which were considerable, for a third-tier Master. He was stronger than Ashra, though Gil's own talent far surpassed Demir's—which is why he was a Warden and Demir wasn't.

The commander of the Zakai, a man named Kuzey, was speaking rapidly, his hands gesturing wildly, while Demir stood nodding his head with an intense frown on his face.

"We should make for Janul," Demir said at last, turning to Gil.

Kuzey came forward, waggling a finger at him. "Nabad is closer!"

"Nabad is too near the front line," Demir differed. "There is a good chance it has been sacked already."

"We'll make for Janul," Gil said, silencing Ashra's

commander before he could offer protest. "We need to go forward. Not backward."

The officer grunted, anger darkening his face. It occurred to Gil that he had no business telling the officer what to do; Kuzey's oath of allegiance was to the Sultanate, not the Lyceum. Suddenly unsure of himself, he glanced at Ashra. She stood for a moment in thought, at last inclining her head.

The Zakai officer understood. He immediately lowered his eyes, deferring to his Sultana.

"Our first problem is supply," Gil pointed out. "If we don't find food—"

"Warden Archer."

Hearing his name, Gil turned to find a black-cloaked man standing behind him. When he recognized the face, his jaw dropped in surprise.

"Hadley?" he gasped.

Looking past Hadley, he saw three more mages standing behind him, all members of his own order. It took him a moment to convince himself that what he was seeing was real and not some kind of hunger-inspired hallucination.

"What are you doing here?" he asked.

The tall, dark-haired Battlemage reached up to remove the brooch that held his cloak together. "Prime Warden sent me," he said, and moved forward to drape his own black cloak over Gil's shoulders. "I came to talk."

Gil reached up and caressed the soft fabric, taking intense comfort in both its warmth and symbolism. He shifted his eyes to the Malikari soldiers standing around them, saying, "There's not much privacy around here."

"It's all right." The man handed Gil his brooch. "For the record, the Prime Warden's vexed about your antics."

Gil bit his lip against a potent mixture of sadness and grati-tude that was welling up inside. He nodded in understanding. "I imagine she is. I didn't have a choice, Hadley. They were going to kill all of them, every last civilian. As it was, we left far too many behind."

The mage stepped back, crossing his arms. "You used magic as a weapon. Shouldn't've done that."

"I didn't have a choice."

The man licked his lips, glancing back over his shoulder at the men who had come with him. "Prime Warden's of a different opinion."

"So what?" Gil spread his hands. "Did she send you here to arrest me?"

Hadley shook his head, frowning deeply and breathing out a long side. "I'm here to tell you you're not welcome back."

"Well, that doesn't surprise me," Gil admitted, even though hearing it filled his heart with a deep, throbbing ache. He'd spent his entire life training to be a Battlemage. It was all he ever wanted to be, ever since he was a scared little child. It was what he'd worked his whole life for. And suddenly, just like that, it was gone.

"Shouldn't surprise you," Hadley stated matter-of-factly.

It didn't. "So who's the new Warden of Battlemages?" Gil asked weakly.

"You're looking at him."

That stung. Gil looked deeply into Hadley's eyes, searching there for some assurance that this man in front of him could do a proper job. But for all his searching, he found nothing there to reassure him. The expression in Hadley's eyes was flat and even, lacking the fire he would've liked to see there.

"Congratulations," he whispered. He felt down at his side for the weapon that hung from his belt. Unhooking it, he held it up and offered it to Hadley. "I suppose you'll be wanting this, then."

"No," the man shook his head. "She wants you to keep it."

Gil almost choked in relief. Not just because he would be able to keep the weapon that had once belonged to his father, but also because the news was a subtle sign of Naia's tacit approval.

"Tell the Prime Warden she has my thanks," he said, hooking *Thar'gon* back to his belt.

"I'll do that." Hadley offered his hand, and Gil accepted it. Then Hadley turned away and started walking back to his men. He paused and glanced back. "Keep yourself safe, Archer. Off the record, the Prime Warden's very proud of you."

Gil found the strength to smile weakly. "Thanks, Hadley."

17

DARK ABILITY

As the day wore on, Rylan grew more uncomfortable under the oppressive storm of magic that surrounded them. He found it much harder to pick his way through the winding salt trails without being able to feel the magic field. He had to rely on other senses, the way he had the first time Xiana had led him through this path, but he was by no means secure about it. The salt flats still sprawled ahead of them into the far distance, seeming to have no end in sight.

Ahead of him, Jendo stopped and stood gazing down at one of the bubbling pools.

Rylan asked, "What is it?"

In response, Jendo pointed to the heart-shaped pool that was surrounded by small salt cones that spilled a bubbling froth down their faces. On the far side of the pool, the ochre-stained salt had clumped together to resemble something like a frozen waterfall, spilling acidic ooze from one pond into the next.

"We passed this same pool an hour ago," Jendo informed him with a scowl. "We're walking in circles."

Rylan stared down at the salt pond, realizing the man was

right. He looked around at the poison landscape, finally understanding the true danger of it. In that swampy sea, it was impossible to tell direction, and there was no way they could be sure they were traveling along a straight path. He began wondering how he and Xiana had ever gotten through it before. Of course, he'd had her to guide them.

"I don't know what to do," he said, staring into the green pond with a growing sense of unease.

"We need to start marking our trail," Jendo advised.

He was right. Rylan wanted to kick himself for not thinking of it before. Drawing his knife, he squatted down on the ground and carved a large X into the salt, scraping it over a few times, to make sure the lines were wide enough to stand out. Satisfied, he rose to his feet and wiped his blade off on his shirt. He took his time about cleaning it, knowing what kind of damage salt could do to steel.

"Do you suppose that will work?" He nodded at the marking on the ground.

The old man spread his hands. "I don't have a better idea. Unless—"

His whole body stiffened, a look of fear widening his eyes. *"Get down!"* He dropped where he stood, limbs splayed on the salt.

Rylan followed suit, laying his body flat. Panting in fear, he glanced around, trying to see what had so frightened the old man.

"Are those your ghosts?" Jendo whispered, pointing ahead into the mist.

Rylan craned his neck, trying to see what the man was talking about through the blanket of swirling fog. At last, he saw the movement of distant shadows creeping forward through the mist. He stared harder, trying to make out shapes, but it was difficult. It took him long seconds to come to the conclusion that Jendo was right.

"Yes," he whispered back.

There was a group of white-robed people leading animals through the fog. He counted six of them in all, as well as three long-legged beasts of burden with large humps on their backs of a kind Rylan had never seen before. He watched them until they disappeared into the mist, and only then did he breathe a sigh of relief. Pushing himself to his feet, he stared warily into the fog after them.

"We need to follow them," he said, realizing the situation offered an opportunity.

Jendo frowned. "Are you certain that's wise?"

"I don't know the way through here, but they do. We can let them go ahead a good distance and follow their tracks. The fog will give us cover."

Jendo didn't look pleased with the idea, but motioned him ahead anyway. Rylan didn't like it either but, the way he saw it, they were out of options. Taking his time, he picked out a path around the pools, walking toward the last place he had spotted the robed people, while trying to keep enough of a distance as to not be seen.

Eventually, he found their tracks. Heartened, Rylan felt his mood lift. The Lonesome Ghosts had made Puna Ajaru their home for hundreds of years. Xiana had said they mined the salt flats, using the salt as currency to purchase food and other staples from the borderlands of Zahra. They would have to have trade routes to connect their outposts, and many of those routes would have to lead out of the Scalding Sea.

They pressed on through the mist, following the trail the Lonesome Ghosts laid down ahead of them. It took a of couple hours, but at last Rylan's gamble paid off, and the trail they followed led them to the margin of the salt pools. But as soon as the mist parted around them, the people ahead of them became visible against the horizon.

Rylan froze, shooting a hand out to stop Jendo, then started edging backward into the cover of fog. They stayed there for minutes in the billowing mist, waiting for the group of people to pass out of sight.

When Rylan felt sure they'd moved on, he emerged from the fog onto a flat, parched plain. There, he threw back his head and sucked in a deep breath of clean air, the stress of the day finally crashing over him, exhaustion riding its wake. The sun had set, and the clouds overhead were streaked with the fading colors of twilight.

"Let's stop here," he suggested, "and let them get ahead. I don't want to stumble across their campsite in the dark."

They made their own camp on the margin of the salt fields. There was no fire since they couldn't afford to draw attention to themselves, and besides, there was nothing around to burn. The desert on the far side of the Scalding Sea was just as barren as the wasteland they had left.

The night was too short, and Rylan awoke weary the next morning. Feeling just as tired as he had when he'd lain down to sleep, he packed up his bags and started out again. This time, he let Jendo take the lead, using the position of the sun to determine the direction they should travel. In the distance, the line of a mountain range stretched toward the west, and it seemed to Rylan that Jendo was setting a path toward it, skirting the edge of the Scalding Sea.

They walked on, keeping the acid pools to their right. The desert underfoot was hardpan, a thirsty wasteland that stretched unchanging before them. Their water supply was just about done, and Rylan was growing worried. If they didn't find a stream or at least a spring sometime soon, they were going to be in a lot of trouble.

Up ahead was another obstacle of rocks; only, it wasn't the same kind of lava flow they had crossed the day before. These rocks were made of granite: large, round boulders that looked to have been scattered across the waste by some kind of long-ago deluge. The fragmented landscape sloped downhill. They had to pick their way carefully; it was by no means easy going.

Ahead, Jendo threw a hand up. "Stop."

He sank down slowly, taking cover behind one of the large boulders. Rylan followed suit, ducking down behind another large rock. After a moment, he poked his head up, and looked to see what had alarmed his companion.

Across the rocks were the same group of Ghosts they had followed the previous day. They had stopped there for the night among the rocks, and hadn't broken camp yet. They were gathered around a small fire, their beasts staked out a short distance away.

"Weren't there six of them yesterday?" Jendo asked.

Rylan started counting, fear crawling over his skin like a swarm of insects.

"I count four," Jendo whispered. "So, where's the other two?"

Rylan stiffened, glancing up.

Something smacked him in the face, hard, right above the eye.

He fell back against a rock, his vision flashing white and then black. He threw his hands up just in time to block the next strike when it came. He kicked out with his leg and connected with something—he couldn't see what. Blood was draining into his eyes.

Panicked, Rylan started to reach for the magic field, but stopped himself short. Horrified, he retracted his mind, realizing that he had almost made a fatal mistake. The vortex still raged overhead with all its lethal power.

He heard a smacking noise and a loud grunt. Wiping the blood from his eyes, he turned in time to see Jendo go down, a robed man spinning a staff around to strike him again.

Then Rylan remembered the Hellpower.

He struck out with it without thinking, and the man

attacking Jendo collapsed to his knees with a horrible scream as something like smoke or steam rose from beneath his shredded robes. His companion staggered backward, throwing his hands up.

The act didn't save him. With a strangled cry, he fell, steaming, on top of his companion.

Rylan pushed himself to his feet and stared wide-eyed at the two smoldering bodies. Next to him, Jendo sat up with a groan, hand pressed against his bleeding head. He gaped at the dead Ghosts with a look of horrified shock.

He turned and trained that look on Rylan.

For a long moment, Jendo just sat there. Then, very slowly, he asked, "Do you have any other secrets you want to share with me?"

Feeling suddenly ashamed, Rylan looked away, unable to meet Jendo's eyes. "No."

There was another long, dragging stillness as the old man sat contemplating this new knowledge. At last, he squinted at Rylan and asked, "How does this change things?"

"It doesn't," Rylan said. "I was forced into it. I didn't choose this. And it doesn't matter anyway—my goal's the same."

Jendo drew in a long, exasperated breath, his eyes hardening. "And what *is* your goal?"

Still looking away, Rylan said, "To release the core magic, one way or another. Even if it takes delving into certain parts of me that I'd rather forget."

Jendo nodded. Pushing himself to his feet, he turned to look at the two slain Ghosts whose bodies were still smoldering. "I suppose it's a useful talent. Ugly, but useful." He twisted his lips. "Now, what about their friends?"

Rylan turned to look at the group of Lonesome Ghosts still camped ahead of them. They seem to be going on about their business without any sense of panic or alarm, apparently unaware that two of their companions had been slain.

"I guess we'll take the fight to them." Rylan felt his stomach sour at the prospect of using such a malicious power on more people who had no way of defending themselves against it. He hadn't wanted to kill their companions, but the Onslaught wasn't something that was easily moldable, like the magic field. He couldn't do anything constructive with it, only destructive. It was hard to gauge ahead of time just how devastating any use of it was going to be.

"I don't want to kill them unless we have to," he said to Jendo. "I want you to stay here. Let me try to negotiate."

His remark made Jendo chuckle. "Is that what you call what you just did? Negotiating?"

Rylan turned away, not finding any humor in the situation. Reaching down, he drew his sword and handed it to Jendo along with his dagger. Then, raising his hands, he stepped out from behind the protective shelter of the boulders. It didn't take the people by the fire long to notice him. They leapt to their feet, reaching for weapons.

Approaching them slowly, Rylan kept his hands up and tried to seem as nonthreatening as possible. The people in front of him were wrapped in filthy garments that dragged across the ground, their faces covered by veils so that only their eyes could be seen. As he drew closer, Rylan guessed by their builds that one might be a woman. All four stood with weapons raised, waiting for him to approach.

"I don't want to kill you," he called across the distance between them. "Put your weapons down."

But either the people didn't understand him or didn't believe he was a threat. When he took his next step, one of the men bellowed a war cry and threw his spear.

Rylan acted, burning the spear to ash before it reached him.

The man fell to the ground, where he wallowed and wailed in agony. Rylan couldn't see the damage being done under the linen cloth, but he could see the spreading bloodstains. The next man who lunged met a quicker death. One short shriek was all he was able to get out before he collapsed.

Within seconds, the third person was writhing on the ground, howling in agony. Rylan stood looking on, horrified, despising himself. He wanted to speed their agony but didn't know how. The Hellpower had a sadistic way of choosing how quickly it wanted to kill.

Rylan turned toward the woman, who was the only person left standing. The moment his gaze fell on her, she brought her spear up and scrambled backwards. He took a step toward her, reaching out.

"I don't want to hurt you," he said quickly. "Please! Put the weapon down!"

At first, he didn't think she was going to comply. She was whimpering, scuffling mindlessly backward to get away. She tripped over a rock and fell to the ground, then scrambled away on her hands and knees.

Rylan leapt on top of her, knocking the spear from her hands. He grabbed the spear shaft and raised it over her, wrapping an arm around her neck. She screamed and thrashed, but the threat of the spear overcame the urge to fight. Cautiously, he climbed off her, still holding the spear at a threatening angle.

"Stand up."

At first, she didn't move, just sat wringing her bandaged hands. Rylan looked around for rope or something to restrain her. Finding nothing, he turned and signaled for Jendo then stood over her, hoping the spear would dissuade her from trying to run. The air was already filled with the stench of cooked flesh, and his stomach was already in knots because of it. He didn't think he could bring himself to kill another person, and certainly not a woman.

"What's your name?" he asked.

When she didn't answer, he crouched next to her, resting the spear across his thighs. "What is your name?"

"She doesn't understand you."

He glanced up at Jendo.

Planting his hands on his hips, Jendo stood and considered the woman critically. "What do you intend to do with her?" Irritation abraded his voice.

"Her people must be what's left of Shira," Rylan said after a moment. "Maybe she could help us. Try to say something to her in Shiran. Maybe she'll understand you better than me."

Jendo scoffed. "I lived on this earth thousands of years before this woman was born. It doesn't matter where her language came from, it wouldn't remotely resemble anything I can understand."

Jendo drew his leather pack off his shoulder, laying it down on the ground. Squatting next to it, he started rummaging through the contents. Rylan watched with curiosity, wondering what he had in mind. When Jendo produced the metal band that had once belonged to Varik, Rylan understood.

Jendo offered him the shackle. "Here. Put this on her."

Rylan accepted the artifact with a frown. "She's not a mage."

Jendo shrugged. "Trust me. It'll work on anyone."

The old man would know, Rylan supposed. He held up the manacle and offered it to the woman. "Put it on."

The woman's whimpering became frantic, and she shook her head adamantly. Rylan wished he could see her face beneath the veil. All he could see were her eyes, which were dark and terrified.

"Put it on if you want to live," he insisted firmly.

Her whimpering ceased, almost as though she understood him. With one last sob, the woman reached out and took the band from his hand. Her fingers were shaking so hard that she had a hard time working the clasp. At last, she got the band around her wrist and squeezed it closed.

As soon as she did, her body went rigid, and she drew in a ragged gasp.

Rylan watched her, fascinated, for he knew what she must be experiencing. It reminded him of his own induction into the Unity, the overwhelming sense of belonging to something greater, unlike anything he had ever known. Watching this woman go through an experience he could never have again, he found himself desperately envying her. But he couldn't risk opening himself up to the community, couldn't risk them knowing his secret lies and innermost fears, his intentions of betrayal.

He wanted that back. He wanted *them* back, those comforting voices in his mind.

But perhaps he could have one tiny piece of that experience, using the *A'isan*. The artifact was selective enough to filter his link with the community.

Closing his eyes, he reached out toward her through the *A'isan*, opening himself up to her while, at the same time inviting her inside. For a long moment, his invitation when unanswered, lingering in the air between them. But then, like a young lover timidly accepting a first kiss, the woman let down her guard and opened herself wide to him.

Rylan gasped as he felt her essence pour into him, through him, filling him completely, until he was saturated with her. She was a thing of beauty, of complexity. He felt her terror turn slowly to wonder, then her wonder, to awe.

Shaking, Rylan looked up at Jendo.

"Her name's Shade," he whispered.

18

THE CROSSING

More people had died in the night.

Gil hadn't slept. Even though he was weak and exhausted, he was too cold and too hungry. The hunger pains were terrible, and they kept him awake. Once, he had gotten up in the night to get water, hoping that would calm the ache in his stomach. But although the water felt good going down, it made his stomach hurt twice as bad, as though resentful for tricking it into thinking it was going to get food. He'd crawled back into bed after that, feeling weak and shaky, and hadn't gotten up again.

When the sun finally rose, it took them longer than it should have to rouse the people from their makeshift beds and to get the refugees moving. Some didn't rise at all, and never would again. For those, their icy beds had become their final resting place.

With no camp to break, they got an early start, taking the Great Northern Road across the snow-covered grasslands. Gil walked in the center of the column alongside Ashra, while her new general, the Zakai officer named Kuzey, brought up the rear of the column. Their vanguard was composed of the few

Malikari soldiers who had managed to escape the devastated city and still retained the ability to fight.

The survivors walked at a shambling pace that was lethally slow. Many of the refugees were still without jackets, and frostbite was wreaking a deadly toll. Dead bodies had begun collecting along the side of the roadway. As the morning advanced, the disturbing sight became all too frequent. The nearest city, Janul, was still well over a hundred leagues to the north and east. Gil wondered if any of them would live to see the city gates.

That night, they camped again in the open. The men under Kuzey Agha's command had managed to requisition enough scraps of fabric to improvise a command tent. Ashra took up residence inside, where she presided over tense arguments over supplies and logistics, while Gil and the other two mages with them wandered through the camp to provide healing and hope to those without either. As the sun set behind them, people roamed the fringes of the camp, fruitlessly searching for food in fields of grain that had long since gone fallow. But there was no grain to be had, and even the prairie dogs and ground squirrels had abandoned their burrows.

The next day, the sun rose warmer but then cooled again right away, leaving the ground coated with a dangerous layer of ice. When they set out again on the road, Gil thought that the column of people looked thinner than it had the previous day. Moving in a mental fog, he walked at a shuffling pace alongside Ashra, who trudged with her arms wrapped around herself, tugging her cloak tight about her. To his left walked Demir and Emine, the only two Malikari mages who had managed to escape the city with them.

By the afternoon, Gil was having a hard time walking upright. His fingers and toes throbbed in agony. No amount of magic could keep the pain of hunger at bay. He kept his hands shoved in his armpits, his arms wrapped tight around his body. He couldn't remember the last time he'd stopped shivering. The exhaustion was getting to him. It was growing harder to keep moving, and the side of the road was starting to look all too inviting. He was hard-pressed to remember where his last meal had come from. It took him long minutes to recall the sad remains of Demir's chicken, which they had split.

That had been four days ago.

The sound of running feet made him turn to look back. He saw that a lone soldier was jogging up the side of the road in a stumbling stride. The man slowed when he saw Gil and fell in to walk at his side, breathing hard. He was trembling, his dull eyes looking like two bruises that had been jabbed into his face. Despite the cold, a thin trickle of sweat ran from his temple, carving a clean runnel through the filth that covered his face.

"Great Master," he panted. "Scouts report a large group of soldiers approaching from our rear. Chambray light cavalry. The Ford of Murai lies ahead. Kuzey Agha wants to know what are your orders?"

That was not the news Gil wanted to hear. The ford of the river would be more of a death-trap than a bottleneck. The soldiers from Chamsbrey wouldn't waste such a grim opportunity.

At best, it was an unavoidable massacre.

"They intent to slaughter us at the crossing," he said to Ashra. To the soldier, he said, "Send out scouts. Look for high ground. If we're going to fight a battle, I'd rather we pick our own field, if we can. If worse comes to worse, we'll have to use the rearguard to hold them off long enough to move as many civilians as we can across the river."

The soldier bowed, then turned to stagger back down the length of the column.

Without looking at him, Ashra asked, "What are you going to do?"

Gil hung his head wearily. "I'm going to try to keep us all alive. I'm not going to succeed."

Ashra frowned, her mouth compressing. "Gil... I know you're used to leading," her voice trailed off. "But these are my people. In the future, I want Kuzey Agha to be included in the decision-making."

The sting of disappointment provoked by her words took Gil by surprise. He had been her mentor and, in the past, she had always trusted his judgment. After all they had been through together—after all he had sacrificed for her—Ashra's request felt like a gut punch. He clenched his jaw and averted his eyes from her, not wanting her to read what was in them.

He walked in silence a long moment, chewing on the bitter taste of rejection. At last, he straightened and squared his shoulders. Turning to her, he stated formally, "Perhaps it's time to clarify my place. What would you have of me, Your Majesty? Do you want me in command of our defenses? Or would you rather trust Kuzey Agha with the task?"

Ashra's disappointed scowl made him feel like a twelve-year-old boy. "You're our Battlemage, Gil. Your place is right-fully in command of the military. And if we do end up surviving this war, that's exactly where I want you to be. But this is not an army. This is what's left of my kingdom, and I'll have it subject to no one's command but mine."

"Understood, Your Majesty." Gil responded, inclining his head. "I will defer all future commands to Kuzey Agha."

Ashra shook her head with a look of disgust. "You don't have to defer anything, Gil. Just keep him in the loop."

Gil bowed slightly in acknowledgment, then turned and started away.

Ashra's voice called after him, "Stop bowing. You look ridiculous."

Cheeks scalding with embarrassment, he walked back down the column. So mired was he in his thoughts that he almost didn't notice Demir walking at his side. When he finally acknowledged him, the Malikari mage nodded in Ashra's direction.

"Is she always like that?"

Gil grimaced. "No. Usually, she's worse."

Somehow, the man managed to chuckle. They walked in silence for a time, cloaked in mutual understanding. The column of survivors was smaller by a third than it had been two days before, but it was still a good two leagues long. It moved at a snail's pace, far too slow for safety. He'd been aware that a division of Chamsbrey's army had been trailing them by a day. Apparently, a fresh infusion of horses and reinforcements had allowed them to close the distance.

Gil waited until he was about halfway down the column, a good distance from Ashra, before walking away from the road to join Kuzey Agha's party of officers who were standing in a field surveying the terrain. The plain was entirely flat, save for the occasional sparse tree, and blanketed by snow to every horizon.

If Chamsbrey's general chose to assault them at the ford, they would have to fight cold and die colder. It was a brilliant tactic, one of a series of well-orchestrated maneuvers that had dogged them since the first day. The river crossing would be deadly in far more ways than one. The water would be freezing, and any of the survivors who survived the assault would likely die of cold. It was going to be ugly.

When he reached the group of Zakai, Kuzey Agha greeted him curtly, reporting, "There is no ground that would give us advantage anywhere between here and the river. What are your orders, Great Master?"

Gil shrugged, smiling sardonically. "What would you suggest?"

The white-bearded man nodded gravely, either ignoring his smile or ignorant of its meaning, while at the same time, acknowledging the respect Gil had paid him by asking his opinion. "I say entrench the rearguard and send the civilians across ahead of us."

"They have cavalry," Gil reminded him. "What if they flank us?"

Kuzey Agha scratched the thick whiskers of his chin. "My men and I will defend our rear. You and your Battlemages guard the crossing."

"I'm the only Battlemage we have," Gil informed him, feeling sick to his stomach. "Demir is only a Naturalist, and Emine is a Querer. But we'll make do with what we have."

The general poked two fingers into his mouth and whistled sharply to his men. The group of soldiers around them readied their weapons and their shields, then set off across the field, walking toward the rear of the column, gathering others as they went.

Gil looked at Demir. "I guess we'll head back," he said, nodding back toward the front of the column, where Ashra walked in a ring of Zakai.

Demir cocked an eyebrow. "'Only a Naturalist?'"

Gil issued a wan smile of apology. "If I had three of you, I'd be happier."

"If there were three of me," said Demir, "I still couldn't keep you out of trouble."

"What does that mean?"

"During the battle for the gate, I watched you risk your life—and the lives of all you protected—to save one little boy." Demir raised an admonishing finger. "You must be wiser than that. As you just admitted yourself, you are the only Battlemage we have."

Gil hung his head. Demir was right. His actions at the gate had been rash and thoughtless. He hated thinking of his own life as more valuable than that of a common person. But not admitting that fact was reckless and endangering. The truth was, there was only one of him, and no twenty men could take his place. According to standard military doctrine, one Battlemage was considered to be worth more than an entire battalion of common soldiers. He had to keep remembering that.

Gil walked in silence back toward the front of the column, his gaze focused on the ground, Demir treading silently at his side. When he reached Ashra, he fell in to walk at her side, but she gave no indication that she was even aware of his presence. Perhaps it was just exhaustion, or perhaps she was genuinely irritated and ignoring him. He had no way of knowing which one it was. All he knew was that it hurt.

They walked for another two leagues until the river came into view. All the while, Ashra held fast to her silence. When they reached the water's edge, Gil called a halt, then walked away from the column, taking a quick study of the landscape. The river was not wide, and there was a sandbar in the center of the ford that could almost be considered an island. But the waters were swift, and the river bottom was full of stones. It would not be an easy crossing. Squatting at the water's edge, he stuck his hand into the current. It didn't take a second for his fingers to start aching from the cold.

"Our scouts report the way ahead is clear," one of the Zakai officers reported to his back.

Gil rose to his feet, shaking the water off his hand, and ran his cold fingers through the coarse growth of his new beard. He looked past the officer, back in the direction of the snaking column. The river had carved a shallow hollow out of the ground, so he couldn't see the prairie behind them on the other side of the slope. But somewhere back there, he knew, Chamsbrey's forces were preparing their assault. The faster they could ford the river, the more people they could save. Just standing there thinking about it wouldn't save many lives.

"All right," Gil said. "Start sending people across."

Reaching down, he unhooked his weapon from his belt and held it at his side. He waited, listening to the shouts of the officers relaying his orders. The column started forward, people making their way down the slope to the river's edge. But when their feet broke the surface of the water, they cringed back with cries of dismay.

"Keep going!" soldiers shouted, urging people deeper into the river.

Soon the entire river bottom was full of moans of pain and the sounds of weeping. Gil turned away, unable to stand the sight of children shrieking in pain at the touch of the frigid water. The soldiers drove them forward relentlessly, the civilians splashing toward the island in the middle of the river. A woman halfway across collapsed into the water with a pitiful shriek. Gil turned and started toward her, but a soldier got there faster. He hefted her out of the water and held onto her, but her body was limp and unmoving. The soldier let her go. She slid back into the water and floated away, gently turning with the current.

Gil stared after her, his heart aching in sadness. He glanced at Ashra and saw her standing on the bank, eyes moist at the sight of her people suffering in such agony. Her soldiers continued prodding people on, forcing them into the river. But the people collecting on the sandbar refused to leave it, unable or unwilling to climb back into the water a second time to finish the crossing. The clot of people was slowing the passage, backing things up. Civilians stood crowded in the middle of the icy current, unable to move further. Panicked, they turned and splashed back toward the bank.

Then, from somewhere far away, Gil heard the unmistakable sound of horns.

He felt the hair on the back of his neck stand up. He held *Thar'gon* up against his chest and whispered the Word of Command that activated it:

"Vergis."

At once, the river disappeared, and he found himself on the plain where he had stood earlier with Demir. Only, now, the plain was no longer empty. It was filled with horses and riders charging across the snow, closing on the rear of the column where Kuzey's forces had dug in, barricading themselves behind hastily improvised earthworks. As the horses charged across the plain, the Malikari bowmen loosed their shafts. Horses staggered and started dropping.

Gil almost started toward the fight, but stopped himself. His place was back at the ford. This was Kuzey's command, and he had to trust the commander. Raising the talisman, he closed his eyes and muttered, *"Vergis."*

The land around him shifted, and he was at the river bottom. Tormented civilians still clogged the river as those on the island refused to get back in the water. Growling an oath, Gil started toward the river himself, shouting at the people on the island.

"Move! You can't stay there! *They're coming, godsdamnit!"*

His words did little good. The people gathered on the sandbar refused to abandon it, and no amount of shouting would drive them back into the icy water. Not knowing what else to do, Gil waded into the river himself. The moment the water hit him, the cold knocked the air right out of his lungs. Agony stabbed into him like thousands of terrible daggers piercing his skin from every direction. His muscles locked, and for a moment, he couldn't move. He stood in the current, jaw clenched, moaning in pain. It took everything he had to force himself to start forward.

He got only a couple of steps before a rock turned under his numb foot, and he staggered. Lances of pain shot up his leg. He thought maybe he'd twisted his ankle, but he couldn't tell. His leg was nothing but a well of pain, and he couldn't tell one stabbing agony from another.

Summoning the magic field, he tried feeding warmth into his flesh. For some reason, his efforts just made the pain worse, so he dropped the magic field and pushed himself to move faster through the water, stumbling over rocks and fighting against the current and the people in front of him. When at last he reached the bank, he had a hard time staggering up it. His feet were so numb, he couldn't feel them.

"Keep moving forward!" he shouted at the people gathered on the sandbar, brandishing the morning star. "Keep going! You can't stop here!"

No one listened to him. The people on the sandbar cowered together in a giant mass, weeping and moaning from the cold. He didn't know what to do. He couldn't throw every one of them physically into the water. With a cry of dismay, he knuckled his forehead and glanced around, searching wildly for a solution.

When the answer came to him, he gasped and wanted to hit himself.

"Clear the river!" he bellowed, moving forward to flush the people back. "Get out of the water!"

When he had the river cleared, he raised his hands and used his mind to pull the heat out of the water. Within seconds, the entire river was covered with a thick layer of ice.

With cries of joy, the crowd rushed together off the island, slipping and sliding across the ice toward the far bank.

"Gil!"

He turned at the sound of Ashra's scream just as the edge of a shield smashed him in the face.

19

THE MARKS

RYLAN SAT GASPING, STARING AT THE WOMAN IN FRONT OF HIM with a mixture of admiration and pity. She was in pain—a lot of pain, coming from everywhere in her body. He had the feeling she lived like that every day, and had done so for a long time, perhaps her entire life. Just like the other members of her family that he'd killed—whom Shade was not mourning—she was clothed in a long linen robe that hung from her body like a sheet. The cloth might have been white at one time, but it was so soiled that the color was indeterminable. She wore a gray headscarf that covered her hair, along with a full-face veil, which left only her eyes exposed. Her hands were wrapped with wide strips of cloth that covered her arms like bandages, leaving only her fingers bare.

"Do you understand me?" Rylan asked, leaning forward and peering into the woman's eyes.

"Yes," she answered in a voice that held no fear nor trace of accent.

Amazed and somewhat awed, Rylan glanced at Jendo. "How can it be that easy? Put a bracelet on someone, and they can speak your language?"

The old man gave a knowing smile. "She's not speaking your language."

"What do you mean?"

Jendo lifted his eyebrows. "I don't speak Rhenic."

Rylan was floored by the revelation. Suddenly he realized that he had never questioned why none of the Turan Khar had a problem understanding him. It was as if that all of them spoke his own language—his own *dialect*—with perfect fluency. Now that he thought about it, the idea seemed ridiculous.

"The *A'isan* translates our words for you before you even know you've heard them," Jendo explained. "That's why my voice sounds perfectly natural to you."

"But we're not linked," Rylan protested.

"Oh, you and I are linked, all right." Jendo chuckled. "With that thing on your wrist, you are linked to every member of the Khar society at all times. But for you, it's a passive link, not an active link—unless you want it to be."

Rylan stared at Shade as the new information settled in. He asked Jendo, "What language are you speaking?"

"Nagalan. The language of my birth."

Rylan took another moment to contemplate that, then offered his hand to Shade. She accepted it and allowed him to help her to her feet. Immediately, he felt a flood of shame and horror through the link. The woman reached out and clutched his shirt, her eyes filling with tears

"Father," she gasped, her eyes wide and horrified. "Please forgive me! I didn't know!"

At first, he didn't understand what Shade was talking about. But then he remembered how Talat and Pedra had begged his forgiveness before they were executed.

He took Shade by the shoulders. "Stop. There's nothing to forgive. That was... before. And please, call me Rylan." He swallowed. It was not his intent to bring this woman grief. Removing her hand from his shirt, he let go of her.

"Easy," he mumbled. "Let me have a look at you." Gently, he reached up and touched the veil that covered her face. Very delicately, he started to draw it aside.

"No," the woman gasped. He could feel her shock and fear through the link, along with the deep regret she felt at denying him what he wanted. "It is forbidden."

Embarrassed, Rylan retracted his hand. "Why is it forbidden?"

The woman's hand went up, trailing down the long scarf that covered her face.

"I am Marked." Shade lifted her chin, pride and dignity in her voice.

"What does that mean?" Jendo asked, stepping forward to peer at Shade with curiosity.

"Marked," she repeated, emphasizing the word as though they should both be aware of its meaning. When neither of the men showed any sign of comprehension, she tentatively raised her right sleeve past the bandages that wrapped her forearm, exposing the skin underneath.

Rylan stared down at Shade's damaged flesh with an intense feeling of pity. It was as though she had suffered terrible burns, although the scarring was different. Her skin was mottled and pockmarked, looking etched and eroded. His gaze was drawn to the veil that covered her face, wondering what disfiguration the fabric concealed.

"What happened?" Reverently, he drew the fabric of Shade's sleeve back down to cover the scars. A sense of confusion flowed toward him through the link, as though she didn't understand his emotional reaction, and was further confused about his lack of knowledge of the subject.

"Nothing 'happened,'" she answered, spreading her fingers before him. They, too, were scarred, though the damage was more subtle. "The Marks are a part of me. They are beautiful things. But private things."

Rylan wondered what could create such scarring, if it was a disease like leprosy, or perhaps the result of the caustic air of the Scalding Sea. He dismissed that idea; if the Marks on Shade's flesh were caused by the miasma, her lungs would be similarly damaged.

Somehow, her Marks seemed not to detract from her. If anything, they contributed to her character. Whatever their appearance, Shade's outward disfiguration hadn't scarred her on the inside; instead, the Marks seemed to have made her stronger and more self-confident.

"They are beautiful," he told her, his words provoking a flood of pride that rushed into him through the link.

"Shade, I need you to help us, if you can," he said, glancing back at Jendo. "We're looking for a power source. Not the magic field. Something else. Have you ever heard of anything like that?"

He felt only confusion from her.

"No." Shade shook her head. "I'm sorry. I've never heard of that kind of power."

Disappointed, Rylan scratched his face. "Do you know anyone who might have?"

She appeared to think about it, then said, "Perhaps the Priests of Seer. They have the knowing."

The knowing. That was an odd way of putting it, Rylan thought. Perhaps these priests had access to knowledge that the rest of the population wasn't privy to. It was a good place to start, at least. Better than just aimlessly wandering the streets of Suheylu Ra, hoping they would stumble across the information he needed.

Rylan asked, "Where can we find them? These priests?"

"At the Temple of Seer in Cardish."

He glanced at Jendo, sharing with the old man a hopeful smile. He asked Shade, "How far away is it? Can you take us there?"

The woman looked toward the horizon, bringing her hands up to shield her eyes from the light of the sun. "It's only two days' journey from here, but Cardish is a Ghost city. It is forbidden for anyone not blessed with the Marks to pass through the gates."

That was an obstacle, but it was one that Rylan figured they could overcome. Looking around the campsite, his eyes fell on the body of one of the people he had slain. He walked over to the corpse, looking down at the garment that covered it. It was bloodstained in a couple of places, though compared to other stains that darkened the cloth, the stains of blood didn't seem so bad.

"What if we wear these robes?" Rylan asked. "Then no one would know who we are."

"No," Shade responded firmly. "That wouldn't work. To enter the city, one must expose the flesh of the right arm for all to see. It is the way we identify ourselves amongst each other. Those not Marked are turned away. And those found in the city without the Marks are executed."

Rylan frowned, staring down at the dead body at his feet. He needed to get into that city, and to talk to these priests. Squatting, he pulled back the corpse's sleeve, revealing bandages similar to the ones Shade wore on her arms. Delicately, Rylan started unwrapping the strips of cloth, pealing them back from the man's melted flesh.

"So we would both need scars like that," he muttered to himself.

"I already have them," Jendo said, pulling back the sleeve of his robe to reveal markings like the scars on Shade's arm, just not near as deep or intricate.

Rylan rose to his feet. "How did you get those?"

Lowering his sleeve, Jendo responded, "During the war against the Turan Khar, the building where I worked was damaged, and the conduit beneath it ruptured. I sealed the breach, but it wasn't easy on my skin."

Rylan stared at him in understanding. "Core magic did that to you?" He glanced at Shade, wondering if it was possible that her Marks were caused by exposure to the same thing—a power source she claimed she wasn't aware of. And if that were the case...

"There must be core magic everywhere," Rylan breathed, glancing around, wondering why he couldn't sense it.

Jendo said, "Every city and town was connected to the network of conduits. It is unimaginable that they all survived the centuries intact. For one thing, there was never a volcano beneath that salt flat. I've been wondering how it got there. It could have been caused by a large enough rupture."

Rylan nodded slowly, lost in thought, already a million miles away from where Jendo was in the conversation. He mumbled, "So it's just me, then. I need the Marks."

The old man shook his head with a sardonic smile. "You can't just wish them onto your skin."

Raising his arm, Rylan pulled his sleeve back. "No, but I can make them."

The grin dissolved from Jendo's face, melting into an intense look of concern. "With the Onslaught?"

Rylan nodded, his mind already working on the problem of how to use such a wild and untamed magic to mimic the right kind of scarring pattern. He could feel Shade's sudden alarm flood through the link when she realized what he was contemplating.

"No," Jendo said firmly. "You can make them, but you couldn't heal them. So you wouldn't be scarred—you'd have arms full of open wounds that could fester."

"Sometimes the Marks fester," Shade whispered, her voice full of foreboding.

"Then that's the answer," Rylan decided. It wasn't something he wanted to do to himself, but he was confident that any damage he did could be repaired later, once he was out of the vortex and had access to the magic field. He turned away from Jendo and Shade and paced away, staring out across the horizon. He wondered how far the vortex extended overhead, and how long it would take them to walk out of it.

"Don't be rash, Rylan," Jendo said, starting toward him.

But it wasn't rash. It was the only thing that would get them into the city of Ghosts.

Closing his eyes, Rylan opened himself to the Hellpower and let it seep into him, like oil soaking into a rag. When he figured he'd gathered enough, he pulled back his sleeve and concentrated on his right arm, envisioning the intricate patterns of furrows etched into Shade's flesh.

"No!" Shade cried, lunging for him.

The green glow of the Onslaught appeared around him, crawling over the surface of his skin. The pain was instant and excruciating. Rylan cried out and dropped to his knees, clutching his arm against his chest. Even after he let the magic die, it went on burning, searing like branding irons into his skin. He curled up in a ball and writhed in agony, until unconsciousness mercifully released him.

He woke to pain.

Rylan lay on his bedroll beneath a dark sky that faded to indigo on the eastern horizon. His arm ached intolerably, alternating between throbbing and burning. He clamped his jaw closed and shuddered, deeply regretting his decision. The pain was so much worse than he'd expected. It was incapacitating.

He lifted his arm and stared up at it. Someone had bandaged it with the same wrappings the Lonesome Ghosts used to cover the Marks. But these wrappings were wet with fresh blood. They bound his forearm all the way up to his elbow, leaving only his fingers exposed, which had escaped unharmed, for the most part.

"I always thought Keio Matu was insane," came Jendo's voice from above him, "but I didn't realize that Rylan Lauchlin was too."

Rylan looked up to see the old man standing next to him, his face compressed with fury. He clutched a Ghost spear in his hand, leaning on it as if it were a walking staff, shaking his head in disgust.

A horrified anxiety flooded Rylan's consciousness. It took him a moment to realize the emotion came from Shade. The woman was sitting on the other side of him, arms wrapped around her legs, which were covered by her long and filthy robe.

Gritting his teeth until his jaw muscles bunched, Rylan pushed himself to a sitting position, groaning the whole way up. Shade shot forward to assist him, taking care not to jostle his bandages. Jendo hovered with his arms crossed, staring down at him without sympathy. If anything, he seemed satisfied, as though he thought Rylan deserved every moment of pain he had coming to him.

With great care, Shade drew back the sleeve of Rylan's shirt, exposing his bandaged arm. She glanced at him anxiously, then hunched over and began the laborious and painful process of removing the carefully applied wrappings. Rylan grimaced as the cloth was pulled away from the raw wounds beneath, revealing deeply eroded flesh where the skin used to be.

"These are not good enough," she said, turning his arm first one way then the other, examining the injuries closely. "Now you are Marked, but the wounds are too recent. To look that fresh, they would have to be festering, and they are not."

Jendo stared down at Rylan's injuries with clinical interest, although a look of genuine concern was growing in his eyes. He reached out, as if to touch the raw, oozing wounds, but retracted his hand.

Rylan stared at his arm, not sure what to do. He had maimed himself for no reason if he couldn't convince Shade's people to let him through the gates of Cardish. He didn't know how to duplicate the look of infection, but he did know how to create one. Pushing himself to his feet, he walked across the camp to where the three beasts of burden stood tethered to the ground. He ran a hand down the long neck of one, feeling its coarse fur. The beast made a noise that sounded like a deep, strangled groan and pulled its lips back from its teeth. Rylan jerked back, afraid of being bitten.

"What is it?" he asked.

"A camel." Shade came up beside him and captured the animal's lead rope, holding it so that he could inspect the strange creature.

The camel smelled earthy, like a goat, only different, more pungent. Its jaw worked in a circular motion like a cow chewing its cud. It was fitted with a rope halter tied to a picket driven into the ground. Trailing his hand along the animal's side, Rylan walked back to the camel's hindquarters. Scattered across the ground was a healthy supply of scat.

Bending down, Rylan picked up a hard, round ball of dung. Holding it up, he recognized it as the same fuel Shade's people had used to feed their campfire. It was harder than horse dung, but when he squeezed it, he found it pliant.

Shade looked at him suspiciously. "What are you doing?"

Rylan clenched his fist, smashing the dung-ball with his fingers. He worked it around between both hands, kneading it like dough, until it was a smooth and malleable consistency.

Jendo came forward, shaking his head adamantly. "That's a big risk," he said, staring at the mess of camel dung. "If you get blood poisoning, you could die in a matter of hours, and I can't heal you under the vortex."

Looking up at him, Rylan asked, "Can you think of a better way?"

Jendo made a smacking noise with his lips, looking disgusted over more than just the dung. "No. I can't."

Neither could Rylan. He was out of ideas. So he took the smashed wad of dung and, gritting his teeth against the pain, started smearing it over the raw flesh of his arm.

20

SURVIVAL

GIL FELT LIKE HE WAS SWIMMING, FLOUNDERING UNDER THE surface of some deep water, lost in a dark ocean. He didn't know how long he'd been there, but it didn't matter. Whatever it was, it was too long already. The drumming ache in his head wouldn't go away, and every time he tried fighting his way to the surface, the pain in his head always pulled him back down. It was a long time before he finally broke the surface.

When he did, the pain was excruciating.

"Careful. You have a head injury."

It was Ashra's voice. Gil tried opening his eyes, but the moment he did, light pierced his eyeballs, stabbing all the way to the back of his brain with a brutality that made him retch. He squeezed his eyes shut as hard as he could, choking back bile.

"What happened?" he croaked. The words were slurred. It felt as if his tongue was swollen and too big for his mouth.

"You were beaten unconscious in the middle of the river. Demir dragged you out from under the ice, but he's not a very good healer."

A healer. Gil remembered that *he* was a healer. But the

moment he reached for the magic field, he stopped himself quickly. Healing oneself with a head injury was a terrible idea, at best. The brain was the most difficult organ to work with, and any mistake could be catastrophic. He would have to wait until his senses were more stable.

But Demir wasn't the only other mage among their number. The woman, Emine, was a Querer. She would have knowledge of healing.

"Where's Emine?" he asked.

"She was killed at the crossing."

Gil groaned. The news made him sick. Emine was a kind, gentle woman, and she didn't deserve to die without even a recent meal in her belly. Now they were down to three mages, including Ashra, and only one healer. It wasn't enough.

Gathering his courage, he opened his eyes slowly. The pain was fierce, but not as terrible as before. Squinting, he saw that Ashra was seated next to him. They were in her tent. Reaching up, he felt timidly at the bandage wrapped around his head, the pain making him wince.

"How bad was it?" he asked, thinking back to the river.

"Bad," Ashra answered. "We lost Kuzey Agha and our entire rearguard. Also, they've flanked us. We're cut off from Janul."

It was grave news. Most of the Malikari soldiers who had escaped with them from Karikesh had been assigned to the rearguard. If they were all dead, then there was very little left to protect them.

Ashra whispered, "How are they able to keep coming like this?"

"Because they have supply lines, and we don't," Gil answered. While their own people starved, Chamsbrey's soldiers had a constant stream of food and reinforcements. They also had proper winter clothing and tents to shelter them from the storms.

"Do we have a chance?" Ashra whispered.

The question made his heart ache. If she didn't already know the truth, he didn't want to break it to her. Let her cling to hope. That was all they had left.

"We're not dead yet," he told her, grimacing at the lie as much as at the pain. He extended his hand. "Help me up."

She didn't take it. "Stay down. They're not upon us yet, and you can't walk like this."

He didn't see that he had much of a choice. Even if they weren't immediately threatened, they still couldn't stay there. Their only hope was to keep moving, not just sit and wait to be massacred.

"I'm going to have to walk. We're going to need—"

"You *don't* have to walk," said a voice from behind them.

Gil turned to see Demir standing slightly off to the side. He had something in his hand, but Gil couldn't make out what.

"I saved you a horse," Demir said, moving forward and crouching next to him.

Gil asked, "When did we get a horse?"

Demir held up his hand, and Gil saw he was holding a long rib bone, half-stripped of meat.

"Courtesy of Chamsbrey's Third Calvary," Demir said. "They left behind many horses, mostly dead, for which we are fortunate. Without food, many more civilians would have died in the night."

"Are you hungry?" Ashra asked.

Gil knew that he should be. He hadn't eaten in days. But at the moment, the thought of eating turned his stomach. "Not right now."

"How long has it been since you last ate?" Ashra asked, concern heavy in her voice. She took his hand and squeezed his fingers.

Gil looked down at her hand, considering it. The feel of her fingers was soothing, but it was more than that. The sight of her hand in his sent a warm shiver through him that surprised him.

He hadn't realized his feelings for her had grown so strong. They had slowly crept up on him when he wasn't expecting them, and now...

"I'll eat something later," he whispered, closing his eyes. The pain in his head was worse, and there was a sudden pain in his heart that hadn't been there before. They were all going to die, and he was going to lose her. The thought made his throat constrict.

Leaning forward, Ashra brushed his hair back away from his face. The feel of her touch made his eyes burn. He was growing tired. He lay back down and closed his eyes, turning away from her.

"Why are you here, Gil?" she asked, pulling his blanket up.

"Because this is where I want to be," he answered.

He slept until evening and, even then, only woke because of the wind. The rest of the night proved brutal. A storm moved in and unleashed its full fury over them, burying the camp in a foot of snow. Gil shivered in his blankets all night, despite the tent. The wind blew through the gaps between fabric, and loud gusts shook the entire structure, threatening to blow it over.

When he woke in the morning, he didn't remember much of the night before, other than the cold. The rest was just as hazy as his dreams. Only, the sound of the wind continued outside, relentless, and he knew that the rest hadn't been a nightmare.

His head felt better and, when he opened his eyes, the ambient light in the tent didn't scorch into his brain the way it had the day before. And he was hungry, which was an improvement. The smell of cooking horsemeat made his stomach rumble and ache. Gathering his strength, he fought to sit up.

A wave of nausea rolled over him, but he made it to a sitting position. He sat staring blearily around, trying to get a sense of his surroundings. His vision was foggy, and the lights of the lanterns had bright halos around them. He squinted, concentrating on making the inside of the tent squirm back into focus, but no matter how hard he tried, his vision was still muddy.

He wasn't alone in the tent. Ashra was speaking quietly to Demir and another man, who wore the uniform of the Zakai, someone else Gil didn't know. Seeing him awake, Ashra broke off her conversation and knelt at his side.

Delicately, she adjusted the bandage on his head. "How are you feeling?"

"Better," he answered, though it wasn't quite the truth. His head didn't hurt as much, but the fact that his vision hadn't recovered wasn't a good sign.

"Are you hungry yet?"

Gil assessed the situation with his stomach and came to the conclusion that he might be able to keep food down. He had to try. He was already incredibly weak from hunger, which might account for most of his problem.

"May be something small," he said.

Ashra stood and crossed the tent to the exit, throwing back the flap. The wind gusted in, guttering the lanterns. The air was frigid, making Gil shiver even more. He pulled his blanket up around him, grateful for its warmth. He thought about the hundreds of people in the camp who didn't have a tent to protect them from the wind and felt instantly guilty. He should have thought about freezing the river solid sooner than he had. He wondered how many people had died at the ford because of his stupidity.

Ashra returned with a steaming bowl in her hands and sat back at his side. The smell made Gil's stomach clench with hunger, and his mouth started watering. Ashra spooned him a bite, bringing it to her own lips and blowing the steam from it before offering it to him. He slurped the broth down. The moment he swallowed it, his stomach revolted, and for a moment he thought he was going to be sick. He squeezed his lips closed, bringing a hand to his mouth. After a moment, the feeling passed.

"Another?" Ashra asked.

He nodded.

Spoonful by spoonful, he got most of the bowl down. It took him a while, much longer than it should have. But Ashra was patient and didn't rush him—and didn't press him to eat more when he said he'd had enough.

The tent flapped open, and a young soldier was blown in with the wind. He went instantly to his knees.

"Sultana!" he gasped. "More soldiers have been spotted."

The report sent a chill down Gil's back. He was in no shape to stand, much less defend anyone.

Demir reacted instantly, moving to Ashra's side. "How many are there and how far away are they?"

"They're coming from the east, Great Master. Several hundred, about five leagues out!"

"Are they on horseback?" Gil asked.

The soldier turned to him, apparently noticing him for the first time. "Some," he reported. "But many are not."

Which was good. That would give them more time.

"Send word through camp," Gil ordered. "We're moving out." Leveraging his arm against the floor, he pushed himself onto his hands and knees then tried to get his feet underneath him.

Seeing his intent, both Ashra and Demir rushed to him at the same time. Gripping him by the arms, they helped him to his feet. Immediately, Gil's head reeled, and his stomach lurched.

"Rouse the camp," Ashra ordered. "Get everyone moving north!"

"We can't go any further north," Gil gasped, swallowing bile and squinting against the pain in his head. "We're already on the margin of Orien's Vortex,"

"We don't have a choice."

Hearing that, Gil felt the last of his hope dashed out of him. The vortex would seal their doom. They wouldn't be able to use magic. It was done, then.

They were finished.

Without magic, without the Zakai, there was nothing they could do.

It took him seconds to form the words. "We'll have to surrender and throw ourselves upon their mercy. There's no other option."

"They have no mercy," Demir growled. "Surrender is not an option."

Gil stared at him through a heavy shroud of pain, guilt, and exhaustion. "I'm out of ideas."

"I'm not," Ashra said. "If we are on the margin of Orien's Vortex, then that means we can't be too far from Orien's Finger. Isn't there a transfer portal there?"

Gil nodded, though her words didn't fan his hope. The vortex was enormous, covering league upon league of open prairie. They could still be days from the monolith known as Orien's Finger. There was a transfer portal beneath it, just as Ashra said. But even if they could reach it, they could only send the people through one at a time. It would be a worse bottle neck than the ford... and a more effective killing ground.

"We won't make it," he said. A heavy defeat crept over him, weighting him down. No longer did the throbbing ache in his head seem so terrible. Far more painful was the look on Ashra's face at hearing his words. Her expression collapsed, her eyes tearing up and her face growing pale. She shook her head very slowly, her mouth working in silent denial. He wanted to put his arms around her and comfort her in some way. But then Ashra's expression changed, her gaze hardening with defiance

"We *will* make it," she growled. Turning to Demir, she ordered, "Get Gil on a horse. *Right now.* Get the camp moving."

Before Gil could protest, the big man started pulling him toward the entrance.

"Wait!" Gil exclaimed. "I need my weapon!"

With Demir's help, he recovered *Thar'gon* from a corner of the tent. Then he let the mage help him stagger toward the entrance of the tent. He tried to glance back over his shoulder at Ashra, but didn't get a look at her before the tent flap closed behind him and the chill morning air hit him in the face.

He didn't struggle as Demir took him outside and lifted him onto the back of a gray courser that was absent a saddle. Gil leaned forward and grabbed a fistful of the horse's long mane, wrapping it around his fingers. His hands trembled, his whole body shivering from the cold, and his head throbbed ferociously with every heartbeat.

All around the camp, people were moaning and sobbing as they fled into the fog. Gil didn't stare after them. Instead, he found his eyes drawn to the people who were not moving, those who had died in the night.

"You go ahead," Demir said, pulling his sword from its sheath. "I'm going to stay with her."

"No." Gil shook his head stubbornly. "You'll never get her out in time." He gritted his teeth, reining the horse around. "I'm going to stay and guard your rear—"

"You will not!" Demir cried fiercely, catching the courser's bridal. "I will go—"

"No!" Gil shouted over him, brandishing the morning star. "You're not a Battlemage! But I am—and I'm the only chance she has! Now, obey my order and save your Queen—that is your charge, Master Demir! That is your duty!" Lowering the weapon, he ordered, "Make for the coast. I'll guard your retreat as long as I can."

Demir drew back, nodding wearily and drawing in a long,

shuddering sigh. He brought his hand up to his chest, covering his heart. "May you know the peace of the gods, Gil Archer," he said solemnly.

Gil reined the horse around, leveling his weapon at Demir. "Don't leave her side."

The Malikari mage bowed formally, then turned and went back to the tent. Gil sent the horse forward, directing it back across the camp in the direction of the river. He wanted one, last glimpse of Ashra, but there was no time. He had to position himself between the enemy and the refugees and pray his cracked head would be able to handle enough magic to give Ashra and her people even a small amount of hope.

Clucking his tongue, he urged his mount to a canter.

21

JOURNEY TO CARDISH

THEY LAID SHADE'S KINSMEN TO REST IN THE FROTHING GREEN ponds, which was their way, for each gurgling pool contained water caustic enough to dissolve a body. Standing beside her on a brittle salt bank, Rylan watched as Jendo fed the last of the dead to the acid. He'd expected the bodies to start bubbling immediately, and was surprised when they merely slipped quietly into the water. By the time they were ready to leave, the linen on the first corpse had just started to blacken. Rylan guessed it would be some time before they were fully dissolved.

Shade showed no remorse, even though the people had been her family. Rylan was rather shocked by her reaction; he felt absolutely nothing from her through the link. No grief, no anger. He wondered if it was just an artifact of her new connection with the Unity, but decided it couldn't be. The link with the community inspired great love for those within it, but it did not sever bonds already in the heart.

They loaded the camels with their provisions, then the rest of the day was spent traveling. Jendo and Rylan wore robes and veils scavenged from the bodies. Shade led them away from the salt flats into the desolate waste that was altogether devoid of plant life. The evening was spent camped beside a fire fed with camel dung, which burned with a peculiar odor that wasn't unpleasant.

Rylan's arm throbbed and stabbed him with pain every time he moved it. After the meal, Shade unwrapped the strips of linen to examine the wounds beneath the bandages. The process was painful. The cloth stuck to his arm, so when Shade pulled the bandages off, it felt like his skin was being stripped away with them.

By the time she had the bindings unwrapped, Rylan's eyes stung with tears of pain. He stared down at his ruined flesh that was still slathered with brown excrement, the sight making his stomach crawl with nausea. It was hard to gauge how the wounds were taking to the treatment. He had expected to feel feverish already, but he wasn't, for which he was both grateful and concerned. Cardish was only another day's journey, and if his wounds hadn't visibly festered by then, they wouldn't be admitted.

Satisfied with her inspection, Shade rewrapped his arm using the same filthy cloth. Rylan watched as she wrapped the bandages in a herringbone pattern, explaining how different patterns of weaving the wraps conveyed different attributes of the person wearing them. Rylan wondered what the pattern of her binding said about him, but he couldn't bring himself to ask her.

After the wounds were bound, Shade stayed with him by the fire. They sat in silence, watching the flames dance and pop. Jendo sat on the opposite side of the fire, robed in one of the garments they had taken from the dead. He had been conspicuously avoiding them all day, and wore a constant scowl of disapproval, making Rylan feel like a boy who had earned the disappointment of a father.

Shade raised her arm and appeared to be inspecting the manacle on her wrist. She rotated her arm, letting the light of the fire dance across the polished metal of the band. It was two inches wide, with small hinges and a loop that a chain could be fastened to. It looked more like a bracelet than a shackle, and she could remove it any time she chose to. The band's power over her was mental, not physical. Once connected to the Unity, a person had no reason or desire to leave it.

"Thank you," she whispered.

Rylan felt warm waves of gratitude through the link, which surprised him. "Why are you thanking me?"

"For this." She traced a finger across the smooth surface of the band. "They call us Lonesome Ghosts. I never realized why until now."

"What do you mean?" Rylan asked.

Shade's eyes grew wistful. "My people live in solitude, dispersed throughout the salt flats. Each band has their own territory of salt to mine. We don't share well. We're fighting all the time over who owns which salt field. We don't dare tread onto the salt of another band—it's seen as an aggression."

Rylan try picturing such a society, but couldn't quite imagine how it would work. "So... you live your whole life within one family? Who do you marry?"

"We don't marry."

"Then... what do you do?" Rylan asked, wishing he could see her face beneath the veil.

Shade leaned forward, drawing her robed legs up to her chest and wrapping her cloth-wrapped arms around them. "The women in the band are shared by the men, at least until the men are killed by a rival band. Then the women and children are taken to live with that band."

Rylan stared at her, unable to speak. What Shade was describing was tantamount to a culture of slavery. No wonder she had felt nothing for the people they had fed to the acid pools. Had she spent her entire life being traded like livestock from one group of men to another?

"That's... terrible." He felt a flutter of anger through the link, and thought maybe he had offended her. Just in case, he decided to keep his opinion to himself and not say anything stronger. "So... the conquering bands just keep getting bigger?"

"No." She shook her head. "Bands can only be so big, because each area has only so many resources. Once those resources become strained, the band splits. Old friends become new enemies."

Rylan had a hard time imagining such a society, wondering how people could ever exist happily with such fragile social bonds. "That does sound like a lonesome existence."

"It is."

Rylan shifted uncomfortably. "So, the people I killed... they were not your family?"

"No. The band I was born into was slaughtered when I was a young child. The band that took me and my siblings lasted only four years before they, too, fell to a rival band. Of my original family, I'm the only one who has survived."

That sounded like a brutal existence. And yet, Rylan felt no sadness or even anger coming from Shade through the link. He didn't understand her lack of emotion. He asked, "Do you have any children?"

"No. Sometimes, a woman can be Marked on the inside as well as the outside. It is considered an act of mercy by the gods."

"I'm sorry to hear that," Rylan muttered softly.

She turned to look at him, her dark eyes intense. "I was never sorry. Before I was pronounced barren, I lived every day in fear of becoming pregnant. I did not want to raise children just to watch them be torn from me."

Rylan felt anger drip down his nerves, imagining Shade suffering in such a society. She must have sensed his sympathy through the bond. Leaning forward, she peered into his face as if searching for an answer, then reached a tentative hand up to touch his cheek. Suddenly, her eyes widened, as if she had seen something that shocked her.

"You are much more than you seem," she said softly. "More than just one man. How is that possible?"

"You must be sensing the Unity through me," Rylan guessed.

Shade closed her eyes and leaned her head back, as though savoring an aroma. "I feel them," she breathed, "all of them together, all at once. Such a beautiful feeling!" Opening her eyes, she gazed at him intently. "But that's not what I mean. I sense something else in you. Like there is another man inside you."

Her words made Rylan wince. She had sensed the duality in him, his relationship with Keio Matu. Feeling ashamed, he looked away quickly, unable to meet her gaze.

"This other man I feel," she pressed. "He is very strong. Who is he?"

Grudgingly, Rylan admitted, "His name was Keio Matu."

Shade sucked in a sharp breath. "The ancient Custodian? He lives within you?"

Rylan recoiled in shock. Across the fire, Jendo shot bolt upright as though poked by a spear.

How could she know his name?

Keio Matu had died eight thousand years ago, and his entire society had been erased. It was inconceivable that his name could be known by a woman who had never ventured outside the borders of her own territory.

Rylan stood and strode away from her a few paces. "You know who that is?"

"Of course!" she gasped, rising to her feet, her eyes wide with excitement. "Keio Matu was the greatest man the world has ever known! But he died thousands of years ago—how is it that he has come to live within you?"

Rylan shook his head, glancing at Jendo in amazement. The

man was standing on the other side of the fire from them, arms crossed, watching them intently but saying nothing.

"I went on a pilgrimage to Suheylu Ra," Rylan admitted. "There, I joined with the spirit of Keio Matu. A part of him came to live within me."

"Can I...?"

Moving forward, Shade reached out to him with both hands. Rylan took a step back, not understanding what she wanted. But, reassured from the excitement coming to him through his link with her, he let her take his face in her cloth-wrapped hands. She closed her eyes and leaned forward until her brow touched his. She stayed that way for seconds, the thin veil that covered her face the only thing separating them.

Slowly, she released him and moved away. What he saw in her eyes surprised him. The look of wonder in her eyes had been replaced by a look of grave concern.

"I pity you, poor Rylan," she said, compassion and sympathy flooding into him through the link.

Rylan's chest tightened. "Why's that?"

"I feel his spirit within you," she explained. "It is not content, and it's growing stronger. He is not going to want to stay inside you much longer."

Rylan stared hard at Shade, wondering how she could sense such a thing, when he didn't. He closed his eyes, trying to reach through the prison of his consciousness to feel the man locked deep inside him. But no matter how hard he searched, all he found was emptiness.

"Then he's just going to have to be disappointed," Rylan said, turning away.

That night when he fell to sleep, Rylan dreamed of Xiana.

They lay together on a blanket spread over the ground,

surrounded by an orchard full of trees laden with blossoms. Time froze, and for one infinite moment the feel of her in his arms was the only thing that existed in the world. He breathed in the scent of her hair and ran his fingers over her smooth skin.

He opened his eyes and looked at her.

But it wasn't Xiana he saw. It was Ilia, and she was smiling at him with new hope.

The next morning, Shade had to rouse him from sleep. He had a hard time fighting his way out of the dreams, and a harder time still keeping his eyes open. He was feverish, his whole body drenched in sweat. And yet, he was cold. He couldn't stop shivering.

Shade bent over him, and he could tell by the intensity of her concern how bad he looked. Trying to dispel her worry, he fought himself upright then struggled to his feet. But before he could take one step, a terrible weakness bent his knees, and he staggered.

She caught him with a curse, maneuvering him over to a rock and setting him down on it. Rylan leaned forward, shivering, and wrapped his hands around himself for warmth. With Shade's coaxing, he let her take his right arm and start unwrapping the bandages. They stuck terribly to the wounds beneath, and he tried hard not to cry out as she peeled them away. But no amount of trying could contain the agony he felt as the bandages came off. When she had his arm bear, Shade let out a horrified gasp and brought her hands up to cover her mouth.

The wounds had festered in the night. The smell was pungent and sickening, the flesh caked with drying pus, which was why the bandages had stuck so badly. Jendo came over and, kneeling beside him, drew his arm away from his body and pushed Rylan's sleeve back all the way to his shoulder.

"His blood is becoming poisoned," Jendo growled with a curse. "We must get him to the priests. How far away is this city?"

"Not far." Fear and foreboding clung to Shade's voice.

They broke camp quickly. Rylan climbed onto the back of one of the camels, which sat down in the sand for him to mount before lurching to its feet. He slept on and off as the animal swayed beneath him. Every time he opened his eyes, the landscape around them looked different. Tufts of grass had appeared, and small trees started dotting the plain.

They reached Cardish in the late afternoon. The city of Ghosts was tucked away in a long valley, pressed up against foothills that rose up out of the desert into a range of craggy mountains. The walls of the houses were the color of the sand, built of adobe blocks. The city was bordered by a high wall that had only one gate which was guarded by four pairs of guards. Groups of Lonesome Ghosts were camped in the valley outside the city walls. Smoke rose from many fire pits, filling the air with the scent of burning camel dung.

They came down out of the desert onto a wide dirt road, falling in with other groups of robed men and women leading camels and other beasts of burden heavily laden with woven baskets and leather packs. Rylan let his eyes slip closed, his head lolling to the lurching motion of the camel's gait. The busy noise of a market filled his ears, but he paid no attention to it. All the smells and sounds ran together until they formed a meaningless muddle of sensations.

He finally opened his eyes when his leg was jostled by another camel. Pulling himself out of the fog, he saw they were following a steady stream of people moving into the city through the gate. Looking ahead, Rylan saw that the guards were stopping every person upon entering, questioning them and inspecting them closely before waving them through.

As they approached the guard station, their progress slowed substantially, the stream of people in front of them condensing into a single-file line. Rylan silently willed the crowd to move faster. He was shivering violently, and he rode hunched forward, arms wrapped tight around him. By the time they reached the front of the line, his vision was growing dim. He kept catching himself drifting off to sleep, and it was getting harder to keep his head up.

"State your business."

Rylan opened his eyes and stared ahead dimly.

"This man has the fever-heat," came Shade's voice, drifting through the murky world is if from very far away. "We've come seeking the priests of Seer."

There was a pause.

"He does not look good. Reveal the Marks, and you may pass."

Someone took his arm and peeled the bandage back.

The pain was horrifying. It was the last thing he felt.

22

OUTLAW

Each jarring stride of the horse sent a spear of wrenching pain through Gil's head. Sweat dribbled down his face despite the cold temperature of the air, and every breath he took sounded like a gust of wind in his ears. The crunching sound of his mount's hooves punching through the snow seemed to echo into the great silent distance. He had passed beyond sight of the camp, and the enemy wasn't yet within earshot. But he could see them coming: a long line of cavalry moving across the snow-covered grasslands, lances raised, numbering over a hundred.

There were far more than he could handle on his own in the state he was in. Gil knew he couldn't stop them, but that wasn't his goal. He intended to slay as many as he could before they took him down. He would give Ashra and Demir the chance to get away before the enemy general could deliver reinforcements.

He drew his mount up on the ridge of a low hill and stood for a time watching the line of cavalry moving silently toward him. The horse beneath him snorted and shifted its weight, its nostrils breathing hot steam into the air. Reaching down, Gil ran a hand over the coarse brown hair of its withers, feeling the muscles twitch beneath his touch.

Squinting, he tried to count the number of horses moving toward him, but lost track after a few dozen. His mind fumbled through pain, muddling options as his eyes surveyed the landscape for any natural advantage. There was none. Not even a rock scarp. Just a slow, gradual slope that wouldn't even provide defilade.

There wasn't much just one mage, alone, could do.

But then again, he really wasn't alone. The weapon at his side easily doubled the power he could draw, and dramatically added to what he was capable of. *Thar'gon's* concussive attacks could be devastating—this same weapon destroyed the Well of Tears. If the artifact could demolish a portal to hell, he was sure it would prove devastating against a cavalry charge.

He reached up and gently probed at the wound in his scalp. The bandage was stiff with blood, and his hair was crusted with it. Just the slightest touch made him wince. Normally, he would never have dreamed of channeling magic with such an injury, but it wasn't like he had a choice. Either his magic would work, or it wouldn't. He unwrapped the bandage from his head and tossed it aside, a badge of weakness he couldn't afford.

He summoned Ashra's image to mind, a soft smile forming on his lips. He didn't remember falling in love with her, but somehow along the way, he had. He didn't know how or why he cared for her; all he knew was that he did. Ashra frustrated him on a good day, infuriated him on a bad one, and never did one thing he'd ever asked. She'd been a terrible acolyte, by any measure. The worst he could imagine.

But she wasn't his acolyte any longer. Gil wasn't even sure what she was. Not quite a mage. Not quite a queen. Not quite a lover... yet something far more beautiful and precious than all those things put together.

He could hear the approaching calvary now, a rising

thunder carried toward him by the wind. He squeezed his fingers around the morning star's haft, feeling tears collecting in his eyes. His gaze searched frantically for some means, some tactical advantage—anything to give him more of a chance.

There was nothing.

He listened to the thunder of their horses' hoofs as the column approached. Even though they had slowed their advance, there were still so many that the sound of their passage trembled the air. Gil kept the reins of his own mount drawn tight. He sat with his back straight, holding his weapon like a club, his black cloak announcing to all the world the threat of magic posed by his presence. The soldiers of Chamsbrey would know what it meant, what that cloak stood for. He hoped the sight of it gave them terror.

Instead of breaking into the charge, the ranks of cavalry drew up at the base of the slope.

Three men rode out toward him, the one in the front wearing captain's bars on his sleeve. He sported a thin mustache and a disgruntled frown, but his uniform was pristine, as if it was a new garment just worn for the occasion. He pulled his mount up twenty paces away, then simply sat his horse as the cold prairie air swirled around him, staring at Gil as though taking measure of his mettle. After a full minute, he nodded slowly.

Gil returned the nod, acknowledging his foe.

The captain kicked his mount forward. The man met him at the top of the hill, angling his horse so that they could speak easily. He sat with a rigid spine, his gloved hand resting on the hilt of the saber attached to his saddle. When he spoke, it was with all the self-assurance of a man with an army at his back.

"Grand Master Archer, I presume?"

When Gil only stared at him in silence, the captain went on, "I hereby place you under arrest, by order of His Royal Majesty

Godfrey Faukravar. Drop your weapon, sir, and surrender your-self into my custody."

Gil snorted his disdain, looking at the captain through a bloody clump of matted hair. "You can tell His Royal Majesty to go fuck himself."

A condescending smile passed over the captain's lips. "You can come in alive or dead." He shrugged. "Your choice."

Gil grinned bitterly. "You take me for a fool?"

They knew he was a Battlemage. Which meant the captain was aware they had no way of physically restraining him.

The officer's smile slipped. "Not a fool," he breathed. "All right, then, Grand Master Archer. Let's be honest with each other. We both know you won't be riding off this field today. The only question is, how many others are going to accompany you to the grave?"

Gil brought a hand up and scratched the ragged whiskers of his chin. "What are you proposing?"

"I ask that you lay down that weapon and present yourself honorably to Corporal Harriston behind me." He nodded over his shoulder at a man with a longsword attached to the back of his saddle. "After your head comes away from your body, you have my word: we'll pack up and go home. After all, yours is the only neck we've ever been interested in."

Gil caught his breath. His skin went cold. He stared at the smirking captain in naked horror.

All those lives.

All those wasted lives.

"Just me?" he whispered, his voice cracking. "All this has been for me?"

"That's correct."

Why hadn't they made it known they only wanted him? He would have surrendered. *He would have surrendered!* Gil felt a sudden surge of nausea. It was all he could do to keep from vomiting in the saddle.

Seeing his reaction, the captain smirked grimly, the corner of his mouth twinging upward. "Or you can fight. You'll kill a lot of us, I'm sure. But, eventually, we'll knock you off that horse. And after we've dispatched you, we'll hunt down the rest of your savage friends."

Gil stared at the ground a long moment without moving, his mind clawing against a cage of incapacitating guilt. The little strength he'd had left drained out of him, and he let his body slide limply from the horse. He staggered, catching himself on the gelding, using the beast's mass to support him. His grip on the hilt of the morning star loosened, and the weapon fell from his grasp, its heavy head disappearing in the snow.

His gaze went to the man with the longsword, watching him dismount and move to stand at the captain's side. There was no trace of malice in his eyes, just a cool professionalism that Gil appreciated.

"You could have sent a message," he said weakly. "I would have come willingly."

The captain hocked a glob of spittle that arced away from him before falling to the snow. Then he smiled. "But that wouldn't have been as fun." He pointed at the snow in the place where the spittle had just landed. "Kneel."

Gil's spongey legs carried him woodenly forward, and he went to his knees in the harsh, wet snow. With trembling fingers, he unclasped the brooch of his cloak and let the thick black material slip from his shoulders. As it did, winter's chill gripped him in its cold fist, as though wanting to punish him one last time for his defiance.

Gazing straight ahead in a daze, he whispered, "Why didn't you tell me...?"

Crunching footsteps on snow circled him slowly. Gil bit his lip, shivering uncontrollably as the cold worked its way into him. He willed his executioner to hurry, wishing the sword would fall quickly. The crushing weight of grief and guilt was simply too much to bear. It bowed his shoulders forward, pressing his chin against his chest.

A fist grasped his hair, jerking his head back, positioning his neck at the best angle for the sword strike. When the hand retreated, Gil held himself steady. There was no reason to fight, and he didn't want the headsman to miss his swing.

He heard the captain's voice, "We're ready if you are, Prime Warden."

Gil stiffened. *What...?*

"I'm ready," said Naia's voice from behind him.

23

THE PRIESTHOOD OF SEER

THE CAMEL LUMBERED ALONG, SWAYING IN A DRUNKEN GATE. Rylan was vaguely aware of the commotion of the crowd swarming around them on the city street, but the noise of people sounded muted and distant. He was even more aware of the deep exhaustion that encased him, and the terrible fire burning him from within. His eyelids kept sliding shut, and he kept jerking awake.

Someone shouted something nearby, and the camel lurched to a stop with a moan of protest. With great effort, Rylan opened his eyes just a crack and saw a man, face covered by a veil, shouting and gesturing in anger, while Jendo stood by, holding the camel's lead rope.

He didn't understand what all the shouting was about; all he knew was that he wanted the conversation to end. The only thing he wanted in the world was to get where they were going and collapse into a bed. It felt like his head was getting heavier, and he let it droop to his chest. Sleep was calling to him again in a voice he couldn't ignore. Relinquishing the fight, he let his mind drift.

The ground smacked the back of his head, his vision

exploding in sparks and pain. He lay still, unable to move. All around him were shouts and frantic commotion. He opened his eyes, staring straight up into the sky. Hovering over him was a circle of faces all peering down at him with anger in their eyes.

There was nothing after that for a long time. He was aware of being carried, and every now and then, a sound cut through the blanket of his unconsciousness. Scraps of conversation came and went, and he heard only the occasional few words that were fleeting and out of context. They placed him on something hard and cold that sucked the warmth right out of him, and he started shivering violently, uncontrollably.

The pain sawed into him, searing and throbbing, until it was beyond his ability to cope with. Holding his arm against his chest, he started writhing and moaning. Hands try to hold him still, but he fought them, until he lost the strength to fight. Then he collapsed back against the cold surface they had laid him on and gave in to the agony and despair.

"His arm will have to be amputated." A man's voice. Soft. Flat and without compassion.

Those words provoked a feral panic. Rylan struggled against the grip of the hands that held him.

"Pin him down," the merciless voice directed.

"No!" Rylan moaned, fighting and bucking with the last of his strength.

"Keep him still!"

A horrifying feeling came over him, and his entire body stiffened, his eyes springing wide open. It was as if a hand just reached deep inside him and pulled him on like a glove. He tried to move, but every muscle in his body was suddenly paralyzed.

Until his hand moved of its own accord. It reached up and caught the arm of the priest who hovered over him, scalpel in hand. The man jerked back, but he was no match against Rylan's unhuman grip.

"We've come for the Quintessence." The voice coming from his mouth was his own—but the words were not. "What do you know of it, priest?"

The red-robed man stared down at him with fear in his eyes. He whispered, "I don't know what you're talking about."

"You lie," growled the voice that wasn't his. "You wield it like your own!"

"I know nothing." The man struggled, trying to break free of Rylan's grip. At last he succeeded, staggering back.

"There is nothing I can do for him," the priest gasped, starting toward the door.

Rylan's body came alive, twisting out of the hands that held him. Sitting bolt upright, he shouted, *"Torata mayir fa dagul!"*

The priest stopped between strides as though snapped back by the end of a leash. There, in the doorway, he stood frozen. Slowly, he turned around.

"How do you know those words?"

But whatever had taken hold of Rylan breathed out of him like a sigh, and he collapsed back to the stone, unconscious.

***

The next time he opened his eyes, the red-robed priest was back again. Rylan couldn't see his face through the man's veil, but he could see his eyes. They were dark brown, much like Shade's, though older and harder. The skin sagged over his eyelids, and a spiderweb of wrinkles creased the corners.

Rylan stretched, testing his strength. He was still weak, still exhausted. But the fire inside had subsided. More than anything, he felt a horrible thirst.

Seeing him awake, the priest bent over him and asked, "How is it possible that you have returned to us?"

"What?" Rylan's voice creaked like old hinges.

"The Custodian has been dead for thousands of years. Yet, today he has returned. How is this possible?"

Rylan tried to lift his head but gave up quickly. It was too heavy, and he didn't have the strength. Weakly, he asked, "How... do you know... who I am?"

The priest drew back. He clutched the arms of the chair he had pulled up to Rylan's bedside. "Eight thousand years is a long time. But our memory is longer."

"How?" Rylan whispered, intensely confused.

The man stood up, lacing his fingers together in front of him. That steady gaze stared downward, boring into him. Almost, Rylan could make out the silhouette of the man's face beneath the thin red veil he wore.

"Rest for now," the priest advised. "When you are well enough, we will speak again."

When next Rylan woke, he found Jendo at his side. At first, Rylan thought he was sleeping, but then the mage cracked open an eyelid and looked down at him. With a grunt, he leaned forward and peered into Rylan's face.

"You look better."

"I feel better," Rylan said. The overwhelming exhaustion was gone, replaced by a gnawing hunger. His arm had stopped throbbing beneath the bandages. Indeed, it felt like it had been healing for days.

Jendo's mouth squirmed into a scowl. "That's too bad. The priests should have left a bit of the illness behind to teach you not to be such an ass in the future."

Rylan grinned weakly, struggling to prop himself upright on his elbows. "So how do you go from calling me 'my Lord' to calling me an ass in the span of a day?"

Jendo scoffed, waving his hand at the question as though

brushing it away. "I'm too old to have patience for polite dishonesty. I label things what they are. If you act like a lord, I'll call you a lord. If you act like an ass, then I'll call you an ass."

Rylan couldn't help smiling. The more time he spent around the craggy old man, the more he enjoyed his company. "Fair enough."

Glancing around, he saw that he was lying in bed in a room with whitewashed walls. There wasn't much to the interior, just a stuffed mattress and a small table with a rush light shoved in one corner.

"I take it we made it to the Temple of Seer?" he guessed. "Have you had a chance to talk to the priests about the core magic?"

Folding his hands in his lap, Jendo fidgeted in his seat. "I tried. I'm convinced they know something about it, but it's as if their lips have been sewn shut. But I will say it is truly miraculous how they were able to heal you so quickly within a vortex. Do you believe in miracles?"

"I don't," Rylan responded. With a grunt, he swung his legs over the edge of the bed. "Help me up."

Instead, Jendo picked up a wooden platter and set it down on the bed. "First, you need to eat."

Rylan looked down at the tray of food, all other thoughts vanishing. There was a bowl filled with rice, with some type of meat crumbled over it. He plunged his fingers into it, scooping up a handful and shoving it in his mouth. He chewed quickly, scooping up another mouthful before swallowing the first. Within minutes, the entire tray sat empty, save for a few grains of rice. He had no idea what kind of meat he'd just eaten, only that it was greasy and unfamiliar.

He looked sheepishly at Jendo. "I guess I was hungry."

The old man shrugged. "Healing is hungry business." He returned the tray to the floor and smiled condescendingly.

Rylan asked, "How did they heal me?"

"We weren't allowed to watch," Jendo answered, his eyes going distant. "But the means the priest used had to be arcane. There's no other explanation for your swift recovery."

"Core magic," Rylan surmised. "It has to be." The priest wouldn't have been able to use the magic field under the vortex, and the Onslaught was entirely destructive. Jendo was right; there was no other explanation.

"That was my conclusion, as well."

"So the reservoir itself has to be close." Rylan felt a sudden eagerness to be underway. He glanced down at his freshly bandaged arm, hoping he was well enough to continue the journey.

"Not so fast." Jendo stopped him. "Just because there's core magic here doesn't mean the reservoir is anywhere close. Remember when I told you there were conduits that delivered core magic to cities within the vortex? This might be one of those cities."

Rylan didn't believe it. "Cardish couldn't have existed eight thousand years ago." Nothing lasted that long. Except for Suheylu Ra, but that was an exception, a city frozen in time.

"Cities are often built on top of ruins," Jendo mused, adding, "which might have been built on top of conduits."

Rylan refused to feel discouraged. "That's something, at least. I think it's time to speak to these priests about their 'miracles.'"

Jendo let his gaze trail over Rylan, lingering on his arm. At last, seeming satisfied, he rose to his feet and offered a hand. Rylan let Jendo help him up, leaning on him for support until he felt confident on his feet. He was still weak, but the food had helped.

"Where is Shade?" Through the link, Rylan could sense her presence, and he knew she could sense his. The joy she felt at knowing he was well again made him smile.

He let Jendo lead him down a flight of stairs to the ground

floor. The walls of the temple were made of large sandstone blocks without mortar between them. Chandeliers full of candles lit a large hall at the bottom of the stairs. Along the edges of the room were many statues of human figures that reminded him of the petrified men and women in Suheylu Ra. But these likenesses were made of marble, not brittle stone. They were only statues, nothing more.

They found Shade kneeling at the base of one.

At the sight of Rylan, she shot to her feet and walked quickly toward them. When she reached him, she hugged him close with a gasp of elation. He hugged her back, her joy affecting him through the link. He couldn't help smiling, bolstered by her spirits.

"I felt you..." She shook her head as though shaking off a nightmare. She gave Jendo an uncertain smile, as though not knowing what to say to the old man. Fidgeting, she looked back over her shoulder at the statue she had abandoned.

"The high priest wants to speak with you," Shade informed Rylan. "He's in there."

She pointed at a doorway at the far end of the hall. For some reason, he felt hesitant to walk through it. He dismissed the feeling quickly; he had risked everything to enter this city and speak with these priests. His reaction was irrational.

Nodding his thanks at Shade, he beckoned Jendo to follow him and crossed the floor toward the dark doorway. As he walked, Rylan looked down the row of human images, reassuring himself that they were merely statues carved from mundane stone.

He entered the room and found himself in a dim chamber lit by a pool of water that glowed with a queer golden light, casting distorted patterns of shadow across the walls. On the other side of the pool stood a man in crimson garments, face covered by a long veil, holding what looked like an illuminated tome. Seeing Rylan, he closed the book and simply waited.

With a glance at Jendo, Rylan walked forward cautiously, circling the perimeter of the pool. The man stood next to a long table, the kind that men might gather around, not for meals, but for weighty conversation. Yet the three of them were the only occupants in the room. Perhaps the priest wanted this conversation to go no further.

The man raised his hand, gesturing at the table. "Custodian. Please have a seat."

Rylan paused. The title was nothing he had ever borne in this life, but he recognized it, nevertheless. The priest was addressing Keio Matu, not him.

Wary, Rylan complied, taking a seat beside Jendo, while the priest claimed the chair at the head of the table. The man leaned forward, staring at him closely. Slowly, he brought his hand up and drew the red veil back from his face.

At the sight of the man's features, Rylan stiffened. The priest's skin was hideously pockmarked and contorted, his nose infested with bumps and ridges. His lips look gnawed on by rats, and his ears were nonexistent. But, despite his imperfections, the priest's eyes were kind and frank, putting Rylan at ease.

Licking his lips, Rylan asked, "You speak my language?"

"I speak all languages."

He waited for the priest to elaborate. When he didn't, Rylan shifted uncomfortably. "You have my gratitude for saving my life."

The priest dipped his head gravely. "Of course. I could do no less for the ancient father of my people."

Rylan didn't know how to respond to that, so he didn't. Instead, he looked down at his hand and spread his fingers, flexing them to test the elasticity of his flesh. His skin seemed whole and perfect, bending easily. If anything, it looked younger than it had before.

"You did an extraordinary job," he acknowledged. "How did

you accomplish it?" He looked up at the priest expectantly, wondering if the man would see and understand the question for what it was.

A fleeting smile passed the man's distorted lips. He sat back in his seat, clasping his hands on the table before him. "Let us be candid. You are Keio Matu, and yet, you are not. I spoke at length with the woman named Shade, so I know something of your situation. I also understand you have been twice compromised, and your motives are not pure."

Rylan stiffened at the accusation. Out of the corner of his eye, he saw Jendo sit up straight. He stared at the priest, wondering what the man's intentions were. He actually appreciated that the man had laid out everything he knew, with nothing held back. The priest in red was a capable negotiator.

That, or a capable foe.

Rylan inclined his head, acknowledging that the man had scored a point. "Then I'll also be frank. I need to find the core reservoir. The lives of every mage on this planet hang in the balance."

The priest's gaze turned inward, looking thoughtful. "So it is true. You are indeed an instrument of the Turan Khar."

The words sparked Rylan's anger. "No. I'm no man's tool."

"Then why do you seek the core reservoir?"

"Because confining that magic was the worst mistake anyone in this world has ever made," Rylan snapped. "I'm going to set things right."

"By delivering the core magic to our ancient enemy?"

"Yes." Rylan turned to Jendo. "Tell him what you know of the Turan Khar before the Sky Portal was created."

The old man flicked his eyebrows, as though surprised at having been called on. Lacing his fingers on the tabletop, he looked at the priest and cleared his throat. "For hundreds of years, the Turan Khar existed as a peaceful and benevolent society, but we did have a weakness. We were entirely dependent on the core energy. When Shira locked that power away from us, our civilization started to collapse. Without core magic, we were forced to find an alternative power source. And we found one: the Hellpower."

With a grotesque scowl, the priest concluded, "So the Turan Khar enslaved themselves to the God of Chaos. And to add insult to injury, they have resurrected the soul of our own Custodian to deprive us of the means of our existence."

Rylan's frowned. "Why does your existence depend on core magic?"

The priest explained in a frigid voice, "The land of our ancestors is a barren, polluted place, which is why it is called the Desolation. For a thousand years, this land existed in utter darkness, and before that, it was tainted by the very power that gives us life. Food doesn't grow here, and even the water is impure. Without the core magic and the sustenance it provides us, mankind cannot survive in this place."

"Then why don't you leave?"

"Don't you know?" the man returned.

Rylan took a moment, searching his memories. "No," he admitted.

The man sighed heavily, sagging back in his seat. "Then there is very little of Keio Matu left in you." His gaze turned downward to the tabletop. When he spoke again, his voice was fraught with disappointment. "Since the fall of Suheylu Ra, the duty has fallen upon us, the Priesthood of Seer, to be the keepers of Shira's knowledge. Once, that was your duty, Custodian. Upon your death, it became ours."

"I don't remember." Rylan wished his fingers could dig through his mind and claw the knowledge out.

"That is unfortunate."

Jendo demanded, "Explain yourself."

The priest turned to look at him. "I could. But I don't have to. Every piece of information you need is locked within this man's mind. The Custodian lives within you, and he must be set free."

Rylan stared straight ahead, mired by confusion and doubt. The man was making sense, and yet his words were sobering. "You want me to become him."

The priest nodded. "Only one man knows how to unlock the core reservoir: the same man who put it there."

Rylan felt a slithering cold trace over him. "But if I become him, what will happen to me?"

The priest shrugged dismissively. "Does it matter?"

Rylan thought about it, and the more he did, the more his stomach became unsettled. Once, before all this started, he'd had an identity and a life. But all that had been taken from him. Before, he thought he knew who he was, only to find out the life he had been living was all just a lie. He really didn't have any reason to rail against destiny. The truth was, he'd lost himself a long time ago.

"But if you're dependent on the core magic, how would it benefit you if we release it?" Rylan asked.

In response, the priest raised his sleeve, baring his scars. "Because we are slaves of the core magic, just as the Turan Khar are slaves of the Hellpower. And it is my belief that, if our Custodian is returned to this world, he will find a way to free us all." The priest looked at Rylan with compassion in his eyes. "Keio Mato built the core crystal at the top of the Tower of Morning. But the Tower isn't aligned strictly with our plane, and every fifth sunrise it appears in a different place. I have no idea where it is now, or where it will appear next. You'll have to go to the Temple of Akai. That's where you'll find the map room that predicts the Tower's location."

Jendo cocked an eyebrow. "Akai's called the 'Hidden Temple' for a reason. Even in my time, few knew where Akai was located."

The priest looked at Jendo with a knowing smirk. "But *you* know where it is. Don't you?"

In response, Jendo folded his arms, glowering at the priest with an expression that could have soured milk. "I know where it is," he admitted grudgingly, "but that's only half the equation."

The priest pointed at Rylan. "The other half is right there."

24

——————

DELIVERANCE

Gil awoke, but not to death.

But also not to life.

When he opened his eyes, he found himself in a wash of candle-fed light, the smell of decay filling his nostrils. Looking around, he found himself gazing up into shadows that went on forever, deep into eternity. Beside him rose a wall that was honeycombed with vaults, disappearing overhead in unending shadow.

He wasn't in pain, for which he was grateful. And it seemed he still had a head to lift.

He was lying atop a raised granite slab, the kind a body might be laid out on for burial. Leveraging his weight on his elbows, he fought to sit up. Looking around, it took him a moment to realize where he was: somewhere deep within the Catacombs of Death. Had he died, then, and his body been taken to this place? Did he still have hope of life, or was this just some transient state? He licked his lips, taking comfort in the feeling of saliva on his skin. It reassured him that he was still alive.

"Welcome back."

Gil turned in the direction of the voice and was startled to see Naia sitting next to him on the granite slab, smiling at him kindly. He gaped at her in shock, unable to do anything but blink. The Prime Warden had changed since the last time he'd seen her. The lines of her face were deeply set, as though she had aged years since he had left her in Karikesh.

"How am I alive?" he asked weakly. Bringing his hand up, he touched the place on his temple where the scalp wound had been. There was nothing there; the injury had been erased. He ran his hand over the back of his neck, half-expecting to feel a scar.

"You are alive because I willed it," Naia said. "The captain and his officers were paid well for their silence. As for the remainder the men under their command... Before their view, the body of a slain Battlemage was carried away by the priests of Death."

"Why would you go through all that?" Gil asked.

"For one thing, it absolves the Lyceum of your crimes," Naia answered. "But more importantly, it gave Captain Horner a reason to turn back with honor, having accomplished his mission."

"So both the Lyceum and the captain save face." Gil smiled acidly. "Creative."

"It was the only way to save the civilians. It was mostly you they were interested in. The general has sent his forces up the coast, sacking towns along the way, and he didn't want you making it to Janul. He didn't want to face a Battlemage with an army behind him."

"Then I suppose I should thank you," Gil said, rubbing his eyes. His gaze wandered around the periphery of the enormous hall. All around them, tall candlesticks and reliquaries sprouted from the floor. Other slabs of granite adorned the chamber, most exhibiting cadavers draped in discolored shrouds. Gil shivered, looking down at his own body. Other than the bloodstains on his shirt and trousers, there was no sign he had been laid out on a bed of death.

Naia sighed wearily, rubbing her eyes. "No. I should be thanking you. You protected the weak while the rest of us could only look on in guilt. While I was occupied with diplomacy, you were fighting to save lives."

He wondered why that had been the case. Naia's hands had been tied only because she'd allowed them to be. It wasn't like her, to choose politics over civilian life.

"And where did diplomacy get you?" he asked.

Naia's face became thoughtful. "It got us somewhere. We were able to secure the release of the remainder of the women and children."

"What of the men?"

Naia closed her eyes. "Executed."

"All of them?"

"All of them."

Gil grimaced, his hands curling into fists. Not long ago, he had despised the Malikari. They'd invaded his homeland and displaced his people, driving them from their ancestral farms and villages, sacking their towns. He had demonized Rylan's father for trading sides to help them. He had never understood such an act of treachery. Not until he had committed such an act himself.

He no longer thought of Darien Lauchlin as a war criminal. Now, he understood the man. Just like Rylan's father, he had seen through the cloud of war to the other side and gain clarity, and, like Darien Lauchlin, he'd done what was right.

"So what now?" he asked, gesturing around.

"We're left with very few options. All the kingdoms of the Rhen have united in an alliance unlike anything we've seen in modern history. They are gathering forces from as far as Southwark, intending to cleanse the north of the Malikari. They want to drive them back into the Black Lands—or into the sea.

Whichever; it doesn't matter to them. They are blinded by vengeance."

"Can we stop them?"

Naia shook her head. "Not without help."

Pushing himself up from the stone slab, Gil rose to his feet. His legs felt stronger than he'd expected, and he didn't waver over his feet. As ever, Naia's work was thorough, relieving him of all trace of injury. He had never met a more competent healer.

Standing, Naia said, "The Malikari are at a distinct disadvantage. They've lost their centralized leadership. Their cities are trying to field armies, and even the rural areas are sending men to flesh them out. But they lack leadership and coordination, so they won't be enough. The population of the North has never been dense. There aren't nearly enough soldiers to oppose the numbers the Allied Kingdoms are able to field. If the Malikari hope to prevail, they will have to look for help from elsewhere."

Gil raised his eyebrows. "Elsewhere?"

"The Black Lands."

Gil frowned inwardly. "I thought the Black Lands were emptied."

Naia turned and paced away a short distance, to another granite slab littered with charnel. Reaching out, she traced her fingers over a yellowed human skull, gazing down at it wistfully.

"They were emptied, but not completely. When Quin returned there before the end of the war, Bryn Calazar still retained a small population."

Gil thought about it. If there really were people still inhabiting the Black Lands, perhaps it was a place the Malikari could flee to. That would be the best solution all around—give the Kingdoms back their land. Have the Malikari return to where they came from. Then everyone could be satisfied.

"Then why don't they just go back?" he asked.

"They can't. As they are now, the Black Lands can't support that many people—and they won't be able to for hundreds of years. The best you can do is seek help from the people who are there. They may have enough soldiers to make a difference."

Gil breathed a sigh of resignation. "All right. Can you get me there? Are there transfer portals that could take me to Bryn Calazar?"

"You don't need a transfer portal. These Catacombs go anywhere there is a temple of Death. And Bryn Calazar was riddled with them."

Gil reached down to his belt, realizing in a stab of panic that he was absent his weapon.

"*Thar'gon*," he gasped.

"Still on the ground where you dropped it," Naia reassured him. "No one but you could lift it—except for Hadley, but he knows better than to touch it."

"While I'm alive." Gil echoed. He thought about it. He could leave the weapon there. He felt certain nothing would happen to it. But then... What if he forgot where it was? What if he was never able to find it?

"I have to go back for it."

"I'll take you to it."

Gil smiled at her gratefully. "Thank you."

He followed Naia to the nearest portal, exiting the surreal world of the dead through a marble shrine erected in the middle of a snow-draped grassland. Pausing in the doorway of the shrine, Gil saw that Naia had not come alone. Four mages and their horses lingered outside. Seeing him, they came forward and greeted him solemnly.

Gil stood for a moment looking around, content just to be alive. His gaze settled on the sunset over the wine-colored mountains in the distance. He'd never thought he'd see them again.

They walked away from the shrine through the snow. The place of the staged execution wasn't far. Which made sense; otherwise, the priests would have had a difficult time hauling his body a long distance. Naia led him to the place just outside the grove of trees, to the hill where he had met with the captain.

"It's somewhere here, beneath the snow," she said. "I'm just not sure exactly where."

Gil closed his eyes, reaching out from within. He had a strong bond with the weapon, as if he were attuned to it. After a moment, a patch of snow to his right began to glow. He sprinted toward it, plunging his hand deep into the snow and closing his fingers around the ice-cold haft of the talisman. He held it up, staring at the morning star with infinite relief. Cradling it close against his chest, he felt comforted by its touch.

Looking back at Naia, he saw that her attention was directed at something behind him. He turned to see what she was looking at.

And froze, his gaze falling on the woman who stood staring at him with tears in her eyes.

"Ashra..." he whispered.

25

THE ROAD TO AKAI

THEY LEFT CARDISH IN THE EARLY MORNING, BEFORE THE SUN had crested the horizon. The priest accompanied them through the dirt-paved streets of the city that were strangely empty. The smell of cooking fires hung in the air, and the occasional voices echoed hollowly through the alleys. Even though the sky was still dark, the city was not lost in shadow, for it was lit by street-lamps spaced out at regular intervals, one on every corner, hung from thin copper poles that were green with verdigris. The lanterns cast a pale blue light from beneath their glass chimneys, creating glowing orbs that chased back the shadows.

As he walked, Rylan found his attention drawn to the lanterns, thinking that there was something peculiar about them. The streetlamps back home burned whale oil, which produced a clear, bright light. These lanterns, with their ghostly blue glow, shed a color of light unlike any he had ever seen. Rylan changed course, making his way across the street to the nearest lamp. There was something unnatural about the quality of light that rubbed his insides the wrong way.

He wanted to reach up and touch the glass, to find out

whether or not it was hot. But something stopped him. He retracted his hand, turning back.

"Is that... magelight?" he asked.

"No," the priest said, coming to stand at his side. "It's corelight."

Rylan peered deeply into the lantern with a mixture of curiosity and trepidation. "Unlike magelight, the corelight collected in a dense ball that didn't waver like a candle flame, but glowed steadily. It formed a perfect globe of light around the lantern that ended abruptly, as though sliced off by the surrounding shadows.

Rylan glanced down the street, counting streetlamps. There was one on every corner, along with others on alternating sides of the street. He counted sixteen just within view.

"I thought it was all locked away," he said. "Where is this coming from?"

Reaching a hand up, the veiled priest touched a finger to a pane of glass. From within, a thin filament of energy shot out from the center of the lantern to dance along the inside of the glass, as though attracted to his finger.

Lowering his hand, the priest explained, "What little core energy we have comes to us through ancient ducts buried in the ground. Most are broken. The one under Cardish still functions."

Rylan reached up and set his fingers upon the glass. Immediately, streaks of energy shot out to needle the pane beneath his touch. He flinched, anticipating pain, but all he felt was a slight tingling sensation in the pads of his fingertips. Staring at the flickering dance of energy, he whispered, "It's beautiful."

The priest nodded and said ominously, "But it comes with a heavy price."

"The Marks," Rylan whispered, retracting his hand.

"The core magic is not compatible with living flesh," the

priest said gravely. He set a hand on Rylan's shoulder, drawing him back toward the center of the street.

Rylan asked, "If it's so dangerous, then how did you use it to heal me?"

"It can be used sparingly, and with acute precision. Our entire civilization depends upon core magic, even though it poisons us. We have adapted to the conditions of this environment, but that adaptation has taken its toll."

As they walked, Rylan glanced behind to make sure his two companions were still with them. Jendo strolled along with his gaze fixed on the ground ahead of his feet, his back bent under the weight of his pack. Shade walked at his side, glancing nervously about the street.

The priest accompanied them to a small caravansary outside the city gates where their camels had been kept. After some discussion, it was decided that two of the camels would be left behind, one in payment for Rylan's healing, the other in exchange for food and supplies.

While Shade and Jendo loaded their packs onto the remaining camel, Rylan lingered behind with the priest. He seemed a kind man, and Rylan was grateful to have met him.

"Take the western road to the mountains," the priest directed. "You'll find the ruins of Akai among the cliffs."

"You have my gratitude," Rylan said, offering his hand.

The man stared down at his hand as though he didn't know what to do with it. "What is your name, boy?"

The question took Rylan off guard; he hadn't realized he'd forgotten to introduce himself. "Rylan Lauchlin."

There was a long gap of silence while the priest stood there staring into his eyes. When at last he spoke, his voice was lowered so that only Rylan could hear. "This journey is unlikely to end well for you. Try to make peace with your ghosts along the way."

Rylan nodded, looking down.

The priest turned away, leading his two camels back toward the city gates. Rylan stared after him, a deep sadness weighing on his heart, dragging him down.

They took a road that led away from the city toward a line of mountains that rose from the desert like a jagged row of teeth. Rylan was grateful just to feel healthy, although he had yet to remove the bandage from his arm to examine the damage he had caused. He was reluctant to, though not because he dreaded seeing the disfigurement. Every time he thought about his arm, he was reminded of the streetlamps. He was afraid to see the kind of healing such a poisonous magic could accomplish.

The desert sprawled ahead of them, vast and parched. There was sparse vegetation along the side of the road, thickening the further they went. But there was still no green in sight; every leaf was the drab color of the desert, as though the dirt had infused even the vegetation with its essence.

They broke for lunch in the afternoon, then turned west onto a path that led upward into the foothills. The landscape changed around them, growing stonier and steeper. The color of the dirt evolved around them, darkening. The mountains ahead climbed higher until they loomed over them, casting a wide shadow across the plain. The path they were on followed the contour of the foothills, at last turning into a narrow canyon between sloping ridges.

They paused at the entrance to the canyon, stopping to rest. The sandstone walls surrounding them rose hundreds of feet. High up, the occasional stunted pine grew from cracks in the rock faces. In the thin strip of land between cliffs, a dry streamed ran downhill between patches of scrub oak and red-barked mesquite. It was the most vegetation Rylan had seen since entering the Desolation.

"This valley used to be beautiful," said Jendo, coming up to stand at his side.

"You've been here before?" Rylan asked.

"When I was first married, I lived not too far from here. My home was just a day's journey beyond that ridge." He nodded toward the south. "This entire area was a dense forest." His gaze scanned the surrounding cliffs, filled with a deep sadness. "No more."

Rylan couldn't help feeling responsible, even though he knew it wasn't his fault. "I'm sorry. You really did lose everything."

The old man shook his head. "No. Within the Unity, I gained much more than I lost. So much more. I will never miss the life I led. What I do miss is all that Keio Matu stole from this continent. He should have surrendered. Then what was left of Shira would have been absorbed into the Unity, and all this would still be beautiful and alive." He gestured around. "By collapsing the Sky Portal, Keio Matu destroyed all of this. He did far more than end a city full of lives that day."

Hearing that, Rylan looked away.

"Let's go," Jendo prompted. "The sun's going to be setting in another couple hours, and we've got a long way to go."

Rylan gave the camel's lead a good tug to start the animal moving forward. It balked, digging its feet into the dirt. It took quite a bit of effort to get it started.

Shade walked at his side. She hadn't spoken to him in hours, and he could sense through the link that her mood was tense. He didn't know why. He wondered if the priest had said something to her. She had seemed different ever since they had left the temple in Cardish.

The canyon walls narrowed around them, becoming a trail that led steeply up into the mountains. The higher they went, the more reluctant the camel became, and Rylan found himself having to tug it along. Eventually, he decided the animal was causing more bother than it was worth. At that point, they unloaded the baggage and sent the beast huffing and moaning back down the path.

From there, they bore their own supplies to the top of the ridge, to a place where twisted and anemic pine trees dominated the scenery. Still, the dirt trail rose ever upward, following the ridgeline. As they ascended into the mountains, the air cooled around them. Looking back, Rylan could see the sprawling desert stretching away to the flat horizon. To the east, night was already falling. Cardish's corelight lanterns glimmered at them from the desert, like a lost jewel twinkling from the depths of an ocean.

Eventually, as twilight faded to darkness, the trail ended in front of them, blocked by a great wall of rock that towered higher than the sky. Rylan glanced at Jendo, seeking clarification, but the old man just scratched his head.

Hesitant, Rylan took a few steps forward, gazing up at the impervious wall of rock that swallowed the sky. In frustration, he let out a deep sigh and flung his hands out at his sides. Their path was blocked.

"What is that?" Shade asked from behind him.

Turning, Rylan followed her gaze. There, on the ground, was a glowing patch of sand. Rylan walked toward it warily, pausing on the margin. He crouched beside it, hesitantly reaching out to touch it. But before he could press his fingers against it, dozens of grains of sand flew upward and stuck to his fingers, drawn to his hand like iron filings to a lodestone.

Rylan flinched, jerking back. He cast a startled glance at Shade, holding his hand up to his face. His fingers were covered with sand that glowed energetically with blue light that streamed outward from his fingers in sharp rays.

"Core magic," Jendo whispered, squatting beside him. He

touched a finger to Rylan's hand, watching as some of the grains hopped from Rylan's fingers onto his.

"What do you think it is?" Rylan asked.

"I think it's a sign that we've found what we're looking for," Jendo replied, staring down at the glowing patch on the ground.

Confused, Rylan looked around, not seeing anything that looked like the ruins of an ancient temple. He frowned at Jendo. "What are we looking for, exactly?"

The old man gestured up at the towering cliff. "Akai was hard to find, even in my time."

Rylan frowned. "Then how do we find it?"

Jendo pointed up at the cliff. "It's there." Then he pointed at the glowing patch of dirt. "And there. It's all around us." Then he pointed his finger at his head. "Especially here."

As Jendo spoke, the hairs on the back of Rylan's neck stood up. He turned slowly, his eyes wandering over the landscape, looking for anything that seemed out of place.

"I see it," Shade said, her eyes growing wide and staring fixedly at Rylan. Bending over, she scooped up a handful of glowing sand and cast it right at him.

Rylan threw his hands up reflexively. But the grains of sand shot through the air, hissing past him, and stuck to... something.

Rylan opened his eyes and looked behind him, pausing only to gasp. He started backing away, at first slowly, and then quickly.

Moving back to where Shade and Jendo were standing, he stopped to gape at the outline of a freestanding arch, made visible only as a glowing outline of sand hanging suspended in the air.

Rylan edged forward cautiously, walking toward the glimmering apparition. The arch was only a little taller than he was, slender and elegant, coming to a scalloped point two inches above his head. Hesitantly, he reached out, and passed his hand through the opening of the arch.

Halfway in, his hand disappeared.

Rylan retracted his hand, shaken. He raised his fingers before his face, half-expecting them to be missing. But his hand was still there, still attached to his wrist. He flexed his fingers just to make sure.

He glanced back at his companions in wonder.

Jendo came forward and, just as Rylan had done, passed his hand through the arch. It, too, disappeared, then reappeared as he withdrew it.

Rylan picked up a stone from their path and tossed it in. There was a faint shimmer in the air as it disappeared. Rylan wondered what would happen if he walked behind the arch and threw something in from the other side.

He decided to find out. Cautiously, he walked around it.

"Be careful," Shade called out to him. "There are rules operating here you don't know."

Rylan walked behind the arch, then stopped and turned. Looking back through the outline revealed by the glowing sand, he saw Jendo and Shade standing on the other side. He scooped a rock up off the ground and tossed it in. It disappeared in a glimmer of light, just as the first had.

Returning to his companions, Rylan considered the arch. "Well, there's only one way to find out what's on the other side."

Jendo looked profoundly skeptical. He stood staring at the arch with a dark and troubled expression, one finger drumming his cheek. "If we go in there, there's no guarantee we'll come back out. Think of the rocks. *They* didn't come back."

Rylan chuckled. "Did you expect them to? Anyway, we didn't come all this way just to stand here staring at that arch. I think it's obvious I need to go in there. Alone."

When Jendo started to protest, Rylan went on quickly, "This isn't about you. This is about me and the vile man I have locked inside me. If that doorway leads me to him somehow, then I have to go in there. But no one else has to take the risk."

"You don't have to go in there on your own," Shade said. "That's why we're here with you."

"No." He didn't want her going in there. He didn't know what awaited him through that arch, but he feared it. "Let's camp here tonight," he said at last. "That will give me the evening to think about it."

Shade nodded, though she looked anything but relieved, and Jendo turned and walked away from them. Rylan swung his rucksack off his shoulder and set it on the ground. Without waiting to see if the others would follow suit, he started unpacking his provisions and turning out his bedroll. He could feel Shade's eyes on him as he worked, but he didn't look up at her. Instead, he sat on his mat and dug out some strips of camel jerky the priest of Seer had given him.

Eventually, Shade came to sit beside him while Jendo busied himself with setting up a campfire. Rylan avoided her eyes, turning his attention back to the archway that still glowed with the glimmering lights of hundreds of grains of sand. The longer he peered at it, the more he feared it. Into that arch was the last place in the world he wanted to go.

Rummaging in his sack, he found a small carving of a woman. He'd almost forgotten about it. He had carved the little figure while on his journey to Suheylu Ra with Xiana. He'd been bored and started whittling a piece of wood with his knife, not really intending to make anything. Lacking direction from his brain, his knife had done the work all on its own. The result was a faceless woman who meant everything to him.

"Who is she?" Shade asked, staring down at the wooden figure in his hands.

"My wife," Rylan replied, squeezing his fingers closed around it.

Shade put her hand out, and grudgingly, he handed her the

carving. She took her time examining it, at last handing it back. "She is lovely."

Rylan felt a knot tighten in his throat as he tucked the little carving back into his sack. "Aye. She was."

Shade scooted closer and peered at him in understanding. "I would like to tell you a story."

Rylan found it hard to lift his eyes to her.

"When I was young, there was a man who lived among us," Shade told him. "His name was Auger, and he had the mind of a child, and a childish love of everyone. He had been raised by his elder brother, a fierce warrior whose sword every man on the salt plains feared.

"Then one year, a new band formed, made of young men who had been driven from their own tribes. These men had no women and no salt, so they went from place to place striking family bands and then running before anyone could retaliate. They never had the strength or the honor to take over the duties of the males that they killed, so instead of establishing their own salt fields, they continued roving and killing and stealing the food from others' plates.

"When they came to my band, they did the same as they did everywhere else. They slaughtered the men and most of the children, and forced themselves upon the women. At first, they spared Auger, for it is known that the gods repay cruelty to cripples and the witless kind for kind. But eventually the lure of the game at last overcame their prudence, and they decided to make sport of him. They made him an offer: they told Auger that if he doused himself in oil and lit himself on fire, then they would cut his brother's bonds and set him free. So that's what Auger did. He doused himself in lamp oil and threw himself into the campfire.

"As he died in the flames, his persecutors were true to their word: they cut his brother's bonds and released him. But

Auger's brother only took five steps away from the camp before they shot his back full of arrows."

Her voice trailed off, leaving Rylan to stare in dismay into the empty space left behind by her words.

"Why are you telling me this?" he asked, greatly unsettled by her story.

Shade peered at him. "Because you need to hear it."

26

EMBASSY

Gil stood frozen, gaping at Ashra in shock. She just stared back at him for seconds, then she sprang forward, crushing him in a strong embrace. Startled, he hugged her back, the feel of her touch sending a thrill of emotion down his spine. The smell of her hair was nostalgic, bringing his emotions sharply into focus.

Clumsily, he released her. He stepped back and ran his gaze over her. Ashra was thinner than she had been back in Karikesh, the bones of her face protruding more than they had. But she was still beautiful, maybe even more beautiful now that he looked at her through eyes colored by sentiment. A sense of euphoria crept over him at the knowledge that she was unharmed.

"They said you were dead," she whispered. She looked at Naia, who stood behind Gil, surrounded by the mages of her retinue.

With a warm smile of affection, Naia moved forward and took Ashra into her arms, kissing her tenderly on the cheek. Pulling back, she smiled. "I'm so proud of you," she said.

Tears rolled down Ashra's cheeks, and she wiped them away.

Gil looked past Ashra at the trees that lined the top of the hill behind them, wondering where Demir and the rest of her Zakai were. Ashra shouldn't be standing there alone, with no one to guard her.

Nervously, he asked, "What are you doing here?"

She looked at him with an uncertain expression, as though hesitant to reveal her true motive. "I was looking for that," she said in a soft voice, nodding at the weapon in his hand.

Gil frowned at her in confusion. "How did you know it was here?"

Ashra gestured at the snow-covered ground, which was pockmarked by many deep footprints. "It's where your tracks ended."

That made sense. He nodded. "Where's the camp?"

"On the other side of the river."

"You shouldn't be out here alone," he chided her.

Ashra shrugged apologetically. It was the kind of look she never would have given him as his acolyte. She extended her hand in a gesture of invitation. "Let's go back to camp and talk over a fire and a meal."

Gil couldn't argue. He let Ashra lead Naia ahead. She glanced back at him, making sure he was following, then set off up the hill and into the line of trees. They crossed a small brook, the smell of woodsmoke permeating the air. The sounds of people became louder, drifting toward them through the trees.

As they wound their way through the camp, people glanced up at him with vacant looks on their faces and grief in their eyes. A woman rose ahead of them and bowed. Another woman rose and followed suit, then suddenly people all around the camp stopped what they were doing, turned toward them, and bowed their heads. It took Gil a moment to realize who they were bowing at: the Prime Warden had entered their midst, the white cloak on her back announcing her presence. The refugees in the camp looked upon her in reverence, their faces brightening with hope. Naia smiled and dipped her chin as she passed, muttering greetings.

The sight of Demir emerging from the command tent brought a smile to Gil's lips. At the sight of him, Demir stopped in his tracks, gaping as though he were looking at a ghost. He probably thought he was. His gazed jerked from Gil to Ashra, as if he was trying to discriminate between the living and the dead. At last, he threw his head back and laughed heartily. Surging forward, he yanked Gil into his arms, clapping him on the back.

"You were dead!" He exclaimed in wonder. "I saw you! You were dead!"

"You saw what you were supposed to see," Naia said with a smile. "I'm sorry, but the deception was necessary."

"I am happy to be wrong!"

Demir led them into the command tent, which was larger than Gil remembered. More cloth panels had been added, so that now several people could stand within it comfortably. The interior was lit by the warm glow of magelight and smelled powerfully of body odor.

"Please," Ashra said, inviting them to sit.

While Naia made herself comfortable, a woman wearing a headscarf came forward, offering them cups of hot tea. Gil held his with both hands, letting the cup warm his fingers.

"What do you intend to do?" Naia asked Ashra without any preamble.

At first, Ashra seemed taken off-guard by the question. But, gathering herself, she answered the Prime Warden just as directly, "I would lead these people to Janul, a city with strong walls that can protect them. From there, I will seek to muster an army."

Naia lowered her teacup. "Unfortunately, that's no longer possible. The armies of the Kingdoms are advancing up the coast. Janul fell two days ago."

A slight gasp passed Ashra's lips. "They have advanced that quickly?"

"Alas, they have. There was little to stop them. Many of the coastal towns have fallen. The closest city left standing is Bel Arun. But it, too, is likely to fall soon. The army that besieged Janul is continuing north. They will be reaching the walls of Bel Arun in just a few days."

Ashra stared grimly into the depths of her teacup, her teeth worrying her bottom lip. After long moments, she looked up at the Prime Warden with renewed determination in her eyes.

"Then I will lead these people to Bel Arun and take command of this war from there."

Naia raised her cup to her lips, taking a delicate sip. "Bel Arun will not stand before the armies of the Kingdoms. Without reinforcements, it too, shall fall. Gathering those reinforcements needs to be your priority."

"What would you suggest I do?" Ashra asked, her eyes fearful.

Looking at her, Gil realized that, at that moment, Ashra needed his help more than ever. "Naia has suggested that we appeal to Bryn Calazar for reinforcements from the Black Lands."

"The Black Lands?" Ashra glanced at Naia. "There are still people in the Black Lands?"

"A few stayed behind," Naia responded, absently smoothing a wrinkle in her cloak. "I have no idea how many there are now, or whether they'll feel any loyalty toward their brothers and sisters in the Rhen. But if it's possible to leverage their support, then I suggest you try."

Gil protested, "The Black Lands are on the other side of the

Shadowspears, and the pass is blocked. Reinforcements could never get here in time."

"They could, if we brought them through a transfer portal," Naia said.

Taking a deep breath, Gil glanced at Ashra. "Allow me to lead a delegation to Bryn Calazar. If I can get them to agree to an alliance—"

"But what kind of alliance?" Ashra frowned. "There are many types of alliances. I would not be open to all. We know nothing of these people."

Naia set her hand on Ashra's in a reassuring gesture. "It has not been so many years since the people of Malikar fled the Black Lands. Some of the refugees you chaperone may have relatives still living there. It's possible even some of your own relatives were left behind."

Ashra nodded, her eyes thoughtful. "Of course, you are correct." Her gaze wandered over the wall of the tent behind Gil, staring blankly. At last, she turned to Naia, lifting her chin. "Very well. I'll go."

Gil shook his head. "You can't go. You're needed here. There must be a continuity of command. Send me and I'll—"

"That's what generals are for." Ashra glared him to silence. "I want to see for myself what kind of people we're getting into bed with."

"She's right," Naia said, taking a sip of her tea. "She must be there. But I do believe you should go with her, Gil."

Gil didn't like it. "But who will take over here?"

Ashra looked to Demir, who was sitting along the wall of the tent next to Gil. "Master Demir, I charge you with leading our people to Bel Arun. Gil and I will meet you there shortly with reinforcements from Bryn Calazar."

Naia smiled and nodded, looking satisfied. "Then it is settled. On the morrow, I'll escort you and Gil through the

Catacombs to the Temple of Death in Bryn Calazar. But it will be up to you to make your way from there."

Scowling in irritation, Gil raised his cup. "So be it," he said, and knocked back the last of his tea, wishing it was something much stronger.

The next day dawned clear and crisp. Gil roused, anxiety tightening his stomach to the point that even hunger eluded him. He left the tent and stood before the heat of one of the fires, warming his hands and gazing absently into the flames. The sounds of the waking camp stirred around him. People rising from their blankets walked to the edge of the encampment to make their morning water. Gil nodded at them as they move past.

He forced himself to eat a grilled trout, though the fish didn't sit well on his stomach. Thinking of the journey ahead tied his nerves into knots. They were taking a great risk, walking into the unknown, just the two of them, and he didn't like gambling with Ashra's life. Even though he trusted the Prime Warden, he still couldn't set aside his fears.

They said their goodbyes—or threats, in Demir's case. By the time they made their way out of camp, Gil was more than aware of what creative tortures Demir had in mind for him if he let anything happen to Ashra.

They followed Naia to the shrine of Death and soon found themselves within a cold, macabre ambience suffused with candlelight and the stench of myrrh. It took only a moment for Naia to unlock the vault behind the altar, exposing hidden stairs that led down deep into the chambers below the shrine. From there, they entered the portal into Death's Passage. He didn't think he could ever grow used to the empty halls and corridors inhabited only by bones and marble monuments.

Two months ago, he hadn't even known of its existence, and now he was using it just as if it were a transfer portal.

They didn't have to go far to find the exit to Bryn Calazar. Naia led them quickly through the echoing corridors, seeming to know exactly where she was going. They paused before a dark portal that led to something that look like an abandoned shrine. There, Naia halted and stepped aside. Gil realized that was as far as she would be accompanying them.

"This is it?" he asked.

"It is." Naia gestured at the portal. It reminded Gil of looking down through the surface of a pool into the depths of the water below. On the other side, he could see a dim chamber lit by heavy chandeliers, built of large granite stones that seemed to sag with age.

"What do we know about this place?" Gil asked.

Naia answered, "As far as I'm aware, no one has ventured into the Black Lands from the Rhen in twenty years."

"My father sent a few emissaries north of the pass," Ashra said in a faraway voice. "They never returned, so he stopped sending them."

The information didn't make Gil feel any better. Glancing back through the portal, he asked, "So we have no idea what we'll find?"

The Prime Warden shrugged. "No. We know that the sun shines in the Black Lands once more, but the Great Migration emptied those lands thoroughly. Very few people chose to remain behind."

Gil scratched his cheek. "So we have no idea what we're walking into."

Naia said, "You must be ready for any possibility. There is also the chance that whoever now rules the Black Lands will see your arrival as an opportunity to expand their empire. Whatever happens, please try to *negotiate* your way out of the situation."

Gil grinned nervously, taking her meaning. "That's assuming they're willing to negotiate. What's stopping them from locking us in a dungeon and marching an army through the pass?"

Ashra shot him a look of irritation. "We're not helpless, Gil."

"No," Gil allowed. "But they may have mages of their own."

"That's a possibility," Naia agreed. She turned and drew Ashra into an embrace, kissing her cheek. She did the same for Gil, whispering in his ear, "It's her time to rise and fly free and far. You need to let her."

Gil's eyes went to Ashra, who stood staring at the portal, her concentration bent on the shadows on the other side. He nodded, knowing Naia was right.

27

THE TEMPLE OF AKAI

RYLAN STOOD AND DUSTED OFF HIS PANTS, CASTING A RESENTFUL glare at the archway revealed by the glowing grains of sand. The map room lay somewhere on the other side of that arch, and there was no sense putting it off any longer.

He glanced at Shade and found her staring at him. He could tell by the look on her face that she was reading his every emotion. Embarrassed, he tried to stuff his fear deep down inside, someplace she would never find it. Taking a deep breath he started toward the portal.

"Wait!" she gasped.

But he'd waited long enough. Sucking in a deep breath, Rylan closed his eyes and stepped through the arch.

The light changed.

The scent of pine disappeared, and the air warmed substantially.

He stood in the deep silence of twilight, in what looked like the courtyard of a Southern-style villa. Stone walls surrounded him on all sides. The courtyard was paved with flagstones, and the gurgle of a fountain in its center was the only sound that echoed through the vast stillness of the world. Ahead, a scalloped blue door looked like it led into the interior of the villa.

Rylan stood for a moment trying to understand his surroundings. Something about the villa seemed wrong, but he couldn't put a finger on it. It took him a little while to realize that the entire courtyard was an impossibility. The water of the fountain trickled upward instead of down. Bending, he picked a pebble up off the ground. Opening his hand, he was not surprised when it floated.

A thought came to him from out of the dark recesses of his brain, dredged up from Keio Matu's faded memories, of a culture which had existed thousands of years before Shira that had used magic to store troves of knowledge inside the minds of its own people, only locked away. Those who needed to access that knowledge could do so only if they knew the prerequisite key. Such a key unlocked the vaults constructed within their mind, the very same way a person might gain access to a locked room within a library.

Looking around, Rylan wondered if this was the same kind of mind-vault. Was that where he was, trapped within his own head? And if he was, where would the vaults within his mind lead him? He looked around the courtyard, wondering what to do next. He doubted he knew the key to open the door. He took a step forward, noting that his footstep produced no sound. The only thing that disturbed the silence was the constant babbling of the fountain.

There was only one way to go. The door to the villa lay ahead, waiting. He crossed the courtyard toward it, moving around the fountain. When he reached the blue door, he found it locked.

He stared at the door, considering it grimly. It was made of riveted wood, painted deep blue, the color of lapis. He was sure that door was where he needed to go. He turned back and looked around the courtyard, wondering if he had been mistaken, but there were no other exits. The portal that had brought him here was gone. The only way out of the courtyard was through that one blue door.

He didn't know what else to do, so he decided to knock.

Lifting his hand, he rapped three times upon the wood, the sound echoing hollowly through the stillness. Then he waited, feeling soft fingers of trepidation creep down his spine. Seconds went by, and yet nothing happened. Just as he was about to turn away from the door, he heard the click of the latch.

The door creaked open just a fraction.

It was enough. Rylan felt his stomach sink as he stared into the darkness beyond that crack in the doorway.

Slowly, he pushed the door open on creaking hinges, exposing a great darkness beyond. No light spilled into the room from the doorway, as though the light of the courtyard simply stopped at the threshold. The only thing he could see inside the room was a great totality of darkness.

Gathering his courage, Rylan stepped across the threshold.

The door closed behind him on its own and, suddenly, he was encased by shadow.

A thunderous booming noise resonated through the darkness as if from a great distance, like the sound of a vast metal door closing somewhere else in the world. The way the sound echoed, Rylan got the impression that he was standing within an enormous chamber, one whose walls and ceiling soared hundreds of feet to either side. The echo of the noise continued for impossibly long seconds before finally fading to an all-consuming silence.

Another resonating *thud* made Rylan jump. He had the eerie feeling that, somewhere far away, another colossal door had just slammed shut.

The sound of it echoed as though traveling down an impossibly deep mineshaft. And this time, when the echoing thunder faded to silence in the distance, it didn't disappear completely. Instead, it was replaced by a high-pitched droning noise that increased in intensity.

Somewhere in the distance, another door slid open or shut—he couldn't tell which. Then another. Then another, sounding much closer. It was like he was standing within some enormous clockwork machine that was opening and closing possibilities while he stood there gripped in the paralyzing darkness of indecision.

From somewhere deep inside, a terrible awareness seized him: he was on limited time. The darkness around him was shifting and changing, and if he allowed too much time to pass, the only path of escape would move on without him.

He didn't know where to go, just that he had to start going *now*. He started forward into the darkness in the direction of the echoing rumbles. Eventually, he reached what felt like a metal wall blocking his path. He felt along it, feeling for a door, but didn't find one. Not knowing what else to do, he knocked on the wall. The sound echoed hollowly. He walked along the wall, knocking as he went.

Nothing happened.

Until something did.

To his left, a door slid open, admitting a wash of light into the chamber. He still couldn't see the walls or the ceiling around him, but the light coming through that doorway marked a path that he could follow, and his feet turned in that direction eagerly. He rushed toward the opening, the door closing behind him cutting off the sound of echoing possibilities.

Rylan stopped and turned around slowly. He was in a large, circular room lit by magelight that swirled close to the floor.

There were four doors, one on each wall. He had no idea which one to take.

Another echoing thunder broke the silence, coming from without. Rylan now had the feeling that he stood deep within a maze, and that maze was constantly shifting around him. Every second of delay was costing him. Looking from door to door, he clenched his jaw in indecision. They all look the same, and there was no way to tell one apart from the other. He felt his pulse kick up as he began to panic.

From somewhere inside him came a nerve-tingling urge to use the door on the right. Rylan didn't need to be told twice, for he knew where that feeling had come from. Walking toward the door, he felt a shiver of hope. Somewhere deep inside him, Keio Matu was stirring, coming alive, at least enough to guide him through the mind-vault. Even as he felt the maze moving around him, the thought gave him some comfort.

But when he reached the door, it wouldn't open.

Panicked, Rylan started rattling it, practically ripping it out of its door frame, but, still, it wouldn't budge. Then his eyes fell on a small metal plate on the wall with six tiny wheels on it.

He felt sure it was some type of a locking mechanism, but he had no idea how it worked. His hand went to the wheels, and he started turning them, first one direction and then the other.

Nothing happened. The door wouldn't unlock.

Desperate, he tried wiggling the wheels back and forth. At last, one slid to the side. He tried sliding the other five in the same direction.

Nothing.

He tried again, sliding the wheels back and forth, trying different patterns. Then he paused, caught in the grip of a cold and eerie feeling. His hand moved as if of its own accord, sliding the wheels into place. The door clicked and popped open.

A satisfied feeling bubbled up from within him, a feeling that couldn't be his own. Rylan started forward, but then stopped himself, feeling suddenly confused. For just a second, he had forgotten what he was doing there. It took a moment for him to regain his bearings. As he moved forward again, fear gripped his throat in a chokehold.

Shaking, he opened the door and moved through, letting it close behind him. Confronting him was another room with another puzzle. The sound of the thundering doors and sliding walls followed him here, goading him on. This time, there were only two exits from the room, and somehow, he knew one would lead to certain failure. Suddenly, it became clear to him that the price of failure was a lifetime locked away within the maze. For that was the true danger of this temple, and the reason why Akai had stayed hidden for so long from the rest of the world. The unwary who ventured within became entrapped inside these vaults, never to return.

Taking a deep breath, Rylan decided to place his trust in Keio Matu. As he did, he felt another colossal door sliding open. And, somewhere else, another door sliding closed with a finalistic *thud.*

By the time the echoes faded, he knew he needed to choose the door on the left. He didn't understand how Keio Matu could have known. Perhaps there was some pattern to the puzzles that the Custodian was aware of that he was not.

Confident that the man would not steer him in the wrong direction, Rylan opened the door and stepped through.

And almost fell into darkness.

He stifled a cry as the door slammed close behind him. He was balanced on a ledge only as wide as the balls of his feet over a wide vertical shaft that dropped forever into darkness. The shaft continued upward, soaring away into eternity. There was just enough light to see, though he couldn't tell where the light came from. The walls on every side of the shaft were riddled with doors, but there was no obvious path between them. He didn't know how he would get from the ledge he stood on to the nearest door, which was across the shaft from him.

The ledge shuttered and gave way, sliding back into the wall, and suddenly he was falling.

Another platform slid out from the wall, catching him instantly.

Rylan crouched on all fours, shivering in fear. He felt certain he was going to keep falling, down into the shaft, falling forever and ever, never-ending. Quivering, he regained his feet. The echoing *thuds* of doors reverberated up the shaft, increasing in urgency.

He took a step forward. The platform under him disappeared, and this time, there was nothing beneath him to break his fall. He barely got his hands out in time to catch himself on a ledge that appeared spontaneously. If he had missed the ledge, he would've fallen all the way down.

He dangled there over the shaft, legs kicking in the air, panic quickly overcoming reason. Groaning, he pulled himself over the lip of the ledge with all the strength he possessed, using his elbows to shimmy himself forward. By the time he rolled over onto his back on the ledge, he was shaking so hard, all he could do was lay there panting, but he didn't have time for that. There was no reason to expect the platform to remain.

He pushed himself to his feet and stood leaning against the wall on trembling legs. He felt a strong impulse to turn to his right and step off the ledge, but there was nothing there but a long fall into darkness.

Remember...

He had two choices: trust the voice in his head or fall to his death the next time a platform slipped out from under him. He decided to trust the voice.

Biting his lip, he stepped off the platform just as it disappeared beneath him. He fell only a foot before connecting with another platform sliding out from the wall. Catching his breath, Rylan opened himself to the next impulse welling up from inside him.

Forward.

Without hesitation, he walked off the platform into empty air.

And fell.

Only to be caught by the next ledge materializing beneath him.

Left.

He stepped off the ledge onto a ramp that climbed up the wall of the shaft. The sound of another massive door opening or closing echoed vastly from the distance.

Faster.

He jogged up the ramp, making his way toward a door high up the wall on the other side of the shaft.

Jump.

He leapt off the ramp as a section of it gave way beneath his feet. He landed on another ramp that had been invisible just a second before. Reaching the door, he burst headlong through it, throwing his body on the floor of the room on the other side. He lay there, shaking, until the sound of another monstrous door shuddered him off the floor in a growing panic. He stood there in the middle, turning in circles, glancing about frantically within a pool of blue light.

Once again, he had forgotten what he was doing there.

For long seconds, it didn't come to him. Desperate, he clawed his way back through a lifetime of memories that didn't seem real, searching for the one all-important memory that would tell him what was happening, what he was supposed to be doing. As he pawed through them, he started remembering little bits and pieces of his life. His education. His parents.

Meeting the woman he loved. Moving to Suheylu Ra. Being elected Custodian.

Rylan shuddered. Those weren't his memories. They were someone else's. Panicked, he forced himself back down into the muddle of his mind, digging deeper for memories of his own. They came to him tediously and incompletely. A picture of his daughter's face, though lacking features. The farmhouse where he'd grown up, though he couldn't tell what color it was. His son's funeral—he stared through tears of frustration at the flowers that fill the shrine, trying with all his might to figure out what type they were.

Horrified, he realized what was happening. The more he relied on Keio Matu's memories, the more he was losing his own.

But now he remembered why he was there, and time was running out.

The map room was close. Just ahead. If he could reach it quickly enough, he could still get out in time.

He moved toward the room's only exit.

The door wouldn't open.

It was another puzzle lock. Groaning, Rylan brought trembling hands up to wipe the sweat off his face. He would have to use the man's memories again. This time, though, he would protect himself. He would hang onto his own memories at the same time and wouldn't let them go.

Keeping his wife's image fixed in his head, he closed his eyes and opened his mind.

He felt Keio Matu take over.

Instantly, his hand started working, flipping levers and turning dials until the door popped open. Without hesitation, he slid through and pulled the door closed behind him, drawing up with a gasp.

He was in the map room.

Only, it didn't look like what he had expected.

It was a wide chamber, filled with mist. He couldn't see the walls, the ceiling, or the floor. It was almost like standing within a cloud. Suddenly, he remembered he was supposed to be thinking of something. Remembering something. His wife's name.

Groping through the mist of his mind, he struggled to recall it.

Ilia.

No. That wasn't her name. Ilia had been Keio's wife, not his. Rylan strained harder, but no matter how hard he tried, his own wife's name would not come to him.

"*No...*"

He was losing himself. Frantic, he tried dragging an image of his daughter's face to the forefront of his mind.

He could not. He had no idea what his own daughter looked like.

Rylan balled his hands into fists, hitting his thighs in frustration. He had to get out of there, *now,* before the man gained control. Before he was erased completely.

But first, he needed to access the map. Only, he had no idea how the map room worked.

The fog...

Keio's voice in his mind made him shudder, for now he understood the true price of hearing it.

Use the fog...

Of course.

This place wasn't real. There was no such thing as a Temple of Akai. This entire place was just a mnemonic. Sometime long ago, the construct of the temple had been implanted in Keio Matu's mind, making accessible any knowledge he could ever need, as well as protecting that knowledge from those who would try to wrench it forcibly out of him. The Temple of Akai existed within him. Nowhere else.

"Show me the Tower of Morning," he commanded the mist that fogged his mind.

And it did.

The parting of the mist did not reveal a map. The location of the Tower had always been known to him, and now the veil obscuring that knowledge had been lifted. The understanding was there, along with all the other knowledge he had lost. Every drop of it. No longer was he divorced from himself, living in the shadows of someone else's awareness. After eight thousand years, he could finally be free.

Almost...

Even though he had managed to swim to the forefront of his thoughts, there was still the matter of the other man who could resurface at any time.

He couldn't let that happen. He couldn't take the chance that man could ever suppress him again.

He already knew what to do with him.

With the mist cleared from the room, he could see two doors set into the far wall. He already knew where each of those doors led. The door to the left would take him back through the portal of his mind. The door on the right would trap him within it forever. It was a last-ditch protection, should anyone try to steal his memories.

Purposely, he selected the door on the right. Only, it wasn't himself that he intended to trap.

The moment he opened the door, he felt the silent scream of the man inside him. There was a flash, and then darkness.

He stood for a moment with his hands out, fighting for stability as the world wobbled beneath his feet. But then, slowly, that motion stabilized, and the world returned around him as though it wakened from a dream.

A woman sitting on the other side of a small fire rose to her feet. Even though her face was covered, he could see recognition and relief brightening her eyes. Instantly, she started toward him but then froze. She brought a hand up to her head, as though some profound thought had occurred to her.

"Rylan?" she gasped, peering at him with fear in her eyes.

The sound of that name filled his mouth with a bitter taste that made him want to spit it out. His mood darkened.

Taking a step toward her, he growled, "I'm not Rylan."

28

BRYN CALAZAR

GIL STEPPED OUT OF THE CATACOMBS INTO THE BASEMENT OF THE temple. As he stood waiting for Ashra, he let his eyes wander over the dim shadows in the chamber, which looked tarnished by centuries of dust and neglect. Sagging cobwebs hung from chandeliers that emanated a feeble light that flickered inconsistently like a skipping heartbeat. There didn't seem to be any signs of other people. He turned toward Ashra as she came through the portal and stopped next to him, pausing to take in her surroundings.

"Doesn't seem like a going concern, does it?" he asked.

"Death's temples rarely are," she said dismissively, her gaze drawn upward to the roof. "Most people try to avoid them, for obvious reasons."

"For very *good* reasons." Raising his hand, Gil gestured at a stairwell on the far wall. "After you, Your Majesty."

Ashra flashed him a vexed look as she passed by. "Is there something upsetting you, Gil?"

"Other than the fact that you're here, risking your life, no."

She scowled in response. He followed her up the stairs into

the main shrine of the temple. There were still no people about, not even priests, which surprised him. The far end of the shrine glowed dimly with the flickering lights of candles. From somewhere high above, he could hear the flapping of wings. A bird must have flown in through the doorway and couldn't find its way back out again, soon to be another addition to Death's collection of souls.

They walked to the temple door. There, Gil paused, feeling hesitant about opening it. On the other side of that door was a world no outsider had ever seen. He wondered if the Black Lands were still black, or if the dark soil had been bleached by the return of sunlight. He'd heard stories of the dark, soot-encrusted streets of Bryn Calazar, and was anxious to see what changes the last twenty years had brought.

"Go ahead," Ashra urged him. "Open it."

Gil lifted his hand to do just that, but fear of the unknown stopped him. There might be people outside on the street who wouldn't take well to the sight of foreigners. Being Malikari, Ashra might be able to blend in, but there was no way he could. His blond hair would give them away instantly, not to mention the black cloak he wore on his back. Taking a deep breath, he applied his weight to the door, swinging it open on rusted hinges.

A bright glare of sunlight jarred his vision, making him wince. Blinking, Gil moved forward into the wash of light, opening the door wider. Then he drew up to stand on the temple steps, taking in a view that was entirely unexpected.

A modest-sized city lay before him, layer upon layer of brilliant white walls capped with blue tile roofs, tumbling down away from the temple toward a harbor the same azure as the sky above it. A pleasant breeze tugged at his hair and played with the edges of his cloak. The cries of seabirds made him glance up, breaking the spell.

He looked at Ashra, marking the shock and wonder in her eyes that had to be an echo of his own. Then he looked back to the city. Below the temple steps, people moved along the street. There were none of the crowds he had come to expect in cities like Karikesh or Auberdale, but still, there were far more people on the street than he would have ever expected to find in an area that was supposed to be depopulated. The citizens of Bryn Calazar were dressed in a bright variety of colors, many wearing shawls or tall hats on their heads. People pushed carts or pulled wagons behind them. The air was warm but not humid, and the sun seemed very direct. Gil could feel its comforting rays on his skin, a welcome sensation after so many days exposed to ice and snow.

"This is not... what I expected," he muttered, lacking better words to express what he wanted to say.

"Nor I," Ashra whispered.

She moved forward down the steps, and he trailed behind her. Reaching the level of the street, they stood there for a moment, watching the people passing by: men and women, children running alone or in groups. The cries of birds, the barking of dogs, all the typical noises of a city.

He followed Ashra into the street and waded into the current of foot traffic. At first, the people walking by seemed to pay them no mind, keeping their eyes on the ground in front of them. But soon, the occasional passerby caught a glimpse of his face, their eyes widening. The stares they were getting were becoming harder and more penetrating. It didn't take Gil long to feel exceptionally uncomfortable. Within minutes, the skin of his back was positively tingling with apprehension.

"They've marked me as a foreigner," Gil whispered.

"Did you think they wouldn't?"

The comment made him bite his tongue. He tried reassuring himself that the attention he was gathering wasn't necessarily negative. They had come here for a reason, to meet with the ruler of this city. His foreign looks might help land them an audience faster—either that or get them killed.

Ashra smiled at someone walking by, at the same time muttering under her breath, "Remember. You are an emissary."

Gil gave a dry smile.

They followed the street toward the harbor, though Gil had no idea where they were going and doubted Ashra did either. To their left rose an enormous step-sided ziggurat with a small building at the top that might have been a temple. Trying to seem inconspicuous, Gil nodded at it, pointing it out to Ashra.

They turned onto a narrow street that ran uphill toward the ziggurat. Tall white walls bordered the street on both sides, occasionally laden with flowers and vines. There was absolutely no sign of the long darkness this land had endured, as if all signs had been completely scrubbed away. Everywhere he looked were bright colors and greenery. Flowerpots hung from second-story windows, palm trees line the streets, and, far in the distance, acre upon acre of orchards marched in straight rows over low, rolling hills.

As the street narrowed, the foot traffic around them thinned. The stares of the citizens moving around them grew longer and harder, and Gil noticed that more people seemed to be reacting to the color of his cloak. He wondered if they knew what the cloak symbolized. From the reactions he was receiving, he thought they did.

Three men stepped into the street, blocking them. Gil drew up sharply, almost running into the tall, black-armored man who stood in front of him holding a spear in one hand and a shield in the other, a conical helm on his head. All three men had bearded faces that looked chiseled from stone, their eyes as hard as granite.

One of the men barked something in Malikari.

Guessing his intention, Gil immediately unhooked *Thar'gon* from his belt and, squatting, laid the weapon down on the ground in front of them. He raised his hands, glancing nervously at Ashra. She appeared hesitant, her arms held away from her body, as though she had started lifting her hands and then thought better of it. Her gaze flitted between Gil and the guards, making her look indecisive.

Two of the guards moved around him. One held Gil's hands firmly behind his back, while the other frisked him thoroughly for weapons, quickly finding his eating knife. The other man stood where he was, looming like a gargoyle in front of them, his dark eyes pinned on Ashra. At last, when the men seemed satisfied that he was unarmed, they released his hands.

"You are a mage of your people?" The oldest guard asked in thickly accented Rhenic.

Before Gil could say anything, Ashra answered for him, "He was. But not any longer. Now he's a mage of *my* people."

Gil glanced at her and shock, surprised she would say such a thing. It left the door open for many more questions than he wanted to answer standing on the street.

"A turncoat, then," the man decided. His gaze rolled over Gil with a look of contempt. "A coward."

Ashra lifted her chin defiantly. "Gil Archer is a hero to my people. He saved thousands of Malikari lives."

The man harrumphed, dismissing the conversation. He gestured broadly at the city around them. "How did you get here? These lands are sealed off from the Rhen."

Ashra shrugged. "We are mages. We go where we please. The two of us are emissaries who desire to speak with your ruler."

The guard raised his hand to his face, scratching his beard beneath the chinstrap of his helmet. He turned to the man next to him and said something Gil didn't understand.

The other man bent to pick up the spiked morning star, and acted surprised when he couldn't budge it. With a frustrated look, he tried harder. When that didn't work, he grabbed onto it with both hands and pulled with all of his weight until his face burned red.

The talisman didn't budge.

"It's a magical artifact," Ashra informed them, looking smugger than Gil thought was prudent, considering the situation. "Gil's the only one who can lift it."

The guard let go of the weapon, stepping back with a snarl. "Then bring it along."

Gil reached down and scooped *Thar'gon* off the ground with one hand, to the frustration of the guards.

The first one motioned them forward with a jerk of his head, falling in beside Ashra, while the other two brought up the rear. No words were spoken as they moved through the street, passing long blocks of tall walls and tiled rooftops, until at last they came to the bustling square in front of the ziggurat. There, the older guard shouted for the people to move out of the way, leading them to the long, staircase that climbed all the way up the front of the pyramid. The terraces of the ziggurat created a very gradual slope with a footprint wide enough to span an entire city neighborhood.

"What are your names and titles?" the older guard asked, starting up the stairs.

"I am Master Ashra ni Sayeed. And this is Grand Master Gil Archer of the Order of Battlemages."

Gil felt relieved that she hadn't provided her title.

She didn't sound out of breath, even though Gil was starting to feel the climb in his legs. The steps were wide, but there were so many of them. It took them minutes to reach the temple at the top of the pyramid, which had the look of a granite mausoleum with a low-hanging roof supported by strong columns. Without stopping, they were led past the guards that warded the entrance, who stared straight ahead without making eye contact. Within, they were led into the interior via a narrow hallway that sloped gradually downward.

Candles spaced along the wall disrupted the shadows. The sounds of their footsteps echoed off the stone floor. As they were taken further down into the bowels of the pyramid, a growing apprehension tightened Gil's stomach. He was starting to sweat, even though the interior of the ziggurat was cool. He brought a hand up, pushing sticky hair out of his face.

At last, the guards came to a halt in front of a massive, elaborately carved door.

"Wait here."

With that, the first guard pulled the door open a crack and whispered to somebody inside. A gut-twisting stillness settled in to encase them. Though Gil strained his ears, he could hear no sounds coming from the other side of the door. He waited, shifting nervously, glancing back and forth between Ashra and the guards. At last, the door opened, swinging wide.

The men who had brought them remained without, while a new set of guards waved them forward. Walking at Ashra's side, Gil found himself in a throne room. It was a large circular chamber with a dais at the far end. In the place of a throne there was a sofa occupied by a man in a white cloak, his legs spread wide, his hands resting on his thighs. His head was wrapped in a turban, and he was clothed in long, indigo robes.

Gil drew to a stop alongside Ashra at the base of the dais, staring up at the man wearing the cloak of a Prime Warden, who sat regarding them with intense interest.

One of the guards accompanying them announced, "Prime Warden, I present to you Master Ashra ni Sayeed and Grand Master Gil Archer."

"*Sultana* Ashra ni Sayeed," Ashra corrected, her voice ringing off the walls.

A man moved away from the shelter of a wall to stand at the base of the dais. Loudly, he proclaimed, "You stand in the presence of Andigar Shadeem, Prime Warden of the Lyceum of Bryn Calazar."

It was only when Ashra moved to bow that Gil remembered his manners and prostrated himself upon the floor in the customary abasement that was required in the presence of a Prime Warden. He remained there as the seconds dragged by, wondering how long they would be forced to remain in that position. Thankfully, it wasn't as long as he had expected.

"You may rise," said a mild, welcoming voice.

Gaining his feet, Gil watched the Prime Warden stand and walk toward them with eyes only for Ashra. He descended the steps and came to stand in front of them. Only then did Gil realize how tall this man was, standing head and shoulders above him. Though he seemed young for a Prime Warden, Andigar Shadeem carried a formidable presence that dominated the room.

The man's dark eyes flicked downward to the morning star worn at Gil's side. "Is that *Thar'gon* you carry, the weapon of Byron Connel?" He gazed down at the talisman with a reverent expression.

Gil licked his lips, feeling tense enough to snap. "It is," he answered. "Once, it belonged to Byron Connel. Now it belongs to me."

The young Prime Warden cocked his head, staring at him with intense interest. "Then, are you Warden of Battlemages among your people?"

Gil spread his hands, not knowing what to say. He glanced at Ashra. "The title was recently revoked."

Prime Warden Andigar Shadeem raised his eyebrows. "And why was it revoked?"

It was Ashra who answered. "Because Grand Master Archer defied the rules of our Lyceum in order to rescue the people of Malikar from slaughter at the hands of the Kingdoms."

"Is that so?" The man crossed his arms, looking gravely concerned as he turned back to Gil. "So, you admit to being a traitor."

Before Gil could respond, Ashra interjected, "Grand Master Archer saved thousands of Malikari lives."

The Prime Warden raised a hand to his face, tapping his mouth with one slender finger. His gaze travelled over Gil's face, as though attempting to assess his character. He didn't look pleased by what he found. He asked, "And what is the punishment for treachery among your people?"

Put off by the question, Gil snapped, "It's not treachery when it's condoned."

The man sucked in a cheek, nodding slowly, appearing to be lost somewhere in the space between speech and thought. At last, he took a step back with a nod. "Very well, then. Sultana Ashra ni Sayeed, Grand Master Archer. Welcome to Bryn Calazar."

With a wave of his hand, he indicated a small room off to the side of the dais, partitioned from the rest of the chamber by a silk curtain. He led them into the room, a servant parting the drape before them. Within was an intimate space defined by cushions set against the walls, clustered around a low table. The Prime Warden sat down upon a cushion, leaning back against the wall. Servants came forward to serve them while Gil and Ashra took their seats.

"Let us drink," Andigar Shadeem announced with a gracious smile, raising his glass.

As he drank, Gil's gaze lingered on his host's face. The man's features were perfectly chiseled, as though carved from flawless stone. Gil thought he was perhaps the most attractive man he'd ever met, and he did *not* like the way Shadeem was looking at Ashra.

Taking a sip from his cup, the Prime Warden said, "Congratulations upon your ascendance, Sultana. Please tell me, what has become of Sultan Sayeed?"

He knew of Ashra's father, which told Gil that Shadeem

wasn't as cut off from the rest of the world as they had been made to believe.

Ashra said, "Sultan Sayeed fell gloriously in battle against an enemy who called themselves the Turan Khar. I am his daughter."

The Prime Warden bowed his head gravely. In a low voice, he murmured, "From the Atrament we all come and back to the Atrament we all return. You have my deepest condolences, Sultana."

There was a moment of silence that lingered like a wall between them. It was broken only when Ashra took another sip from her wine cup. "Thank you, Prime Warden. Unfortunately, our war with the Turan Khar weakened our defenses, and the rulers of the Kingdoms took advantage of that situation. They have mounted a campaign of genocide against our people. They seek to either slaughter us all or drive us back into the Black Lands. We came to ask for your assistance."

Andigar Shadeem considered her gravely, a look of deepest concern returning to his face. Gil was still trying to figure out how old the man was, unable to put a number to his years.

"I am sorry to hear of your troubles; however, this is not my war to fight. Almost twenty years ago, your father fled this land with the bulk of Malikar's population. Those who chose to remain behind did so for reasons of their own, and those reasons haven't changed. We will not deploy our armies south of the mountain divide."

Gil could almost feel Ashra's frustration. She set her cup down on the table in front of her and leaned forward, her expression intense. "My people are losing this war. They need allies. The blood of Bryn Calazar runs through Malikari veins. There is no more logical ally for us to turn to."

The Prime Warden issued a consoling smile. "The Black Lands have stood alone for thousands of years, and we have no desire for that to change. We also have no enemies, and have no need of allies. Especially allies that already abandoned us once." He looked genuinely regretful.

Ashra drew in a deep, troubled breath and released it slowly, nodding in defeat. "I understand. Very well. I will return to Malikar. Thank you for your time. And your wine."

She moved to rise, but Andigar Shadeem raised his hand, stopping her before she could.

"Please let me finish. I rule these lands not only as monarch, but also as Prime Warden, as has always been our way. As monarch, I cannot lend you my armies. But there is something I can do to help you. As Prime Warden, I can lend you my Battlemages."

"No." Gil interrupted immediately, before Ashra could respond. "With all due respect, the use of magecraft for the purpose of war is expressly what my own Prime Warden is trying to avoid. The people of the Kingdoms rightfully fear mages leading the armies of Malikar."

Andigar Shadeem turned to look at him with a gaze powerful enough to stop his breath. A terrible shiver ran over him, and Gil stilled himself, realizing it would be very unwise to provoke this man.

"If that's the way the Kingdoms feel, then use magic to your advantage," Shadeem challenged. "Give them reason to fear Malikar's mages once more. That would go further toward securing your borders than any threat of military might."

Gil stared at him without answering. Shadeem returned the look, unblinking. It was Ashra's voice that made Gil break his eyes away.

"Thank you for the offer, Prime Warden," she said. "It is most gracious."

Andigar Shadeem sat back and considered her with a benevolent smile. "Of course. It is the least I can do. Please, let me extend to you my hospitality. Allow me to provide you with accommodations for the night, so that you might rest. I would also be honored if you would accept my invitation to join me this evening for dinner."

Ashra smiled back, holding his eyes with her own, seeming far more comfortable in this formidable man's presence than Gil felt.

29

THE CUSTODIAN

Keio Matu moved past the woman with rigid strides and came to stand over the old Nagalan man sitting beside the fire. Like the woman, this man seemed slightly familiar, though he didn't know anything about him, not even his name. Yet the sight of him provoked a visceral reaction. The man rose slowly, fixing him with a wary gaze.

"If you're not Rylan, who are you?" the old man asked, regarding him the way one might regard a viper.

"You know who I am." He wasn't in the mood to fence.

The Nagalan man—*Jendo,* that was his name—drew back with a look of revulsion on his face. "You are Keio Matu."

Keio nodded in affirmation, then paused to examine the man's reaction. But Jendo had none. Taking careful note of that, he also noted the silver manacle around the man's right wrist. He'd seen such a wristband before, on the arm of the gray man who had attacked him in the Guardian Tower. A cold feeling ran like liquid down his back, making him shiver. He looked to his own arm, noticing the silver band that encircled his own wrist.

His chest tightened as though a giant hand was squeezing

his ribs, expelling the breath from his lungs, leaving him feeling dizzy. Keio brought the band up before his face, examining it closely. It was perfect, seamless, without any sign of latch or hinge. His vision reddened at the sight of it, and white-cold anger seared his nerves. He wanted to rip the thing off and cast it away as far as he could. But something stopped him, a lingering memory from the man he had defeated.

Rylan's memories were still with him, though he could sense them already fading, like dreams upon waking. He paused and took a moment to sift through what few memories he could still access, and came quickly to the conclusion that the band on his wrist was not a threat. *He* was *its* master, not the converse. He could make the band serve him and, through it, he could make the Turan Khar serve him.

Keio felt a smile growing inside him, though he didn't let it show on his face. He lowered his hand, returning to his study of the Nagalan mage. There was something about this man that egged him, something important. Again, he sifted through the memories of the man he had set aside, coming to the conclusion that Jendo might be much older than he appeared. Which brought another realization: *he* was much older than he remembered.

Keio froze.

Looking upward, he gazed at the cliffs, his eyes wandering over them. They looked familiar. They were the walls of the mountain temple that most people thought of as Akai. He stood on its doorstep, where he had stood before, many times in his life. Only, something was vastly different. He turned in place, taking in the totality of his surroundings. The vegetation looked unfamiliar. This canyon had contained one of the world's oldest groves of aspen, but now it stood clad only in scraggly conifers. He tilted his head back and drew in a deep breath of air, finding the scent of it utterly foreign. This place was wrong. It was not the place he remembered.

Then he realized: it wasn't the mountain that was wrong; it was him. *He* was wrong, out of place.

The world had moved on.

Looking down, he realized he was clutching a pendant he wore on a necklace about his neck. He lifted the pendant to examine it, and his breath caught. It was the opal artifact he had given Ilia as an engagement gift. The sight of the pendant brought tears to his eyes. He felt them gathering, hot and scalding, blurring his vision. Releasing the necklace, he fought to clear his vision, not wanting these strangers to see him weak. He had to be strong, not only for himself, but for all the world. He had been brought back for a reason, and he felt certain he wore that reason on his wrist.

A memory flickered across his vision, an image of a little girl with dark waves of hair. For just a moment, a crushing feeling of loss broke against him like a wave, and he nearly staggered. The feeling wasn't his; just a residual artifact left behind by the man he had condemned, like the spastic twitching of a dismembered limb.

When the emotion had passed, he turned back to the old man. Softly, he said, "You are a traitor."

Jendo nodded as though conceding a point, his eyes hard and cold and angry. "I am. But so are you."

It took Keio a moment to figure out what the man was talking about.

Suddenly, he was back in the Guardian Tower, his wife dead at his feet. He stood at the focus of the Circle of Convergence, drawing on enough power to eliminate the Sky Portal. The realization exploded into him with all the force of apocalypse: he had killed all of them.

Everyone left in the city, all of the people he had sworn to protect. He had sentenced them to die along with him. And if that memory wasn't enough, looking at the Nagalan man in front of him drove home the terrible irony of his action.

The Turan Khar hadn't perished that day.

It had all been in vain.

The realization was crushing. It squeezed tears from his eyes and, this time, he couldn't fight them back. He turned away from the vile man with his accusing gaze, unable to face him in his defeat. After all the lives he had sacrificed, the Turan Khar had still won.

Wiping the moisture from his eyes, he whispered, "I've been gone a long time, haven't I?"

"We both have," the old man stated in a gruff voice. "Eight thousand years."

Another staggering revelation. They were too many, and they were coming much too fast. He felt a numbing panic welling inside him, weakening his knees. It was too much to take in, too much to digest. He had failed in too many ways. He closed his eyes, brushing away the last of his tears.

"The man who freed me..." he whispered, "he was looking for something."

Jendo responded slowly, "Yes. Do you remember what? And why?"

Keio grimaced. He didn't like wading through Rylan's memories, where he felt like a trespasser. Rylan had been looking for the containment crystal, although he'd had no idea how to release the energy it contained, or how dangerous such an action would be. He had been desperate for it. Why? Heaving a sigh, he realized he would have to go swimming deeper into the grief-filled swamp of that man's mind.

Finding a rock beneath the inadequate shelter of a scrubby pine, he sat down and held his head in his hands. Closing his eyes, he emptied his mind of his own thoughts and dove in as deeply as he could, scavenging what fading memories he could salvage before they disappeared forever. They came to him like flotsam drifting on a current, seemingly random: the praise of a kind mother, the gift of a sword, the denial of a father. The awakening to a new plane of knowledge that was the embodiment of the Turan Khar. In the span of seconds, he absorbed what he could of Rylan Lauchlin's life, while the rest of the man drained through his fingers like spilt water.

When he felt that he'd collected as much as he could, Keio Matu opened his eyes. He understood now why that man had been so desperately searching for the containment crystal. It was the one thing the Turan Khar needed to save their repugnant society, the one thing he had to deny them at all cost.

Raising his head, he looked up at the man named Jendo, who stood studying him gravely as if contemplating murder. For a moment, he considered killing the man. He felt certain this man had once lived in Shira, but that was before he had been collared by the Khar. Now, he was merely an enemy. An obstacle.

But death was final. Already he was beginning to regret setting aside the man who had held him hostage. Rylan's memories were useful, and he wish he had been able to collect more of them before they washed away. Now he was left with only what he had managed to save in that short amount of time, and his knowledge of this world was limited. He would have to rely on these others to get by.

Looking at Jendo, he decided to stay his hand.

Rising to his feet, he told him, "You will accompany me to the Tower of Morning."

Jendo's eyes narrowed suspiciously. "Do you know where it is?"

"Yes. Right now, it's in the Appos Mountains, somewhere above Karadun."

The old man sucked at his lips, looking exceptionally distrustful. "Karadun is downwind of Suheylu Ra. The air is heavily tainted there."

"That's where the containment crystal is." Standing, Keio dusted off his hands on his trousers, the action feeling somehow symbolic. Trudging past Jendo, he went to where Rylan had left his equipment and, squatting, started loading it back into the rucksack.

Jendo came up behind him as though stalking him. Keio didn't bother to look back at him, for the old man was no threat. If he died, the core energy would be lost forever to the Turan Khar. He was the only person who knew how to unlock the containment crystal.

Crossing his arms, Jendo said, "Rylan already spent an entire day breathing contaminated air in the dead zone you created around Suheylu Ra. The Appos Mountains are beyond it. We would have to cross the dead zone, and the body you're wearing would never survive it."

"So be it."

Keio stood up, swinging the large pack over his shoulder. He knew what manner of taint had to be lingering in the air, and was familiar with its nature. It was a form of energy released when magic and anti-magic collided. Such contamination would never decay, and would forever haunt the place. And Jendo was right: there was only so much of that poison the human body could stand.

But it wouldn't kill him immediately, so it didn't matter.

"Let's go," he growled, and stood waiting for the other two to gather their things.

Jendo moved wordlessly to comply, but the strange woman made no move toward her belongings. Instead, she approached him, stopping before him and peering into his eyes with a look of intense loathing. He took in the sight of her coarse garments: filthy linen robes that were rent and frayed in many places. He wondered why she covered her face with that veil. There were cultures that covered their women, but none were on this continent, and she didn't look like she was from Aeridor. Her arms were covered with strips of cloth that looked like bandages, the same as he wore on his own arms. She also wore the metal shackle of the Turan Khar.

"What happened to Rylan?" she asked him.

The name brought a stab of anger, and he turned away from her. At least he thought it was anger; it felt a little like guilt.

"Rylan's dead."

The woman stiffened. For a moment she just stood there. Finally, she sighed. "Then I will mourn him."

"Do what you will."

He moved away from her, heading toward the trail that led down the mountain. As he walked, a little leather purse bounced uncomfortably against his leg. Pausing, he untied it and opened it up, dumping the contents into his hand. Only one item came tumbling out: a small wooden carving of a woman.

He held the carving up, considering it for a moment. It was crude, the work of an amateur. He saw no reason to keep it. With a flick of his wrist, he tossed it to the side of the road and stuffed the pouch into his pack.

***

He led the other two out of the canyon and back down onto the plain. As they rounded the last ridge that flanked the valley, Keio stopped, frozen in mid stride.

Ahead of him was a wasteland that seemed to stretch the entire length of the world. He stood with jaw slack, every scrap of thought smacked from his head and every drop of energy flushed from his body. His mouth went dry, and a brutal cold froze his spine.

The enormous forest that had covered the interior of the continent was gone, reduced to baked dirt. A brown haze clung to the air, distorting the view. In all his life he had never seen such a grotesque corruption of nature. It defied his every concept, and his mind screamed that it couldn't be so.

But it was.

He dropped to his haunches, right there on the trail, and then fell back to sit in the dirt. He shed the heavy pack from his back and brought his knees up to his chest, leaning forward to cover his eyes with his hands. He stayed locked in that position, barely noticing the others moving around him, setting up camp. Every few minutes, he summoned enough courage to glance up at the wasteland of his own creation. The damning view scalded his eyes, searing the image into him like a smoldering brand.

No one bothered him, for which he was grateful.

He sat there until darkness fell like a stroke of mercy.

He woke the next day to the first sunrise he had seen in eight thousand years. The sun rose like a blood clot to shed its gory light over the wounded plain. He didn't want to look at it—the sunrise felt corrupted and condemning, like everything else here—so he kept his gaze averted, cast downward at the ground.

They broke the camp in silence and continued out onto the dusty hardpan that had once been the boreal forest of Elandel. Keio led the way, for he knew exactly where he was going. For to him, ancient Shira was like yesterday. He remembered nothing of all the years he had spent encased in stone. They had fled past him in a blink, until he had awoken to the quasi-reality that had been his existence within the mind of another.

When they had traveled an hour into the waste, he stopped and lifted his waterskin to his mouth and wet his lips. Looking at Jendo, he decided it was time to try to engage the man in conversation. He would need the old man in the future, and would have to cultivate him.

"Tell me of our enemy," he prompted.

The old man chuckled, sensing his feint. "They aren't my enemy. And you'd know all about them if you opened yourself up to that." He nodded at the band Keio wore on his wrist.

Keio responded with a scornful grin. "I'm no fool. I won't allow my mind to become enslaved like yours."

Jendo scrunched up his mouth, shaking his head surely. "I'm not enslaved. And neither would you be. The Khar civilization is superior to any the world has ever known. But I think you'd have to experience it firsthand to understand."

"There is no justification for what they've done," Keio growled. "The Turan Khar are a cancer that rots the earth."

Jendo stopped and turned toward him, gesturing out at the corrupted landscape. "Can you justify what you've done, Custodian?"

The rage that speared through Keio was intense, so consuming that he couldn't help recognizing if for what it really was: guilt.

That knowing infuriated him all the more.

Instead of answering, he quickly dodged past the old man, grazing his shoulder roughly. As he went by, Jendo snaked out a hand, catching him by the strap of his pack.

"I don't think you understand," the old man growled, shoving him back with surprising strength. "If you hadn't sequestered the core energy, the Turan Khar would've remained peaceful. You created your own enemy, Custodian."

Keio tried to wrench free, reeling that the old man could possibly know a history only known within the walls of the Guardian Tower.

"Who are you?" he gasped.

Releasing him, Jendo arched a smug eyebrow. "I'm Jendo Mahr, Arch-Dedicant of the Priory."

Keio's jaw dropped. *"You?"*

One corner of Jendo's mouth wormed upward. "That's right."

A cold breeze blew past him, ruffling his hair and flapping the sleeves of his linen robes. Keio shivered forcefully. Or perhaps he trembled. "How is it that your face is unknown to me?"

"Because we never met face-to-face, you and I. But I'm the Man behind the Mask."

Keio's insides stiffened. Jendo Mahr had been more than just a revolutionary. He had almost single-handedly toppled the entire Sanctuary by himself. He was the puppet master behind a broad network of anarchists who had, for years, fought against the power of the Wise Counsel, long before the Turan Khar ever became a threat.

"A traitor, indeed," he murmured.

Jendo shrugged. "I had my failings. Sometimes, when we peer through a closed window, we are so focused on the view that our eyes ignore our own reflection in the glass."

It was Keio's turn to cast a scornful grin. "That's an elegant way of admitting failure."

"Believe me, Custodian. Your failure was far greater than mine."

Enraged, Keio swept his hand back. But before he could land the punch, Jendo caught his wrist quick as a snake strike, gripping it with the kind of strength that no old man should ever possess. Very calmly, he shook his head.

Then he let go and continued up the path.

Keio stood panting, watching him go, trembling in rage. He glanced sideways and found Shade staring at him accusingly. His lips drew back from his teeth, ready with a curse. But instead he snarled, turning to follow Jendo across the desert, the woman trailing behind in his wake.

They walked all day and into the evening, feet crunching on the petrified bones of the dead earth. When the last light faded in the sky, they stopped and set about the process of making camp. Somehow, Jendo found enough scattered camel dung to build a fire while Shade went to find water to replenish their empty waterskins.

Instead of lingering around the camp, Keio walked away from it, staring off in the direction of what used to be called, in his language, the Emerald Valley. It was to there they were heading, toward Suheylu Ra, or, rather, to the mountains on the far side. He wondered what he would feel, confronted with the ruins of the city he had brought to destruction. Just the thought made his heart ache. He vowed to skirt the ruin. He had enough guilt already weighing on his soul, enough to bury him. He stood there for a long time as the stars slowly revolved above him. At last, exhaustion got the better of him, and he slunk back toward the camp.

Along the way, he found Shade kneeling beside a small mound of what look like rubble.

Coming up behind her, he noticed she was building something, arranging blocks on a pile of other scattered blocks, forming what looked like some kind of trail marker or perhaps a small shrine. Standing behind her, he watched her fashion a square cist in the rocks. Bowing her head gravely, she placed something within. He got only a glimpse of the little carving of the woman he had tossed aside earlier before she covered the cist with a flat stone, sealing the cracks up with dirt.

"What is that?" he asked, wondering why she would waste the time burying such a trinket.

Pushing herself up from the dirt, she whisked her hands together, brushing them off. She glanced at him severely, her eyes shooting daggers at him from beneath the shadows of her veil.

"It is a memorial for Rylan," she said coldly then turned and left.

Staring down at the marker-stone, Keio grunted, just happy the man was gone.

30

ANDIGAR SHADEEM

Gil looked around at the guestroom the Prime Warden had provided for him, feeling smaller and less important by the second. The room around him was enormous, octagonal, with a vaulted ceiling encrusted with gold and walls paneled with deep mahogany. A chandelier dripping with many colored lanterns hung from the ceiling, casting a dizzying kaleidoscope of light across the walls. The furniture was just as ornate and sumptuous. The bed was wide enough to sleep six people not even crammed together, and there was a wardrobe that proved to be supplied with tunics and coats, vests and sandals. There was even a bath with a tiled washtub and a separate water closet.

Gil had never seen such wealth, and certainly would have never expected to see it in the Black Lands. For moments, all he could do was stand there gazing around. Not even at the king's palace in Karikesh had he ever seen such a place that screamed authority and affluence.

It was all very intimidating, and the more he thought about it, the more uncertain he felt. They were in a house of a very powerful man, and he felt at a tremendous disadvantage.

After minutes of gawking, he realized he needed to put the clothing in the wardrobe to use. The garments he had worn out of Karikesh were nothing but tattered, filthy rags soaked in his own blood. He couldn't remember the last time he had bathed. His skin was stained brown, especially around his fingernails and in the creases of his knuckles. He couldn't stand the smell of himself, which was never a good thing.

He drew a bath and immersed his body in hot water, leaning back against the tile and closing his eyes. It was all he could do to keep from falling asleep as he let the hot water sooth his tired muscles. There was a variety of soap, and he lathered himself up well and scrubbed off the grime with a horsehair brush.

When he rose from the bath, he toweled off and dressed out of the wardrobe, selecting a knee-length tunic the color of a deep ocean. Given the choice between the provided sandals or his old boots, he chose the boots, using magic to refurbish them to the best of his abilities.

A knock on the door pulled him from his thoughts. When he opened it, he found a woman he didn't recognize standing in the doorway.

It took him a full second to realize it was Ashra. She had bathed and cleaned up, her dark hair spilling in loose waves about her shoulders, and she was wearing a deep red gown with wide sleeves and a matching shawl. She was stunning in a way he had never seen her before. For a moment, he forgot to breathe.

"Can I come in?" she asked, waking him from his trance.

"Of course." He felt heat rise to his cheeks. He moved back out of the way and closed the door after her. Feeling incapable of trusting his voice, he motioned her toward one of the sofas that lined the wall.

Smiling, Ashra gathered her skirts and reclined on the cushions, looking from the neck down very much like a queen.

Only, her face remained her own, her eyes kind and compassionate, and for that, Gil was grateful.

"It's good to see you hale," she said, her eyes scanning him over. "I've been worried about you."

Gil dismissed her worry with a timid smile. "I've been worried about you too. Although it seems my fears were not justified. You're made of stronger stuff than I am."

"Hardly," Ashra scoffed, pushing a silken lock of raven hair back from her face. "You have been every inch a Battlemage. Without you, every person we rescued would have been lost several times over."

He refused to believe that; his very presence had done them more harm than good. He opened his mouth, but he didn't know what to say. He could only stare at her, as though her beauty had chased his thoughts away.

She patted the fabric of the sofa, inviting him to sit. He sat beside her, probably too close, so he edged away a bit. Then it occurred to him that she might have noticed him pulling away, and she might be offended. He wondered if he should scoot back again. Paralyzed by indecision, he sat with his hands clenched in his lap, looking at everything in the room but her.

He thought of their host, the Prime Warden, and a sharp stab of jealousy caught him off guard. Gil stiffened, surprised by the intensity of the feeling. He silently berated himself, ashamed. This was not the time nor the place for jealousy, and Ashra was certainly not a woman he had any right to feel possessive of. What she needed from him had nothing to do with affection.

Fighting to clear his mind, Gil asked tightly, "Have you thought about his offer?"

"I have."

"And?"

"I think it's the only chance we have."

She was probably right, and yet he was still troubled.

Beneath his jealousy, another feeling was growing, a cold feeling, something akin to dread. He couldn't even name it, much less tell what caused it.

"What about Naia?" he asked.

Ashra stroked a lock of hair absently. "I don't think Naia would object."

"I think you might be wrong about that." He sat forward, trying to keep his emotions off his face.

"I'm not," Ashra assured him with an easy confidence. "Naia's hands are tied, but that's even more reason why she might welcome this. She has always been a bold defender of Darien Lauchlin, even after he led the invasion of the Rhen. I never understood why until now. Right now, the roles are reversed, but it's still the same war, and a very similar situation. And your people are being just as merciless as mine were."

Gil didn't know what to say to that. He couldn't argue with anything she said. His understanding of the Kingdoms' war with Malikar was very much different than it had been.

"At any rate," Ashra went on, "even if Naia doesn't support us, if given a choice between preserving the reputation of mages or the lives of people, I'll choose the people."

Gil searched his own feelings and found that he agreed. He whispered, "As will I."

She took his hand, a gesture that surprised and stunned him. He stared at her slender fingers around his, her very touch provoking emotions he knew he shouldn't be feeling. He swallowed heavily, struggling to fight them back down. But they wouldn't go. Somehow, they became stuck in his throat, forming a tight knot.

"Thank you, Gil," Ashra said. "You've done so much for us already. Whoever would have imagined that Gil Archer would become a champion of Malikar?"

Not knowing what else to say, he muttered, "I'm far from a champion. I'm just a soldier."

"I disagree." She smiled warmly, squeezing his hand.

There was a knock on the door. Cursing the interruption, Gil rose to answer it.

A long-robed servant greeted him with a bow. "The Prime Warden requests the honor of your company at dinner."

Ashra rose from the sofa, adjusting the drape of her long shawl. Gil waited for her to go first, then walked at her side, following the servant down long flights of stairs to a chamber that must have been close to the pyramid's base. Within, an intimate space had been created with opulent rugs, long drapes of colorful silk, and intricate tapestries.

Andigar Shadeem rose from his cushioned seat, a golden goblet in his hand, and bid them be seated around a low table upon which a feast had been presented on silver bowls and platters.

"Thank you for allowing me the pleasure of your company," Shadeem announced with a warm and gracious smile. "Please, sit. Eat!"

Ashra thanked him with a shy smile that made Gil's back stiffen.

Gil sat on the wall across from the Prime Warden and Ashra and stared at the spread of food while a servant provided him with a drink. A tray with a bowl of water and a rolled cloth was offered him, but he had no idea what to do with it. His eyes went to Ashra. She made a swirling motion with her fingers that ended with patting her face. It took him a moment to understand.

He dipped his fingers into the bowl, giving the appearance of washing them, then spread the water over his face, blotting himself dry on the towel. Across the table from him, he saw that Ashra and the Prime Warden were doing the same thing. An odd custom, but one that seemed logical, considering it looked as if they would be sharing the meal directly from the bowls the food was presented in, without individual plates.

"I hope everything is to your liking," the Prime Warden said.

Ashra scooped one of the rice dishes into her mouth with her fingers, closing her eyes as if savoring a delicacy. "It's delicious."

The Prime Warden's smile seemed sincere and pleased.

Relaxing back in her seat, Ashra said, "I'd like to know about the Black Lands, Prime Warden. How many people were left here, and how did you survive?"

Shadeem drained his cup. Before he could set it down, a servant appeared beside him to replenish it. "Not many people chose to stay," he said, "and those who did were mostly from this city. Some simply did not believe that their lives were in jeopardy. Others could not bring themselves to leave behind the homes their families had lived in for generations. Fortunately, the skies cleared, and the sun shone down on us. What a joyous day that was, the day the sun rose for the first time in a thousand years! For weeks, there were celebrations in the streets. But after that, we got busy.

"Even though the sunlight had returned, the only places plants could be grown were the ancient lightfields the mages had always tended. Any other soil would not sustain crops; it had been barren for too long. So, for the past two decades, we have been gradually expanding our fields and sowing seeds. It has been a hard labor, and slow, but it has been a labor of love. We have experienced much success. The river delta is once again green with fields of grain, and the hills are clothed in orchards."

Ashra scooped up a strange, prickly fruit from one of the dishes. "That is a miraculous work, Prime Warden. I would love to see it."

The man positively beamed. "And you shall! Tomorrow when the sun rises, I would be honored if you would let me take you to the orchards and show you myself."

"I would like that, Prime Warden." Ashra smiled.

Staring into her eyes, Andigar Shadeem lowered his goblet. "Please, call me Andigar."

Gil squirmed in his seat, staring down at the food on the table as a means of averting his eyes. He had made only a half-hearted attempt to eat it, for the food had lost its flavor. The growing warmth between Ashra and the Prime Warden was provoking more than just jealousy. He was developing a loathing for the man that went deeper than that. There was something about his eyes Gil didn't like, and it went further than just the natural desire of a man for a beautiful woman.

"And what of Malikar?" Shadeem asked. "Describe to me the full nature of your troubles."

Ashra did. The whole while she was talking, Gil stared down at the platters of food, forcing himself to take slow bites, chewing and swallowing automatically, not really listening to any of it. He was too lost in his thoughts, trying to dissect his own innermost feelings.

"Have you considered the proposition I made?" Shadeem asked.

The question drew Gil's focus back to the conversation. His eyes locked on Ashra, who had finished eating and was lounging back on her sofa with her wine cup cradled in her hand. "I have to admit I find it intriguing."

Their benefactor spread his hands, the gesture seeming to encompass the entire ziggurat that surrounded them. Perhaps the entire city. "I am a simple man, Your Majesty, with a singular goal. And that goal is to return the Lyceum of Bryn Calazar to its former grandeur. I would like to extend to you an invitation."

He set down his napkin and smiled. "Sultana, you have convinced me that the Black Lands need not stand forever alone, and neither do our brothers and sisters in the Rhen. I have no armies to send you. However, allow me to send my

Battlemages to the defense of your people. Allow us to help secure your borders and drive the invaders from your lands. Then join with me in alliance. Our two peoples are like two trees that share the same roots. And we would stand stronger together than we could ever stand on our own."

Gil was in the middle of raising a spoonful of curried lentils to his lips when the Prime Warden turned his attention to him.

"Grand Master Gil. It seems a true shame that you are no longer welcome among your own people. Let me assure you, a man of your stature would be very much appreciated here. I would be honored if you would consider joining the family of mages I have gathered here in Bryn Calazar. As yet, there are only a few of us. But I believe that, given enough time, we have the capacity for greatness. Please forgive me for asking directly, but what tier are you?"

Feeling embarrassed, Gil lowered his spoon. "Sixth tier, Prime Warden."

Andigar Shadeem nodded slowly, his eyes distant and contemplative. "You are by far the most powerful mage among us, and no doubt well-trained. Should you decide to join our Assembly, I offer you the position of my Warden of Battlemages. "

Gil ducked his head, feeling almost ashamed, though he didn't know why. Perhaps it was because of the feelings of doubt and jealousy he had been brooding over throughout the meal. "Prime Warden," he said softly. "I'm humbled."

Andigar Shadeem turned back to Ashra. "What do you say, Your Majesty, to my offer of alliance?"

Ashra took a long sip of her wine then paused for a moment, staring down into the cup. When she looked up again, the smile that brightened her face sliced Gil's heart. "It is a very gracious offer, Prime Warden. I would like to accept, provided the terms are just and fair."

Andigar Shadeem inclined his head very solemnly then,

reaching across the short table, took Ashra's hand into both of his. "I assure you, any treaty will include only those terms you agree to in advance." Turning to Gil, he asked, "And what of you, Grand Master? Would you join us here at the Lyceum?"

Gil glanced up from his plate to look at Andigar Shadeem and Ashra, who sat with hands still clasped, cementing the bond they had just proclaimed. Staring at Shadeem holding Ashra's beautiful hand, Gil felt his resolve solidify. "I appreciate the offer, Prime Warden," he said, staring deeply into Ashra's eyes. "But my place is with my Queen."

He watched Ashra's expression change as she slowly realized the words he had said and sat contemplating all their infinite layers of meaning. With a look of shock, she slipped her hand away from Andigar's.

If Shadeem noticed her reaction, he didn't let on. With a magnanimous smile, he said to Gil, "It is our loss, of course, though I find I can't blame you. Perhaps, after Malikar is once again secure, you will reconsider."

"Perhaps," Gil said softly.

Looking as uncomfortable as Gil felt, Ashra pushed her plate back and rose from her seat. "This has been wonderful. Thank you for your generosity, Prime Warden, but I am simply exhausted."

Following her up from the floor, Shadeem bowed formally. "Of course, Your Majesty. Thank you for the pleasure of your company. I will have my servants show you back to your rooms. Tomorrow, I will show you the orchards. I am excited for you to see firsthand what our long years of labor have built."

"I'm looking forward to it," Ashra said with a broad smile.

Gil felt a brief stab of jealousy, followed by a flush of relief. Ashra's smile hadn't made it all the way to her eyes.

31

IMPASSE

Keio Matu stood at the edge of the desert, overlooking a wide expanse of forest. The limbs of the trees below swayed mildly in the wind, cresting like the swells of an ocean. He closed his eyes and breathed deeply of the comforting smell of the forest he loved so much. Somehow, it was the one thing on this continent that remained preserved, as though the forest had been lost in time, just as he had been. The sight of it awakened memories that were razor sharp and cut deep. In the distance, he could see the ruins of Suheylu Ra poking up out of the canopy like distant islands in the sea of green. He tried to look past the decayed bones of buildings that had once been so familiar, now barely recognizable. What disturbed him most were the spikes of the Watcher towers, many grotesquely twisted and warped.

The tallest structure, surpassing all the rest, was the remains of the Guardian Tower, which spiked out of the forest, a dark, cylindrical spire that had managed to weather the years intact. The sight of the Guardian brought on an intense pang of shame, dredging up memories he had no wish to confront.

They followed a steep trail down off the plateau.

Keio refused to look at either of his companions, unwilling to meet their eyes. He could feel their accusations needling him in the back, sharp as spear points. When they reached the forest floor, he felt an intense relief. Almost, he could pretend that none of this was real, as though the apocalypse of his own creation had never happened. He walked ahead of the others, picking his way carefully through the dense undergrowth, in the direction of the wide, paved road that had once bisected the city. He couldn't be sure the road would still exist after so many thousands of years, but seeing the miraculous preservation of the rest of the city gave him hope.

The forest proved to be just as peaceful as he remembered, full of moss and fungus, and scented with leaves and loam. The only thing missing was the sound of the forest life that had once been ubiquitous. The canopy that loomed overhead had once shivered with the flutter of bird wings and quivered with the scampering of squirrels and raccoons.

Now only a haunting silence filled the air, encasing the forest in gloom. He understood why. It was the poison in the air. No animal could survive it more than a day or two. Soon, it would be affecting him too.

They hadn't gone more than a league into the forest before they came across the first of the Twelve Watchers. Blackened and twisted, it thrust out of the canopy like a mangled candle, its megalithic blocks of diorite having melted into lava, which had flowed down its sides to form dark, wax-like beads. Keio could only imagine the horrendous amount of energy it had taken to heat that kind of stone to its melting point.

They passed the distorted tower and walked on, past more crumbled ruins that appeared in their path, seemingly just to torment him.

Eventually, they came across the road. Keio was grateful to see that the paving stones had remained intact, defying time and every whim of nature. No stone laid by man should survive so many millennia, and yet these had.

Instead of turning toward the city, he led them in the direction of the Appos Mountains far in the distance. It would take days to reach their destination, and at least one of those days would be spent traveling through the contamination that poisoned the air.

He thought he could feel the taint already working its way through his skin, though he knew that was impossible. The damage he was taking was subtle, and would have to accumulate for more than just a few hours before he would start to feel its effects. Keio smiled bitterly, finding it somewhat ironic that the same ancient event would kill him twice. Somehow, it seemed fitting. The devastation he had so far witnessed eclipsed anything he could have ever predicted.

He had much to atone for.

As the day wore on, his attention kept wandering to Shade, for he found her fascinating. He wished he could see her face, the desire fueled by more than just morbid curiosity. He knew that the veil masked some kind of physical disfigurement, but that wasn't what he was interested in. He wanted to know what kind of people had survived from his time. Shade's ancestors had been Shiran. It was fair to say that her entire society had been molded from the ashes of the devastation he had caused.

He glanced down at her hands, trying to glimpse the skin of her fingers, which were the only part of her body not covered by cloth. But she was moving, and he couldn't get a good look at them. He wanted to know the nature of the damage that had been done to her, to all her people.

Noticing him looking, she turned to confront him, her brown eyes drilling him with accusation.

"Are you trying to see my Marks?" she asked in a voice sharpened by anger. Reaching down, she unwound the strips of cloth that bound her arm, peeling them back. Moving closer, she offered her arm to him.

Keio turned it slowly, his eyes skimming the terrible pock marks and ridges that had eroded the landscape of her skin. He had seen terrible burns before, but this was different. This was not scar tissue. It was some kind of deformity.

"This is your doing," she accused, snatching her arm back.

He reminded her, "Without core magic, your people wouldn't have survived a thousand years of darkness. It kept you fed when the sunlight failed." He watched her rewrap the protective cloth, noticing how carefully she arranged the intricate pattern of the material.

When he started moving forward again, Jendo fell back to walk at his side, fixing him with a glare. "If you hadn't locked the core magic away, there never would have *been* a thousand years of darkness. The Turan Khar wouldn't have needed to carve a portal to hell to find an alternate power source. The sooner you realize the consequences of what you've done, the better off this world will be."

"Why?" Keio demanded. "No amount of regret on my part will change the past."

"You still don't get it, do you?" Jendo scoffed. "You can't change the past, but you *can* affect the future. If you release the core magic, not only will you provide the Turan Khar with the energy we need to become independent, but you will also be helping Shade's people by emptying the conduits. The core magic was never meant to be contained. It's wild and untamable, like nature itself. You should have never tried to keep it in a cage."

Keio knew the old man was right. It was one of the reasons why he was poisoning his body to rupture the containment crystal. It had been a mistake to try to tame such a hostile magic. But it was a mistake he could rectify.

What Jendo didn't understand was the danger posed by the

Turan Khar, which was just as big a crime against nature. *Human* nature. The Khar society was an abomination, robbing its citizens of freedom and agency. Jendo just didn't realize it because his prison was comforting, just as it was confining. In giving himself over to the will of the Unity, he had lost himself.

And that was the true danger of the Turan Khar. To Keio Matu, the damage their society was capable of was far greater than anything he had ever done or could ever do. He would shatter the containment crystal. And then, just as he had before, he would send their entire society back to hell where it belonged, this time forever.

They walked on, following the road ever westward. The forest maintained its consistency around them, infinitely silent and infinitely preserved, just as Suheylu Ra.

An hour later, a terrible pain stabbed into Keio's middle. Every muscle in his abdomen constricted at once. His whole body stiffened reflexively, and suddenly he was on his knees vomiting forcefully onto the paving stones of the roadway. When he thought he was finished, he vomited again. And again, until all he was able to bring up was clear liquid.

Trembling, he rose unsteadily to his feet, spitting a globule of bile onto the ground and wiping his mouth on his sleeve. Tears leaked down his cheeks, and his body was suddenly covered in a cold sweat. When he realized his two companions were staring at him, he forced himself to walk forward as though nothing had happened, turning his head to spit another wad of vomit-tasting filth from his mouth.

"You're becoming ill," Jendo said, taking long strides to keep up with him.

"I'm fine."

"You are not. The poison is eating away at you. You can't free the core energy if you're dead."

"I'll make it there." Keio raked a hand across his brow, mopping sweat out of his eyes.

"Perhaps," Jendo allowed. "But you will go no further."

Keio shrugged. "I won't have to."

They walked in silence after that. His stomach was still unsettled, though manageable. After a while, the trembling and weakness went away, and he felt almost hale again, except for a powerful thirst that all the water in his waterskin could not quench. Every so often, he caught Jendo and Shade trading glances of concern.

When they stopped to rest, Keio cast his aching body down against the trunk of an oak tree, leaning back in the space between two great roots. Shade came to him and offered him her waterskin. It was a compassionate gesture that surprised him, especially knowing how much she despised him.

"Why are you here?" he asked, handing the waterskin back.

She stood for a moment over him, considering him gravely. "Since I was a child, I have never known love." Raising her arm, she displayed the iron shackle encircling her wrist. "This band means more to me than all the salt in the Scalding Sea. It's given me the family I never had. I would do anything for them."

Keio picked up an acorn from the ground and rolled it around in his palm. "When we destroy the containment crystal, it's likely to bring half the mountain down. There's no reason for you to die with us. There's nothing you can do to help."

"There is," she insisted flatly. "Despite what you think, you need me."

Keio wasn't sure what she meant by that. She wasn't a mage, so her presence served no purpose. From what little he knew of her, Shade seemed a fine woman. There was no reason for her to waste her life. "Jendo's enough. He will make certain I get there."

She stared at him sideways from under her veil. "You called him a traitor. He is not your friend."

"No. He is not my friend. But I can trust him to walk me to my death with a smile on his face. In that, Jendo will not falter."

The expression in her eyes changed, softening. She sank down beside him, finding a seat on a gnarled tree root. "What does Jendo have against you? Were you rivals?"

With a flick of his wrist, Keio tossed the acorn away. It bounced a few times, like a stone skipping off the surface of a pond. "Jendo was a subversive. He was the leader of a political faction who called themselves the Priory. It was their belief that magic would be the downfall of mankind. Their ideology was popular among the masses, who feared that the mage class was becoming too powerful. The Priory was heavily funded and had a great deal of influence, so their voices were hard to ignore. Especially his voice."

"Why him?"

"He was the Man Behind the Mask. I can't begin to tell you all the troubles he caused us."

"Did he really wear a mask?"

Somehow, he sensed she was smiling under that veil, if only slightly. Finding another acorn, he tossed that one too. "No. We named him that because no one knew who he was. He always spoke through mouthpieces and acted through proxies. We worked for years to discern his identity, but our efforts were never successful. We always assumed he was a common. I would have never guessed he was a mage."

Hearing the crunch of dead leaves, Keio looked up to find Jendo approaching.

"Is there something you'd like to say to me, Custodian?" the old man asked, his eyebrows raised.

"There's nothing to be said." Keio picked up another acorn, twirling it between his fingers. "You abandoned us when we were at our most desperate. When we needed the cooperation of the Priory most."

Jendo squatted beside him, resting his elbows on his knees. "But magic wasn't the solution. It never was. Since the beginning, magic was the root of Shira's problems."

The old man was simply wrong. About everything. "You crippled us," he snarled.

"No. *You* crippled us." Jendo raised a finger, pointing at him accusingly. "The Turan Khar were too powerful. All the magic in the world couldn't save Shira. The only answer was surrender. But your pride wouldn't allow that, would it, Custodian? And so our nations bled."

He snatched the acorn from Keio's hand and tossed it away. "You're going to have to start accepting your own part in what happened. I'm beginning to think that's why I'm here. To help you understand your role in these events, so that history doesn't repeat itself."

Keio glared at him.

"What do you mean about history repeating itself?" Shade asked.

Jendo turned to look at her. "Why do you suppose he's willing to poison himself to reach the Tower? Do you think he really intends to return our power source?"

A cold anger was brewing in Keio's gut, a seething resentment that made him want to punch Jendo. It took every effort of will he could muster to stay his hand.

"Of course he's not," Jendo said with a sharp glance at him. "So that begs the question: what is his motive?"

"If you think you know, then just say it," Keio snapped.

"Oh, I don't *think* I know. I *do* know." Jendo rose to his feet and said to Shade, "The Custodian here wants to finish what he started. He intends to use the core magic to destroy the Unity."

Shade glanced at him in alarm. "Is that possible?"

Keio asked, "If you know this, then why haven't you tried to stop me?"

Jendo rest his weight against the rough bark of the oak tree, the condescending smile never slipping from his face. "Because killing you won't get me what I want. I don't know the way to the Tower."

"And even if you did, you couldn't unlock the containment crystal."

"That too," Jendo allowed. "And knowing what you know of me, why haven't you tried to kill me?"

Keio ground his teeth. "Because, unfortunately, I need you too. It takes two mages to unlock the containment crystal."

"Well, then." Jendo chuckled, as though he found the entire situation humorous. "I suppose we're at an impasse."

32

A GIFT

A KNOCK AT THE DOOR WOKE GIL FROM SLEEP. BEFORE HE COULD stir from his covers, the door opened, admitting a female servant carrying a tray. Groggy, he sat up and swung his legs over the edge of the bed, rubbing his eyes and trying to smear his vision back into focus. The servant didn't speak, but merely set the tray down on a table in the center of the room. She bowed once and then left, the door closing behind her softly.

He yawned, stretching his arms and legs. He had no idea how long he'd been asleep, but it felt like forever. The light in the room was dim, for there was no window, just a lantern. It was impossible to tell what time of day it was or how long he'd slept.

Rising, Gil went to inspect the tray and found it laden with bread and fruit. Warm tea steamed from an earthenware cup, filling the room with its fragrance.

He sank to his knees beside the table and started ravenously attacking the bread. He hadn't eaten well at dinner the night before; the rapport between Ashra and Shadeem had soured his appetite. He ate as much as he could from the tray, but couldn't finish the entire portion. Apparently, days spent without food shrank the stomach.

He rose and went to pull his clothes on, but before he could, another knock at the door interrupted him. Hastily, he grabbed his tunic off the floor and pulled it on over his head. He stabbed a foot into his trousers then hopped around until he got the other leg in.

He opened the door to find Ashra already walking away. She turned back at the sound of him opening the door. Self-conscious, Gil reached up and scrubbed at his hair, wishing he'd woken up in time to clean up a bit.

Ashra looked like she'd been up for a while. Her hair was elaborately coiffed in an intricate nest of curls and braids. At her neck hung a large pendant on a golden chain set with a large sapphire contained within a bed of emeralds. She walked toward him, pausing before him and opening her mouth to speak.

"Now he's giving you gifts?" he asked, interrupting her. Reaching up, he took the pendant into his hand, lifting it slightly to examine it. The sapphire was enormous and flawless, multifaceted. It looked perfectly at home around her neck.

Ashra smiled, the old light glistening in her eyes. Reaching up, she tugged the pendant out of his hand. "You sound jealous."

Gil grimaced, embarrassment rushing to his cheeks. He stepped back away from her and struggled to collect his spilled feelings off the floor.

"I'm not jealous," he growled. "I'm concerned."

Ashra snorted. "Well, don't be concerned. Gifts between diplomats are common and appropriate."

Appropriate. Unlike his feelings, which obviously weren't. He wanted to hit himself over the head for allowing himself to be so transparent. She had to be aware of his feelings for her, or she wouldn't be accusing him of jealousy. If she had wanted him, she would have acted already. The fact that she hadn't told him his sentiments were not returned.

"Well, then," Gil grumbled. "That's very nice of him."

Ashra looked at him sideways. Evenly, she said, "Yes. It *was* very nice of him."

Gil turned and paced away a few steps, not knowing what else to do. He felt like running and hiding in his room; nothing he could do or say was right. Without looking at her, he asked, "So what is the plan for today?"

"Andigar is going to show me around the city, then, this afternoon, he wants to introduce us to his mages."

Gil hadn't missed the fact that he hadn't been invited on the city tour, an exclusion that made him stew even harder. It was obvious that 'Andigar' had intentions with Ashra that went beyond diplomacy. Gil couldn't blame the man for finding her attractive, but he at least could have paused to assess Ashra's situation before swooping in.

Stiffly, he asked, "Shouldn't we be getting back to the war?"

"We will tomorrow. After I make my decision."

He wondered if that decision would include an offer of marriage. The thought came from out of nowhere, but it resonated. Gil's eyes widened, and he glanced nervously at the pendant. A jewel like that would make an excellent gift of engagement. It was common among royalty to use marriage to forge alliances. And that's what Ashra was: royalty in need of an alliance.

Suddenly, he felt physically ill.

Another servant appeared in the hallway, approaching them with eyes lowered and hands clasped in front of her. She drew up before them and bowed stiffly.

"Your Majesty. The Prime Warden awaits you."

Again, Gil felt the sting of the non-invitation.

Ashra must have seen his disappointment on his face, for she placed a hand on his arm and muttered, "I'm sorry, Gil. I'm sure he meant nothing by it."

"It's okay," he muttered, turning away. "I'll find something else to do."

Opening the door to his room, he slipped inside without waiting to see if she had anything further to say. Closing the door behind him, he leaned back against the wall, wanting to bang his head against it. He let his gaze rove over the ceiling, considering the swarming gold embellishments. The entire room was a chaotic confusion of patterns that precisely echoed his mood. He needed out of it.

He considered replacing his wrinkled tunic with another from the wardrobe, but then he thought about where the clothes in the wardrobe had come from.

From *him.*

Gil wanted to rip the tunic right off his body and throw it on the floor. But his old clothing was far too damaged to mend, even with magic, so he would have to suffer the mortification of wearing the wretched man's gift. He sat on the edge of the bed and pulled his boots on, his thoughts drifting to Ashra. After all he had done for her, all he had *sacrificed* for her, her lack of empathy toward his feelings bothered him.

If Ashra was going on a tour of the city with Andigar Shadeem, then he was determined to take a tour of his own. He wanted to find out more about this man and the city he ruled. For, deep down in his gut, he didn't trust the Prime Warden. He needed to make sure it wasn't just jealousy giving him that feeling, or if his suspensions had been provoked by something more nefarious.

Picking up the last of the bread from the tray, he wrapped it in cloth and shoved it in his pack. Then he hung his weapon from his belt and let himself out.

It took a bit of wandering through hallways before he finally found an exit. Emerging from the temple at the top of the ziggurat, he paused at the edge of the terrace and stood there, letting the warm breeze soothe his skin while he looked out over the city. The view was extraordinary. He had always thought Karikesh was beautiful, but Bryn Calazar surpassed it entirely. Every roof in the city was tiled with blue, every wall glistening white. Foliage and palm trees sprouted from every corner and lined every street.

The thick, cool air had a heavy odor of salt. He closed his eyes and relished it. The scent was peaceful and clean. Distantly, he could hear the sound of the waves breaking against shallow reefs beyond the mouth of the harbor.

He took the long flight of steps down to the level of the street and merged with the foot traffic, letting his feet carry him wherever they wanted. He had no fear of getting lost; the ziggurat was the largest structure in the city, visible from every quarter. He was more concerned about knowing where to look to dispel his suspicions. Whatever Shadeem's motives were, he wasn't sure he would find them in Bryn Calazar's streets.

He wandered into a marketplace that captured his interest, for the city's trade and industrial situations were as good a place as any to start looking for chinks in Shadeem's armor. It wasn't anything permanent like the Kazri Souk back in Karikesh. Instead, it seemed like a scattered cluster of various transient merchants who filled a large square, spreading their wares out on rugs under portable awnings, or displaying their trinkets arranged on the beds of carts. There was a general bustle of people moving through the market, and a healthy amount of noise. The calls of hawkers, the sounds of haggling, and the noise of live animals all filled the air.

A vocal rooster dashed across the street in front of him, wings extended, a child chasing after it. The boy didn't look as if he stood a chance of catching it. With a loud flapping of wings, the bird took to the air and glided across the square, alighting on a cart before taking off again. The boy dove through the crowd after it, earning himself a series of reproachful cries.

Gil recoiled as someone waved what looked like a trencher of overcooked squash in his face. The smell hit him instantly, making his mouth water, but he had no money, so he waved the man away. Undeterred, the street vendor ran after him. Gil turned and hurried in the opposite direction, but the man was persistent, jogging along at his side and forcing the trencher back in front of him.

"I don't want it," Gil said firmly, shoving the trencher away.

The man disappeared with what sounded like a long string of curses, probably off to assault someone else with his charred plate of squash. Mercifully relieved of the man's company, Gil paused and looked around, letting the swarm of people flow around him. To his left, a woman with a bright shawl was minding a cart full of baskets loaded with fruit. Three half-naked children stood in front of the cart, waving fruit over their heads, bodies twisting back and forth in obvious boredom. On the other side of the street, an old woman sat weaving something on a small loom with a wide variety of folded textiles displayed beside her.

Gil worked his way through the crowd. His attention was drawn to a merchant's stall that was loaded with small trinkets of various types and colors. Walking over to it, he squatted beside a rug full of assorted jewelry. His eyes wandered over the pieces, at last coming to rest on a silver necklace with a filigree pendant. Unbidden, his hand moved toward it.

Suddenly angry, he clenched his fingers and stood up. What was he thinking? Another pendant couldn't solve his problems, even if he had enough money to afford it. He turned and trudged heavily away, putting a good distance between himself and the merchant's stall. Without thinking, he let his feet carry him out of the market. He wound his way aimlessly around a maze of streets, weaving through foot traffic and goats pulling carts.

He paused at the top of a terrace with a good view of the ocean. Below, many small boats bobbed on the surface of the sparkling water. A few larger ships were under sail, heading into or returning from the open sea. He stood there for minutes, captivated by the scene.

"What do you think of the city?"

Startled, Gil turned to find a willowy, dark-haired woman standing behind him. Her thick mane of wind-tossed hair was held back by an enameled comb, and she wore a billowing dress the color of sunflowers. She looked very young, barely out of her teens, but there was something about her that made her seem older. Pushing her hair out of her face, she smiled at him shyly.

"The city?" Gil repeated, wondering what her purpose was. "It's interesting."

She moved to stand beside him, setting her hands on the wall, leaning over to look down at the harbor. "This part of the city used to be known as the 'Soot District.'"

Gil looked around at the bright white walls surrounding them. "I don't see any soot."

The woman grinned. "It's not sooty anymore. Ever since the skies cleared, we have gotten away from using so much coal."

Gil remembered learning wood had been a rarity in the Black Lands, where there was too little sunlight to grow anything that couldn't be directly eaten. Animals had been all but extinct for lack of the grain to sustain them. Thinking of the carts and livestock abundant in the market, Gil was glad to see things were changing quickly for the better.

"I'm Cerille Davore," the woman said, placing her hand against her chest.

"Gil Archer." He flashed a meager smile. "Cerille... Pardon, but that doesn't sound like a Malikari name."

"It's not," the woman admitted. She turned her head slightly, her hair spilling over her face before she could push it back. "My mother was from the Rhen."

"How did you end up here?" he asked.

"My father was a soldier. He was one of the few who returned to Bryn Calazar after the skies cleared. He brought my mother back with him. I grew up here, in the Soot District. My home was right over there, down that street."

She nodded in the direction of a small road that curved away from the market, bordered by walls made of limestone blocks. Gil looked back to the woman, amused, wondering why a complete stranger would feel the need to show him the street she grew up on.

"Now I live at the Lyceum," she said casually.

Gil blinked, taken aback, then peered at her harder, suddenly seeing her in a different light. "You're a mage?"

"That's right," she said with a delighted grin, as though she had succeeded at playing a trick on him.

Gil stared at her hard, watching her long hair ripple in the wind. "You came looking for me," he guessed, a sour taste filling his mouth. He'd liked Cerille better before he'd known she was a pawn of Andigar Shadeem.

"I was sent to bring you to the Lyceum. The Prime Warden wants me to introduce you to some of the other mages."

Gil sighed, rolling his eyes. "He doesn't relent, does he?"

"No, he doesn't," she said with a little smile. "The Prime Warden isn't one to take 'no' for an answer."

Which darkened Gil's mood more. "And if I refuse to come?"

An incredulous look sprang to her face, like she couldn't

believe he would ask such a ridiculous question. "I'm not going to hit you over the head with a stick! Either you come or you don't."

With that, she walked away a few steps before turning back.

Gil cast one last glance back down at the sparkling harbor, wishing he could just ignore her. But all the wishing in the world wouldn't make Andigar Shadeem go away.

He let her lead him onto the street she had pointed out earlier. He found himself staring at the houses that lined the road, wondering which one had been hers.

"The Prime Warden said you are a powerful Battlemage," Cerille said unexpectedly. "He also said you are confused."

Gil grunted. "Confused about what?"

"About your purpose."

That struck him wrong. "What did he mean by that?"

Cerille shrugged. "He said you're still trying to see the world through the eyes of a man."

That was a bizarre answer. Frowning, Gil asked, "So, I'm not a man?"

"No." She scrunched her face up, as though mocking a foolish question. "You're a Battlemage, and Battlemages serve only one purpose. They are weapons."

"So, I'm just a weapon, then?" Gil muttered. "Is that what I'm reduced to?"

Cerille stopped. "Look at me."

He forced his eyes to meet hers.

"It's as I thought," she said. "You are no stranger to war. You have the eyes of a man who has killed other men. Perhaps many other men. So you tell me, Gil Archer. How much humanity do you think's left in you?"

He stared at her a moment without responding, her words slowly seeping under his skin, poisoning his insides. Making him angry. Making him think.

"I'm more than just a weapon," he snapped, wondering who this woman really was.

Cerille raised her eyebrows. "But less than a man?"

Gil nodded. No matter how much he wanted to deny it, she was exactly right.

"Come on," she said with a sudden smile. "Let me show you the city along the way."

33

THE SICKNESS

THE DAY WORE ON. BY AFTERNOON, KEIO'S STOMACH WAS rebelling against him, becoming increasingly nauseous and sending sharp pains shooting throughout his abdomen. He walked clutching his middle, jaw clenched, forcing himself forward by brute force of will. What made it worse was that he knew they weren't out of the contamination zone yet, so there was no relief from the damage his body was taking. At the rate he was deteriorating, he feared he would not live to reach the Tower of Morning.

They were still encountering the occasional ruin. Structures from the past appeared along the side of the road, although they were becoming progressively more deteriorated. Many buildings resembled scattered piles of stones that had been eroded by vegetation. Very occasionally, they came across an intact structure.

As they walked, the forest was changing. Broadleaf trees were taking a foothold, appearing now and then in the gaps between evergreens, becoming more plentiful the further they went. Rough-barked oaks and beeches, bare-limbed maples and birches, soon dominated the canopy. Keio was startled by the rustle of a songbird taking flight, the first sign of animal life they had encountered since entering the forest.

The road started to narrow, the paving stones increasingly broken or missing, the path invaded by opportunistic plants. Even though that slowed their progress, Keio looked upon it as a sign they were leaving the toxic air behind. The realization sped his feet; he was eager to be out of it. He was also hoping that the vortex of magic above them would end soon. Perhaps, once they were out from beneath it, he might be able to reverse the damage he had taken, at least to some limited extent.

The trees parted, revealing a large, dark pond. Keio turned off the path and walked toward it, pausing when he reached the shore. The pond used to be part of a much larger body of water, but the rest of the lake had apparently dried up. The water was different than he remembered: darker, murkier. Small bubbles gurgled to the surface from deep down below, and the air above it stunk.

The change in the lake was profound and, to Keio, it seemed symbolic. A great sense of loss came over him. Tears gathered in his eyes, and this time, he didn't rub them away. Since coming back to this world, he hadn't taken the time to mourn, and he was starting to feel the emotional effects of that. For a moment, the sense of loss became almost intolerable, a crushing weight he didn't think he could bear. The lake was just further confirmation that it was long past his time. He didn't belong here.

Pausing next to him, Shade asked, "What is it?"

"This lake was called Jenia. There was a small fishing village here. At least, I think it was here. The waters have moved since the last time I saw it." He felt a tear run down his cheek. "I met my wife here."

Shade said nothing in response, but stood beside him looking out at the lake. Keio didn't say anything further;

instead, he stood grieving in silence, feeling as though he were standing over Ilia's grave.

"I shouldn't be here," he muttered at last, wiping his eyes. "This isn't my time."

The sound of crunching leaves told him that Jendo had left the road and was coming over to join them.

"Perhaps the gods are giving you an opportunity to right the wrongs of your past," Jendo suggested in his smug-as-ever voice, a tone that was starting to grate on Keio's nerves.

"I think you're right, old man," he said in a biting tone. "I should have used the core energy to collapse the rift instead of the magic field. But now I've got a second chance."

Jendo looked at him, his stare long and searching. "How does one act of genocide justify performing another?"

The question, like the man, was exasperating. "Why don't you apply that same logic to your own kind? How many civilizations have the Turan Khar destroyed or consumed?"

"All because of you." Jendo spoke as though he were lecturing a five-year-old on the same topic for the millionth time. "If you do what's right, we can return to a peaceful existence."

Keio stood in silence, gazing out at the lake. For just a moment, an image of Ilia came to mind, the way she had looked on the day he had met her. He had gone fishing with his brother, and was just returning with his basket full when he heard a scream followed by a splash, followed by the ringing sound of laughter. They had dropped their baskets and jogged to the shoreline, where they found a pair of women, swimming fully clothed in the water, splashing each other in the lake.

He remembered standing on the shoreline watching them, enjoying their fun. Until the pair noticed them standing there, staring. For a moment, he and his brother had stood frozen, looking at each other as though mortally embarrassed. Then the two women had burst out in a fit of laughter that had ended with an invitation to come swim. The image faded in his mind, leaving only an acute, aching grief.

"Maybe you're right, old man," he said softly. "Maybe I really am the monster you claim me to be." Turning away from the lake, he trudged back toward the road, Jendo hurrying to catch up.

"But that doesn't absolve the Turan Khar," Keio said, lifting a finger. "Everything about your Unity is contrary to human nature and human dignity. That band on your wrist deprives you of your individuality. Tell me, how many times since you put that thing on have you pursued your own dreams and goals?" He scoffed, letting out a dark chuckle. "The puppet master has become the puppet. Quite the irony, don't you think?"

Jendo shrugged. "That's an easy claim to make, looking from the outside in. But you don't understand, and you never will. Unless you open yourself up to that." He pointed at the band on Keio's wrist, the silver *A'isan*.

The idea was so ridiculous, Keio wanted to laugh. "I'm not going to enslave myself just to see the world through your eyes."

He hurried his pace, seeking to get away from the man. Once back on the road, he led them in the direction of the foothills that had become visible above the tree line. It would take the rest of the day to reach them, he figured. He would push on until evening if he had to, anything to put a good distance between himself and the lake.

By late afternoon, the forest was starting to thin around them, and by the time the sun was going down, they emerged from the trees into a large meadow of tall, green grass. A small herd of whitetail deer looked up at the sight of their party, stiffening, ears perking in their direction. For seconds the deer stood frozen, then returned immediately to their grazing. To Keio, it was a demonstration of just how rare the sight of man was to these creatures, if they had ever seen a man at all.

When they started out into the meadow, the deer finally bolted, deciding not to trust these new, two-legged creatures who were in invasion into their territory. Keio watched their hindquarters bobbing up and down as they bounded away, tails high, disappearing into the trees.

As they crossed the meadow, signs of life appeared everywhere around them. Swarms of gnats rose from the grass to pester them, and once, they flushed a pheasant out of hiding. When the last of the sunlight had faded from the sky, bats appeared overhead, flitting across the twilight.

They camped in the center of the meadow, clearing enough space to build a fire. Keio rolled out his blankets away from the others and sat hunched over upon it, holding his stomach against a deep, aching pain. The taste of blood kept filling his mouth, and whenever he spit, his saliva was slightly off-color, tinted pink. He thought maybe his gums were bleeding. It didn't surprise him, but it did worry him enough that he didn't want to eat.

Standing up, Shade moved around the fire to sit beside him, offering him a cup of tea. Keio took the cup from her hand and just held it for a moment, enjoying the warmth. When he took a sip, the tea hit his stomach like a brick, making him retch. He handed the cup back to Shade, shaking his head, his eyes watering.

Unwinding some of the wrappings from her arm, she reached out and placed the naked skin of her wrist against his forehead. Seeming satisfied, she lowered her hand. Then she sat back and relaxed there in silence beside him.

For minutes, neither of them spoke. Keio stared down at her disfigured skin, his eyes wandering over her Marks, finding the sight of them deeply unsettling. Not because of their grotesque appearance, which he was getting used to, but because he knew he was responsible for them. His gaze rose from shade's arms to her veiled face. He couldn't help wondering what the rest of her looked like. Hesitantly, he raised his hand toward her, but froze with his fingers within inches of her face.

"Go ahead," she whispered.

Moving slowly, with great respect, he released the veil and let it fall aside.

Keio's breath caught at the sight of what lay beneath. He didn't say anything, just sat quietly, staring at the grotesque contortions of skin the veil kept hidden, struggling to hide his revulsion.

She felt it anyway, through the link. But there was no shame in her eyes. She held her head up, her expression defiant and full of pride.

"The core magic did this," he said, then added, "I'm sorry."

Her jaw tightened. "Rylan thought the Marks were beautiful."

The statement made him angry and, not for the first time, he was glad the man was gone. Rylan had been wrong to placate Shade. He shouldn't have catered to her delusion that such corruption was anything but a crime that had been committed against her.

"I don't see anything beautiful," he snapped. "What I see is a wrong that needs to be righted."

Her eyes flashed in anger, hot and searing. She lifted her veil and tucked it back in place, but before she could stand, he caught her arm, preventing her from leaving.

"Wait."

She glared at him in silence.

He had to make her understand. "I realize that the Marks are accepted and appreciated in your culture. But they are still a disfigurement. A corruption. Just like the poison that's killing me."

"I don't care," she said tightly.

"I do." A powerful wave of guilt came over him. She had to understand—he didn't deserve forgiveness. And by denying the corrupt nature of the Marks, that was exactly what she was doing: forgiving him. He couldn't have that.

Leaning forward, he stared deeply into her eyes, silently begging her to understand. "I truly thought it was the answer. The way to elevate the whole of our civilization above the mundane. We were so close. Don't you understand? We were on the cusp of becoming a society completely transformed by magic, free of all natural constraints. The Turan Khar had already succeeded, in a way. The Unity they constructed allowed their society to transcend the limitations of human experience. Somehow, they had found a way around all the flaws and the ugliness that mar all of our interactions. I didn't agree with their philosophy or methods, and I never will. But I envied their accomplishment."

He dropped his eyes to the ground. "That's why I did it. I wanted the same for us—only, better. Something more human. I didn't think about the price." His voice trailed off. He stroked his thumb across the dents and weals that covered the back of her hand.

He sat back and said nothing more.

34

THE LYCEUM

Gil had expected Cerille to lead him back to the ziggurat. But instead, she took him on a winding tour of the city that, hours later, ended on the far side of the harbor, at a tall cliff that rose hundreds of feet above the waves. There, what looked like a palace was under construction, a large portion already completed. It was a stunning piece of architecture, with golden domes that climbed one upon the other, surrounded by tall minarets and arcaded walkways. While the construction was astonishing, it was the sheer size of the structure that stole his breath. When completed, it would be the largest building in the world, dwarfing even the great temples of Glen Farquist.

"The Lyceum?" he asked.

Cerille nodded. "It is a duplicate of the ancient Lyceum that stood here before the Desecration, built right on the old foundation. The Prime Warden's master builders have access to original diagrams of the old Lyceum, to make certain every wall and angle is exact in every detail."

"What's he going to do with it?" Gil wondered, staring at the cascading domes. "You can't possibly have enough mages to fill it."

"The Prime Warden is hoping to attract more." She smiled shyly. "Like yourself. He wants to restore the Lyceum to its former grandeur. It's a worthy goal."

"It is." Gil's attention was still riveted on the magnificent structure above them.

They turned off the street onto a wide brick path that wound around the cliffs above the harbor, eventually arriving at the Lyceum's gates. Cerille led him into the main courtyard, where they stopped so that he could appreciate the splendor around him. They stood in a plaza paved with white marble tile surrounded by enclosed walkways. The large golden dome ahead of them dwarfed anything Gil had ever seen. Just that single dome was larger than the entire palace of Karikesh. Cerille had to tug his arm to get him moving again. Gil walked forward, staring at the domes and minarets that surrounded them, many encased by scaffolding.

"This is unbelievable," Gil whispered.

"It is." Cerille smiled. "Wait until you see what's inside."

She led him through the massive doors into the central dome. Immediately, shadows fell around them, encasing them in the dim light that spilled from stained glass windows set overhead above layers of galleries. The dome itself was held up by several ornately carved pillars. The ambiance was surreal, at once intimidating and uplifting at the same time. He turned slowly, his gaze moving over the walls, finally coming to rest on the floor.

His mouth fell open.

In the center of the floor was a Circle of Convergence. It had to be the same Circle that had existed a thousand years ago; the knowledge of crafting such tremendous artifacts had disappeared from the world in the Desecration. There existed only five Circles of Convergence that Gil knew of, and three of those were dead. There was one in the ruins of Aerysius, another at the top of Orien's Finger. Yet another had been lost somewhere in the Black Lands; the last was on the Isle of Titherry. Quin Reis had managed to repair the Circle on the island, as well as the one in Aerysius. How the Lyceum's Circle had been repaired, Gil didn't know, and he wondered who had performed the feat. Quin was the only master Artificer that he knew of, and Quin was dead.

Moving forward, he walked to the margin of the Circle and stood gazing down at it. It was made of red tiles arranged in the pattern of an eight-pointed star. There were two stars, actually, one oriented toward the four cardinal directions, as well as a smaller star oriented toward the intercardinal points. The lines of the stars glowed with a mercurial light. It was those lines, Gil knew, that gave the artifact its power. A Circle of Convergence worked by gathering the lines of the magic field together at a single point, focusing the power of an entire vortex and filtering it into a form that could be used by one mage.

Cerille grinned, watching Gil's reaction. "Wait here while I go get them."

She moved away, her footsteps ringing hollowly throughout the dome as she crossed the Circle of Convergence to the far wall and disappeared through a doorway. Gil remained behind, pacing the margin of the Circle. He could feel it through his feet, pulsating slightly, like a living thing with a detectable heartbeat. He couldn't help himself. He followed the lines of one of the stars all the way to the Circle's center, until he stood right over the focus, in the position of command. There, he closed his eyes, reaching out with his mind to probe the Circle of Convergence beneath his feet.

Hearing his call, the Circle responded.

All around him on the floor, the rays of the stars brightened. Gil felt a stirring of power stronger and purer than anything he had ever known rush into his body through his feet. At his side, *Thar'gon* began glowing. It was all he could do to restrain himself from using that immense amount of magic to do something... anything.

With a gasp, he broke his connection with the Circle and staggered away from the center, panting. Beads of sweat trickled down his face, his hands trembling. He looked back at the quieting Star, terrified and euphoric at the same time. The amount of power it was capable of drawing was truly terrifying.

"Gil," Cerille's voice called from the other side of the dome.

He flinched, startled, struggling to clear his thoughts.

She was walking toward him, accompanied by two men who wore robes of the deepest indigo blue, a silver eight-pointed star embroidered into the breast. He wore the same symbol on the back of his own cloak. It was the universal symbol of magic and mages, the very star of the Circle of Convergence.

Gil watched their approach warily, not trusting them. These were the first mages he had ever met that had been trained by someone other than Naia and Quin. These were Andigar Shadeem's men, and they would be advancing the Prime Warden's agenda. Besides, Gil thought, he still had no idea what that agenda was.

The three mages halted in front of him. The younger of the two men had shoulder-length black hair and a hawkish nose and wore a beard that was impeccably trimmed. The other man was older, bald, his features ragged and angular. Gil could almost feel the magic that radiated from his body. He was powerful, Gil acknowledged. Almost as powerful as he was. And the man was very aware of it. He stood casually, arms folded in front of him, a dour frown on his face.

Cerille smiled warmly. "Gil, I'd like to introduce you to Master Laith Saheen and Grand Master Jed Dagher."

Gil nodded slightly, his eyes lingering on the older of the two men.

"Laith and Jed are Battlemages," Cerille added.

He could have guessed that without her telling him. Both men had the look of warriors. Gil wondered if he projected that same kind of dangerous presence. He'd never thought about it before, but one look at Laith's face told him he did. The young man was staring at him as if either awed or terrified—or undecided between the two.

The older man, Jed, moved forward and offered his hand stiffly. "Prime Warden says you're thinking about joining our number."

"Oh, he does?" Gil asked, accepting the offered hand, deciding not to contradict the man. After all, he had told Shadeem that he might reconsider after Malikar's borders were secure.

Stepping back, Jed raked his gaze over him. "You're stronger than both of us. If you decide to speak the vows, you'd be our Warden."

Gil wanted to wince at the word 'vows.' Two vows had once been required for the Rhen's mages. The Acolyte's Oath was still in use, but the Oath of Harmony had been abandoned. It had forbidden mages from using magic as a weapon under any circumstance, no matter how dire. It had been a crippling vow, and Naia and Quin had abandoned it for good reason. Gil wondered which vows the mages of Shadeem's Lyceum were made to swear. Looking at Jed, he couldn't imagine it would be an oath of peace.

Folding his arms, Jed asked, "What kind of training did you receive in the Rhen?"

"I was trained by Grand Master Quinlan Reis," Gil admitted, figuring the two mages should be familiar with that name, considering Quin had been one of the men who had destroyed the Well of Tears and returned sunlight to the Black Lands. "Quin was the closest thing we had to a Battlemage."

The two mages glanced at each other with eyes widened by surprise.

Gil managed a smile. "He made sure I'm capable."

"I don't doubt you are," Laith said quickly. "Quinlan Reis... Such an honor. Then, you must have the knowledge of the ancient Lyceum—there is so much you could teach us! And Quinlan Reis was also an Artificer. Did you learn that skill from him too?"

"No." Gil shook his head with candid remorse. "He didn't believe mages should be trained to more than just one Order. He said most people couldn't master more than one skill set—and those that could were just too damn dangerous," he added with a grin. "I think he was talking about himself."

"He's probably right," said Laith. "I had a mentor who was an Empiricist, so I learned a bit of that too. I had a knack for it, but I never learned enough to consider myself a master of the craft." He grinned. "I guess that means I'm not too damn dangerous."

"And what about you?" Gil asked, looking at the older, sour-faced man. "Are you dangerous?" He had said it in jest. But he was also keen to know what the man's reaction to the question would be.

Jed eyed him sideways. "I kill things that need to be killed."

Gil asked, "And how do you determine what needs to be killed?"

"It's not my job to figure that out."

The way he said it made Gil feel cold. It made him think of Cerille's questions back at the marketplace, when she had asked him how much humanity could possibly be left inside him. Perhaps she was thinking of Jed when she had asked such a question.

Looking past the Battlemage, Gil noticed a strange, glimmering light that instantly caught his attention. It was coming from an orb that seemed to hover in midair, glowing as if suffused with an entire galaxy of stars. Tiny forks of energy danced across the inside surface of the sphere with a low, vibrating hum.

"What is that?" Gil asked, crossing the Circle toward it. "It's not magelight."

He approached the hovering orb, but stopped well away from it, wary of the strange energy. This close, he could feel it on his skin, a strange, shivering feeling that made every hair on his body stand up all at once. He moved forward and reached out to touch it. As he did, the tingling sensation increased to a frantic vibration that made his entire hand numb.

"It's core magic," Cerille said, moving to stand beside him.

"What is that?"

He retracted his hand and then reach back out again, feeling the tingling sensation return. The energy of the orb seemed to be doing much more to the air around it than simply illuminating it. Gil stood with both hands out, as if ready to collect the light with his palms. Small, jagged forks of energy shot from the glowing orb, arcing toward his fingertips. He couldn't feel them, or if he did, he couldn't tell. His hands were already tingling painfully, as if the blood of been cut off to them for a while, and was only just returning.

Cerille walked forward, coming to stand at his side. "Core magic is the purest magic in the universe." She touched a finger to the surface of the orb. A jagged spear of energy shot toward it and danced briefly across the glass before flickering away. "We've been collecting it, drop by drop, for twenty years. Even after all that time, this is all we have ever managed to gather. There was much more once, but no records tell what happened to it. It just disappeared from the world a very long time ago. What's left is just the residual. But even that residual energy is potent enough to work true miracles."

Gil retracted his hands, staring down at them in trepidation. Whatever the core magic was, he didn't like the feel of it. It was entirely different from the magic field, and felt somehow discordant, as though it were out of tune with the rest of the world.

If such a small fraction could make his skin crawl as badly as it did, he didn't want to know what more would be like. He turned away from the globe and moved back toward the Circle of Convergence.

"You've given me a lot to think about," he said, glancing back at Cerille and her two companions.

Laith and Jed still stared at him, Jed with a hard-as-nails glare, and Laith, with a look of awestruck reverence.

"I'd better get back," Gil said.

Laith walked forward and immediately offered his hand. "Well met, Gil."

Jed didn't bother. With a snort and a nod, he turned and strode away, limping slightly across the Circle toward a door on the very far side of the tremendous hall. Gil watched him go, wondering how far a man like that could be trusted. He'd met seasoned soldiers in his time. But the coldness he sensed in Jed was a different sort entirely, a complete disregard of life.

He turned and followed Cerille out of the dome. She led him out of the Lyceum grounds and back down the hill into the city, navigating the winding streets toward the ziggurat. She made small talk along the way, using scattered smiles and fleeting apologies to smooth his nerves. If Cerille could be believed, Jed was harmless but notorious for acting like an ass. But it wasn't Jed that Gil's thoughts kept returning to. It was the core magic. Everything about it seemed unnatural, and it chilled him more than Jed's hostile arrogance. He couldn't get his mind away from it all the long way back to the ziggurat.

By the time he returned to his own room, he felt exhausted, and his brain seemed muddled. He found a couple bottles of wine waiting for him, a gift from his host. Picking up a bottle, he stared down at it, seeing the wine as less of a gift and more of a consolation prize. Nevertheless, he pulled the cork out with his teeth. He was just raising the bottle to his lips when he was interrupted by a knock at the door.

He set the wine down with a groan.

Gil wasn't surprised to find Ashra in the hallway, but he wasn't happy about it either. The sight of her sent a knife of anger through his chest, stabbing right for the heart. He stood and stared at her, unsure of what to say.

"May I come in?" she asked.

He motioned her forward and returned to his seat and his bottle of wine, while she claimed the cushion next to him. He poured himself a cup of wine, then poured one for her without bothering to ask if she wanted any.

"How was your tour?" he asked, passing her the cup while avoiding her eyes.

She murmured a polite thank-you, then took a sip of the wine. "It was eye-opening. Andigar has some excellent ideas that would benefit both our nations. And the terms he proposes are... quite generous."

There was something about her voice that he didn't like, a peculiar hesitation. Perhaps she knew he wouldn't like the terms 'Andigar' was proposing. There was a good chance he wouldn't, Gil figured, and tossed back a healthy swig of wine.

"So, you've decided to accept his offer, then?" he asked, trying his best to sound impartial.

Ashra brought a hand up, absently fingering the sapphire pendant at her neck. "I have."

A knot of jealousy tightened around his throat, making it difficult to swallow the wine in his mouth.

"Congratulations," he mumbled and, tilting his head back, finished what was left in his cup. He immediately poured another, sloshing a bit into Ashra's cup to top it off.

Ashra flinched, staring down at the splashed wine soaking into her gown. She glanced up at him, her mouth wide open in bafflement.

"What was that?" she asked. "Are you *jealous?*"

Instantly regretful, Gil settled back in his seat, raising his cup and using it like a shield to hide behind. "I just think you're trusting him a little too easily."

She leaned forward and pushed the cup aside, peering deeply into his eyes. "You are," she gasped, her eyes widening. "You're jealous!"

The anger that seized him was sharp and brutal. "I'm not," he spat, and, setting the wine down roughly on the table, rose to his feet. He turned his back on her and walked toward the door, seeking an escape. But before he could reach it, she bolted up after him.

"Stop!" she ordered. *"And turn around."*

Gil did as she asked, jabbing her with an insolent look. She approached him slowly, her accusatory gaze cutting across his emotions.

"How long have you had feelings for me?" she demanded, slipping between him and the door.

Gil couldn't believe she had actually asked the question. Could it be possible that she didn't know? He hadn't exactly been forward with his feelings, but he didn't think he'd hidden them all that well either.

"It doesn't matter," he muttered, stepping back to gain some distance.

She moved around him, cornering him against the door-frame. "Why didn't you tell me?"

He spread his hands, feeling exasperated. "Because no good can come from it. You're a queen, Ashra. I'm just a soldier. We're not even supposed to be on the same side!"

"And yet, here you are," she said almost accusingly.

He took a deep breath, wanting to fling his hands up. "I've been here all along."

She blinked once. Twice. Her eyes slipped to the side, her shoulders sagging. Her face went blank. "I... I didn't know..."

"Would it have made any difference?"

She didn't answer. Her eyes remained fixed on something on the floor, the expression on her face evolving through a series of emotions before settling on something that looked like regret. But her lips didn't move, and for that he was almost grateful.

"Then there's my answer," he said, wishing he hadn't left his wine back on the table. "Look. If you want to form an alliance with that man, it's not my place to tell you otherwise. But please just let me know what you want from me. Do you still want me by your side, knowing how I feel about you?"

She brought a hand up and twisted a lock of hair between her fingers, something she only did when she was extremely aggravated or upset. "I can't tell you what to do."

"Yes, you can," Gil said, his anger cooling a bit, now that he had a definite answer. "I've already thrown my lot in with you. For better or for worse, you are my Queen. I don't say that lightly, and it's not an emotional decision. It's simply a fact. So, as my Queen, what would you have of me?"

She stared into his eyes a long moment, her expression beseeching. "Gil..."

He crossed his arms and stood waiting for an answer.

Taking a step back, she whispered, "I'm sorry."

It wasn't the answer he was hoping for, but it was *an* answer. Moving around her, he strode back over to the table and scooped up his wine. "I'm going to sleep," he said wearily with his back to her. "Good night, Your Majesty."

She lingered in the doorway a few seconds before leaving, the door shutting quietly behind her. The moment he heard it latch, Gil brought his hand back and let the wine cup fly. It hurled across the room and shattered against the wall, showering the rugs with dark wine and sharp pieces of ceramic.

35

THE MOKONA HIGHLANDS

Someone was shaking him awake, but Keio was sleeping way down deep, floating in the darkness, and it was too hard to climb back up. He didn't want to fight his way back to consciousness.

The urgent shaking wouldn't stop and kept pulling him upward, no matter how much he wanted to slip back down.

Keio opened his eyes into a world of pain he didn't want to exist in.

Moaning, he raised his hands to his face to fend off the light that poked fiery daggers into his eyes. The world was so distorted that he couldn't make out who it was that was trying to wake him. The figure was just a dark blur against a bigger, brighter blur. He tried closing his eyes again.

"Rylan!" someone called. But that wasn't his name, so it had no meaning to him, and therefore didn't register. The shaking continued, relentless.

"Keio!"

That name sprung him back. He made an effort to focus his eyes, and the blurred body bending over him coalesced into

Shade. She was not the woman he had been hoping to see. Somewhere, down deep in the dream, he had left Ilia, and he wanted to get back to her. But this woman wouldn't leave him alone.

"Let's get you to the fire," she said, reaching under his arms to steady him as she pulled him to his feet.

He shambled on trembling legs toward Jendo, who sat making breakfast over the campfire. The man looked up as he approached, an immediate frown sagging his face. Keio sat down hard, rattling his insides. He sat shivering, staring into the flames, the smell of cooking meat making him queasy. When Shade tried stuffing a soggy piece of bread into his hand, Keio shook his head, waving it away.

"I'm not hungry," he said.

But he was thirsty. He saw his waterskin lying next to a pile of supplies across the campfire. Heaving himself up off the ground, he made his way around the fire toward it. He picked the waterskin up and shook it, but it was empty. Shade replaced it with another, and he chugged at the water as though it were lifeblood. He stopped drinking well before his thirst ended, not wanting to make himself more ill. Nodding his thanks at Shade, he returned to the fire.

"Deteriorating faster than you thought you would?" Jendo asked mildly. Leaning forward, he used a knife to turn over a strip of meat that was sizzling in his skillet. "I'm not surprised. In total, you spent more than two days in the contamination zone, and one of those days was spent in Suheylu Ra itself, where the poison is very concentrated."

Keio tried to ignore him, shivering while keeping his gaze fixed on the dancing flames in the campfire. The old man seemed to be gloating, and he didn't want to give Jendo the satisfaction of knowing that his words scared the hell out of him. For the old man was right.

Still hunched over, tending his meat, Jendo said, "Perhaps

you should tell us where the Tower of Morning is, in case you don't make it."

Keio said through chattering teeth, "If I don't make it, then knowing where the Tower is won't do you any good. You won't be able to unlock the containment crystal by yourself."

"You could tell me how," Jendo suggested, leaning forward and spearing a strip of meat with his knife. He held it up with a satisfied smile, rotating it on the tip of the blade as though admiring his handiwork.

Keio's sneered, shaking his head. "Oh, no, old man. We're in this together, you and I."

Jendo pulled the meat off his knife and brought it to his lips. He held it there, blowing on it as it steamed. "Well," he said, biting off a piece. "We'll be passing out of the vortex later this morning. That should help."

It would help. Possibly. If it wasn't already too late.

They broke camp and headed toward the foothills of the mountains in the distance. Jendo and Shade had lightened his pack, distributing many of his possessions among the two of them, which made the going easier. The forest thickened around them once again, only this time, filled with animals. The grove they walked through was dim and musty, and light came down in slanted rays that dappled the ground.

After hiking for a couple of hours, they came across another ruin. This time, it was the remains of an ancient fortress perched atop the spur of a hill. The keep appeared thoroughly overgrown, with vines and roots infesting its walls. Trees grew up through cracks in its fortifications. It didn't look as old as the other ruins they had passed, and Keio didn't remember it, which meant it had probably been built sometime after he had been gone from the world. As they passed beneath its shadow, the forest seemed to grow quiet.

On the far side of the keep, they passed a thin waterfall that emerged from under the curtainwall of the fortress and plummeted hundreds of feet into a pool contained in a shallow grotto at the base of the cliff. There, along the shoreline, Keio paused and stood still, staring down into the pool. Way down deep, a light glowed from the depths of the pool and shone upward, making the surface of the water shimmer.

"What is it?" Shade asked, coming to stand beside him.

Keio backed away from the pool and looked around the surrounding grotto. Much of the moss growing up the cliff above the water had taken on a deep, blood-red pigment, as had the leaves of the surrounding trees. A black, slimy fungus clung to the rocks above the pool. Above the water, just in front of the waterfall, a hole had appeared in the air, a darkness deeper than shadow, that was slowly rotating. Keio's gaze locked on that twisting shadow, and his breath caught in his throat.

The hole in the air was a result of the collapse of a core conduit. It was a rip in the fabric of the world, a doorway to another place. Probably not anywhere in this world. For, unlike the magic field, the core magic wasn't constrained to this planet. That rent in the air could lead somewhere as far away as the stars themselves.

When Shade started toward the grotto, he reached out and caught her arm. "Don't go in there."

Her eyes went wide, fixated on the spinning darkness. She asked, "What is this place?"

Keio scan the grotto again, wondering about the blood-red appearance of the vegetation. "That's core magic. Somewhere beneath this pool is a conduit that's ruptured."

"We should leave here," Jendo said, taking Shade's other arm and leading her away.

Keio remained behind, drawn by the spectacle of the shadowy hole in the air. To him, that gaping wound repre-sented everything wrong in the world. The power that created it could have delivered his civilization to new heights of human experience, far greater than any other society had dreamed of achieving. But some things weren't meant for perfection, and thus was the nature of humankind.

Regretfully, he turned away and followed Jendo and Shade out from under the lee of the grotto. The ground was getting steeper, and the forest around them was once again dominated by evergreens. Ahead, the mountains loomed over them, summits hidden by dark clouds that had been advancing toward them all morning, cooling the air and thickening it with humidity.

Walking at his side, Jendo asked, "So, how do you intend to do it?"

"Do what?"

"Destroy the Unity."

Keio glanced at him, surprised by both the timing and the directness of his question. He decided to humor the man with an answer, knowing the information wouldn't do Jendo any good. "When I collapsed the Sky Portal before, your entire society was sucked into the Netherworld by the very magic that sustained you. Unfortunately, that had an unintended consequence: you endured through time, just as I did. And also like me, you returned. I'm not going to let that happen again. This time, I'm going to use core magic to collapse your portal. There will be no coming back, not for either of us."

Jendo's face darkened with a skeptical frown. "You're not that powerful."

Keio sneered. "The man who previously occupied this body made a compact with Xerys. Which is convenient for me, for I have access to the entire triune of magic. And, through this"— he held up the *A'isan* on his wrist—"I can summon the collective power of every mage in the Turan Khar. Is that powerful enough, old man?"

Jendo halted, the color in his face draining by slow degrees until he stood gazing at Keio with bloodless skin and hollow eyes. "You will kill us all."

Keio issued a triumphant smile. "In one stroke, I can free this world of the Onslaught, the core magic, and the Turan Khar. Isn't that what you wanted, Puppet Master? A world free of magic's oppression? I'll deliver your wish before I end."

He stood gazing into Jendo's face, eager to see what his response would be. It was a long time before it came. The old man stared at him slack-jawed, eyes vacant.

"I was wrong," he finally whispered.

"I know," Keio said. "But it doesn't matter anymore."

He walked away, leaving Jendo to his despair. He turned south, following the ridgeline, which continued ever uphill into the foothills. Every once in a while, the piercing cry of a hawk knifed through the air. The clouds closed in overhead, and the air took on enough of a chill to make him long for a jacket. But all he had was the thin linen robe, which though perfectly suited to the Desolation, didn't do much to keep the chill of the highlands at bay.

Toward midafternoon, Keio began to feel ill again. His stomach had troubled him on and off throughout the day, feeling twisted and knotted. It was the pain, more than anything, that weighed him down. It was constant, and therefore exhausting.

They stopped to rest at a tumbled scree of debris that had fallen from the cliffs to impede their path. Grateful for the excuse, Keio cast his aching body down upon a rock and leaned forward, panting and gripping his middle. Shade and Jendo took their rest some distance away, leaving him to his pain, which was fine. He wasn't interested in their company.

Absently, he hiked up the hem of his robe and scratched an itch on his leg. The action didn't do a lot of good, except for making his leg itch even worse. Scowling, he scratched harder and was surprised when his fingers came away bloody. He held his hand up, staring in shock at what looked like small clumps of bloody flesh that had collected under his nails.

Lifting his robe, he stared down at his leg and saw that it was bleeding—a lot. Dismayed, he ripped a strip of linen off the hem of his garment and held it against the injury. He sat there gritting his teeth, the cloth pressed tight against his leg. After minutes, he removed his hand to check the wound, only to find it still bleeding.

Jendo and Shade had already risen and were shouldering their packs, but he couldn't leave yet. He couldn't walk without getting the bleeding under control first. Shade must have noticed that something was wrong, for she came toward him and knelt at his side. She lifted the bloody wad of cloth away from the wound, bending over to examine the injury.

"This is bad," she said.

She let go of his leg and, setting her pack on the ground, rummaged through it, at last producing fresh linen bandages and more cloth to use as a compress. Keio bit his lip as she went to work on his leg, while Jendo did his best to conspicuously ignore them.

"I think we need to stop here for the night," Shade called over her shoulder to Jendo. To Keio, she said, "If you walk any farther today, this is just going to bleed more."

He didn't want to stop there, not this close. They had to be almost out from under the vortex, which meant that in only another few leagues, he would have access to the magic field and the means of healing himself at least partially. Not completely—the taint of Suheylu Ra could never be fully healed. Wholesome flesh could only be grown from wholesome flesh, none of which he had anymore. The best he could do was slow the progress of the damage. But whatever he could do, he would have to do it soon.

While he sat on the rock pressing the bandage against his leg, Shade went to fetch water from a stream. Jendo disappeared into the brush and didn't return until an hour later, carrying two dead rabbits slung over his shoulder. Tossing them down, he took out his knife and began gutting the animals while Shade started the fire the way she did every night, with a piece of flint struck against firesteel.

Jendo braced the rabbits over the fire, tending them the way a new parent watches over their firstborn. Keio sat staring off in the distance, his thoughts murky, nursing his leg. The afternoon was fading to twilight, and the sounds of the birds fading with it. Overhead, the clouds celebrated their domination of the sky with a crackle of thunder.

Across the fire, Shade began singing. The sound was so unexpected that it startled him. But her voice was clear and pleasant, carrying over the crackle of the fire and out into the dimness of the evening. He couldn't understand the words of the song she sang. All he knew was that it was a haunting refrain, and it stirred his soul.

"What was that?" he asked when she was finished.

"It's a Urati song about the long darkness."

"You sing it beautifully," Keio said. "It gripped my heart."

On the other side of the fire, Jendo let out a wry chuckle. "So a song can grip your heart, but not the plight of an entire society?"

Keio scowled. The man never let up, and was wearing on his nerves. He was like a relentless hammer, each strike driving the nail a little further in. Keio was beginning to hate the man, and not only because of his unending jabs. More than anything, he hated him because some of the things he said were starting to sink in.

36

A UNITED MALIKAR

When Gil woke, his head throbbed reprovingly, as though trying to pay him back for a night of abuse. He didn't remember having *that* much wine, but apparently it had been more than enough on an empty stomach. When he sat up, he felt vaguely ill. He moaned and rubbed his temples, working his dry tongue around his mouth. A little magical healing made him feel a bit better, at least physically. But magic could only treat the symptoms, not the disease. That, he'd have to get over on his own time.

Casting off the covers, he saw that he'd slept in his clothes. He stood up slowly, blinking, gazing blearily around. There were three empty wine bottles sitting on the table, and the remains of the cup he had tossed were still scattered across the floor. He headed to the bath, where it took him forever to make his water, his stream a never-ending font.

A knock at the door made him sag. He dreaded opening it, not wanting to face Ashra—and certainly not wanting her to see the state of the room. He opened the door only a crack, using his body to shield the interior from view.

But it wasn't Ashra in the hallway.

It was Cerille.

The woman leaned forward and peered at him with a befuddled expression, her eyebrows knitting together. "What happened to you?"

Gil realized he probably looked like something scraped off the ground. He rubbed his eyes with the heels of his hands. "Nothing happened."

The disbelieving frown on her face told him that answer wasn't working.

"I came to check on you," she said. "You slept through the ceremony."

Squinting, Gil blinked his confusion. "What ceremony?"

"The signing of the treaty." Cerille frowned harder at him. "Didn't the Sultana tell you?

Gil shook his head. Of course, she hadn't. After last night, he doubted Ashra would be telling him much of anything ever again.

"They're wrapping things up," Cerille said. "The Prime Warden was hoping you'd attend."

Gil glanced down at the clothes he was wearing, which were wrinkled from bed and stained with wine. He wasn't prepared to go anywhere. Running a hand back through his hair, another over the whiskers on his chin, he decided there was no quick way to solve the problem.

"Just give me one moment," he said, then ducked back into the room, closing the door behind him quickly before Cerille could get a view of the interior.

He picked his way barefoot across the floor, managing to gouge a piece of shattered ceramic into his big toe. Inhaling sharply, he hissed a curse through his teeth and plucked it out. Limping, he struggled out of his clothes on the way to the wardrobe and dragged a fresh tunic from a hanger, pulling it on over his head. He went to the washstand and poured a pitcher of water into the bowl, using his hands to splash it over his face and wet his hair. He scooped a handful of water into his mouth, swishing it around.

That was as good as it was going to get. Wiping his face dry on his shirtsleeve, he opened the door and sidled out into the hallway, shutting it quickly behind him. Cerille must have figured out what he was trying to do, for she looked at him oddly, trying to peer around him.

"Are you hiding a naked woman in there?" she asked.

Gil chuckled bitterly. "I'd have to attract one first."

Cerille frowned at him critically for a second, then beckoned him forward with a jerk of her head. "Come on. We're keeping them waiting."

"Why doesn't the Prime Warden use the Lyceum for formal ceremonies?" he asked. "I mean, that's why you're building it, right?"

Turning a corner, Cerille glanced at him. "The Lyceum is still under construction, and the Hall of Assembly isn't ready yet. This temple has been used for all matters of state for the past few hundred years."

"It's just a bit oppressive, is all." Gil ducked under a doorway that was not quite tall enough for him to walk fully upright. He followed her down a spiraling stairway all the way to the ground floor, then down a narrow hallway lit by golden magelight.

The hallway ended at a large, circular chamber that was just as dim as the rest of the place. There, the magelight clung to the ceiling and the walls, making Gil feel like they were floating through a hazy curtain of fog. A ring of people stood at the far end of the room, all wearing floor-length indigo robes. As Gil entered, all eyes turned toward him, and he felt instantly self-conscious. He moved forward slowly, following Cerille into the center of the room.

He noticed Ashra standing off to one side wearing a brocaded gown and a headpiece made of many gold chains. A teardrop-shaped sapphire hung suspended in the center of her forehead, glimmering in the dancing mage light.

She stood beside the Prime Warden, the treaty they had signed spread out before them on a pedestal. As Gil approached, her eyes sought his. He looked quickly away, red warmth flushing his cheeks.

"Grand Master Gil," the Prime Warden greeted him in a raised voice. "Thank you for joining us."

"Thank you for having me," Gil said, his gaze roving over the faces of the mages that surrounded them in the hall. There were many more than he had expected, perhaps thirty or forty, in all. He'd had no idea so many had been left behind in the Black Lands.

"Come forward," the Prime Warden directed, beckoning with his hand. "Please. Stand with us."

Gil moved forward cautiously, crossing the floor to stand at Ashra's side. He could feel her eyes tracking him, but he couldn't look at her. Instead, he kept his gaze trained on Andigar Shadeem, and he didn't care what the man might be reading into his expression. When he reached him, Shadeem took him by the shoulders in an embrace that was much too intimate for Gil.

"Have you given thought to my offer?"

"Thank you, Prime Warden," Gil said, drawing back, "but my place is with Ashra."

Shadeem's smile reminded him of a cat grinning at a bird. "If you become my Warden, then you will be at her side," he argued. "The Sultana has accepted my proposal to become my bride. Together we will rule a united Malikar."

Stunned, Gil glanced at Ashra for confirmation, but her eyes darted swiftly to the floor. He stared at her in shock for a moment, his brain fumbling to form words. He wanted to punch Shadeem, and it took everything he had to restrain his fist. Taking a deep breath, he considered his options, realizing he didn't have any.

Gil drew himself up stiffly and said in a rigid voice, "Congratulations to both of you. May the gods bless your union." Struggling to keep his voice even, he said to the Prime Warden, "Thank you again for the offer, but I am sorry, I will have to decline."

He turned to Ashra. "Your Majesty, I will come with you to Bel Arun. As I promised, I will fight at your side until Malikar's borders are secure. But after that, I'd like my own command."

The smile Ashra gave him was forced and full of sadness. "Of course. Thank you, Gil. You've already given me so much more than I deserve."

Already turning to leave, Gil muttered, "I know."

He retreated out of the room, his angry strides carrying him down the hallway and up the long flights of stairs, ignoring the sound of footsteps rushing to catch up with him. He chanced a glance back over his shoulder, dreading it was Ashra. With a mixture of both relief and irritation, he realized it was Cerille.

He ignored her as long as he could, trying to pretend he didn't hear her. When he finally arrived at the door to his guestroom, he turned sideways and slipped through it ahead of her. Before he could close the door, she rushed up to him and pushed it open. Once inside, she stopped dead, taking in the spectacle of the devastated room.

"By all means, please come in," Gil spat, closing the door forcefully behind her.

Cerille turned toward him. "What's it going to take to change your mind?"

"I'm not going to."

"Why not?" she asked, acting as though she didn't see the shattered cup and wine stains.

"In all honesty? I don't like him."

"You don't have to like him to serve him."

Gil scowled. "I don't trust him."

"Well, that's different," she said, glancing down at the mess on the floor. She lifted a foot, setting it back down again carefully. "Why don't you trust him?"

"Gut feeling. Why *do* you trust him?"

She smiled. "Because he's given me every reason to trust him and no reason not to." Turning away, she picked her way carefully across the broken ceramic on the floor, toward the table where a bottle of wine sat half-full and uncorked. Picking it up, she took a sniff. Wincing, she set the bottle down with a look of disgust.

"Without Andigar there wouldn't *be* a Lyceum of Bryn Calazar. Most of our parents were Lightweavers who were left behind during the Great Migration. And when the sun came out, they all found themselves in a world they didn't understand and where they were no longer needed. Andigar brought us together and gave us direction and hope. He gives us purpose."

"Well, I'm happy for you," Gil said flatly, wishing she would leave. "Try to understand something. I left my home—somewhere I had a purpose. Somewhere where people needed me. I gave that all up to come here, and I didn't do it for Andigar Shadeem."

"You did it for Ashra, and now she's rejected you," she said matter-of-factly.

"Is it that obvious?"

Bending, she picked up the wine-stained tunic he had slept in. "Your broken heart is bleeding all over your shirt." Wadding it up, she tossed the tunic into the corner of the room.

Gil could feel his cheeks heating. Enough was enough. He strode to the door and opened it wide for her.

She took the hint. Moving past him, Cerille said, "You'll get over her. In the meantime, take my advice. Don't make any decisions until you *are* over her. Understand?"

"Fine," Gil growled, starting to close the door behind her.

She shot her hand out, catching the door before it could latch. "Good. At least you can recognize common sense when you see it."

Gil turned and leaned back on the solid wooden door, letting his weight push it the rest of the way closed.

37

KARADUN

KEIO GAZED UP AT THE TOWERING EFFIGY THAT LOOMED OVER them, feeling a cold shiver in his heart. It was the statue of a Greater Elephant, the kind that had once been common to the savannas of Aeridor, used for millennia to bear armies on its back. The elephant towered two hundred or more feet above the roadway, its trunk lifted defiantly above its head. It was carved from dark gray diorite, the same material as the Watchers, and had once been polished to a satin finish. On its back, it wore a tasseled blanket, and stood grasping an object in its trunk: an elephant goad, which the creature raised triumphantly. One of the elephant's ears had broken off, along with a piece of its rump, and the statue's once-smooth surface was dull, pitted and scratched.

"The Vanadian Colossus," Jendo announced, studying the massive effigy that dwarfed the cliffs behind it. "It still exists."

Keio grunted. "This elephant was standing here thousands of years before you and I ever walked the earth. I'm sure it will still be standing here thousands of years after we're gone."

"I suppose it will," Jendo muttered.

The elephant stood planted over the opening to a flight of

stairs that had been carved into the cliff, marking their ascent into the Appos Mountains. The cliffs on either side of the stairs were likewise carved in bas-relief imagery, depicting scenes that hearkened back to a time before even Keio's memory. They were all relics of some lost Nerian civilization that had risen and fallen thousands of years before his own.

His own people had always avoided this area. It was a dangerous place, full of mysteries that all the minds in Shira had never been able to explain. The Tower of Morning was one such mystery. The mountains themselves had been carved hollow by the excavations of men delving for precious minerals. The ancient Nerians themselves had carved and molded the mountain landscape to suit their purposes, using arcane magic to forge the mountain city of Karadun—until that self-same magic rose against them.

Keio had ventured into the ill-fated city once before, so he had a good idea of what awaited them there. With that experience in mind, he pressed forward with dread toward the staircase. Many scholars had given their lives to unravel the mysteries of ancient Karadun. Not one scholar Keio was aware of had ever completed their work, and every attempt to map Karadun had met with disaster.

Jendo gestured at the rock-hewn stairs that lay ahead. "Are you going to be able to make it up there?"

Keio had been wondering the same thing. He reached up and rubbed the back of his head, which had been aching worse than his stomach ever since the morning.

"I'm going to have to, aren't I?"

Shade turned from the statue to survey him critically. "You are becoming frail," she said without a trace of emotion in her voice. "How much longer until we reach this city?"

Keio let his gaze travel up the side of the mountain, to where the stairs ended at a fortress whose façade had been carved directly into the cliffs themselves, looming thousands of feet above the valley.

"The Tower is somewhere to the south right now," Keio's said. "Maybe a day. Maybe two."

The look Shade gave him spoke volumes of doubt. "You'll never get there. I will be surprised if you make it up the steps."

"I will make it," Keio assured her. "The vortex ends at the base of these cliffs. Once we're beyond that I can use the magic field to ease the sickness, at least long enough to get us there."

Jendo shook his head. "You can't heal the taint."

"I can't cure it," Keio agreed, "but I can slow its progression."

He started forward, walking under the shadow of the Colossus. As he passed beneath its legs, he felt a warm gush of fluid running down his face. He brought his hands up, catching large drops of blood pattering from his nose. He stopped, tilting his head back and holding his nose, trying to get the bleeding under control while his two companions stood watching him. It took some time, longer than it should have, but at last he got the bleeding to stop.

"Let's go before I have to carry you up there," Jendo growled, starting forward with his hands clasped around the straps of his pack.

Shade moved to Keio's side, taking his arm.

"I'm fine," he said, pulling away.

"You are not," Shade snapped. "You are dying, and we can't afford to lose you yet."

Grinding his teeth, Keio allowed her to steady him as they mounted the staircase hewn from the tawny stone of the cliffs. The steps weren't as bad as they looked from the ground. They ascended in a gradual incline, each step longer than it was tall. But even still, the climb was grueling. The staircase went on relentlessly straight ahead, bisecting the cliffs at a consistent angle, rising hundreds of feet above the valley floor. Keio ran out of breath not even a quarter of the way up and had to stop and sit, panting like a dog caught in the heat. His body was covered in a cold sweat, and he shivered as though chilled.

The break didn't seem long enough. Jendo urged him back onto his feet, and Shade gripped his arm and pulled him forward again. He managed another couple hundred steps before his nose started bleeding again, this time much more profusely. They had to pause on the steps while he fought to get the bleeding under control. Exasperated, he decided to test the strength of the magic field, to see if they were out from under it.

As soon as he opened his mind, a bolt of energy slammed into his head that nearly knocked him down the stairs. Keio groaned, clutching his head in his hands, blood raining from his nose. The field was too hot to work with, but it was taming. He thought that maybe, by the time they reached the top of the stairs, he could use it to stop the nosebleeds.

They ate lunch right there on the stairway, then continued their journey up the steps. This time, Shade walked on one side of him while Jendo took his other arm. He grudgingly walked between the two of them, their combined support helping immensely. He made it nearly the rest of the way up the stairs before having to halt again to rest.

"It's not much farther," Jendo said.

Keio sat on a step, leaning back with his elbows on the stair above him. He peered up at the sky through the thin gap between the cliffs. Heavy clouds hung low, moving quickly when viewed against the reference point of the mountains. The air was getting colder, making him shiver harder.

With the help of his companions, he managed to make it the rest of the way to the top of the steps. Once there, he bent over his knees, panting to catch his breath. The bas-relief fortress they had seen from below lay ahead of them. Its entrance was a tunnel that led straight back into the heart of the mountain, guarded by twin stone lions with folded wings, one to either side of the gate.

"Carathiel Fortress," Jendo uttered.

The name provoked a cold feeling of dread that tickled Keio's spine. Of all the many ruins of Karadun, Carathiel Fortress had been studied most extensively, for it was the first of the thirteen fortresses encountered by would-be explorers venturing into the ancient city and likely was the only keep that was truly stable. Few visitors made it past Carathiel's walls to report what they found on the other side. The streets of Karadun were not static. Rather, they shifted over time, so that the likelihood was low of encountering the same fortress or passage in the same place. Such fluidity in structure would have many benefits that Keio could think of, not the least of which would be defensive.

"What lies within?" Shade asked, peering with a fearful look into the darkness of the tunnel.

"Who knows?" Keio answered, for he didn't. Time changed things, and enough time had passed since the last time he had walked Karadun's dim streets that he couldn't vouch for what they would find. He was armored only with the knowledge he had managed to unlock in Akai, a basic understanding of the map as it existed at this moment.

He could only hope it didn't shift again before they reached their destination.

"Let's go."

He pulled himself upright, which was no easy task. Clutching his middle, he started forward into the dim shadows of the tunnel. As the darkness closed over him, it felt like they were walking into a cave. The tunnel was made of arched walls of stone that curved overhead, almost like a sewer. Every so often, a square opening in the ceiling let in light from shafts bored down through the rock of the mountain. The light did little to illuminate more than just a small area beneath the shafts. The space between was cloaked in a thick blanket of darkness.

The sound of their feet echoed loudly off the walls. The air was moist, and it cooled quickly around them. Soon it was chill enough that he could see his breath before his face. The tunnel led straight ahead for hundreds of feet, deep into the heart of the mountain. Keio could almost feel the weight of the rock pressing down on top of them, the weight of an entire mountain and all its thick layers of snow.

As they walked further into the tunnel, the light shafts became fewer and farther between, until eventually they disappeared altogether, and utter darkness encased them. Keio glanced back the way they had come, and saw the entrance to the tunnel now as only a distant point of light.

It was time to try again for the magic field.

He closed his eyes and reached within, but before he could cast his mind out, a beautiful blue-green mist appeared in the passage at their feet. Surprised, Keio glanced at Jendo. The old man didn't acknowledge him, instead turning to start forward again, sending the glowing mist ahead to light their way. With Shade at his side, Keio's started after him.

The long tunnel ran ahead for some distance, at last opening into a chamber that had once been an enormous hall. Stories above, massive chandeliers composed of many concentric iron rings hung from the ceiling, glowing with a hazy light that filled the room, driving back all but the firmest shadows. Keio stared up at them, wondering how many centuries their candles had continued burning.

Jendo let his magelight die. He stood looking upward, mouth open, his gaze crawling over the surface of the walls. The room was enormous, like a cavern. Two waterfalls spilled into it from opposite sides of the room, their water collecting in a reflecting pool that spanned the center of the chamber. To one side, steps led to a high platform, where a canopied throne overlooked the hall.

"What happened to this place?" Shade asked. "Why was it abandoned?"

Keio answered, "The Nerians were a very powerful race of mages whose entire society was sustained by magic. But their creations turned against them, and something bad happened. Something bad enough to drive every inhabitant out of the mountains, never to return. They left all this behind. All of their magic, all of their knowledge—it's all still here."

"Then why hasn't it been plundered after so many centuries?" she asked, moving forward to gaze up at a balcony that appeared to be floating in midair.

"People tried," Keio answered. "No one ever succeeded."

"Why not?"

Keio exchanged ominous looks with Jendo. "Because Karadun was built to hold her secrets close. The entire city is booby-trapped with magical wards. Nearly every person who's ever come here never came back out."

"What about us?" Shade asked.

Keio spread his hands. "Fortunately for us, I'm one of the very few people who managed to escape alive."

38

LACK OF PURPOSE

GIL TOOK THE REST OF HIS MEALS IN HIS ROOM.

When the knock on the door finally came, he was unsurprised. He opened it to find Laith and Jed standing outside in the hallway, armed in breastplates, swords strapped to their waists. He stood for a moment in silence, considering the implications of their arrival. He realized with a grim sense of resolve that he would have no choice but to go with them. This was his decision, he had to remind himself. He had given his word to Ashra, and he intended to keep it.

"The guard is ready to move out," Laith reported. "The Sultana is waiting below, but the Prime Warden would like a word with you before we leave."

Gil gritted his teeth. Andigar Shadeem was the last person he wanted to speak with. He had been hoping for a quiet exit, so he would never have to look upon the man again. That obviously wasn't going to happen.

"Let me get my things," he said with a sigh and closed the door.

He pulled on his boots and strapped *Thar'gon* to his waist. He thought about the armor both Laith and Jed wore, and regretted he didn't have his own. This was war they were marching off to, the same war he had left, and it hadn't gotten any less dangerous. The Lyceum's two Battlemages were more prepared for it than he was, but Gil wouldn't stoop to begging Andigar Shadeem for one damn thing—even if it was a life-saving thing.

Fully dressed, he joined both Laith and Jed in the hallway. They led him down to the stairs and corridors of the ziggurat, all the way to the Prime Warden's throne room. But, Gil discovered, Shadeem's throne was empty. The two men led him past the dais, toward a doorway in the far wall that looked like a servants' entrance. There, Laith motioned for Gil to enter, then stood back against the wall with Jed.

Moving forward cautiously, Gil nodded his thanks at the two Battlemages, then knocked upon the door.

"You may enter," issued a low, baritone voice from the other side.

Gil obeyed. Entering the room, he found himself in what looked like the Prime Warden's personal quarters. It was a large sitting room just as elaborately decorated as his own guestroom, but more than twice the size. Gil took a step forward, his gaze wandering the walls. The feel of the place conveyed a wealth of power far beyond anything in Gil's experience. Andigar Shadeem stood waiting for him in the center of the room. Seeing Gil, he moved to a chair, beckoning him forward to sit next to him.

"Thank you for coming," he said pleasantly. "Please have a seat."

Gil complied, removing the morning star from his belt and setting it down upon the floor. He sat studying the Prime Warden, taking in Shadeem's richly embroidered robe, the same worn by the other mages of the Lyceum. A necklace of many draped chains hung down his chest, sparkling in the lantern light.

Sitting back in his chair with his legs spread, hands resting on his thighs, the Prime Warden told Gil, "I wanted to tell you that I'm sorry things didn't work out the way you were hoping they would."

"I'd say they worked out fine," Gil responded tightly. "Ashra has secured her empire and gained a husband. And it looks like the people of Malikar have found themselves a new champion."

He couldn't keep the rancor out of his voice—not that he was trying very hard. He couldn't conceal his loathing for the man. He wondered what it was about Shadeem that provokes such hatred in him. It wasn't just Ashra. He was jealous, true, but he didn't think he would have this kind of reaction if the Prime Warden was just another suitor. There was something more going on, something far deeper. He wished he could put his finger on it, but he couldn't.

"I mean, I'm sorry things didn't work out for *you*," the Prime Warden clarified, his voice as soft and smooth as silk.

"I had no expectations," Gil said, his grip tightening on the armrests of his chair.

The Prime Warden smiled. "I'm happy to hear that. When this war is over, I do want you to reconsider my offer. You can't go back home. You're a Battlemage; you have but one purpose. What will you do?"

"I don't know."

Andigar Shadeem stood from his chair and, turning his back on Gil, paced across the room to the hearth, where he stood for a moment staring down into the flames with his hands clasped behind his back. "We need someone with your training. Someone with your skills." He turned back to look at Gil. "You would have a good life here. You would have a purpose. When this war is over... consider it."

"I'll think on it," Gil lied.

Shadeem flashed him a friendly smile, as though

completely ignorant of the depths of Gil's hatred. "That's all I ask."

Gil took that as the end of the conversation. He stood from his chair and made for the door. As he moved past the Prime Warden, Shadeem offered his hand. "Go in peace, my friend."

Gil looked down at his hand, hesitating, not wanting to take it. But he reminded himself that he had no real reason to despise this man. He had to admit, the Prime Warden could be acting out of nothing but sincerity, and every bad feeling he had could be the product of his own jealous imagination.

Rigidly, he shook the man's hand.

Exiting the room, he followed Jed and Laith down to the ziggurat's portal chamber. There, soldiers of the City Guard were already waiting to accompany them. The transfer portal gleamed from beneath a cross-vaulted arch. It wavered and beckoned, its dancing light casting harsh shadows across the walls.

They waited for Ashra.

It was long minutes before she arrived in Shadeem's company. Gil stood seething, waiting and watching as they took their time about saying goodbyes. Shadeem held Ashra by the shoulders, pulling her close, kissing her forehead. Gil averted his eyes, unable to watch, feeling like someone had just poured a bucket full of cold water over his head. His gaze went to the light of the transfer portal, wanting nothing more than to plunge into it.

"You take with you my heart," Shadeem said, smiling fondly into Ashra's eyes. "Come back to me soon."

In response, Ashra kissed his cheek. She turned toward the portal, her eyes avoiding Gil. Clenching his jaw, Gil moved to her side and took her hand with no small amount of sadness.

They entered the transfer portal together. The world shivered and shifted, the light of the portal swelling to a blinding brilliance.

Gil let go of Ashra's hand. He stepped out from the light of the portal, finding himself in what looked like a large, spherical cave carved out of black stone, the walls set with glittering crystals that shimmered like stars.

More soldiers had arrived ahead of them, a highly trained escort Shadeem had sent with them to protect his betrothed. The transfer portal glowed again, and Laith and Jed came through. Ignoring Ashra's presence, Gil moved past her to the door.

He left the portal chamber and walked out into the light of afternoon, gazing out across a snow-covered valley rimmed by high cliffs that were blackened by fire. Turning, he saw that he was standing at the base of a thin pillar of rock hundreds of feet high ending in a flat peak high above.

Orien's Finger.

He'd never seen the landmark before, but the sight of it filled him with trepidation and awe. The pillar of rock had a Circle of Convergence at its peak, the one Darien Lauchlin had used to summon a firestorm that had immolated tens of thousands of soldiers. Gil stared around at the charred cliffs, now understanding them better. An empty stillness clung to the air, an eerie quiet that spoke of death and graves. Gil shivered. This was a haunting place. He wanted to leave it.

He walked away from the pillar of rock and out into the grasslands beyond, where the rest of the guards Shadeem had loaned them awaited on horseback. He made his way to the front of the column, where their own mounts stood ready for them. Within minutes, they were mounted, and the order was given to move out.

Looking out across the plain, Gil looked to the east, toward the ocean and Bel Arun. He wasn't sure, but he thought the distant brown haze on the horizon might be smoke.

39

THE THIRTEEN FORTRESSES

KEIO HELD A BLOOD-SOAKED RAG TO HIS NOSE, WISHING WITH ALL his heart that he could stop and rest. But he couldn't. They didn't dare stop, not here between fortresses in the open city, which was never a safe place to be, even in the best of times. And this definitely was not the best of times. Much had changed in the past eight thousand years.

The city existed in a permanent state of eternal twilight, as though time here never moved. Yet Karadun was showing its age more than he'd thought it would. The last time he'd walked these ancient streets, the city had already been abandoned for thousands of years, yet had experienced little deterioration because of the extent of its magical infrastructure.

This time was different.

Chunks of ragged buildings littered the streets, along with various other scattered debris. There was no vegetation or animals to be seen; Karadun was like a ghost city. After treading blocks full of echoing stillness, a slow, creeping doubt begun working its way into Keio's skin. Looking around at the remains of shattered buildings, he realized that it wasn't age that had destroyed them, but rather something else.

Something had gone wrong.

Very, very wrong.

The eternal twilight hadn't changed since the last time he'd been there. What was different was the amount of destruction. It was almost as though the city was rotting from the inside out. The buildings looked like hollow corpses, decaying where they stood. They weren't weathered by the elements; rather, it was like some disease was rotting them.

The street they followed crossed a flat valley between two ridges of the mountain. The air was moist with roving mist that made it hard to see more than a few blocks away. Out there in the open between fortresses, Keio felt exposed and vulnerable. There were things in the city that were better left alone or altogether avoided. Judging from the deterioration of the buildings, he wasn't confident that those things had remained contained.

The people of ancient Neria had been a race of mages with an unquenchable thirst for knowledge and not enough sense to know when to stop looking for it. They had created things of magical technology that had grown beyond their understanding, and they had lost their mastery over them. At some point, their creations had gotten out of hand, and had risen against them. There were reasons why magic shouldn't be relied on too heavily, especially for mundane tasks. It had a way of taking on a life of its own, and that life was not always in the interest of its creators. In Karadun, the Nerian's magical creations had started serving themselves instead of their masters. The resulting holocaust had ended the Nerian Empire.

Keio was not pleased that the Tower of Morning had chosen to make its appearance in Karadun. Of all the places on the continent, this was the one that had the greatest capacity for disaster.

Shade came to walk next to him, appearing greatly concerned that his nose was still bleeding. "It hasn't stopped?"

Pulling the cloth away, Keio confirmed that the blood on it was still fresh. He replaced the cloth and shook his head.

She glanced back, motioning Jendo toward them. "Can you try healing him?"

The old man pursed his lips and sent a sour glance her way. "There's nothing I can do. All magic can do is work with what's already there. But his tissues are so far gone, they don't know what they're supposed to be anymore."

It was a good way to describe what was happening to him, Keio figured. He was a competent healer himself, though not as good as Jendo, who had studied in the greatest school of healing the world had ever known. If, between the two of them, they couldn't keep him on his feet, then nothing would. Which made his sense of urgency all the more desperate. He had to reach the Tower of Morning before his body failed him completely.

"How much farther is it?" Shade asked.

That was the problem. He couldn't say. Their journey through Karadun could take anywhere from hours to several days, depending upon how the fortresses aligned.

"We probably won't be getting there today," he answered.

He took the rag away from his nose and wrung the blood from it. The look on Shade's face as she watched the blood splatter to the street conveyed her doubts. She didn't think he would live to see the next day, and he was starting to agree with her. A growing panic was building in his gut, gripping him harder every hour that went by.

"Up ahead." Jendo pointed. "Isn't that another fortress?"

Peering ahead through the fog, Keio made out a tall, crenellated curtainwall.

"It is. But I have no idea which one."

"Does it matter?" Shade asked.

"It does. Some of the fortresses are more hostile than others. Which ones we'll encounter in which order all depends on how they line up each time the city rearranges itself. If this is one of the corrupted fortresses, we will have to move through it as fast as we can."

"We need a place to shelter for the night," Jendo said. "Sooner rather than later."

Keio grinned breathlessly, looking up at the permanent twilight. "I'm afraid this is as much night as were going to get."

"You know what I mean." Jendo glanced at him in irritation.

Shade asked, "What is the danger of staying outside?"

"There are things here that rove the streets," Keio answered, even though he was out of breath. "The kinds of things that should have never been created in the first place. If we run into them, we'll be sorely pressed to defend ourselves. Most of them are capable of wielding far more magic than either Jendo or me. But most of the fortresses here have defenses against them. That's why we need to find a fortress that hasn't been compromised."

The keep ahead of them was growing larger and more intimidating, its walls towering above the streets. Its white turrets rose several stories higher than the curtainwall, looking, for the most part, intact. Whatever evils that haunted Karadun had left this particular fortress pretty much alone. The looks of it gave Keio hope.

The moat gate was open, admitting them into the castle's outer ward. Inside the courtyard, it was hard to tell that the fortress had ever been abandoned. Everything seemed fresh, although still. Keio walked forward, his boots scuffing the dust under his feet. There was clean hay spilled in the dirt next to a building that once might have been a stable. The whole place looked eerily ready to receive its population back.

"Time doesn't move here at all, does it?" Jendo asked.

"No." Feeling suddenly weak, Keio motioned toward one of the castle's tall turrets. "I think I'll ... I'll..."

His legs gave out from under him.

Shade didn't catch him in time. He felt to his knees then collapsed forward to the ground. They rolled him over, and he watched through a swirling fog as both Shade and Jendo bent over him, speaking frantically, their voices fading in and out. The old man had his eyes closed, his hands pressed against Keio's chest. He could feel a tingling warmth spreading through him, the feeling of Jendo's power creeping through his body. But he could tell from the sluggishness of the healing that it wasn't doing all it should.

Jendo opened his eyes and sat back with a grim expression. "You're not going to make it another day. I doubt you'll make it through the night."

Keio felt too dizzy to really process what the man was saying. He closed his eyes, wanting just a moment to lay there and rest.

Taking his arm, Jendo shook him roughly. "Get up. You can't sleep here."

Between Jendo and Shade, they hauled him to his feet and walked him forward. He had a hard time keeping his legs moving as they steered him toward the entrance to the tower. He lurched like a drunken man, staggering as much as walking.

Overhead, the swirling mist flickered as though illuminated by lightning. In the distance, there came a high-pitched screech. Shade glanced back then hurried forward with a fearful expression.

The tower door was made of wood that had been partially eaten by dry rot. Shade tugged hard at it, but it didn't want to give. Jendo came forward and gave it a good jerk. Trembling on its hinges, the massive door finally relinquished its hold on the doorframe and groaned open, kicking up a swirl of dust into the air that made Keio cough.

They got him across the threshold into the base of the tower, but that was as far as he could go. There, they let him collapse to the floor, where he curled into a ball, clutching his aching middle. Shade started to work on setting up a space where they could shelter for the night. Fortunately, there was a large hearth built into the wall at one end of the room. Shade created firewood by kicking apart broken furniture. While she built the fire, Jendo made himself comfortable, leaning up against a wall with a book in his hand.

Keio lay there until his head cleared and his stomach felt good enough to sit up. But when he raised his hands, he didn't like the looks of them. His skin was pink and blotchy, like he had spent too much time in the sun. Underneath, he could see the sinuous pattern of his veins beneath his skin, which looked more prominent than usual. Curious, he pressed his fingers firmly against his arm. When he pulled them away, the pads of his fingertips were red with fresh blood.

Keio shivered. He was bleeding through his pores, which meant the blood vessels in his skin were breaking down. Jendo was right. He wouldn't survive the night, and that thought brought despair.

Leaning back against the wall, he stared deeply into the flames of the hearth. He was terribly thirsty, and his breathing came shallow and rapid, which made him afraid he was also bleeding on the inside. He closed his eyes and reached within, probing himself with his mind. He almost wished he hadn't. His organs were shutting down. Concentrating hard, he tried summoning enough magic to salvage what he could. It didn't do much good, but it was better than nothing. Perhaps, if he could keep up the concentration to maintain a consistent supply of healing, he could push his death back a few hours.

Shade walked toward him, carrying a cup of water. He accepted it with gratitude, but needed her assistance just to hold it. He drank every drop before handing the cup back to her. She sat down next to him. Taking a fresh cloth, she used it to dab the sweat from his brow. She gasped when the cloth came away red.

"Your skin is bleeding without being cut." she whispered.

"I'll make it," Keio insisted, although there was little conviction in his tone.

Sitting back, she looked at him with fear in her eyes. "I don't know which I'd rather see: you living to reach the containment crystal, or death taking you before you get there. I think I'd rather death take you now."

That didn't surprise him. She had never seen worth in him, which he understood. "You see me as a threat to everything you love," he said. "I'm surprised you've helped me get this far, in all honesty. Why have you?"

Shade lifted her chin defiantly. "Because you were once the Custodian of Suheylu Ra. Your people must have had great faith in you to put you in that position. You made a grave mistake that had tremendous repercussions, but you must have learned from that mistake. You have been here now for days. You've walked across this land and experienced the damage you caused. You've also come to know Jendo and me. You know that we're not evil, and you know neither one of us deserves an eternity in hell. You're a good man, Keio, and you mean well." She drew in a deep breath. "I don't think you'll do it."

He was feeling weak and didn't know if he had the strength to argue. But he had a stubborn streak, so he decided to try. "Why do you think the Turan Khar deserve to live? All they do is conquer, and what they can't conquer they slaughter. That is their way. That has *always* been their way. How can you support that?"

"You're wrong." Jendo lay aside his book and rose, walking over to them. He crouched next to Shade, staring at Keio as though he were a rat cowering on the floor. "How long did the Turan Khar exist before they attack Shira?"

"I don't remember exactly. Hundreds of years."

Jendo nodded slowly. "And in those hundreds of years, they were the most peaceful nation on earth. Am I correct?"

Keio shook his head weakly. "That doesn't mean they'll just go back to being peaceful. They've become vampires, living off the blood of others."

Jendo made a dismissive gesture with his hand. "Only out of necessity. Do Shade and I look like vampires to you? Think about it. If there's even one small chance that you're wrong about us, then you know you can't go through with it. It wouldn't be morally right."

With that, he walked back to the fire and his book in a limping gait. Keio stared after him, wondering why he hadn't noticed Jendo's limp before and wondering where it had come from. He tried remembering the journey across the city, but could conjure only dim recollections. He was exhausted.

He turned back to Shade. "If it's possible... If you'd let me... I'd like to see your face again."

Her brow pinched in anger and suspicion. "Why?"

"I just want to see you again," he whispered.

Her stare and her expression did not falter as she reached up and untucked the corner of the fabric that held her veil in place, letting it fall aside. Her eyes held his in an iron grip that didn't waver.

Keio sucked in a breath. Not because of the twisted features, the scars and lumps, the grotesque deformation of her lips, all of which, strangely, didn't extend to her eyes. Shade's eyes were left perfectly unblemished. Perfectly beautiful. He couldn't believe he hadn't noticed that before.

"You think I am ugly," Shade accused, still holding his gaze.

"No." Lifting his hand, he touched her scarred cheek. "Even all this can't make a beautiful person ugly."

A lump formed in his throat and started squeezing. For Jendo was right—neither of his two companions deserved an eternity in hell.

"Thank you," he said, dropping his hand.

Shade replaced the veil, tucking it in. And then she rose

and left him, moving back across the room to join Jendo by the fire.

Tears gathered in Keio's eyes, though he tried to force them back. But the weight of his failure was crushing, and it squeezed the moisture right out of him. He raised a hand to his face, wiping his eyes.

When his fingers came away bloody, he wept harder.

40

SULTANA

The sun had already set, the plains stretching dark and flat beneath a sky streaked with melancholic hues. The riders that went before them were but black silhouettes against the sunset, and those that came behind trailed like a dark rope. Before them was Bel Arun, its high walls and towers smothered by sunset, the lights of its windows reflected by the dark waters of the ocean.

To the south, across the plain, were other lights—the lights of campfires of the Army of Chamsbrey, only a half day's march from the city walls. Gil took in the size of the army with trepidation. There were far more campfires than he had been expecting. There was more than just one army down there. Another kingdom's forces must have arrived.

Gil looked back down the small column of guards Shadeem had provided them, which seemed suddenly thin and frail. He caught Ashra's eye and, just for a moment, they exchanged a look that conveyed an entire conversation's worth of doubts and regrets. He broke his gaze away, regretting the slip, vowing not to let it happen again.

Wrapping the reins of his horse around his fist, he kicked

the animal to a trot, riding ahead to where Jed and Laith rode at the column's head. Laith acknowledged him with a nod, while Jed merely glanced at him with an irritated look. Their eyes were drawn to the encampment to the south whose size dwarfed the city it was preparing to consume. Their meager column of guardsmen would add little support to Bel Arun's defenses. They followed the road down off the hills, a thin sliver of moon setting behind them over the mountains to the west.

It took them another hour to gain the city gate, which was already closed and barred for the night. Gil rode out ahead of the column, taking stock of the city's fortifications. Bel Arun was guarded by a series of double walls reinforced by circular towers and protruding bastions, with a large fortress that protected the entrance to the port. A flooded moat ran around the outside section of the walls, which towered eighty or so feet above the surrounding plains.

The city gate was warded by towers and accessible only by a drawbridge that had already been hoisted for the night. Soldiers patrolled the walls above the gate, while others looked down from the tops of the surrounding turrets. Fires were lit along the tops of the walls, providing light and warmth for the defenders, as well as flames to ignite incendiary weapons.

They looked like they knew what they were doing. But seeing the size of the army approaching, Gil doubted all their preparations would be enough. Bel Arun was simply not large enough to mount an adequate defense against an army that size.

He drew his horse up just beyond the moat and simply waited as, overhead, soldiers scurried into position above the gate.

"Hoy there!" someone called down to him. "Who the hell are you, and why the fuck are you here?"

Gil grinned. He shouted up at the gate, "Grand Master Gil Archer! I'd like to have a word with your commander!"

He waited then, as there seem to be some disagreement on the wall about exactly what to do about him. He'd wondered what the commanders would think, seeing a small army approaching their walls, demanding to be let in. He couldn't blame them for their caution.

There was some shifting of bodies at the top of the wall. At last, a man came forward to view him through one of the crenels. After a moment, he removed his helmet and waved down at him. Recognizing Demir, Gil smiled in relief and waved back. Demir motioned him forward, pointing next to him on the wall.

For a moment, Gil was uncertain what he meant. Then he realized the man must have remembered *Thar'gon's* transfer ability.

Climbing down from his horse, Gil raised the weapon and focused on a small stretch of the battlements to the left of the gate where no one was standing. He'd always wondered what would happen if he materialized in the same space as a person —or in the middle of a wall. So far, that hadn't happened. Perhaps the talisman had some safeguard built into it.

Closing his eyes, he whispered, *"Vergis."*

The ground shifted, and suddenly he stood on the walkway above the gate.

Soldiers jerked back, raising their weapons in shock, but lowered them again as Demir scrambled forward, catching Gil up in a mighty bearhug, exclaiming, *"Ishilzeri!* As ugly as you are, you are a beautiful sight!"

Demir let him go, and Gil turned to look at the man standing beside him, a capable-looking officer with a white-streaked beard that squirmed out from beneath the shadows of his helmet.

"Grand Master." He effected a stiff bow, for the Malikari

never did anything without great formality. "I pray you are not here to negotiate our surrender?"

"I'm not." Gil nodded in the direction of the small column of men he had brought with him from Bryn Calazar. "The Sultana has secured some reinforcements. With your permission, we'd like to bring them into the city."

The man's face pinched with anxiety. "Is the Sultana with you? Is she safe?"

"She is," Gil assured him. "Now, let's *keep* her safe by lowering the drawbridge."

"Of course. At once!"

The officer jerked a bow, then turned and started shouting commands down to his men in the courtyard below. Immediately, the wall beneath Gil's feet trembled, and a loud clattering of chains rattled the air. The drawbridge shuddered downward with a dragon's deep groan, spanning the width of the moat.

Satisfied, Gil nodded his thanks at the commander and whispered *Thar'gon's* Word of Command. A second later, he was standing beside his mount. Gil steadied himself against the side of the horse, for a moment feeling dizzy and disoriented from the two rapid transfers. Then, pulling himself into the saddle, he rode back and drew to a stop in front of Ashra, who sat her mount at the head of the column next to Laith and Jed. Nodding at her curtly, he reported, "The gate stands open, Your Majesty."

Ashra dipped her chin. "Thank you, Grand Master."

The column started forward. Gil turned his horse to ride alongside the other two Battlemages. He rode in silence, listening to the creek of his saddle, his gaze focused on the fires burning on the walls while his stomach felt like it was chewing rocks.

They passed over the drawbridge, their horses' hooves clattering over the boards, and entered the city by way of the arching gate. They left the bulk of their men in the courtyard, while soldiers came forward to guide Ashra and her entourage to the main keep.

As they made their way through the narrow city streets, Gil couldn't help admiring the freshness of the buildings that surrounded them, each constructed of seamless limestone, all built within the past twenty years. Bel Arun's streets ran along narrow terraces that tumbled gracefully toward the ocean.

They dismounted at the gate of the fortress and were escorted to the main hall, where they were met by the resident ruler of the city, a grotesquely fat man in a velvet cape, who stood from his throne and nearly toppled over in a pathetic attempt to kneel before his Queen. At the same time, every person gathered in the hall fell to their knees and abased themselves before the woman who was both mage and sovereign.

Walking gracefully forward, Ashra mounted the steps to the dais and claimed the throne the fat man had relinquished. She sat back in her seat, looking quite at home, her firm gaze sweeping over the room. At last, her stare fixed on Gil and held there. It took him a minute to realize what Ashra was waiting for, and when he did, he felt his cheeks heat.

Before the woman he had sworn his allegiance to, he went to his knees and bowed forward, prostrating himself the way he would before only a Prime Warden, the other mages around him following him to the ground. It was the Malikari way, to treat every mage as though they were monarchs. Ashra's status, especially, demanded no less than complete obeisance from all present in the room.

"Arise."

All within the chamber rose to their feet and stood in silence, awaiting her command.

Ashra turned to the corpulent governor of the keep. "You are Neval son of Mesut, Bey of Bel Arun and Sanajuk Province?"

The man bowed as deeply as the thick rolls of his belly would allow. "I am, Your Majesty."

"Thank you for welcoming us into your city," Ashra said.

"You came and the gods brought you!" The man gestured expensively. "The armies of the Kingdoms are but a day's march from our gates!"

"I have brought with me reinforcements from Bryn Calazar," Ashra informed him. "And, better yet, I have brought three strong Battlemages to defend your walls." She raised her hand to indicate Gil and the two men who stood at his side.

The governor's breath caught, his eyes widening. *"Ishilzeri!* The gods have listened to my prayers! I will send my officers to have your men situated within the walls, and I will order my kitchens to prepare enough food to fill every stomach, for surely the battle will be brought to us tomorrow. And I beg you, my Lady, to join us in a feast of gratitude tonight."

Ashra inclined her head graciously. "A most generous offer, but let us save our stores for the men who will fight tomorrow."

The governor's disappointment was palpable. "Then I will have my servants escort you to my finest rooms."

Ashra raised her hand, stopping him. "We are all very tired, but there is no time to rest. Assemble your commanders. We have a battle to plan."

The governor bowed again, then turned and started issuing commands in terse Malikari. The hall was quickly cleared and tables brought forward to gather around. Within minutes, officers began trickling in, slowly filling the chamber.

The governor waved forward a man in a tall hat, whose uniform dripped with decorations. Everyone fell silent as the officer approached the dais and prostrated himself before his Queen.

"This is Emdad ul-Calazi, my Captain of the Watch," the governor announced.

"Greetings, Captain," Ashra said. "Allow me to introduce

you to my own commander, Grand Master Gil Archer. You may report to him."

The captain moved around the long table and, approaching Gil, bowed humbly before him. "I and my men are at your disposal, Grand Master."

Gil glanced at Ashra. After all that had transpired, he hadn't expected her to put him in charge of the city's defenses. But, looking at the captain and his men awaiting his orders, his feeling of shock dissipated rapidly, replaced by gratitude. He glanced back at Ashra with a look of thanks.

Then maps were spread out across the tables, and all thoughts of anything but war quickly disappeared from his mind.

Hours later, Gil finally felt he had a good enough understanding of the city's defenses to know for certain they were going to fail. Even with Bryn Calazar's reinforcements, they did not have enough soldiers to adequately man Bel Arun's walls. If they were going to successfully defend the city, they would have to do it with magic, not numbers.

So he decided to get some sleep.

He thanked the captain and the governor and ordered Laith and Jed to find a bed, knowing getting even a few hours of rest was the best way his mages could prepare for the coming battle. Upon his request, the governor provided them with guestrooms. The room he was issued was modest and practical, containing only a sturdy bed, a washstand, and a private but drafty garderobe that emptied into the moat far below. Exhausted, he sat down on the bed and pulled his boots off.

A knock at the door interrupted his action.

He didn't want to answer it, figuring that whoever it was

could only bring problems. Vexed, he tossed his boots on the floor and opened the door.

It was Ashra.

Seeing her, Gil froze. She had changed out of the gown she had worn on the ride, and stood before him in a blue robe that covered only a thin linen shift. She appeared hesitant, her kohl-lined eyes staring at him intently.

She asked, "May I come in?"

"Of course." He stepped back out of her way, opening the door wider.

She moved by him, her gaze wandering over the walls and the scant furniture in the room, finally coming to rest on him with a look much softer than it had been earlier. Sometime during the night, her eyes had lost their fiery spark.

"I came to say thank you," she said. "You didn't have to come but you did." She licked her lips, looking intensely uncomfortable, as if she didn't want to be there. He couldn't blame her. He couldn't figure out why she was.

Gil brought a hand up to rub his eyes, already wishing she would leave. All her presence did was drive the hurt deeper. He said wearily, "I already told you. I cast my lot with yours."

Ashra nodded, for a moment looking like she was going to leave. But then she hesitated.

"I don't love him."

Her words stung Gil like a slap. He stiffened, feeling hot and raw with anger. Fighting it back, he said tightly, "I get it. At your level, marriages are political."

She stared into his face, her eyes pleading forgiveness. "This union will provide Malikar with a Lyceum of its own and a powerful ally to the north. It's too important for me to pass up just because I love another man."

"I under—"

The word caught in his throat and stuck there.

Gil froze, every muscle in his body locked rigid with hurt. She might as well have taken a dagger and twisted it into him.

"Why are you telling me this?" he whispered.

Tears spilled down her cheeks, her lips trembling. "Because I wanted you to know."

Gil closed his eyes, shaking his head and fighting back tears of his own. "Well, now I know." He drew in a weary breath. "Only, it just makes it worse."

"It doesn't have to."

He frowned. "What do you mean?"

She took his hands. "Political marriages aren't meant to be monogamous."

It took Gil a moment to realize what she was offering. When he did, his lips curled in revulsion. "No." He jerked back from her, anger coursing hot in his veins. "I can't share you with him."

He wanted to rail against the injustice of it all. More than anything else in the world, he loved her, and now he knew she loved him back. And yet it didn't matter. Ashra was royalty, and there was simply no place in her life for someone like him. He felt the hot sting of tears on his face. Ashamed, he turned away from her.

Ashra caught his shoulder, gently turning him back around. She moved in close, gazing deeply into his face, her eyes pleading with his.

"Then just give me tonight," she whispered.

Gil winced. It was too much.

He almost ordered her out.

But then he broke.

He took her in his arms and kissed her. The kiss ended softly, gracefully. He pulled back, his eyes searching hers. What he saw in her face was everything he could ever want and everything he couldn't have.

Damn it all.

He gathered her in and kissed her again, passionately. Her hands slid around his neck, the soft curves of her body pressed against him. She was beautiful and untamable, but in that one moment, she was his. He knew he couldn't keep her, but that just added to the urgency.

He gathered her in his arms and laid her on the bed. Lying beside her, he let his lips explore hers, his hands stroking the full length of her body.

He pulled back just enough to gaze into her eyes. He could have stayed that way forever, just looking at her. In her eyes, Gil saw the same longing that he felt.

Caressing her cheek, he whispered, "I love you."

"I love you too," she replied.

She pressed her mouth to his in a kiss that wandered across his jaw and found its way to his neck. He pulled his clothes off then helped her out of hers, collapsing on top of her. Her body felt luxurious beneath him, naked and soft, her breath warm against his neck, her breasts firm beneath his hands.

He paused, trembling. "Are you sure this is what you want?"

"Yes," she whispered.

Reaching down, she pulled him inside her.

41

SHADOWS OF THE GLOAM

JENDO WOKE THEM EARLY, AT WHAT SHOULD HAVE BEEN THE HOUR before dawn, had dawn ever occurred in this place. Keio felt better. The rest had done him good, but more than that, the frequent healings Jendo had applied to him during the night seemed to have bought him an extra day. He no longer had a metallic taste on his tongue, and blood no longer leaked from his skin. He even managed a small appetite when Shade offered him cheese and bread. He ate hesitantly, fearful of how his body might react. When the food stayed down fine, he was relieved.

They left the fortress through the keep's eastern turret. The tower didn't face east anymore, as far as Keio could tell, although it was impossible to tell the true direction. Outside, the city was still encased in permanent twilight. There was no wind, and the clouds hung still overhead. The buildings around them cast no shadows, for there was no light behind them. Keio wondered what the source of the ambient light was. It came from everywhere and nowhere.

He stood in the street, taking his time about determining their course. There were few reference points that he could recognize, but at last he found one that he thought he could trust: another one of the city's great fortresses, high up on a cliff overlooking one of the mountain's high passes. He thought he knew which keep it was: Arangel, the Moonlit Keep. He had seen it before during his last trip to the city. Back then, Arangel had appeared closer to Karadun's gates. But, just like everything else around them, Arangel's location had shifted.

As they cross the city toward the fortress, the silence and stillness seemed to deepen around them, and an uneasy feeling grew within Keio's chest. They walked down a street that had once been covered by great windows of colored glass that had extended for many city blocks. Broken glass littered the streets, often at sharp angles. They were forced to pick their way carefully through the jagged slivers, which slowed their progress drastically.

Keio heard a shuddering, inhuman wail that sounded like it came from the mouth of a tortured giant.

"What was that?" Shade gasped, turning in place and peering about sharply.

Keio halted and looked back the way they had come, his eyes scanning the street. The fortress they had taken shelter in was gone. Mysteriously, another fortress had taken its place, this one made of dark stone, with sharp and narrow features, architecture that was characteristic of a later period.

The city had shifted again beneath their feet.

Whirling back around, he glanced up at the cliff and saw that the fortress there had also changed. In place of the Moonlit Keep, a different fortress had appeared above them on the mountainside.

Keio's insides went cold.

Above them upon the cliff, a towering spire of dark granite had appeared, its sides encrusted with fortifications and turrets. The top of the monolith had been dislodged from the rest and was hovering hundreds of feet above the highest towers, bound there by heavy chains that anchored it to the rest of the fortress. Upon that floating rock blazed a shining beacon that glowed brighter and more radiant than the sun: the containment crystal.

Staring up at the Tower of Morning, Keio shivered. The map room had told him it would appear here, but he had been almost afraid to believe it. Even now, part of him wanted to doubt the tower's reality. A breeze came up from out of nowhere, increasing to a frigid wind that lashed his hair against his face. The wind had a smell to it that he recognized. Sweetly pungent, like the odor in the air after a stab of lightning.

"Hurry," he barked, and started toward the opening of a side street.

He couldn't run; his body was too damaged, and there was too much sharp glass on the ground. Sensing the danger, Jendo surged ahead of him, picking up a metal rod from the ground and using it like a staff to knock jagged shards of glass out of their way.

"There's something behind us," Shade called, glancing back.

Keio gripped her arm. "Don't look. Just keep going."

He wasn't sure what was behind them, but just as Suheylu Ra had been protected by the Watchers, Karadun had been protected by magical sentries. But somewhere along the way, something had gone wrong, and Karadun's guardians had turned against her. Unlike the Watchers, they were still operational, which explained why so few people who entered Karadun had ever made it back.

"There!" Keio pointed toward the end of the street. "We will make our stand there."

Jendo hurried forward with his metal staff, while Keio limped after him, leaning heavily on Shade. The wind was forceful, pushing at their backs as though eager to help. But Keio knew better. That foul-smelling wind was not their ally.

They reach the cliff at the end of the street and turned, putting their backs against it. The clouds had thickened, threatening a downpour. Thunder rumbled, shuddering the ground, and ragged lightning speared down in jagged forks.

The road beneath them trembled. Little fragments of glass started jittering, and suddenly the entire street resonated with the sound of tinkling glass, like thousands of tiny windchimes chiming together all at once. An enormous discharge of lightning crackled across the sky, followed by a deafening peal of thunder that made him flinch.

Then *it* appeared.

He had no name for it, and yet he recognized it when he saw it. There was nothing corporeal to define the sentry; it was a moving shadow that emerge from the fortress behind them and drew slowly toward them up the center of the street. He might not have noticed it at all, had he not been looking for it.

The sentry that stalked them had no physical body; it was an object of pure shadow. Lightning struck it, and for a moment, a glow of ionized air haloed its form, giving it an almost definite shape. The gleam of energy lasted only a second and then was gone, absorbed into the body of the shadow-guardian. What the creature would do with that energy, Keio couldn't guess, but he feared it greatly. Against such a monstrosity, they didn't have the power to defend themselves, should it choose to attack.

And he had no doubt that it would.

Somehow, the guardians of Karadun had been alerted to their presence. There was no running from something like that. No fighting it, either.

Time had run out for them, and he was down to only one last choice.

He glanced toward his two companions, his gaze clawing at their faces in indecision, wishing he could peer deeper inside, deep down into their souls. He needed more time to be certain, lest he make the wrong decision. He wanted to scream. He wanted to wail. He wanted to rail against fate, not that it would do any good.

When two more sentries appeared alongside the first, he wanted to cry.

But then Shade took his hand.

"I have faith in you," she whispered.

He didn't know why she'd say such a thing, at such a moment, but it didn't matter. Her misplaced faith in him was enough to seal his decision.

Closing his eyes, Keio Matu opened himself wide to the *A'isan*. Then he reached into Jendo and seized the old man's power, claiming it for himself.

"What are you doing?" Jendo cried.

But Keio couldn't respond. He stood frozen in the grip of a crushing maelstrom of emotions, the collective uproar of an entire society astonished by his unexpected appearance in the middle of it.

His mind reverberated with the clamor of myriad voices that cried out together then faded slowly into silence, giving way to a burgeoning whisper of hope. He didn't want to open himself wider than he already was, but it was impossible not to. At first, they merely trickled in, these numerous souls, pressing their spirits against his in eager welcome. Gradually, he became aware that there was nothing to fear. He opened himself wider, letting them in faster, until he was carried away by a flood of joy and welcoming acceptance. Every doubt and every fear he'd ever had was erased completely, until all that was left was boundless empowerment.

As the tide of emotions slowly receded, one remained: the heartfelt gratitude of an old man who had almost given up hope for him.

Keio Matu turned to face the shadow-guardians of Karadun with galvanized determination, drawing on both Jendo's might and his own, their combined power bleeding from his body in a shimmering aura.

The shadow-guardians swept toward them, blotting out the twilight, sucking the light out of the air. Keio raised his arms, meeting shadow with magic. Thunder shook the ground, and an explosion of sparks detonated above them, quickly gobbled up by darkness. Shade screamed, throwing her hands up to ward her face.

Using every scrap of power he could summon from Jendo, Keio wove a web of light around them all, then turned the remainder into an attack.

The guardians roared like enraged demons, bleeding together like ink to coalesce into one terrible force that gobbled up every drop of energy Keio threw at it. Hungrily, they attacked his light web, rending it like wolves ravaging a kill.

Realizing his error, Keio quailed. He stood for a moment paralyzed, at a loss for what to do. For now he understood what he was up against, why no mage had ever survived a confrontation with the shadow-guardians of Karadun. They were creatures of living magic, and they *fed* on magic. He could throw the entire collective power of the Khar Unity at them, and they would only grow stronger.

Shivering in terror, Keio realized that all the magic in the world wouldn't save them. He couldn't use magic to fight magic.

Then a thought slammed into him so hard it knocked the wind from him.

He could use anti-magic.

Dropping the magic field, Keio reached instead for the Hellpower. With a resonating shriek, the shadow-guardians flinched back, the skies strobing their anger. The entire twilight took on a pasty, otherworldly hue, reflected in the shattered glass in the street and the walls of the ruins surrounding them.

Closing his eyes, Keio reached deep into the darkest place he could find within him, a place buried deep and nearly forgotten. From that terrible place, he called forth the fury of the Onslaught, hurling it at the shadow-guardians. They shrieked in rage and pain as the green torrent of hell slammed into them, sucking the life out of them. They flinched away, bellowing a monstrous wail, but they weren't quick enough. He was already preparing his next assault, and when he released it, a gush of putrescent energy raged out of him, devouring every trace of magic it encountered.

Overhead, the clouds released a torrent of lightning that pummeled the city like a shower of jagged spears that rained down for long seconds, obliterating every last shadow that remained.

Releasing the onslaught, Keio staggered, feeling the last drop of energy drain from his body. He fell to his knees, and would have landed on his face, had Shade not been there to catch him, easing him down onto a bed of shattered glass.

He lay panting, staring straight up at her as the world dimmed and faded.

"No!" Shade cried.

Vaguely, he was aware of Jendo's hands on him. A flood of warmth penetrated his body, spreading out to every limb, bringing with it a relief so profound that he almost choked with gratitude.

But it wasn't enough.

"Stay with me," Jendo gasped.

He could feel the old man's terror through his link with the Unity, and Shade's as well. He was still dying, and even all of Jendo's great skill couldn't save him. Tears filled his eyes, and he almost gave in to desperation.

But then he felt something else inside, a growing sense of warmth that pushed aside all his weariness and dampened his pain. Suddenly, a frightening deluge of healing jarred into him, ripping through his body with the might of a dozen suns, ramming his lost strength back into him with brutality. Keio cried out as every distorted fiber in his body squirmed back together all at once. Every muscle contracted, his organs seizing. His heart trembled, and his mind spun dizzily. His vision went dim as every color in the world swarmed together at once.

Then it was over as quickly as it came.

Opening his eyes, Keio found he was lying cradled in Jendo's arms, some of his health and vigor returned to him. Some, but not all. He was still dying—just not as quickly as before.

The old man scooped him up into a tight embrace, hugging him fiercely. Still holding him, he lurched to his feet, pulling Keio up with him. Keio stood trembling, leaning heavily on Jendo, reveling in waves of pride and forgiveness that still flooded into him through his link with the Unity.

"What happened?" he whispered. "It felt like hundreds of mages healed me all at once."

"They did," Jendo responded with a candid smile. He held up his arm, indicating the band on his wrist.

Keio understood. Somehow, the mages of the Unity had come to his aid, delivering healing to him through the *A'isan*. He was the Warlord of the Turan Khar, and his people had forgiven him, offering him their strength when his own had failed. It was a heady feeling. A humbling feeling. He was awash in the combined forgiveness of an entire society that surged forward to embrace him.

Tears ran from his eyes, and this time, they weren't tainted with blood.

42

—

THE BATTLE OF BEL ARUN

GIL ROSE QUIETLY FROM THE BED LONG BEFORE DAWN. ASHRA LAY sleeping on her side, one hand curled on the pillow beside her face. He paused over her, gazing down at her peaceful features, a great sadness filling him. It took everything he had to turn away.

He dressed as quietly as he could then scooped his weapon off the floor. Closing the door behind him, he paused in the hallway outside his room and leaned with his back against the door. He closed his eyes and drew in a long, shuddering breath that ached in his throat. He wanted more time with her.

But they were out of time.

He roused Jed in Laith and then found the castle's armory. The armorers took his measurements then came back with a padded gambeson and a chain mail hauberk made of alternating rows of solid and riveted links. He was handed a conical helm fitted with more ring mail. Two armorers helped him gear up then gave him a pair of gauntlets to wear.

Gil stood outside, working his arms, trying to get used to the weight of the new armor, until Jed and Laith came to join him. With full armor, the two Battlemages looked fearsome. Gil couldn't help wondering if the armor had the same effect on him, hoping it did. He would need every scrap of advantage he could find, and intimidation sometimes made the sharpest weapon.

They left the keep and headed toward the main gate. The sky was still dark, the city lit by bonfires that crackled on the tops of the turrets and along the walls, several blazing in the square behind the gate. With Jed and Laith behind him, Gil mounted the steps to the top of the walls, there crossing the battlements to get a view of the flat plain below.

The view was much the same as he had left it. To the south, the campfires of the enemy still glowed. It was still well before dawn, and yet already he could make out the sharp outlines of the Craghorn Mountains to the west and, in the east, the sky above the dark expanse of ocean was just beginning to warm. The sea breeze was up, scattering his hair into his eyes. Turning into the wind, he moved toward a brazier.

He pulled his gauntlets off and held his hands above the flames. The rings of the mail were cold, and they sucked the heat out of him even through the padded gambeson. He warmed his hands over the fire, which crackled and popped, sending sparks shooting high into the air. The other soldiers around the fire, all city regulars, stood casting glances his way and shifting nervously over their feet. Perhaps they weren't used to mages. Or maybe he did look formidable, after all.

"Grand Master."

Gil looked up to find the captain of the city guard standing across the fire from him. The man looked weary, as did they all. Gil doubted any of them have gotten much sleep.

"All is being readied," the captain reported. "The oil is heating, and the fire pots are being prepared. We stationed the bulk of the archers along the southern walls and left the western walls lightly manned, as you asked."

"Thank you," Gil said. "My guess is, they'll be here an hour after dawn. We still have time. Make sure every man knows what is expected of him. We'll be taking the brunt of the attack," he said, indicating Jed and Laith, "but we won't be able to keep them off the south wall. You might want to add more hoardings if you have them, along with anything you can get up there to toss down on their heads. When we start going down, you will have to shift resources quickly. Make sure each man has two assignments and knows when to be where."

"It will not come to that," the captain stated firmly, as though the loss of a Battlemage was an impossibility. Gil didn't see it that way. He saw it as inevitable. In order to be the most effective, Jed, Laith and himself would have to be positioned outside the city walls. He knew he could do a lot of damage out there to anything coming at him, but he also knew there was only so much magic he could handle at once, even with the talisman.

"It *will* come to that," he assured the captain. "Hopefully, later rather than sooner. But regardless, make sure the men are ready when it does happen, and know what to do."

"It shall be so," the man said gravely. "Is there anything else?"

Gil swallowed, feeling suddenly, profoundly sad. He had walked into battle many times in the last two months. Never before had he been so certain he wasn't going to walk back out again. He glanced to the east, to the ocean, where the sunrise was starting to paint the sky above the water a deep vermillion.

"Tell her that I love her," he said.

Raising his hand to his chest, the captain bowed solemnly.

The warm glow of daybreak filled the sky, but the air above Bel Arun only cooled. As the sun crested the horizon, the wind sweeping down from the north took on a biting chill. The braziers along the walls did little to hold back the relentless cold. Gil's fingers ached, and his lips were chapped and cracking by the time the armies of the Kingdoms took up positions just out of bowshot from the city walls.

A banner rippled overhead, and the flames of the bonfires crackled, whipped by the wind. But other than that, the ramparts were still and silent. The only other sound was the great noise of the armies below. Unlike the Malikari, the soldiers of the Kingdoms knew little of discipline. The army of Chamsbrey had few regular soldiers kept on the king's payroll, its ranks supplemented with conscripts and civilians serving the mandatory two years required of every male who came of age. Judging from the banners and insignias below, spread out across the field, both the Northern and Southern divisions of the King's Royal Army had arrived in time for the battle, and they had been joined by armies from Southwark and Lynnley. It was the greatest force ever assembled by the Kingdoms within recent memory.

All for one city that was little more than a seaside community.

No, he knew better than that. These armies hadn't been assembled merely to topple the walls of Bel Arun. Their purpose was much greater: to liberate the whole of the North from the Malikari and to drive Ashra's people back into the Black Lands—or into the grave. Looking down from the battlements, Gil knew there was little they could do against such a force. His thoughts drifted to Ashra, and he prayed that the gods would be with her long after he couldn't be.

"Grand Master, it is time," the captain informed him.

Gil nodded his thanks at the man then turned, beckoning to Laith and Jed. The two Battlemages came toward him, the fires of the braziers reflecting off the metal of their armor. It was said each Battlemage was worth one thousand of the enemy. Gil hoped that today, each one of them would be worth far more.

Otherwise, Bel Arun would fall, and the North would fall with them. Ashra's people would be slaughtered and starved.

He couldn't let that happen.

He *wouldn't* let that happen.

Donning his helm, Gil buckled the chinstrap as he walked, making his way toward a bastion that protruded from the tower overlooking the gate, but he halted when a soldier stepped in front of him, blocking his path.

"Please, Grand Master," the soldier said with an apologetic bow. He held out his own shield, offering it to Gil. "Take it."

Gil didn't know what to say. If his own magical defenses didn't hold, there was little this one shield could do to defend him. Nevertheless, the gesture was so simple and compassionate, he thrust his arm through the straps of the round shield with a word of gratitude.

With Jed and Laith walking behind him, he crossed the bastion and took up position behind the protection of a merlon and surveyed the field below. He raised his hand and pointed down at the strip of snowy ground between the moat and the front ranks of the besieging armies.

"There, there... and there." He indicated three positions spread out along the length of the western wall. "I'll take the south tower. Laith, you guard the north wall. Jed, you've got the gate. Try not to lose it."

"You're the one who's mobile," the abrasive man growled. "If you see me going down, take up my position."

Gil nodded. The gate was the prize they had to defend above all else. He'd decided to put Jed in front of it because, between the two Battlemages, Jed was much more powerful than Laith. Gil had positioned himself at the southwest corner of the city, where the enemy would be coming at him from two directions at once. He would need every scrap of advantage *Thar'gon* could give him, and all the luck the gods thought he deserved.

He took a deep breath then transferred *Thar'gon* to the arm holding the shield, offering his hand to Jed. The Battlemage took it with an expression of contempt, while Laith clasped Jed's other hand. The moment they were connected, Gil close his eyes.

"*Vergis,*" he whispered.

The wall shivered.

Snowy ground appeared beneath their feet, and he released Jed's hand.

They stood on the plain just outside the city gate, about halfway between the flooded moat and the front lines of the enemy. Gil nodded at Jed and Laith, then shifted *Thar'gon* into his right hand and pulled the heavy shield tight against his body. He turned and walked away, headed for the southwest corner of the city. Behind him, Jed stood firmly where he'd left him, while Laith made his way to the north to defend his length of wall. As they walked, loud jeers broke out all along the enemy front lines, as soldiers raised their weapons, taunting them, daring them to come closer.

The ranks of soldiers started to advance before he reached his position. Beneath his helm, Gil started to sweat, his mouth going dry. He raised his weapon, gripping it tight—so tight that the morning star's head trembled. He stood alone, and he was more aware of that fact than he'd ever been of anything else in his life. He didn't want to die here today. What terrified him more than anything else was the thought that, if he fell, then the wall behind him was likely to fail, and his death would doom Ashra too.

Thought of Ashra solidified his resolve, steadied him and filled him with a calm sense of purpose. Her life, as well as every life in the city behind him, was in his hands. Failure was a luxury he couldn't afford. Too much depended on him.

He beat *Thar'gon* against his shield and reached out from within, grasping the magic field.

"Come on," he snarled at the oncoming ranks.

With his mind, he wove a web of shadow around himself the way a caterpillar weaves a cocoon, sealing himself within it. Layer upon layer, he built it up, reinforcing it until the daylight around him warmed and dimmed, as though he looked out upon the battlefield through the lens of sunset. No arrow or spear could penetrate such a thick mass of energy. If they wanted him, they would have to separate him from his shadow.

Let them try.

With a resounding battle cry, the lines of enemy in front of him broke into the charge.

They closed the distance swiftly, spears raised, a mass of armored and bellowing men converging on one point, with him at the focus. Gil stood his ground, letting them come.

Closer.

Come closer.

He raised the weapon in his hand, drawing it back over his shoulder. Still, he waited. Then, when they were almost upon him, he swung *Thar'gon* with all his might at the enemy lines.

BOOM!

Scores of men lifted and flew backward through the air, slamming into the charging ranks behind them, plowing them down. Gil swept the weapon again, swinging the morning star around in a wide arc.

BOOM!

Screaming men were flung like ragdolls through the air. Body parts fell from the sky like hail, and a heavy rain of blood splattered the battlefield.

Gil twisted, bringing the weapon around full circle.

A solid wall of air connected with the front ranks. The entire mass of bodies lifted and sprayed backwards. Clods of dirt shot high into the air, blotting out the sun. On the ground, chunks of armor mixed with chunks of men and pieces of horses.

Gil dropped the kite shield. It wasn't serving him, its mass just weighing him down. Grabbing *Thar'gon's* hilt with both hands, he swung the weapon around again, tearing a great rent through the army ahead of him.

A cloud of arrows eclipsed the sun and came pelting down on top of him. Broadheads ricocheted off his shadow shield, shafts splintering in the air. Others found purchase in the bodies of dead and dying soldiers littering the ground around him.

More men found their courage and closed the distance between them. Gil drew his weapon back, then swung it around with another thunderous *BOOM!*

The explosion of air that shot out from the morning star gave him a couple seconds of relief, pushing back the enemy line another fifty feet. He fell into a rhythm, repulsing wave after wave of enemy soldiers. He kept it up for minutes, or perhaps hours—he didn't know which. The passage of time was inconsequential, and it was the last thing from his mind.

He glanced back at the gate, to where Jed was making his stand. The Battlemage stood with his hands held high, a globe of fire blazing over his head. With a mighty cry, he hurled it at the enemy ranks charging his position.

A massive firestorm ripped across the battlefield, tearing through shield walls and armored horses. Men howled and wailed and thrashed in flames. Others ran screaming across the battlefield, trailing smoke after them in fiery wakes. While they flailed and died in the flames, Jed conjured another terrible fireball.

Gil broke his attention away right before another charge barreled into him. He swept *Thar'gon* down, aiming at the ground beneath the onrushing men.

The entire battlefield convulsed, throwing hundreds of men off their feet. Those who got back up were met with another concussive blast that ripped through armor and flesh, separating bones from meat.

Gil staggered and almost fell, the exhaustion of battle catching up with him. Clenching his jaw, he caught his balance just in time to repulse another deadly wave.

An explosion of flames suddenly enveloped his shield, so violent that he almost dropped it. Staggering, Gil fell to his knees as another flaming projectile exploded around him.

At first, he didn't understand what was happening. It took him a moment to realize they were flinging pots of Hell's Fire at him with their trebuchets.

He wrenched himself up off the ground and staggered forward, sweeping his weapon around in great arcs through the air, carving out a passage before him paved in blood. He moved swiftly, so that the men tending the trebuchet couldn't recalculate their aim fast enough. The fiery assault stopped.

But not the physical one.

The soldiers redoubled their efforts, now coming at him from all sides, wave after wave, pinning him down.

He couldn't keep up. He couldn't last.

His head throbbed with the pain of exhaustion.

Gritting his teeth, he put every last effort into carving his way out. He trudged across the battlefield, a one-man war machine, boring his way through the enemy ranks ahead of him. Making for the trebuchet, he cleaved a pathway through the living, leaving behind him a swathe of ground soggy with blood. When he reached the siege weapon, one sweep of *Thar'gon* reduced it to splinters of wood.

He glanced back over his shoulder and saw Jed floundering. The Battlemage was surrounded by a tightening ring of men, and he wasn't beating them back fast enough.

He couldn't let Jed fall.

Relinquishing his own position, Gil raised *Thar'gon*, shouting, *"Vergis!"*

The battlefield shivered and disappeared.

A crushing mass of bodies replaced it.

A spear took him in the side before he could recast his shadow-shield. Gil went down, barely maintaining his grip on the morning star. A wall of soldiers collapsed on top of him, and he sucked in all the energy he could then cast it violently back out again. Bodies flew in every direction, exploding in the air.

Healing the rent in his side, Gil staggered to his feet. He turned slowly in a circle, readying himself for the next wave.

It didn't come. Through a thick screen of smoke, the only enemies he saw surrounding him were the wounded and the dead. Other than himself, only Jed remained standing near him on the battlefield.

Grinning in euphoric relief, Gil limped toward him. Just as he reached him, he staggered from exhaustion and practically collapsed. He reached out and caught himself on the Battlemage's shoulder.

He didn't see the sword that ran him through, parting the links of his hauberk like silk.

He didn't feel the pain at first. His legs simply gave out from under him, and he collapsed to the ground. He lay there for seconds, staring upward in confusion. At first, he didn't recognize the length of steel sticking out of him for what it was.

Gil fumbled for the magic field, but it wasn't there. He tried to catch hold of it, but it simply drained through his fingers like water.

Incredulous, he reached his hand up and grasped the sword protruding from his chest, trying in vain to draw the blade out of him.

In response, the steel twisted, ripping his flesh open wider.

He cried out in agony, then went limp, sagging back against the snow. The pain in his chest disappeared, and he couldn't feel his legs. He stared straight upward into Jed's scowling face.

Then his eyes lowered to the hilt of the sword: a hilt he recognized.

"How?" he whispered.

Somehow, Jed was holding Quin's sword. The only sword in the world with the power to dampen a mage.

The Battlemage sank down at his side, his hands still on the sword's hilt, maintaining the pressure.

"You're dying," Jed growled. "This is what it feels like when your life is running out of you. But before your last drop of blood hits the ground, you have one last choice to make. You can commit your soul to Xerys, and I'll spare the life of your woman. Or you can refuse. But if you do, I'll take Ashra's soul in your stead. Which will it be?"

Gil gazed up at him in horror.

No...

No.

Not Ashra.

He gasped, "I don't know the words..."

Jed grinned, his lips peeling back to reveal chipped, yellow teeth. "You don't need to know the words. Just repeat after me."

43

THE TOWER OF MORNING

With Shade and Jendo's help, Keio made his way up the hill toward where the dark monolith erupted from the canyon between mountain ridges. A winding ramp spiraled around it, in some places boring directly through the center of the pillar. Fortified structures grew from its sides like lichen: crenellated walls and high turrets, guard towers, bulwarks, and tall palisades. It was as though an entire fortress had been disassembled, the pieces separated and then crammed into the sides of the tall column of rock.

Above the stone pillar hovered the containment crystal, fixed to an enormous rock held in place by two great chains attached to the two highest towers of the fortress.

As he walked, Keio stared at the core crystal with no small amount of trepidation. He had no idea how he was going to make it there.

With Shade and Jendo's help, he mounted the ramp that wound upward around the girth of the stone pedestal. Fortunately, it wasn't as steep as he had feared. He managed to make it a couple of turns around the pillar before he started to tire. By then, the city was far below them, spread out across the ground like a map. He paused to catch his breath at the edge of the path, gazing out over the ruins of Karadun. All thirteen fortresses were arrayed before them, peppered throughout the enormous city and the cliffs surrounding it. Even as he stood watching them, four of the fortresses shuffled positions with an arcane groan.

"How do you feel?" Shade asked.

"Better than I should," Keio replied with a weak smile.

He could feel the whole of the Unity bolstering him, still feeding him strength through the *A'isan*. Without that link, he knew there was no way he could have made it this far. Their faith in him was humbling and also terrifying.

For the second time in his unnatural life, an entire civilization of people dependent on him, and this time, he could not fail.

He turned away from the cliff and glanced up at the sides of the monolith still above them. Stony towers protruded from the rocks, clinging to them like fungal outgrowths. Part of the fortress was directly ahead: a single tower with a large gate that appeared to be closed and barred. Jendo, who had walked ahead, was already approaching it. By the time Keio and Shade caught up with him, the old man had already found a small wicket gate set into the wall beside the main gate, and had it open.

"So, now you're a picklock?" Keio asked.

Jendo grinned with no small degree of pride. "I didn't become the Man behind the Mask by simply healing the sick. Besides, it was already open."

They passed through the gate into the interior of the circular tower. The room at the base of the tower contained racks of weapons and armor, all looking ready for use without signs of oxidation or even dust. Keio walked up to a large battle axe that stood propped against the wall and admired the blade, which looked sharp enough to cleave a head off and still retained a smooth, oiled patina.

"The Tower of Morning exists apart from time," he said. "That's why I chose it. It was the perfect place to contain an eternal energy source, and at the same time, keep it protected. Gods, I was so wrong."

"You didn't know," Jendo said softly. Placing a hand on Keio's shoulder, he steered him away from the weapons rack toward a posterior door that led back to the winding ramp.

As they left the tower behind, the ramp became steeper, broken intermittently by flights of stairs. Keio found himself tiring faster, and had to pause to rest more frequently to catch his breath. By the third such flight of stairs, his nosebleed started again, hot blood coursing down his face.

A warm tingling sensation washed over him, and he knew that his brothers and sisters in the Unity were doing everything they could to keep him on his feet. But all their collective strength could only do so much. By the time they reached the fortress at the top of the tower, Keio's legs were trembling so hard that both Jendo and Shade could barely support him upright.

The ramp ended in a high curtainwall with a portcullis that stood raised. The last of the stairs cut right through the wall and passed beneath two guard towers on either side of the gate. The top of the tower was bathed in brilliant light: the radiant glow of the containment crystal shining down from above. Keio craned his neck to look up at it, squinting and shielding his eyes against the glare. He couldn't see the crystal itself, just the great, floating mass of rock that supported it.

That rock had once been part of the Tower but now levitated in the air above it. The energy of the containment crystal had ripped the top of the fortress right off, along with its rock foundation. Now, the only thing holding the upper fortress in place, and keeping it from rising further, were two great chains anchored to the Tower's highest turrets.

"How do we get up there?" Shade asked.

"We don't." Keio wiped the blood off his face. "We have to bring it down to us." He turned to Jendo. "It will take both of us working together. I need you to climb that tower." He indicated the south anchor. "There's a winch at the top that lowers the upper fortress."

"That must be one hell of a winch," Jendo muttered.

"It is. Fortunately, it's operated by magic. There's another one on the tower ahead of us. Turning both winches at the same time will crank the chains. We have to bring it down far enough to shatter the crystal."

"How do we do that?"

"If we channel enough energy into the reservoir crystal, it will shatter and release the core energy."

As soon as he stopped speaking, a terrible pain wracked his body. Keio doubled over, clutching his middle. Both Jendo and Shade dropped to his side, the old man feeding him healing energy that eased the pain somewhat, but a terrible surge of nausea gripped him and, leaning forward, he vomited onto the rock pavement of the courtyard, bringing up bright red blood that coursed down his face and saturated his shirt.

Jendo pressed his hand against Keio's forehead, closing his eyes. Keio could feel the mages of the Unity doing what they could to stop the bleeding. Perhaps it would work, but most likely anything they could do would be very temporary.

Turning to Shade, Keio told her in a shaking voice, "You need to go. Now. Take cover in the lower fortress. When the reservoir shatters, all that core energy will be released all at once. The fortress might shield you."

Shade's eyes filled with moisture. Through the link between them, he could feel her grief and regret, and was surprised by their intensity. He didn't deserve any of it, but he was thankful. More thankful than he'd ever thought to be.

He looked at Jendo, wishing he could spare him too.

"I'm sorry," he said to the old man. "I wish this could turn out differently for you."

Jendo merely shrugged. "In all honesty, I never expected to get this far." He gave a wry chuckle. "Who would have ever thought that the two of us would end up together in this? What a pair we make!"

Keio summoned a feeble grin. "They say that adversity makes strange bedfellows.vIt seems that desperation makes for even stranger ones."

He offered Jendo his hand, who accepted it firmly. Instead of shaking it, the old man pulled him forward into a tight embrace. "I didn't have much hope for you," he said, gripping him hard. "Thank you for proving me wrong."

When Jendo let go, Shade moved in to take his place, lowering her veil to kiss his cheek. "Thank you," she whispered. "I will make sure the world knows about this day, so that your name does not go down in infamy."

"Just survive," Keio told her. "That's enough. Now, go."

She gave him one last kiss then turned and left, jogging back toward the stairs. Keio watched her go, feeling a potent mixture of happiness and grief. With help from Jendo, he climbed to his feet. Above, the reservoir crystal hummed a loud and throbbing drone. Its harsh light washed the entire court-yard with an ethereal brilliance that made it hard to see.

He gave one last nod to Jendo, then started toward the north tower, which was the closest. The pain inside him was terrible and growing worse as he walked. He found the tower door ajar and pushed it open the rest of the way. The interior was lit by a strange light that seem to come from every direc-tion, but had no single source. The air was devoid of dust and had a peculiar, sweet odor to it, and the walls echoed hollowly with every footstep he took. When he found the tower steps, he was grateful to see that they were wide. He wished he had time to stop there and rest but knew that he didn't. Instead, he applied the last of his strength to the long, laborious climb.

Before he reached the top of the stairway, the agony became unbearable. He fell to his knees on the stairs, where he knelt panting, blood leaking from his face onto the stair above of him. He felt weak and shaky and his thirst was rampant, all symptoms of fatal blood loss. Trembling, he tried to stand, but collapsed instead.

He lay there for moments, drowning in misery, his eyes drizzling bloody tears of despair down his face. Then anger got the better of him. Gritting his teeth, he got his hands under him and wedged his body up off the step.

Determined, he started crawling forward.

He could feel the collective dismay of the entire Khar society through his connection with the *A'isan*. His fear and doubts were being broadcast, and the hopelessness of the situation was becoming apparent to all. The healing coming back to him through the link was the only thing that kept him moving, though it was no longer enough to sustain him. Crawling forward inch by inch, he dragged his ruined body up the last turn of the stairway.

At last, he crossed the threshold onto the roof of the tower, where the great chain that held the upper fortress was anchored, groaning and creaking under the strain. Staring at the chain, Keio felt defeated. It was easily two feet in diameter. The winch that operated it was affixed to the top of the tower, and normally would take the combined strength of a dozen or more mages to crank it.

Somehow, he would have to use his bond with Jendo to turn both winches at the same time. But now, more than ever, he didn't think he had it in him. He could feel the last of his strength draining out of him, and he knew he was bleeding heavily on the inside.

He didn't have much time.

Staggering, he managed to push himself to his feet. Bracing himself on the stone wall, he made his way around the circumference of the tower over to the mechanism of the winch. It was a simple contraption, just an iron wheel with a handle attached, as though meant to be turned with the strength of a single man, and yet, the force it would take to turn that crank would break the backs of a thousand men.

Gripping the handle tightly, Keio closed his eyes and reached for the magic field through his link with Jendo. From the other side of the fortress, he could feel the old man's approval and support. And, through the *A'isan,* he could also feel the acute anticipation of the Unity, as every soul in the community collectively held its breath, pinning all its hope and faith on him.

With all the strength he could muster, Keio turned the crank. The metal handle shuddered, rattling violently in his grip. A terrible, wailing moan rose from deep inside the tower, as though the ancient mechanisms within the turret were crying out in mortal anguish. Slowly, with a shrieking groan of gears, the crank began to turn.

Keio grimaced, diverting some of the power he had gathered back to Jendo, enough to operate both mechanisms at the same time. The shrieking cries of metal filled the air, mixing with the deafening hum coming from the containment crystal above, creating a deafening cacophony that hurt his ears.

He glanced up at the crystal floating above them and saw that it was working. Slowly, inch by inch, the crystal's rock foundation was lowering. Closing his eyes, Keio redoubled his efforts. The pain inside was awful. Groaning against the effort, he applied everything he had left in him, lowering the crystal inch by agonizing inch.

Until his strength failed.

With a cry, he collapsed to the roof of the tower, where he lay, his blood spreading across the stones in a widening puddle.

No...

He was so close. So close. Above, the noise coming from the crystal had risen in pitch to a shrill whistle. The base of the upper fortress hovered level with the tops of the anchor towers. It was almost grounded, though not quite.

And yet, there was nothing he could do. The crystal was still too far away.

He stared down at the *A'isan* on his wrist, which burned his skin from the heat of the power moving through it. Then, from somewhere deep in the back of his mind, a memory twitched to the forefront of his brain, a conversation dredged up from Rylan's past:

Through the A'isan, the Warlord is linked to every member of the community. Theoretically, you could draw on every mage of the Khar Unity.

Even with Jendo's aid, he didn't have enough power to shatter the core crystal.

But the rest of the community did.

Keio gasped as the answer hit him like a blow to the face. The mages of the community had already done what they could to heal him. But what he needed from them now was their power itself.

Closing his eyes, he reached through the *A'isan*, summoning the power of every mage in the entire collective. Afraid of taking more than his human body could channel, he drew on it slowly at first, filling himself to the point of pain, then to the point of agony.

He forced himself to take in more.

And more. And more, until he screamed and shrieked from the terrible anguish of it.

And then he let it all go, hurling every drop within him at the reservoir crystal.

It exploded.

The light hit, overwhelming his sight.

The sound of the explosion tore through the air, louder than every thunderclap that had ever shaken the earth.

And then the shockwave hit, shattering everything in its wake.

Shattering him.

With a gasp, Rylan Lauchlin opened his eyes. It took a moment for his vision to clear, the afterimage of a tower seared red into his vision. Blinking tears of pain from his eyes, he struggled to focus on the dark silhouette hovering over him. It took long moments for the features to condense into the face of a man he knew and recognized.

Quinlan Reis stood over him, offering him his hand.

"Welcome to hell," he said with an unwelcoming grin.

TO BE CONTINUED

GLOSSARY

acolyte: apprentice mage who has passed the Trial of Consideration and sworn the acolyte's oath.

Aeridor: lost continent somewhere in the Southern Hemisphere.

Aerysius: ancient city where the Masters of Aerysius once dwelt. Destroyed when the Well of Tears was unsealed.

A'isan: silver artifact worn by the Warlord of the Turan Khar.

Akai: legendary hidden temple in Zahra.

anti-magic: the magic of the Netherworld. Variously known as the Hellpower, the Onslaught, and dark magic.

Appos Mountains: mountain range in western Zahra.

Arangel: one of the Thirteen Fortresses of Karadun.

Archer, Gilroy: sixth tier Grand Master of the Order of Battlemages.

Archer, Kyel: father of Gil Archer. The man who destroyed the Well of Tears. *(deceased)*

artifact: heirloom of power that has been imbued with magical characters or properties.

Ashra ni Sayeed: daughter of the Sultan of the Malikari Empire and acolyte of the Lyceum of Karikesh.

Atrament: the realm of Death, ruled by the goddess Isap.

Auberdale: capital city of Chamsbrey.

Black Lands: what was once Caladorn, now a sterile wasteland.

Carathiel Fortress: one of the Thirteen Fortresses of Karadun.

Caston: Battlemage of the Lyceum of Karikesh.

Catacombs: place of burial that exists partly in the Atrament.

core magic: residual magic left over from the creation of the universe.

Curse, the: term used to describe the darkening of the skies and earth of the Black Lands.

Dagher, Jed: fifth-tier Grand Master of the Order of Battlemages of the Lyceum of Bryn Calazar.

dampen: to shield a mage from sensing the magic field.

damper: an object that has the ability to dampen a mage from sensing the magic field.

darkmage: a mage who has sworn loyalty to Xerys.

Darl: people indigenous to the continent of Tur and Northern Zahra.

Daru: Nation on the continent of Zahra.

Davore, Cerille: mage of the Lyceum of Bryn Calazar.

Death's Passage: *see* **Catacombs.**

deizu: a mage.

deizu-kan: a Battlemage.

deizu-sum: the most powerful of mages.

Demir: third-tier Master of the Lyceum of Karikesh.

Desecration, the: the apocalyptic event created by the Well of Tears.

Desolation: *see* **Mokona Desolation.**

dracipiter: winged demon of moderate intelligence.

Emdad ul-Calazi: Captain of the Watch of Bel Arun.

Emine: mage of the Order of Querers.

Emmery: former Kingdom of the Rhen that was conquered by the Malikari.

Empress: ruler of the Turan Khar.

Farash: mage of the Turan Khar, a member of the Warlord's cadre.

Farlow: town in Chambsbrey near the city of Auberdale.

field lines: currents of the magic field.

Glen Farquist: holy city in the Valley of the Gods.

Grand Canal: canal that bisects the city of Karikesh.

Grand Master: any Master of the fourth tier or higher.

Guardian Tower: ancient focus of magic in Suheylu Ra.

Hadley: fourth-tier Master of the Lyceum of Karikesh.

Hellpower: *see* **Onslaught.**

Holisgrave: colonel of the Northern Division of Chamsbrey's Royal Army.

Isaerae: Empress of the Turan Khar.

isan: in a *kaiden* pairing, the mage who controls the link.

kaiden: a pairing of mages accomplished by linking their power through a chain-like artifact.

Karadun: ancient city of Neria built in the Appos Mountains.

Karikesh: capital of the Malikari Empire.

Kingdoms: free nations of the Rhen that are not part of the Malikari Empire.

Kazri Souk: the world's largest market in Karikesh.

Knibbs: general the Army of Southwark.

Kuzey: officer of the Sultanate's elite officer core.

Lauchlin, Darien: the Last Sentinel of Aerysius. Conquered the Northern kingdom of Emmery to create the Malikari Empire. Former Servant of Xerys. *(deceased)*

Lauchlin, Rylan: son of Darien Lauchlin, Warlord of the Turan Khar.

Leven: Battlemage of the Lyceum of Karikesh.

Lonesome Ghosts: various tribes of the Mokona Desolation.

Lower City: portion of the city of Karikesh south of the Grand Canal.

Lyceum of Bryn Calazar: ancient school of magic in the nation of Caladorn that was destroyed in the Desecration.

Lyceum of Magic in Karikesh: school of magic founded after the destruction of the Well of Tears.

Mahr, Jendo: mage of the Turan Khar, a member of the Warlord's cadre.

Mahzar: second-tier Master of the Lyceum of Karikesh.

Malikari Empire: Empire formed after the conquest of the Rhen by the people of Malikar.

mage: a person with the ability draw power from the magic field.

magelight: magical illumination that can be summoned by a mage that takes on the signature color of the mage's magical legacy.

magic field: source of magical energy that runs in lines of power over the earth.

Marks: disfigurations of the flesh borne by Lonesome Ghosts as a result of long-term exposure to core magic.

Maro: mage of the Turan Khar, formerly of Shira.

Marshall, Amina: daughter of Rylan Lauchlin.

Marshall, Clemet: adopted father of Rylan.

Master: any mage; more specifically, a mage of the first through third tiers.

Matu, Keio: Custodian of the Wise Council of Suheylu Ra.

Mokona Desolation: desert on the continent of Zahra formed by the Desecration.

Murat: officer of the Karikesh city guard.

Murkaq Square: large central gathering area in Karikesh.

Nagala: nation in ancient Aeridor.

Natural Law: law that governs the workings of the universe that can be strained by the application of magic, but never broken.

Nazapor: capital of the Turan Khar.

necrator: demonic creature that renders a mage powerless in its presence.

Neria: civilization of mages with an unquenchable thirst for knowledge.

Netherworld: realm of Xerys, God of Chaos.

Neval son of Mesut: Bey of Bel Arun and Sanajuk Province.

Nogato, Shiro: Warlord of the Turan Khar.

North: the Northern kingdoms of the Rhen, including Emmery, Chamsbrey and Lynnley.

North City: portion of the city of Karikesh north of the Grand Canal.

oki: the silk of the whisper butterfly.

Onslaught: the corrupt power of the netherworld, also known as the Hellfire.

Orders: different schools of magic among the Masters of Aerysius and the Lyceum of Bryn Calazar.

Osan, Ilia: mage of ancient Shira, wife of Keio Matu.

Pedra: mage of the Turan Khar.

potential: the ability in a person to sense the magic field.

Prime Warden: leaders of the Assembly of the Hall of either Aerysius or the Lyceum.

Priya: the Prime Warden's acolyte.

Puna Ajaru: a large volcanic caldera filled with pools of sulfuric acid. Also called the Scalding Sea.

Quintessence: *see* **core magic.**

Raising: Rite of Transference, during which an acolyte inherits the legacy of power from another mage.

Ranick: Battlemage of the Lyceum of Karikesh.

Reis, Quinlan: former Servant of Xerys, now the husband of Prime Warden Naia Seleni and Warden of Arcanists.

Renquist, Zavier: ancient Prime Warden who created the Well of Tears.

Rhen, the: portion of the Southern Continent south of the Black Lands.

Rhenic: common language spoken throughout the kingdoms of the Rhen.

Rite of Transference: *see* **Raising.**

Rothscard: largest city and former capital of the Kingdom of Emmery; renamed Karikesh by Sultan Sayeed the Conqueror, who made it the capital of the Malikari Empire.

Saheen, Laith: third-tier Master of the Order of Battlemages of the Lyceum of Bryn Calazar.

Sanctuary: birthplace of magic in ancient Shira.

sayan: in a *kaiden* pairing, the mage who submits.

Sayeed ibn Alborz: Sultan of the Malikari Empire, known as Sayeed the Conqueror.

Seleni, Naia: former priestess of Death, now the Prime Warden.

Sentinels: an extinct order of mages that was chartered with the defense of the Rhen. Sentinels swore an Oath of Harmony to do no harm.

saturation: Battlemage tactic of overloading with magical power in anticipation of creating an enormous discharge of force.

Shade: woman of the Lonesome Ghosts.

sharaq: ancient system of honor code of the Malikari people.

Silver Star: ancient symbol of mages, indicative of the focus lines of the Circles of Convergence.

Servant of Xerys: darkmage who has pledge fealty to the God of Chaos.

Shadeem, Andigar: Prime Warden of the Lyceum of Bryn Calazar.

Shira: ancient fallen nation on the continent of Zahra.

Sky Portal: a portal to the Netherworld created by the Turan Khar.

Soulstone: ancient artifact created by Quinlan Reis as a storage receptacle for a dying mage's legacy.

Suheylu Ra: fallen city of ancient Shira.

Talat: mage of the Turan Khar

temples: various sects of worship. Each temple is devoted to a particular deity of the pantheon.

Temple of Seer: Temple of Wisdom in Cardish.

Thar'gon: magical talisman that can only be wielded by the Warden of Battlemages.

tier: additive progression of levels of power among Masters. The higher a Master's tier, the greater that person's ability to strain the limits of Natural Law.

Tower of Morning: tower that appears in a different location every fifth sunrise.

transfer portal: portal capable of transferring a person from one location to another instantaneously.

Transference: process by which an acolyte inherits the legacy of power from another mage, resulting in the death of the Master who gives up his or her ability.

Tur: the northernmost continent.

Turan Khar: the combined peoples of the Empire of Tur.

Valdivora: sword once borne by both Darien Lauchlin and the ancient conqueror, Khoresh Kateem.

Vanadian Colossus: ancient stone statue of an elephant erected at the base of Karadun.

Varik: mage of the Turan Khar, a member of the Warlord's cadre.

vitrus: the Gift that allows a mage to touch the magic field.

vortex: cyclone of power where the lines of the magic field superimpose and become vastly intense.

Warden: the leader of one of the magical Orders.

Warlord: mage in charge of the armies of the Turan Khar.

Watchers: stone towers that formed the defense grid of Suheylu Ra.

Waterfront: area of Karikesh just south of the Grand Canal.

Well of Tears: well that unlocked a gateway to the Netherworld. Created by Zavier Renquist and destroyed by Kyel Archer and Quinlan Reis.

Wise Council: governing body of ancient Shira.

Word of Command: a word that, when spoken in proximity, activates a spell.

Xerys: God of Chaos and Lord of the Netherworld.

Xiana: mage of Daru Provence.

yori: a type of robe.

Zahra: continent in the northern hemisphere.

Zakai: officers of the Tanisar corps that form their own distinctive social class.

Zanikar: magical sword and artifact created by Quinlan Reis.

THE PANTHEON

Alt: God of the Wilds
Athera: Goddess of Magic
Deshari: Goddess of Grief
Dreia: Goddess of the Vine
Enana: Goddess of the Hearth
Isap: Goddess of Death
Om: God of Wisdom
Xerys: God of Chaos
Zephia: Goddess of the Winds

THE ORDERS OF MAGES

Order of Arcanists: order of mages chartered with the study and creation of artifacts and heirlooms of power.

Order of Architects: order of mages chartered with the construction of magical infrastructure.

Order of Battlemages: order of mages chartered with martial applications of the magic field.

Order of Chancellors: order of mages chartered with the governance of the Assembly.

Order of Empiricists: order of mages chartered with the theoretical study of the magic field, its laws and principles.

Order of Naturalists: order of mages chartered with the study of Natural Law.

Order of Querers: order of mages chartered with practical applications of the magic field.

Order of Sentinels: extinct order of mages chartered with watching over and protecting the Rhen in a manner consistent with the Oath of Harmony. Replaced by the Order of Battlemages.

Order of Harbingers: extinct order of mages chartered with maintaining watch over Athera's Crescent.

ACKNOWLEDGMENTS

Thank you to the Terrible Ten. You know who you are.

#nocabal